PRAISE FOR VIVIAN AREND

"If you've never read a Vivian Arend book you are missing out on one of the best contemporary authors writing today."
~ *Book Reading Gals*

"The bitter cold of Alberta, Canada, is made toasty warm by the super-sexy Coleman brothers of Six Pack Ranch."
~ *Publishers Weekly*

"Brilliant, raw, imaginative, irresistible!!"
~ *Avon Romance*

"This story will keep you reading from the first page to the last one. There is never a dull moment..."
~ *Landy Jimenez*

"I definitely recommend to fans of contemporaries with hot cowboys and strong family ties.."
~ *SmexyBooks*

"This was my first Vivian Arend story, and I know I want more! "
~ *Red Hot Plus Blue Reads*

"In this steamy new episode in the "Six Pack Ranch" series, Trevor is a true cowboy hero and will make any reader's heart beat a little faster as he and Becky discover what being a couple is all about."
~ *Library Journal Starred Review*

ROCKY MOUNTAIN FREEDOM

SIX PACK RANCH, BOOK 6

VIVIAN AREND

ALSO BY VIVIAN AREND

The Stones of Heart Falls

A Rancher's Heart

A Rancher's Song

A Rancher's Bride

A Rancher's Love

A Rancher's Vow

The Colemans of Heart Falls

The Cowgirl's Forever Love

The Cowgirl's Secret Love

The Cowgirl's Chosen Love

Holidays in Heart Falls

A Firefighter's Christmas Gift

A Soldier's Christmas Wish

A Hero's Christmas Hope

A Cowboy's Christmas List

A Rancher's Christmas Kiss

A full list of Vivian's contemporary print titles is available on her website:

www.vivianarend.com

This is a work of fiction. Names, characters, places, and incidents either are the product of the author's imagination or are used fictitiously, and any resemblance to any persons, living or dead, business establishments, events, or locales is entirely coincidental.

Rocky Mountain Freedom
Copyright © 2013 by Arend Publishing Inc.
ISBN: 9781999063450
Edited by Anne Scott
Cover Design by Damonza
Proofed by Sharon Muha

This is for my friends and family who have taught me that: love is love, no matter what that looks like, that promises are to be kept, and that people are more valuable than things.

PROLOGUE

July, Red Deer, Alberta

ain wrapped around his temples, the rush of blood through his veins echoing in his ears. Travis Coleman whipped his head up to track his attacker and stars danced before his eyes as chastisement for moving too fast after the recent blow to his head.

He raised his hands into a defensive position and waited with anticipation for the next bit of punishment to land. The dim lighting in the back alley wasn't enough to show all the debris underfoot, and he stumbled before finding his footing.

"Stop."

The order rang from Travis's left, and both he and his opponent turned to see a powerfully built blond race toward them.

By the time Travis recognized his friend, there was no time to shout a warning. Cassidy's forward momentum brought him between Travis and the other fighter, an agonized grunt exploding from the man's lips as Cassidy's fist sank deep into his gut. Cassidy slammed his free hand against the stranger's shoulder, toppling him to the ground.

Shit.

Cassidy whirled to grab Travis, his green eyes bright as he examined the damage. "You okay?"

Travis tossed off the assisting arm, lurching around Cassidy's bulk to offer a hand to the man he'd been fighting. His sparring partner had already scrambled crablike into the shadows and escaped.

"Dammit, what'd you go and do that for?" Travis spun toward his friend. The motion was too rapid after the hits he'd taken, and he staggered.

Cassidy caught him, pushing him against the nearest wall for support. "He was beating the shit out of you. I thought interrupting was a good idea." He leaned in closer and grinned momentarily. "I arrived too soon. You've still got a pretty face."

Travis shoved his friend's hands away. "Next time ask before you butt in."

"Too big a man to ask for help? Even to save yourself from being pummeled?" Cassidy pulled out a handkerchief and offered it. "Your nose is bleeding like you're some kind of virgin sacrifice, and we both know how wrong that is."

Travis took the faded blue fabric and held it tight to his nose to stop the flow. His grip covered his entire lower face and stopped him from having to respond. Silence was a fine thing because there wasn't much he could say right now. Not without telling Cassidy more than he wanted to.

"Where the hell you been, anyway?" Cassidy folded his arms over his chest, biceps bulging the denim of his jean jacket. "We were supposed to meet at Traders. When you didn't show up, I figured you'd found someone to fool around with, or you plain forgot."

"I left a message," Travis insisted. Not a very detailed one, true, but he had called.

Cassidy pulled out his phone and cursed, shoving it back into his pocket with a rueful sigh. "Dead."

"Ha, see? I'm surprised you still have that thing. Isn't it time you lost this one?" He needed to change tack—distract Cassidy from asking any more questions that had no answers.

Only his friend ignored the bait and narrowed his gaze, a glitter of brilliant green flashing out. "You called to tell me what? That instead of meeting to shoot some pool, you'd decided to drive an hour to the cheesiest dive we know so you could find some asshole to fight?"

Travis backed away as Cassidy crowded him, suddenly gone fierce with not a trace of humour left on his face.

"Shut up," Travis snapped. "It's not like that."

"Looked a lot like that to me," Cassidy snarled. "You got a death wish, T?"

The lingering rush of adrenaline, the sweet tease of forbidden pleasure that accompanied the pain...

Travis shook his head to rid himself of the sensations. He attempted to muscle past the solid body blocking him. "None of your damn business."

Cassidy caught him by the shirtfront and shoved him into the wall again. He pinned Travis in place with a rock-solid forearm across the chest, leaning in with his full weight to create a trap.

It was all kinds of fucked up that Travis had to clench his teeth together to stop from moaning as lust roared through him.

Cassidy got right in Travis's face. "I'm your friend, and that makes it my bloody business."

Travis wanted to look away. Wanted to hide, but it was impossible. He was caught, mesmerized by the full force of Cassidy's stare.

Eerie silence filled the air, nothing but their accelerated breathing and the distant sound of early-morning traffic.

"Son of a bitch." Cassidy barely mouthed the words, easing the pressure on his left arm as he slid in closer. He planted his right hand on the wall to the side of Travis's head as their chests brushed.

Travis didn't dare breathe. Any movement might increase the contact between them.

The temptation was far, far too enticing.

Cassidy held him captive. Silent. Motionless except for that all-too-intuitive gaze, until Travis was ready to scream.

He dug deep to find the strength he needed to push away the longings he'd kept hidden for so many years. Shove them aside for yet another day. It was either that, or he was going to flip them around, slam *Cassidy* into the wall and start grinding their hips together. Put his teeth to the strong column of tanned flesh rising from the plain white T-shirt.

Maybe close the gap between their gasping mouths and cut off their rapid breathing as he kissed the goddamn daylights out of his best friend.

His dick hardened further at the thought until interrupted by the reality of what he was considering.

His best fucking friend.

Oh hell, what was he going to do?

"*Jesus.*"

A new voice, loud and getting louder.

Travis nearly folded to the ground as Cassidy spun and stepped away. He deliberately put himself between Travis and the newcomers, one of them uttering curses that rose like twisted prayers into the pale dawn sky.

The man who Travis had been tussling with earlier stepped forward, a sneer cracking his broken smile.

One word. One word was all he uttered.

"Fags."

The insult broke both the silence and the stillness. As if released from restraint, the man in the middle lunged and swung at Cassidy. He dodged right only to get hit by a wide-handed blow from the third man.

That's all Travis had time to see before he had to duck from his own attacker.

The light didn't help. Shadows moved out of synch with punches. A fight in the near dark, without even numbers, without respite given.

This time he hated the intoxicating rush that drove through him. This setting? This situation? It wasn't about sick, twisted pleasure anymore, not for Travis. Not when some of the punishment fell uninvited upon his friend.

Cassidy grunted in pain, swore, and a body tumbled to the ground at his feet. Dust puffed up like miniature tornados.

A curse rang from Travis's left, followed by the sound of fists meeting flesh. A pained gasp, low and masculine, rushed out as feet scuffled in the gravel of the back alley.

Deep shadows played with blood-red-tinged light as the morning sun reached tentative fingers into the darkness. A heavy body bumped him on one side. He caught at them, using them as a support to stay standing.

Angry voices filled his ears, but the words were unclear. The only thing sharp enough to focus on was the throbbing line of hedonistic pleasure tapping his unwilling nerve endings.

Sick bastard.

Travis squinted in an attempt to clear his vision, lurching to the side as bare knuckles grazed his already bruised cheekbone...

...and jerked himself awake.

He glanced around to get his bearings while his ears rang with unexpected stillness. The familiar log walls of his cousin's rustic cabin came into focus. He was leaning on a small log table, a firm chair under his ass.

The rest of his morning's escapade returned in a rush.

The other men racing away as the lights of an RCMP cruiser flickered red and blue on the alley walls. Travis struggling with Cassidy deeper into the darkness, manhandling him into his truck and driving like a madman toward the only place he knew he'd find silence and sanctuary. A safe haven with no questions asked.

Thank God for Gabe Coleman. Cousin or not, the man knew how to keep his mouth shut. Travis stared out the window and waited for inspiration to strike.

Whoever the hell said it got easier as you got older had shit for brains.

He stepped across the kitchen floor and downed a glass of water before making his way to the tiny side bedroom. He leaned on the doorframe, his heartbeat so rapid he was on the verge of falling over from the head rush. A couple deep breaths later he straightened. He had to find the strength to get out the other side of this fucked-up morning even though it was barely eight a.m.

Cassidy lay motionless on the sturdy log-frame bed, his blond hair in sharp contrast against the dark blue pillow, his skin pale. Bruises were rising fast, and before the day was out he would have a shiner to rival the one Travis wore. Maybe two.

The chair Travis had moved beside the bed earlier called his name. He lowered himself gingerly, enough aches and pains making themselves known he felt like an old fart and not a twenty-five-year-old. It was only temporary pain haunting him, though. He'd be better by tomorrow.

Cassidy rolled partway, and the sheets pulled free. Damn it all, why had he shown up uninvited? Guilt at having led his friend into trouble hurt more than the rest of Travis's physical distress.

Guilt for a whole lot of other reasons as well. Naked skin was now visible, and Travis couldn't look away. Not from the muscular chest, the firm curve of biceps as Cassidy shifted to lay one flexed arm over his forehead.

Or farther down the bed where the thin fabric still covered his hips but didn't disguise the size of the man resting flat out on the mattress. Couldn't hide the muscle and bone that was more than his friend. Even now looking him over, Travis wanted to sweep his fingers down the entire length of him and touch. Feel.

Taste.

He squeezed his eyes shut and tried to will away his erection, but it was like hoping for a snowstorm in the middle of the summer. Hell had no intention of giving up its torment anytime soon.

"Travis?" His name croaked from Cassidy's dry lips.

Travis slipped off the chair to his knees beside the bed. "What do you need?"

Cassidy coughed lightly. "Water."

Travis hurried to the kitchen and returned, dropping to the edge of the mattress and reaching around Cassidy's shoulders to help him sit up.

His friend leaned against him as he took the glass, his heated chest pressed to Travis as his fingers shook slightly. "Fuck, I'm like a little girl here."

"You got beat on, asshole, what do you expect?"

Cassidy grimaced as he swallowed. He pushed the half-empty glass at Travis then looked him over closer. "Did you even get hit after I interrupted you?"

He'd gotten his share, but... "You were a bigger target. All that blond hair made you an easier target in the dark. You should have worn a toque."

Cassidy closed his eyes and breathed out slowly. "The room is spinning."

"Lie down, you shit. My cousin Tamara is on her way to check you out—she's a nurse." He tried to push Cassidy to the mattress, but his friend resisted, glancing around the room and out into the main cabin.

"Where's your other cousin?" Cassidy frowned. "I did see him, right?"

Travis ignored the heat radiating from Cassidy. "He and his fiancée went for a ride."

"Damn nice he took me in, I suppose."

"He's the best." Travis hesitated, then figured this much at least needed to be said. "He's a good guy. Knows how to keep a secret."

Cassidy snorted. "Oh, because we all need people in our lives to help keep secrets, don't we? Or is that just you?"

Shit. "I don't know what—"

"I'm not an idiot, T. I see what's going on around me. I know more about you than you're willing to tell, but since I'm a friend I keep my mouth shut."

Travis's mind raced. What exactly did Cassidy know? What did he *want* Cassidy to know?

What do I want?

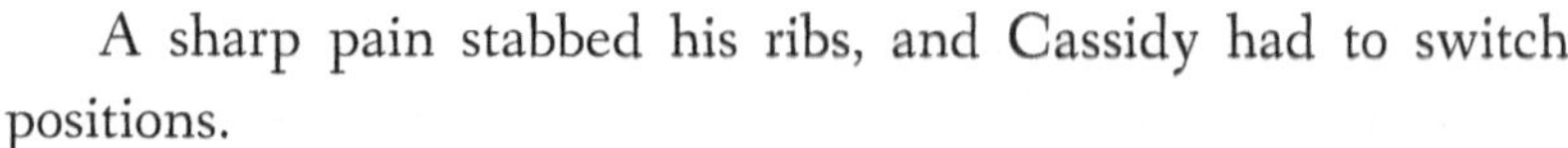

A sharp pain stabbed his ribs, and Cassidy had to switch positions.

He didn't want to move. If he moved he might distract Travis, and the bastard finally looked as if he was about to admit something. At this point Cassidy didn't much care what Travis confessed to as long as he made some forward motion.

He held out a hand, hating how his fingers shook. "Help me. I need to stand for a minute."

Travis curled his fingers around Cassidy's and eased him upright, his arm slipping around Cassidy's waist for balance until he hit vertical.

The room spun again.

"Whoa, hang on." Travis caught him tighter as Cassidy slumped forward, all control gone.

"God, so weak."

"Yeah, you're a right wimp, you are." The words came out tight, Travis's voice rigid. Cassidy blinked to clear his vision. Travis's face was only inches away from his, both of them breathing hard.

Dammit, it was happening again. Cassidy straightened in the hopes a rib would pop out of line or something and send enough pain to stop blood from heading to his groin.

Too late and too little. His cock hardened, his body itching for more contact. Travis's scent wove around Cassidy and caught him tight. He knew damn well what he wanted.

Too bad what he wanted was the last fucking thing on earth that either of them was going to get.

Thinking about it, though, made him slower than usual. Or maybe it was the ringing in his ears from the fight. For whatever reason Cassidy missed the moment when Travis touched his chest softly, fingertips hovering over bruised muscle.

Not the touch of a sympathetic friend. Softer. More intimate.

Cassidy should have jerked away, should have given every indication what Travis was doing was out of bounds and out of line. Couldn't do it, though.

The lie stuck in his throat as the urge to consume Travis overwhelmed everything. "Oh *hell.*"

"I know," Travis whispered. "I'm so goddamn lost here, Cassidy, I have no idea what I'm doing."

Cassidy shook his head, regretting it immediately as his vision blurred. "You're not doing anything. We're not—"

Travis leaned in and pressed their lips together. Gentle, barely there, probably out of deference for the cuts and bruises. Still a kiss. No mistaking it for some macho tease or a friendly gesture of goodwill. Especially not when Travis eased an arm around Cassidy's back to let their torsos make contact as well, warmth and support oh-so-welcome even as Cassidy's brain screamed a million warnings into the silence of the cabin.

It was no use. His body and mind were at war, and until one found dominance, he had to accept this. Once. Only once.

His tongue found Travis's, and a fiery jolt struck. He moaned and caught Travis by the back of the head, thrusting his fingers into the thick dark hair and tightening into fists to keep the man exactly where he wanted him.

Pains forgotten, secrets forgotten. Right now the world narrowed to desire, lust and aching need.

He tugged at Travis in an attempt to end the kiss. Travis groaned, fighting the pressure in his hair, leaning against Cassidy and using his body to manoeuvre him to the mattress.

Agony and ecstasy mixed into one. Travis stretched over him, a solid, heavy weight Cassidy had longed for months to feel. The pain of the beating he'd taken countered the pleasure enough to sharpen his resolve, and Cassidy tightened his grip and jerked Travis's lips away.

Only inches above him, Travis gasped for air. His eyes had gone dark like midnight, pupils wide and blending into his dark grey irises.

"We can't..." Cassidy hated the pleading in his voice. "This can't happen, T."

"You said you wanted to know my secrets," Travis growled. "Make up your bloody mind."

"It's not a joke," Cassidy complained.

Travis rocked his hips. There was no way to avoid the truth—they both had hard-ons like iron hammers. Another rub together followed, with friction creating the most amazing rush, and Cassidy cursed.

Enough. He had to stop them now. He planted his hands on Travis's chest in preparation to shove him away.

Somewhere outside the room a door squeaked, and a female voice rang out. "Travis? You in here?"

Travis damn near levitated off the bed. "Back here, Tamara."

He dragged a hand through his hair as Cassidy rolled onto his side, biting back a moan of pain at moving so quickly. It was the only position where the state of his cock might stay hidden, though.

By the time a pretty dark-haired woman with cat-rimmed glasses appeared in the doorway, Travis was sprawled in the single chair by the bed. All signs of them having done anything out of the norm were gone, Cassidy hoped.

Hoped like hell.

Tamara let out a huge sigh. "So. The idiots have been at play, have they? There was no official fight club last night, so you had to be out trolling for trouble."

"Shut up, and look him over." Travis moved aside as she shoved a hand against his shoulder, exchanging positions so she could access the bed.

Cassidy gave her his best smile. "There's something you don't see often. House calls in this day and age?"

She smirked as she opened a small bag she'd brought with her. "I don't change bedpans, though. How do you feel? You look like shit."

"Still charming as ever," Travis goaded.

"Not that you'd get to know it, cuz, but I have a lovely bedside manner. Especially for gorgeous blonds who are helpless, not to mention half-naked." She shone a light into Cassidy's eyes as she spoke. "Ignoring Travis. Hey, Cassidy, you remember me?"

"Vividly." He blinked. "You still seeing that doctor who steps on your feet on the dance floor?"

"He's got good hands. Makes up for the feet." Tamara glanced over her shoulder. "Stop hovering, Travis, and get out. I'll call you if I need you. Asshole."

"Brat." Travis hesitated in the doorway, his gaze meeting Cassidy's briefly before flicking away. "Should I make something?"

"Yeah, coffee for you and me. I'll let you know about Cassidy in a minute. I have a shift at the hospital right after this. Now get."

Travis got.

Cassidy grinned. "You're good at bossing him around."

"Sugar, when you've got like a million male cousins all with control issues? You learn to stand up for yourself, or you get shoved in a corner and petted far too much." She wrinkled her nose as she stared at her watch, maintaining a firm grasp on his wrist as she took his pulse. "Still beating. That's a good start."

The entire time she looked him over, Cassidy ignored the noises from the front of the cabin. Focused on whatever the hell he could do to stop the coming train wreck.

Tamara finally left with a warning he probably had a concussion, but otherwise she figured he'd survive. He was too tired to argue. Too tired to do anything but close his eyes and hope that when he opened them there would be a solution to his troubles.

Twice he remembered Travis shaking him, getting him to talk and offering a cold drink. Twice he refused to look his friend in the eye, taking the opportunity to turn his back as soon as possible to let exhaustion send him under again.

When he finally woke, driven by a desperate need to take a piss, Travis was stirring from where he'd stretched out on the couch.

Cassidy ignored him for another moment. Did his business,

then got distracted by the bashed-up face that taunted him from the bathroom mirror.

Green eyes circled with the blooming shades of blue and black only strengthened his resolve, though.

Imagine that. I have something to thank the bastard for after all.

They met in the kitchen area. Cassidy deliberately put the entire table and a couple chairs between them.

Travis's quick gaze took in the defensive stance, and he laughed. "You think I'm going to crawl over you or something?"

Cassidy lifted his chin. "You telling me you don't remember kissing me, asshole?"

"Oh, I remember it plenty. And I remember you kissed me back. So why are you standing over there looking as if I'm a freak when we both know this has been hanging over us for far too long?"

"Nothing's ever going to happen again." The words shot out, sharp. "Shit, Travis, when I was poking you to tell me your secrets I was trying to get you to admit you get a kick from fighting in dark alleys."

"When a person's got all kinds of secrets, you don't get to pick which ones they share." Travis's body language softened. "Cass, come on. I'm going crazy over here. I don't want to fuck things up between us."

Cassidy shook his head. "There is no *us* other than friends. And if you're not going to admit you have an issue with violence, there's not much to the friendship either."

Travis frowned. "What the hell are you talking about?"

"You've got a great family, T. A solid place in the community. I'm not about to let you screw things up for yourself just because we've been hanging out together too long without tossing a woman into the mix. It'll be better if I go."

He didn't expect the laughter. When Travis stopped shaking

his head, he took a step to the right. Cassidy retreated, and this elaborate dance started with Cassidy desperate to maintain the space between them.

Travis growled in frustration. "Don't be an idiot. I know Tamara said you might have a concussion, but how hard did you hit your head? You're leaving?"

"I like women," Cassidy blurted out.

Another snort of laughter escaped Travis. "I noticed. So do I. And they like us."

Cassidy clutched that straw as if it was an unbreakable lifeline. "You don't go around kissing your best friend when what you need is to find a good woman to meet your needs."

"My *needs*?" Travis stared at the ceiling for a moment before shaking his head. "Too twisted and too fucked up and too...wrong to deal with."

"Exactly." Cassidy clutched the back of the chair in front of him, suddenly a lot less in control than he'd been a minute ago. He was positive about one issue. "Only if your needs are gonna get you killed by some stranger, you need to reconsider. If you have some twisted reason you like to get punched, then maybe you should consider asking a friend."

Travis's eyes widened. "Did you just offer to beat on me?"

Cassidy shrugged. "I'm your friend. At least I would stop when you've had enough. I don't want to see you dead, which is why I tracked your ass down this morning."

"Oh, and that was such a good idea, wasn't it? Getting set on by an entire gang. Who got the beating on that one?"

"That's not the point. We wouldn't have been there if you had admitted you wanted my help."

Travis nodded slowly. "And if I admitted I wanted...you?"

Shit, *no*. Cassidy pinched the bridge of his nose. "T, I'm the last thing you really want. Stop making this harder than it has to be."

His friend snickered.

Jeez. "Freak. What are you, twelve?"

"You said it, not me," Travis complained. He sighed. "Look, I need to get to the ranch before Blake and Matt start piling up all the shit jobs as punishment for missing work. I'll be back tonight, and we can talk."

"Not changing my mind," Cassidy warned. "Not about anything."

"We'll talk. Have to pick up your truck as well." Travis pointed at the small counter in the kitchen. "I charged your phone—turn it on so I can call to make sure you're okay while I'm gone. Tamara's orders."

Travis left, and the world seemed a lot colder. Not even a steaming-hot shower was enough to warm Cassidy thoroughly.

After a couple hours of worrying at his dilemma, there was no other solution he could come up with. He sat at the table, flipping through the pages of a book but not really seeing the words. A small bundle of black-and-white fur meowed piteously by his feet until he relented and picked up the kitten, depositing it into his lap.

Cassidy refused to be the one who tore Travis's world apart—and Travis had no idea exactly how hellish the world could get. Cassidy also refused to stand by and watch while a good friend found a way to commit suicide by giving in to whatever grim addiction had him in its power.

If he couldn't help, and could only harm, he'd sit through this talk Travis wanted, then he'd grab his truck and leave. There were other places he could make a living, all of them far enough away he wouldn't have to see his friend dead, or wishing he were dead.

Even if leaving Rocky Mountain House was going to hurt like crazy—

Cut and run was Cassidy's only choice.

1

—————

Nine months later
April, Rocky Mountain House

Gravel crunched under her wheels as she turned down the long back-road approach to his trailer. Ashley Sims slowed her van to keep dust from floating through the windows she'd opened to enjoy the warm spring air.

Things hadn't changed much since the last time she'd traveled this path back in December, other than the obvious passing of the seasons. The snow was gone, but the lay of the land stayed familiar. There was still the same old outbuilding at the far edge of the field, its boards weathered to stately grey. The fence posts skipping past in her peripheral vision with a rhythmic consistency ran straight and true, the occasional old boot or baseball cap tacked to the top.

Inside, she'd turned a few corners, and the sight of buds on the willows and tiny blades of grass fighting to emerge from the broken soil in the field—all of it made her optimistic that she was about to find a new lease on life as well.

Fingers crossed Travis Coleman wouldn't mind providing a place she could temporarily plant herself as she set down some roots. Real roots.

The radio station changed tunes, and she hummed along, tapping her fingers with the beat, smiling as it turned out to be yet another song about drinking.

Country music. Predictable, but soothingly familiar. Like coming home.

She'd just pulled into the yard area outside the singlewide mobile home when the dust rising from the east warned her timing had been perfect. The scent of spring hit her as she stepped outside, closing the door and leaning on the worn blue metal of her van.

His black cowboy hat appeared first, the hum of the ATV's well-tuned engine rising over the ridge and carrying his jean-clad form closer.

If she'd had any worries about her reception, he put them aside quickly as his smile broke out, a flash of white against his tan. Travis parked at the edge of the driveway, threw a leg over the seat and strode toward her, all long-limbed and smooth. His worn Wranglers fit snug in the right places, the edges of his jacket flaring open to reveal a dark T-shirt stained with dirt from his labours.

The breeze picked up and whipped her hair across her face. Ashley pushed the long blonde strands out of her way, smiling as she openly admired him. "Long time no see."

He stopped less than a foot away, lifting his fingers to caress her cheek. "Not true. I saw you last night in my dreams."

The deep tone of his voice sent a shiver over her, and desire struck hard as it always did around him. He slid his hand around the back of her neck and eased in until their bodies brushed. With one small adjustment, he tilted her face upward, control in his grasp. Control that made her want to squirm closer and rub like a needy puppy.

Which was why she had to haul in a little control of her own. Take charge of a few things, the most important ones at least, before this situation went completely off track.

His gaze was locked on her lips. She licked them, pleased when the pupils in his dark grey eyes reacted, widening with lust. "You planning on kissing me, or eating me up for dinner?"

"How about both?"

She shook her head—well, as far as his firm grip would allow her to. "I'm not falling back into your bed, Travis. Not first thing."

"Course not." He grinned. "I figure it should take at least a month before we have to resort to an actual bed."

Ashley should have seen that one coming. "You're a filthy bastard at times, ain't cha?"

"Just the way you like me..."

He moved slowly enough she could have pulled away. He'd never have tried it if she hadn't wanted it in the first place—he wasn't that type.

Maybe it wasn't the smartest thing to do, but hell if she'd deny herself this much of a homecoming.

As he lowered his head, she met him halfway. Firm lips pressed to hers, the soft strands of his hair under her fingers. He let go of her neck and cupped her ass, hoisting her skyward, and she wrapped herself around him tight, compressed against nearly two hundred pounds of muscle and barely restrained passion.

His tongue slipped past her teeth, teasing the roof of her mouth, tangling briefly with hers before he drew back far enough to plant kisses down the side of her neck. His fingers clenched her ass, rubbing her slowly over the growing ridge at his groin. Tendrils of pleasure radiated from her core, and for a moment she was so damned tempted to make this a real welcome back— complete with sticky, exhausting sex.

The kind of intimacy she knew Travis was more than proficient at providing.

He was the one who pulled away first, breathing unevenly but smiling as he lowered her reluctant limbs to the ground, supporting her until she found her balance.

Ashley swallowed hard, her lips tingling, blood pounding in her ears. "You still know how to get my motor running, Travis Coleman."

"Good to know. Come on in, and tell me what you're doing back in Rocky."

She followed him up the couple of steps into the trailer. "You knew I'd be back sometime."

He shrugged, hanging his jacket on a wall hook then holding out his hand to take her coat. "I wasn't hundred percent sure. Figured if you decided it would be spur of the moment. Kind of how you left..."

Travis winked to soften his words, but they were true. She had taken off rather sudden-like.

She didn't get time to go into the whys and wherefores before he ducked away into the back of the trailer, headed for the bathroom.

Ashley moved into the kitchen instead, more familiar touches greeting her. She'd sat in that chair and eaten breakfast. She had washed dishes at that sink. Been bent over that table and fucked until she could barely walk the next day.

Memories that shouldn't be returning sprang up from all corners of the room, and she wanted to smack herself silly.

It wasn't wrong to want to go back to jumping his bones, but damn if she'd get distracted from the real goal. It was past time for merely playing games. Past time for taking nothing but temporary pleasures.

She wandered the small trailer space as she pondered. She wanted it all, a present *and* a future, and that meant being smarter than she'd been the last time she and Travis had gotten involved.

"You want to stay for supper?" Travis asked as he stepped back into the room.

His hair was wet and freshly combed. He'd washed up quickly and pulled on clean jeans and a dark T-shirt that boldly stated *Asshole.*

She laughed. "You wore that on purpose."

"Best birthday present I ever got." Travis grinned. "Truth in advertising."

Ashley leaned on the doorframe to the living room. "You look good, Travis. Your family doing okay?"

"Mostly." He opened the fridge. "You never answered about supper. Am I feeding you tonight?"

She shook her head. "I don't want to trouble you. Just need a few minutes to ask you a favour."

"No trouble. Easier to talk when we're not both fighting our stomachs."

He handed her a head of lettuce, and it was like stepping back in time. She put together a salad while he pulled out burgers and tossed them on the grill outside. By the time the food was on the table, she was glad he'd forced the issue. She didn't have much left to eat in her van.

She took a big bite of the thick hamburger patty and moaned in appreciation. "So good. Thank you for being bossy and making me stay."

"I'm good at bossy, if you remember." His smile teased her again. "And now that we don't have anything else to distract us, you can stop dancing from my questions. Are you in town for long?"

She nodded slowly. "I'm considering buying a place."

"In Rocky? Really?"

"It's got everything I need." It was time to face the bull head-on. "Only I need your help to make it happen."

"How?" He kept eating but paid full attention to her.

The explaining first, favour second. "When I left back in December, I headed south. Stopped in and visited my mom for a while. She's doing really well—got a place in California in this amazing artists' community. I did a little work for them and ended up with some commissions."

He frowned. "For your art? I thought you were doing contract stuff with that advertising agency out of Calgary."

Ha. "The jerk took some of my work and used it in another project without giving me credit. I found out before I left. No way was I going to keep on with him."

"I'm sorry to hear that. Can't you get your rights back or something?"

She sighed. "It's more work than it's worth. Some of the things were scribbles I'd done a couple years ago when I started with him—anyway, it doesn't matter. I moved on, and now I have a chance to make some serious money without having to work for another person."

A smile bloomed, curling his lips until he was full-out grinning. "Being your own boss. Always the best way to make a living."

"You know it."

Travis nodded slowly. "It's a good strategy. What do I have to do with it?"

Now came the favour. "I'd like to shadow you on the job for a while. I need pictures to use as a base for the artwork. I figure if I spend time in the field off and on for a couple months I can get most of what I need, then fill in the gaps with specific studio shots."

"You want me to model for you?" His laughter filled the room. "You've got the wrong guy."

"Oh, I don't think so." Ashley looked him over, top to bottom, letting her appreciation show. "Although you're a little too clean at the moment."

"You need a *dirty* cowboy? Hmmm, this is sounding kinkier by the minute."

She leaned forward, ideas and images filling her head. Somehow she needed to explain this so he could catch the vision.

"I'm not trying for a studio-perfect cowboy, Travis. Not what people on the street imagine, but a real working rancher. I want to take pictures of the most boring tasks and make them come alive. Maybe try one of those twenty-four-hour things, typical activities at all times of day and night. The hushed moments when the world is waking up, and the stinking hot, sweaty times when you're up to your ears in shit. That's the story I think will work with this—hard and hungry and so damn down to earth you can smell the country when you see the pictures." She pulled back, her heart pounding. Travis had this knowing smile, and she bumped him with her foot. "What? Why you staring at me like that?"

"Because you're so full of enthusiasm it's making me twitch. You doing photos only for this? Or are you planning to turn them into digital paintings?"

"Mixed media." It warmed her that he remembered what she'd been playing with before she left. "Might use some photos, some paintings—digital and probably watercolour. I was playing around at my mom's and found out I have a fair hand with clay as well."

"The acorn didn't fall far from the tree, I guess."

Which was lovely when it came to art, but not when it came to other things. She hoped she'd be able to do a few things differently than her parents. "Here's what I'd do—tag along with you for a few days, see what kind of photo opportunities arise. Then I'll know better if I should join you at certain times, or if I should buckle down and hang out for a full week, or something else. In between time, I'll work on the actual projects. I have all my supplies in the van. I can work anywhere."

"Well, so far I haven't heard you say anything that's too twisted." Travis pushed his plate back and eased his chair away from the table. She itched to pull out her camera right then and there to snap a shot of him, the lazy position was so perfect. His dark eyes focused on her as intently as she'd looked him over a moment earlier. "You know not to get in the way, but you might be bored as sin for the next while—calves are dropping, and there's not that much else happening around the place."

The news gave her chills. "Calves? Oh, that's fabulous."

He groaned. "Hardly. Not when I have to wander the dark for the damn cows who decide to hide from us."

"It'll be worth it." Ashley waggled her brows. "So, it's a deal? I can use you for a subject? I'd pay you, of course."

He snorted. "That's ridiculous. Why the hell would you pay me?"

"You would be a model of a sort—I'll need to get signed releases from you and any of the family who are in the shots."

"By the book, Ashley? I swear I don't even know you." His words were light but hit a nerve.

"I still break rules, Travis, only not the ones that would get me lawsuits or jail time." He was going to do it. She knew it, and it was tough to refrain from leaping up and cheering.

"Stop gloating," he teased. "I can see it on your face—you know you've got me twisted around your little finger. Of course you can shadow me, and the family will be no trouble."

Happy warmth flooded her. "I'll get you the release forms. They can sign them whenever it's convenient. And you have my cell phone, so if you've got any timeframes that aren't good, give me a call and we can work around it."

He nodded as he stood to clean the table. "What's your deadline?"

"I've got three. End of June I send in pencil drawings to a company for a calendar. Then July there are some digital paintings for an advertising promo I lined up independently. End of September for the art gallery—that's the key one. They'll sell my projects on consignment for me."

"A gallery? Holy shit, I didn't realize that's who you had this with." Travis nodded. "You're doing real good, then."

"I'm scared shitless, Travis, but yeah, it's a huge opportunity. Opens doors I only dreamed of."

"I'll do what I can to help you make it happen." He turned and caught her by the hand as she finished loading their glasses into the dishwasher. She let him tug her against his body, slipping into his arms like she was coming home. His strong fingers curled under her chin and lifted her head so their eyes met. "Last question, though. You really want to spend that much time together, darling? You did run out of here without much warning. I actually figured I'd never see you again."

And...the moment had arrived. Ashley wasn't going to cut him any slack, not on this topic. "Travis Coleman, you know damn well why I left, and it wasn't anything to do with you and me."

His entire body stiffened. He caught her by the forearms and gently separated them. "I suppose you're right."

Cool air surrounded her as sorrow chilled her further. "I didn't mean to bring up old arguments. I think you and I can work together fine."

"Nothing but business, is that what you're saying you want?"

It wasn't, not by a long shot, but the ball was in his court at the moment. If he wanted to continue to ignore the suggestions she'd made so many months ago, it was his life. "If that's how *you* want it. Whatever works for you."

Travis kissed her forehead before pacing across the living room and picking up the remote. He clicked on the TV and settled on the couch without so much as a glance her way. "You give me a call when you're ready to start."

So. It was going to be like that. All business.

Ashley took a deep breath. "I'll be ready to go in the morning. May as well get started."

He stared at the screen as he flipped channels. "Six a.m. Show up here, and you can ride with me."

He was probably hoping to trigger a few emotions with his attitude and actions, but frankly she was more amused than pissed off. He was deliberately being an asshole? Fine by her. She had no intention of getting caught in any game she couldn't win, so until she figured out her strategy, pretending he'd chased her away was as good a solution as any.

She didn't bother to say goodbye. She grabbed her coat and let herself out. Maybe after a good night's sleep she'd know better how to deal with the stubborn-as-a-jackass Travis Coleman.

2

─────────

$\mathcal{H}$e forced himself to stay seated until her van door slammed shut.

Pig-headed, fucked-up shit that he was.

Once he knew for sure she was leaving, he was on his feet and watching out the window as she slowly backed up and got her van onto the gravel, headed west.

She was right. The trouble hadn't been between the two of them. The trouble had been all his, and no matter how much she insisted on listing solutions, there *were* no easy answers.

It was better she admitted that right off the bat.

And yet as her taillights moved away from his trailer, he couldn't help but wonder if he was being an idiot. Ashley was fire and ice. A goddess in and out of the sheets, with a *live it to the limit* attitude one hundred percent of the time. They had fit, goddamn it. Fit in a way that he'd never had with anyone else. When he was with her, he'd been incredibly happy.

Except for one wretched urge.

If he shoved that broken part of him into the hole it deserved, he could happily spend his time with the woman who loved as hard as she played.

So why hadn't he tried sweet-talking Ashley into spending the night? She would have stayed. He was certain of it. He was still staring when she hit the four-way stop. Instead of turning left into town, she headed right. The only thing down that road was a dead-end at the creek, and she knew it.

He killed the television and paced the living room, monitoring the crossroads closely to see if she turned around and came back. The wait gave him plenty of time to fight with his demons and decide he'd been an idiot to simply let her walk out of the house.

When she hadn't returned within thirty minutes, Travis gave in. He figured he knew her enough, knew himself. He grabbed his hat and coat and was out the door, starting up the ATV and going round the back way, across the fields.

He parked at the final fence post, not bothering to manhandle the gate open. Just left the trike there and jumped the stile. He followed the creek, winter leaves and deadfall crackling underfoot as he moved. The frogs in the stream stilled as he approached, resuming their courting songs before he'd passed more than a few steps away.

The bright rainbow colours of her van shone through the trees, and he smiled. Yeah, she hadn't gone far. He should have known she wouldn't bother getting a hotel room somewhere in Rocky when she was driving that beast of hers.

Before he'd stepped from the trees, he'd already heard the sound of guitar strings, soft and low, merging with the trickle of the creek. The scent of wood smoke was the final touch, and damn if he didn't have a knot in his throat. Familiar memories. Good memories.

She had the van side door open wide, and tiny prayer flags

hanging along the opening flapped in the light breeze. A few feet away Ashley sat in a folding lawn chair beside a portable hibachi. She'd built a small fire in the raised metal bowl, a waft of smoke rising and curling around the rustic campsite.

He walked as carefully as he could over the spring-moistened leaves, but they still crunched an announcement. She lifted her face toward him, a far more welcoming smile greeting him than he deserved after being a jerk back in his trailer.

Her fingers didn't falter on the strings. "You come to give me hell for trespassing?"

"More like hell for not inviting me to join you." Travis stepped closer to the makeshift campsite. He spotted a second lawn chair leaning against the wheel well, and unfolded it, settling himself next to her to listen to the music and the sounds of the water.

Ashley ignored him, staring instead into the trees sheltering them, spring buds trembling in the breeze. Above them, the azure sky faded before changing to the purple tones of dusk.

Travis slowed his breathing as he mentally ran through all the reasons this was a bad idea, but the same damn conclusion kept returning time and again.

He didn't want to hurt her, but damn it, he *wanted* her.

She finally put the guitar aside, leaning it against a stump she'd dragged over to use as a side table. She stirred the coals with a small chunk of two-by-four then laid the piece of scrap lumber on the glowing embers. Dusky red flames slowly licked the soft white wood.

Tendrils of heat slipped over his body as well—burning him with a need that only she could quench.

"Invite me to stay the night, Ashley." He caught her gaze over the fire and refused to look away.

He couldn't stop his hunger from tingeing his words, curling around them both in imitation of the thin blue-grey line of smoke rising from the wood. His craving was more in line with the red-hot coals glowing in the bottom of her makeshift fire pit.

She lowered her voice, whispering softly like an echo of the running water. "I don't want to see you dead."

They were the same words she'd spoken so long ago, but maybe because he'd gone without her for four months he was more willing to listen. She'd had only one damn request back before things had gone to hell. One ultimatum.

After all this time he still didn't have a solution. "I don't want to be dead either."

Suspicion stained her next question. "Are you going to stop fighting like I asked? Find some other way to deal with the... needs...you get?"

Fuck it all. "I can't promise that."

She sighed, once again avoiding his gaze. "Then the answer is no. We'll hang out together around the ranch, but I'm not fooling around with you, or doing anything else."

She picked up the guitar, and this time the tune drifting from under her fingers wasn't light and relaxed, but discordant and edgy. As if she was playing her mood on the strings.

Dammit. "You're serious."

She tilted her head, and her hair fell in waves around her shoulders. His body tightened as he looked her over, admiring the soft curves he knew so intimately.

The determination in her expression was new. The touch of pain in the depths of her eyes. She'd always been stubborn, and willful, and hot-tempered, but this was more like a solid wall he wasn't going to be able to climb. Miles from the light and happy-go-lucky woman he'd spent time with in the past.

"Travis, I *can't*. I still want to have fun and enjoy life, but I promised myself I wouldn't fall back into the same old habits. I'm changing for reasons that are important to me. So, do I want to spend time with you? Hell, yes, but not if it means there's a chance I'll have to go identify your cold, dead body when a situation gets away from you. I can't...I can't take the thought of that. And I won't."

"But you have no problem shadowing me all hours of the day and night for the coming months."

Her fingers crushed the guitar strings and the tuneless *twang* scraped his nerves. "If you want to change your mind and tell me no, I'll understand."

"That simple, huh? You'll find someone else." Travis fought to keep his anger from building. She wasn't saying anything ridiculous, only not what he wanted to hear.

She laughed softly, the music resuming—this time a far more melodious refrain. "Life's pretty simple when you come down to it, Travis. We do things to make ourselves happy. We try our best. When situations change, we change with them. I want to use you and the Six Pack ranch as my models, but if you say no, then I'll look elsewhere."

Nothing was simple. "You make it sound like I'm being childish."

"Never said that."

Travis rose to his feet, frustration poking him hard. Only what he'd seen played out in his family over the past few months kept his lips sealed before he said something he'd regret. It'd been all too clear what hastily blurted words could do to a relationship as he'd watched one of his younger brothers cut himself off.

She'd mentioned wanting to move in a new direction, and he could appreciate that. He wanted the same thing, but damn, pulling back on the issue of them as a couple was going to kill him.

He took a few steps away before forcing himself to speak

softly. "I want to help you. Come by a little earlier in the morning, and you can have breakfast with me. Use the shower if you'd like. I promise to keep my hands off."

"I appreciate it. Night, Travis."

The rosy glow of the fire shone on her pale skin, turning her into a kind of pixie or goddess of the flames. He turned his back and walked away.

Because that was all he could do.

Her throat tightened as Travis left, but in the middle of her sorrow she was happy, in a kind of far-too-grown-up way.

It hurt to turn him down, but it hurt less than losing him would. The ache in her heart was still fresh and raw, and she stared into the fire and soaked in its warmth until she could push the pain aside.

Ashley settled her junk back into her van for the night. She'd taken out the front passenger seat and turned the area into storage for her guitar and a small plastic dresser for her clothes, leaving her enough room in the back for a mattress, a tiny kitchen and her computer.

With a set of solar panels on the roof to charge her batteries, and a small portable toilet for emergencies, she was totally independent—high-tech, low-tech camping at its finest.

Except for the shower. She'd take Travis up on that offer happily.

Crazy birdsong woke her. Ashley pulled on sturdy jeans and yanked her hair back into a ponytail, shoving it under a wide-brimmed hat she'd picked up at a market in California.

The scent of eggs and coffee made her stomach rumble as she knocked on his door at five thirty sharp.

"It's open," he called.

Ashley stepped in, the warmth from the wood stove enveloping her like a morning hug. "Hey, Travis. I brought some muffins to add to breakfast."

"Sounds good." He nodded toward the table. "If you hurry, you can shower before it's ready. You got about ten minutes."

"That's all I need. Thanks."

She scooted down the hall and washed up quickly, far too comfortable in his home. And yet—the familiarity wasn't a bad thing. They had a past, there was no denying that.

It was the future she wasn't so sure about.

Fed, watered and wrapped up warm against the weather, Ashley climbed on the ATV behind Travis, slipping her arms around his torso. She settled her camera bag against her back. Tightened her hat straps under her chin. "Where we headed first?"

"Barns. I need to find out what's been happening all night." He got them moving, the soft sounds of nature eaten up under the ATV motor. "If there were a lot of calves born, then the regular chores need doing first. If it was slow, Blake will already have everything done and we might be headed into the fields."

"Sounds fine to me." They rolled over a hill and the wind struck them, far colder than it had been in the creek-side ravine. "Damn, that's a nasty wind."

"Still April. We could have snow next week."

"God, don't remind me." She rested her chin on his shoulder to hear him better as they raced forward, the ATV engine rumbling over their voices. "I enjoyed my time in California, especially being there during the cold snap that usually hits here in January."

"I'm jealous. I haven't been anywhere warm like that for years."

"Maybe someday you'll get a chance. Lots of pretty places to visit."

Travis chuckled and pointed to their right. "Don't have to go far away to find things to look at, Ashley. It would be nice to have them *and* the warm weather."

She took in the cattle moving together across the land, the sparse trees at the edge of the field thickening to full forest as the foothills rose behind the fence line. Small clusters of dark-brown scrub brush contrasted with the greenish-grey grasslands, the occasional outcropping of rock peeking up like miniature castles.

"I agree. Your land is one of the most beautiful places I've ever visited."

Her fingers itched to pull out her camera, but there was time. The sky was breaking to dawn, and while the colours were gorgeous, the details she needed for reference wouldn't be clear until there was more light.

Instead she took mental notes of the shading, the mood created by the rising sun. Those were the things she wanted to make happen in her upcoming projects.

"A few more minutes," Travis announced. "You let me know if you need anything, okay?"

She gave him a quick squeeze. "I will, but for the most part? It's best if you forget I'm there. Do what you have to do, and I'll try to stay out of the way."

He rubbed his cheek against hers. "I don't think I can forget you're there."

Ashley snorted. "Sweet talker."

"Only the truth." They rumbled into the yard, passing the main Coleman house on their right. The field equipment was lined up in a neat row to the side of one barn, all giant metal teeth and enormous tires like crazy alien beasts waiting for their chance to come alive.

Round bales of hay were stacked high to one side. Corral fences ran straight and true, creating boxes outside barn walls.

Everywhere the wood was slightly worn, yet well maintained and tidy.

"You guys keep the place neat," she noted as Travis pulled up beside the barn and parked next to a couple of older Fords.

Travis waved a hand toward the main house. "You try slacking off when you've got a boss like him around."

Ashley turned to see Travis's dad pacing down the well-worn path between the house and the work area of the yard. She smiled. Mike Coleman was the salt of the earth. She'd liked him the minute she'd met him.

He looked up as he drew closer, his frown breaking into a smile. "Well, there's a prettier face than I usually see this time of the day."

"Dad, you remember Ashley?"

He nodded, the grey hair dusting his temples the biggest thing making him stand out from Travis. It was obvious the two were father/son. "Welcome back."

"Thanks, Mr. Coleman. Travis offered to help me with a work project I have—I hope you don't mind if I take a few pictures around the ranch?"

"Not at all." Mike pulled open the barn door, pausing before he entered. "Of course you'll have to join us for dinner in payment."

She grinned. "You got the idea of who owes who mixed up, but I'd love to sometime. I'll explain more later. Don't let me keep you from your work."

Mike winked before twisting toward Travis. "Blake's in the other barn. You want to go take over?"

"Yes, sir." Travis grabbed her by the hand and pulled her with him.

Ashley caught Mike watching them before he disappeared into the barn. Great.

"That was stupid. Now you're going to face a whole lot of questions about me." She hurried to catch up to Travis's side instead of being tugged along like a reluctant little kid.

"Nope."

"Your dad stared after us while you dragged me away all caveman," she complained.

Travis tossed her a leer. "I wasn't being a caveman. I promise, that would involve more hair pulling and a hell of a lot less clothes."

She'd stepped into that one. "Shut up, Travis."

He laughed.

"Hey, if you do need a break or anything, go on up to the house and say hi to my mom." Travis motioned her ahead of him into the smaller of the two main barns. "She'd enjoy getting you a drink and shooting the breeze for a bit. Give her a break in her day as well."

"I'll keep that in mind."

She stopped to let her eyes adjust to the lower lighting, using the pause as an excuse to not say any more about visiting with Marion.

While the older Colemans were the politest people ever, there was something about the way Mrs. Coleman looked her over that made Ashley uncomfortable. As if she'd been judged to see if she was worthy of Travis and found wanting.

When they'd been together the previous year, there had only been a couple events Ashley had gone to with the entire family, but both times she'd felt it. She hadn't given a fuck back then— she was seeing Travis, not his folks, but this time she didn't want to burn any bridges.

She wanted to settle in Rocky. The Colemans were a

powerful part of the community. Getting in either of their bad books wasn't a smart idea.

The barn smelt like all other barns she'd ever been in—earth and shit and warm bodies and sweet straw. She followed Travis deeper in to where they found Blake in a smaller penned-off area. He was wiping down a tiny calf with an old sack, a streak of dirt across his entire forehead.

"You're really getting into your work." Travis leaned on the railing. "What you got?"

"Hey, Travis. Triplets. First was stillborn—I had to pull it before these other two made it. They'll be okay, though." Blake glanced up from his task and spotted Ashley. "Now you're a sight for sore eyes, Ashley."

"Hi, Blake."

Blake let the calf down carefully by its mom before exiting the pen. "I'd give you a hug, only you don't want to stink for the next however long. Good to see you."

"Same."

Travis grabbed a couple buckets from the shelf. "Ashley's going to take pictures of us for some work projects. I said I didn't think anyone would mind."

Blake shrugged as he backed down the hall, wiping his hands clean. "Don't mind at all, only you got insurance on that lens?"

Ashley paused. "Why?"

"When it breaks from taking shots of his ugly mug, of course." Blake grinned as Travis tossed a curse after him. "Hey, Ashley, you planning on being around for a while, then?"

"I hope so."

Blake unzipped his dirty coverall and sat to pull it over his boots. "You want to do me a favour? Jaxi's been talking about having new pictures taken of the girls. I hate the ones they did at the shopping mall the last time—damn fake background with painted daisies on it, or some such nonsense. You feel up to clicking a few shots in our backyard?"

Ashley laughed. "Not a problem. I'll call Jaxi and set up a time."

"Thanks." He yawned, pulling a hand across his mouth at the last minute. "Sorry. It's been a hell of a night."

She smiled and moved farther into the background to let the guys get caught up before Travis headed into his workday. She brought out her camera, switched lenses, then took a deep breath.

This was it. Time to begin.

Ashley looked around for inspiration. Checked the lighting and the angles for shots. One good thing about having a whole bunch of projects to work on, she wasn't stuck following one path. She could allow herself to simply drift for a few days. Take some experimental pictures—see what direction called to her.

She'd told Travis to ignore her and he pretty much did. Blake disappeared, and the barn settled into the soft sounds of animals moving around and the low buzz of the electric lights over the worktables. Ashley took some close-up shots of textures for backdrops. The aged wood of the barn walls up high where they'd remained untouched by hands or animals, tiny fibers sticking upright from the greyish-brown surface. A shot of the smooth curve of a board at hand height, where a million touches had added to the polish and given the curve a high-gloss finish.

She clicked picture after picture of Travis as he used an old coffee tin to scoop oats into feed stalls for the horses. His hands were firm as he pushed aside beasts and checked them over.

He looked up a few times and smiled—the twist to his lips that made her heart pound without even trying. She caught him with the enormous head of a horse nearly resting on his shoulder as the beast nuzzled him for more treats. Travis pushed his hat back into place and patted the creature before moving on to the next task.

Smooth motion, smooth energy.

A sensation of coming home crept up as she worked, ideas percolating how she could make each of her projects into something special. Something that would set her mark on the art world and make it possible to do it for a living.

Her goals were lofty, but she had to follow her dream.

And trailing after Travis and snapping shots of that magnificent backside as a part of chasing her dream?

It wasn't too shabby a life.

3

———

Travis patted the mare on her rump and closed the gate, back from checking the new calves in the far paddock. Exhaustion had soaked into every one of his bones, and it was all he could do to put one foot in front of the other and head through the trees to find Ashley.

Seven days she'd been dogging his steps. If he hadn't been caught up in the frazzle of calving season, he would have been driven crazy by her constant presence.

As it was, he had the filthiest dreams going on and woke up stroking himself, images of her soft body under him filling his brain. But actually going after her and getting her to reconsider them not being a couple?

Maybe come May. After he'd slept for a solid twenty-four hours and could put more than two words together to dazzle her.

He stopped in the middle of the narrow bridge between the main Six Pack land and the second house where Blake and Jaxi had settled. The creek under him was more of a trickle than a flow. Full runoff was still coming as the high mountain peaks remained snow-covered and frozen. Here at the lower elevations the temperatures were milder—thank God—and leaves had already budded in an early spring.

He bit back a yawn and went the rest of the way over to the second ranch house.

A couple of hay bales were arranged by the fencepost between the yard and the north field. Two little girls dressed to the teeth sat perched on top of the bales, and Travis smiled. He wasn't much for kids, but he had a soft spot for his nieces, mainly because it was a fucking lot of fun to see how tied up in knots they, and their mama, got his big brother Blake.

Ashley clicked off shots as Travis's sister-in-law Jaxi arranged the squirming two-year-old tykes and their six-month-old baby sister. Travis paused far enough back he didn't disturb them. Just marveled at the complete western outfits Jaxi had found in miniature. From jeans and flannel shirts down to the teeny boots and hats.

Blake was right. Even Travis who knew shit all about kids and poses thought the setting was far better than the silly pictures currently stuck up on his parents' mantel with the rest of the smiling faces of grandkids and graduation shots from him and his brothers.

Posing in a formal gown and cap hadn't been him.

His cell phone rang, and he turned away to answer it, stepping behind the trucks to stop from interrupting the photo shoot.

"You still not done for the day?" he asked his dad.

"I stopped two hours ago. One of the privileges of getting old." Mike Coleman got to the point. "You free to come up to the house for a bit? We need to chat."

Chat? "I didn't do it."

Mike laughed. "No, you're not in shit."

"*—Mike. Watch your language.*"

It was Travis's turn to laugh as his mom's scold interrupted them.

His dad lowered his voice. "She caught the grandsons cussing and thinks it's all my fault. Now I have to mind my manners all the time. Pain in the ass, I tell you."

"Be thankful she didn't catch them smoking, or she'd take away your pipe," Travis noted.

"Hell, you're right."

"*Mike!*" Marion warned again.

Travis snickered as his dad muttered in the background. "I'll be over in a couple minutes," Travis said. "I have to tell Ashley where I'm going."

He made it to the main house in less than five minutes, stepping past an unfamiliar car in the parking area. The warmth of his childhood home greeted him with familiar scents and sights. The never-ending aroma of coffee in the air, the worn hardwood flooring polished to a spotless shine by his mom.

His father was seated at the long family table, Travis's cousin beside him. Karen's dark hair was pulled back into a typical working ponytail. Her lined jean jacket, thick enough to keep out the cool spring temperatures, was draped over the back of her chair, leaving her dressed in a neat cotton shirt.

"That explains the strange car outside."

Karen tapped the awkward cast covering her lower limb. "Can't drive my truck right now, so the shop gave me a loaner that's an automatic."

"Makes sense." Travis joined them, sitting across from Karen and helping himself to a cup of coffee from the thermos on the table. "Other than the broken leg, how you doing?"

Karen sighed heavily. "Never realized how frustrating a physical injury would be. Not only is getting around more trouble, but me being out of commission is causing other problems. I need some help."

"That's why she's here." Mike leaned back in his chair and gestured to Karen. "I'll let you do the explaining."

Travis frowned. He didn't think Karen would be the one to show up if the Whiskey Creek side of the Coleman family was having issues. His Uncle George was pretty much a tight-fisted captain of his ship—reluctantly allowing his three girls to help at the ranch only because he had to. "You having trouble keeping up with calving?"

His cousin rolled her eyes. "Oh, we're getting by. My dad contacted some friend of his and convinced him to send over his sons to give us a hand."

"Well, that's good." Travis paused at the face Karen made. "Isn't that good? Uncle George wouldn't ask just anyone to come work with your cattle."

"Oh, they're skilled enough, I guess. It's a royal pain in the behind having to put up with strangers around the place, but yeah, it's going okay. Only I have a different issue." She leaned forward, resting her elbows on the table. "Of all the years to try to expand operations, I picked this one. I've been working since last fall on a side project—using some of the Whiskey Creek horses for a new adventure camp in the Willmore Wilderness Park outside of Jasper National Park. My partner and I are all set. We'll be offering trail rides during the spring and summer. I was supposed to go out and check on things on a regular basis—troubleshoot, make sure all the horses we've provided are well cared for and healthy over the entire season. But mostly a lot of office work and grunt labour plus a bit of riding."

Travis nodded slowly. "You won't be getting up on a horse anytime soon, will you?"

She shook her head. "Not until the end of May for sure, and they'll have run at least two camps by then. Not to mention all the setup and organizing at the start. I was supposed to head out after this weekend, but..." she tapped her cast again, "...obviously not."

What a mucked-up mess. Everyone Travis knew was knee deep in spring chores. "You want to know names of people to hire?"

Karen shook her head. "I want to hire you to go in my stead as supervisor."

Travis hadn't seen that one coming at all. "Bullshit."

"You're capable. You're good with horses, and you worked at a camp a few years back, so you know what to expect."

"Yeah, I worked at one, but I didn't run it." Travis's brain flooded with memories from his time away. The chores they'd done on a daily basis prepping the animals for trail rides, caring for them at the end of the day—it hadn't been a terrible job. He'd had a ton of time off from what he remembered.

But supervisor?

"You'd be in charge of ordering supplies and making sure that the head wrangler has everything he needs—I've got everyone else in place, only I can't go and do my job. I'd really appreciate having someone I trust go in my stead."

Travis couldn't stop his grin at her words. "Now you're patting my ego."

"Nope. I call it as I see it. You've got the second-best touch with the horses out of everyone in the Coleman clan, other than me. I am the best." She grinned. "See? I'm not talking you up just to convince you to go. You know there's no way I'd ask someone I didn't trust to be in charge of my babies."

High praise indeed, but there were still a couple of huge issues. "I'm glad you think I'm skilled enough to take over for you, but there's one big trouble. If I'm off doing your job in the mountains, that leaves the Six Pack spread short on help."

"That's why she talked to me first," Mike interrupted. "We

can manage. If it gets rough, we'll convince Daniel to throw in his hand for a short while."

"You can have one of the Marlette boys who invaded my place this weekend," Karen offered. "Heck, you can have all three because I don't want them underfoot all summer long, getting in my way."

Travis paused. He loved the ranch and working with his family, but a change of scenery for a few months might be exactly what he needed. "I don't have to actually lead the trail rides, do I? I don't know that area well enough to feel comfortable guiding."

Karen shook her head. "My partner has that part under control. James and his girlfriend are registered guides, plus Dani's got her medical ticket and they have their own horses, so like I said, the job is mostly coordination and supervision."

"Hell, maybe I'll do it," Mike proposed. "Sounds like less work than I'll be pulling back here."

Karen grinned. "You know it. Why do you think I'm so pissed off I don't get to go?"

Travis laughed. "Dad, you're serious you don't mind me being gone until Karen can take over?"

His father nodded. "Especially if Karen's right and we could get a little help from the Marlettes, we'll be fine."

"Depending on how well I recover, you might end up out there the entire season, Travis," Karen warned. "No use in me going out once you've got the routine down pat."

Shit. It was all making great sense until he remembered his favour to Ashley—he didn't want to leave her in the lurch, but he didn't want to turn down family in need. "I hate to bring this up, but you know my friend Ashley?"

Karen nodded.

"She's doing research for some projects. Taking pictures around the ranch and stuff. I don't know how she'd feel about wandering around when I'm not here."

Karen paused. "Well, she's welcome to come shoot at Whiskey Creek if she wants. Or for that matter, she could go along with you." Her eyes lit up. "Oh, man. You think she would? I mean, I'd pay her, but we could use some photos for the website and to use in a brochure, and—"

Mike laughed. "See? Not a problem, Travis. Ask Ashley if she'd like to go with you, and if she still needs shots around the ranch, she can contact me or Blake or Karen. We'll figure it out however we can."

And this was what family did—they helped each other. There was no reason not to offer Karen the hand she needed. Travis gave her a wink. "I'm yours. Put down the details in writing so I can go over them again if I need them."

Karen sighed in relief. Mike shook Travis's hand then rose and disappeared into the kitchen with his coffee mug.

Travis accompanied Karen to her car. "I promise to do my best for you."

She had to concentrate as she manoeuvred herself behind the wheel, but once she settled, she popped open her window and gave him a smile. "You'll do great. Honest. I trust you. And between you and my head wrangler, you should have a great summer."

She took off before he could ask the wrangler's name, but that was the moment Ashley stepped out from between the barns, her blonde hair shining in the afternoon sun as she strolled slowly, taking pictures as usual.

As usual, his body reacted.

The issue he'd been avoiding he now had to face straight on. Maybe it was for the best. Maybe...getting pushed hard enough to find a new solution was what he needed.

The only thing he knew for sure was he couldn't take off and fight anytime he got the urge this summer. He'd be too far into the bush—too remote for that kind of insanity.

No, Ashley was right. He had to find a new way. It also thrilled him to think there would be no reason for them to be apart anymore—not if he gave in to her demands.

She crossed the yard to his side, stopping to tuck her camera into her bag.

She tilted her head. "You look like you've got a secret."

"I do." He turned her toward the ATV, his palm settling easily in the small of her back. "And if you're a good girl, I'll share with you."

"I'm always a good girl," Ashley teased.

Oh, was she ever. "Come on, I'll take you home and tell you my secret over dinner."

Travis Coleman was up to something. Ashley rocked herself on the swing outside his trailer and watched him at the grill as he turned thick steaks over the coals.

He'd been a gentleman to the hilt ever since he'd brought her home today.

Oh, he'd been polite the other days. Going out of his way to stop when they were in the far fields. Giving her a chance to snap pictures while he filled in his time with small, never-ending ranch chores.

He hadn't once pushed her to take things back to the sexual relationship they'd enjoyed the previous fall and winter.

She wasn't sure if she should be pissed off or pleased he was following her expectations so fully. Pleased—she had to be pleased. She knew that. Until he had his head straightened out.

But damn, she wished he'd make it soon—she was getting tired of her vibrator and fingers.

But now? He'd offered her meals other days. She'd cooked for him as well, falling into an easy friendship that she thoroughly enjoyed. But the glances he was tossing her way this time around? Those said he had plans.

Plans he knew she'd like. A shiver raced up her spine, warmth flushing her skin from more than the shower she'd taken once they reached his trailer.

Travis might have his kinks, but she had hers as well, and he knew it. Knew how to stroke her to a feverish pitch...

She stopped the swing in midmotion and rose abruptly. This? Was where she wasn't supposed to go. Until things officially changed, she was not getting herself all heated up over impossible pleasures.

"It's ready," Travis called, balancing a plate in one hand as he held his other toward her.

Ashley stepped across the space between the trees and the deck. "Can't believe you have a swing out here."

"Nephews stop by sometimes. Jaxi with the girls—I figured it was simpler than having them tear the house apart."

They were inside, seated at the table, the scent of barbecued steaks and baked potatoes filling the air. "You're spoiling me," Ashley teased. She popped the caps on a couple beers and lined them up beside their plates. "There—my contribution to dinner."

Travis laughed. "You can cook anytime."

Their eyes met and heat flashed between them.

Ashley looked away first, digging into the food as if she'd been the one doing manual labour all day instead of merely wandering around taking photos. "You said you had news?"

Travis finished his bite then put down his utensils.

She coughed. "Oh dear, so serious as that?"

He laughed again. "No, I need to show you this."

He reached behind him to the side counter and grabbed a folded paper. There was a hand-drawn horse on the front, and she held her comments, just in case. Sure enough, the paper unfolded to include trip information for the *Trailblazers of Willmore Wilderness Park* with "trail rides and week-long adventure camps". One of the owners had a last name of Coleman. "Family?"

Travis nodded. "My cousin Karen. They're starting up this year, and yeah, I know that's a pretty shitty brochure, but I guess word of mouth was enough they filled their bookings already."

"Good for her."

"She wanted to know if you'd do pictures for them."

Thank God. Ashley could admit the truth. "Oh man, they so need it."

He chuckled. "They do, but there's more. Karen had an accident a couple weeks ago and busted her leg. She needs me to go fill in for her at the camp. There are guides and wranglers, but she wants family to head up her part."

Ashley's stomach fell. "Oh."

He waved a finger in her face. "Don't go leaping to assumptions. I thought about you—I promised I'd help you, and I will. But maybe you can help me as well."

Ashley frowned. "Go on."

Travis leaned back in his chair and crossed his arms. "Uncle George is a bit of an old-school ass. He's got three girls, and the only reason he tolerates them helping around the ranch is that Karen is the most incredible horsewoman. The middle girl, Tamara, has her nursing certificate, but Karen and Lisa want to work the ranch. They want to prove they can make a success of what they try."

Ashley picked up the brochure and held it between two fingers like it was a dirty rag. "This isn't very impressive."

"But it's a start. And all the really important things Karen did right. I hate to see her plans fall apart." He grimaced. "Hate to have Uncle George have another chance to say 'I told you so'."

"So you're going to..." She checked the flyer. "Willmore Wilderness Park for the summer?"

He nodded. "And I'd like you to come with me."

Oh boy. "Really?"

He leaned forward and grabbed her hand. "Really. Does that surprise you? That I like having you around?"

She shook her head. "I'm surprised you're going that easily. The ranch? The chores...?"

"All dealt with. You can stay here if you want. You can move into the trailer for the summer, if that works best for you. My dad and Karen both offered to coordinate shots anytime you need. I just won't be here to help you."

Ashley warmed at his offer, but now her curiosity was on the rise. "But you'd like me to come with you."

"I would." He stroked his thumb over the back of her knuckles. "There will still be horses. Rustic trail rides, if that kind of thing would work for your projects. The mountains and foothills in that area are even more beautiful than around the ranch—although I can't believe I said that. You could probably find some nice creeks and a mountain river or two—it's a bit of a photographer's paradise."

"As well as having another job—taking action shots for a real brochure for Karen's company?"

"That too. I don't know what they'd pay, but it should be fair."

"She's a Coleman, of course she'd be fair." Ashley turned the paper in her fingers as she sipped her beer, considering. Travis went back to his steak, giving her time to think.

She knew what she wanted, only...

"It does sound interesting. I'd love to get right into the heart of the mountains to take pictures." Her mind filled with possibilities—variations on what she'd already been planning for her projects. Additional work in a new area? There were more intriguing possibilities about the situation than negative.

Only...

She lifted her gaze to meet his. "If I come out with you, does that mean you think we'll be sleeping together?"

4

*S*leeping? Travis didn't plan on wasting any time in the first while actually going unconscious around her.

"I want you in my bed, yes."

"So things have changed since a week ago when you told me you couldn't make me any promises?" He saw it—the moment the real situation hit her, Ashley's eyes widened. "Shit. You're going to be in the bush the entire summer. Are you sure about that?"

It was hard to hide his amusement. "What? Now you don't want me to do it? I thought you said I had to give up fighting—well, here you go. I won't be taking off to tear up any bars or go bare-knuckles down at the club."

"Just like that? Cold turkey, and you're not worried? How you going to—"

"Stop poking," Travis snapped. Dammit—that wasn't the response she needed. He tried again, softer this time. "Sorry, didn't mean to be a jerk, but yeah, it's going to be a stretch. I'll have to deal with it, and you know what? Having you there would be a huge help."

She was still staring, but there was a hint of something else in her eyes now. More accepting, only with a touch of fear and sadness that made him want to cradle her close and protect her as he fought to figure out the right path.

He pushed forward. "I don't know all the answers. Either you accept that, and we deal with any shit that comes up, or you tell me to screw off and we keep things businesslike and platonic even though we both know that's not what we want."

"Either, or." Ashley shook her head. "That simple?"

He snorted. "Didn't you say that to me about a week ago? Life was far simpler than I was making it. You believe that or not?"

She frowned, her expression gone cold. "That's playing dirty."

"Your words, sweetheart, not mine. Yes or no?"

"You're a fucking asshole sometimes, Travis Coleman." She went back to her plate, but she was smiling again. Damn, the changes of mood she went through tore him up. All her emotions laid out and up front. Right out there, living on the edge. Nothing hidden with Ashley.

He liked that about her. Liked it a lot.

"You're crazy about assholes. Admit it."

Ashley rose from the table and stomped to the picture window. She stared out, her arms wrapped around her waist as she stood quietly.

"You didn't answer." He followed her, crowding in close.

She stood with her back to him, breathing deeply. Through the open windows the quiet noises of spring surrounded them. The wind in the trees and the occasional birdsong the only things to break the silence.

He waited for her to decide, refusing to give her any more options. It made him a bastard, but not having all the answers didn't change what he wanted here and now.

He wanted her.

Desperately.

Ashley twisted to face him, her head held high, eyes bright with an internal fire blazing. "If you promise not to fight *and* that you'll tell me when you feel the need to fight, I'm yours."

"How the hell does that make any sense?" Travis caught his breath as she planted her palms on his abdomen then slowly slid her hands up to his chest. "I promise not to fight. Isn't that enough?"

She shook her head, distracting him by slipping her fingers around his neck and threading them into his hair. "If you feel the urge to get your head knocked off and you tell me, then maybe we can deal with it without you finding some stupid-ass solution that ends with you sent home to your family in a box."

Frustration, anger, rage. Guilt. All the things he'd been at war with for so long clashed inside. The sick pleasure he got from the pain—he'd done his best over the past months to ignore its intoxicating lure. It would be easier to ignore if he had the sweet pleasures Ashley freely offered to divert him.

He'd been strong enough to deny himself other things; he could deny the urge to fight so he could be with her.

Don't think any deeper, don't confess anything more.

There were things he didn't want to admit, not even to himself.

He slipped his hands around her and settled her firmly against his chest. "Deal."

The flash of fire in her eyes—a challenge, or an acknowledgement this wasn't going to be easy?

Easy or not, it was going to be good.

Her nerve endings tingled in anticipation.

Trust.

Believing he'd keep his word had never been an issue. If it had, she'd never have asked for his promise, would never have attempted to get involved again.

Not when there was so much on the line. Not only her future dreams, but she was serious—she didn't want him dead. Couldn't stand to have someone else put themselves into a position where she could have saved them, and she hadn't.

She stroked the firm muscle under her fingers, the heat of his body pressed to hers making her smile grow. "Thank you, Travis."

His grin bloomed. The one that had tied her up in knots since the first time she'd spotted him across the room. Cocky, arrogant. He could have been the villain tying a damsel to the train tracks or the hero rushing in to save her—she wasn't sure which side he was going to show at any given moment.

The uncertainty was part of what she craved.

Travis's grip on her hips tightened. "You still sleeping in your camper?"

"Yup. Got everything I need to be comfy." She drew one finger down his neck, tracing tiny designs. "I didn't want to disturb anyone."

"You disturb me by breathing," Travis growled. Then he caught her up and connected their mouths, and she didn't care where she was except she was with him, and damn, the man could kiss a woman senseless.

He didn't kiss greedily. Not a frantic, out-of-control attack that would have left her head spinning and lips swollen. He'd given her that kind of kiss before. The soft and the hard. The frantic and the teasing, and she adored them all.

This one threatened to melt her knees right out from under her. Deliberate, even pressure. His lips to hers in a way she couldn't escape but had no intention of fleeing anyway. He stroked his tongue between her lips and tasted her as if she were expensive liquor. Something to be savoured and cherished.

When she could speak again, her words came out breathless, rushed. "The steaks are getting cold."

"I have a microwave." He pressed her torso harder to his, the thick line of his cock tight to her belly. It was all she could do to stop from squirming against him. "You in? One hundred percent?"

Exquisite shivers took her, a flush spreading over her skin from her core outward. She knew what he was asking. What she'd been craving to get from him. "Yes."

His lips were back on hers, hungry now, feasting on each other, their meal forgotten. Travis skimmed a hand under her shirt, the edge of a nail dragging down her spine as he scratched lightly.

Ashley stepped back, grabbed the bottom of her shirt and whipped it over her head.

His gaze locked on her bra. The thrift-shop special. Nothing fancy, no lace or ribbons or sheer see-though fabric. A good, sturdy faded-by-too-many-washes bra.

"Gorgeous," he breathed.

She laughed and lost her pants, stepping out from them to stand in front of him in her all-too-servable plain-Jane undies. "You need to go look at more porn. I'm okay, but I'm nothing special."

"Seen enough porn to know you *are* special." He trickled his fingers up her arm, ever so slowly, as he took her in from the bottom to the top.

Hunger? Need?

Definitely desire.

"I'm yours," she whispered.

"Thank God," Travis moaned as he fell to his knees. He

pressed his lips to her belly button and breathed deeply. "I missed you, Ash, missed you hard."

She stroked her fingers through his hair, amazed to have him at her feet after so many months. Anticipating exactly what they would do next. "I missed you too. But we're okay now."

He tilted his head back, and his dark grey eyes stole her breath. "We're more than okay. Open your legs."

She couldn't stop it. She shuddered, a full-out, torso-quaking rock as his request settled over her.

Request? *Order.* Her limbs were already moving. "I should have taken off my undies as well."

Travis traced his index finger along the edge of the fabric. "I'm pretty sure I can help you with that."

With his hand splayed wide, his thumb reached far enough to skim the apex of her mound. She tilted her hips, trying to make contact between his fingers and where she ached.

It was no use. Travis caught her by the hip and stilled her, continuing to stare intently between her legs as he teased her folds through the fabric.

"Love how you're so eager. Wet in an instant, so slick I could push you up against a wall and slam my cock into your pussy, and it'd be like coming home."

Ashley held on. Waiting for him. Knowing he'd get her there, even if it was in his own sweet time.

Every brush over her clit extended his reach until Travis was rubbing her from front to back, soaking the thin fabric and allowing him to press farther on each pass. He leaned in and put his mouth over her, heat and more moisture pressing against her sex.

It felt good, but barely there. A ghost of a touch. "Please, Travis."

His fingers didn't stop moving. "Please, what?"

"More. Make me come."

He tilted his head back and flames shot through her—his expression of hunger and passion exactly what she wanted to see. Only his words?

Typical Travis.

"Tell me. How. My tongue? My fingers? Want me to find something else to fuck you with?" The edge of her panties was jerked aside and his caress now made direct contact with skin. Wet, needy, aching skin.

Ashley stepped wider, the cold air touching her sex and making sure she knew exactly how wet he'd already gotten her.

"You decide."

His pupils widened, as did his grin. "Good answer."

He hooked his fingers into both sides of the thin fabric of her panties, and they were gone, ripped from her hips, and then she didn't know where they went because he'd stuck his head between her legs and thrust his tongue deep into her core.

He licked her hungrily. Thoroughly. Just enough time spent tormenting her clit, enough teasing everywhere else that she slid rapidly toward release, the anticipation of his touch having gotten her almost the whole way to climax, let alone knowing he was going to fuck her.

His tongue slowed as he switched to flicking her clit lazily, and a moan escaped.

Travis hummed in approval. "You like that, don't you? Me eating your pretty pussy until you squirm. Bet you're already thinking about what I'm going to do next. Wondering if I'll slip my fingers into you and fuck you hard. Or maybe I'll take you right to the edge before I stop and give you my cock."

"Anything, yes." She pulled on his hair, trying to get his lips back to what he'd been doing, but he laughed. Stood and caught her in his arms so he could tumble her to the couch. He rolled her to her back, grabbed her knees and spread her wide. Firm hands slid down her thighs, pinning her in place before he went back to work, the teasing circles and hard laps dragging a cry from her lips.

She loved the uncertainty, the change of pace as he read her body cues and slowed or sped up at exactly the right moment to drive her wild. And when she was gasping for air, on the verge of begging, he sucked her clit into his mouth and broke her—pleasure sweeping in and wrapping her limbs in fire.

He was up and over her in a flash. Cock in hand, slipping on a condom.

When had he dropped his pants? When had he found a condom? Ashley was still seeing stars when he put the thick crown to her core and leaned over her.

She'd expected him to thrust deep, a suitable follow-up to the fire and the intensity he'd prepared her with. Only he adjusted his position, one hand supporting his body over her, the other rising to cup her cheek as he slowly joined them together. One inch, another, the entire time his eyes fixed on hers. His devilish smile making her heart quake as his cock stretched her and filled her with delight.

Nothing in the room registered anymore. Nothing was left to distract her. No chores, no work, no mysterious future. Just him coming home into her body. She was being taken and yet giving at the same moment. And when he sank all the way in, groin flush with her hips, they both sighed.

Then laughed.

"I missed you such a hell of a lot, Ashley," Travis confessed.

She pressed her hand over his where he continued to caress his thumb against her cheek. "I missed you too."

They kissed. Slow and languid, tongues playing softly as he dragged his hips back. Pressed in deep. Fucking her with long, smooth rolling motions. She had no doubts he was enjoying her body, which was fine by her because she was so enjoying his. His tongue, his cock.

He snuck his fingers to her hip and lifted, changing the angle enough to make her gasp as he hit her clit on each stroke. The gentle rhythm made her squirm as tension built again. She dragged in air through her nose and dug her fingers into his shoulders, one leg wrapping around his hip as she tried to speed him—tried to pull him farther into her body at the final moment of each thrust.

He separated their lips and stared down, rocking extra hard, grinding against her clit until she jerked under him, climax rushing her. The intensity caught her by surprise. He continued to thrust through her orgasm. Extending her pleasure, making her shake under him. He closed his eyes and gave in. Hips jolting as he buried himself deep and clung to her.

They rocked together as the aftershocks went on and on. Ashley stroked his hair back from his face, Travis's fingers still clutching her hip hard enough there was no doubt they were together.

Clinging to each other while still connected.

Travis rested his forehead against hers and they breathed each other's air. Then he kissed her. Once. Lips touching fleetingly.

She sighed. "That was fine. That was mighty fine."

Travis rubbed his jaw over hers, rough stubble scraping her skin and sending a signal for goose bumps to rise. "It was. A good place to start."

He pulled out, and Ashley bit her lip to stop from complaining. But the smile on his lips and the fire still visible in his eyes as he looked her over, sprawled lewdly before him, confirmed what she'd figured—they weren't getting back to their steaks anytime soon.

That was fine with her as well.

5

Cassidy had damn near stared a hole in the papers he'd printed out—the ones from Karen Coleman telling him about her accident and the change of plans.

With one email his world flipped. He was about to be trapped for the next four months with the one person he had never expected to see again. The urge to run hit, as if a chastising demon had been set on his heels and there was no way to escape the torment.

Hell. Hell on earth.

He strode forward, the door on the one-room head-wrangler cabin slamming shut behind him as he made his way to the parking area. Around him were the semicompleted shapes of buildings that were being added to the small homestead Karen and her partner had purchased. The cookhouse, shower houses and additional living quarters—everything set in place to be finished over the coming month.

The paddock already had half a dozen horses in it, with the rest of the stock from Whiskey Creek ranch scheduled to arrive once the main season began.

All around him things were progressing well enough he didn't see any reason they wouldn't be ready on time.

A more rustic old-time camp was being established an hour's ride up the trail, but here at the end of the road from civilization was where they would greet the paying customers, and here was where the crew lived when they weren't actively running a camp.

It meant a little more work, having two distinct camps, but it was easier for accessing supplies and caring for the horses while creating a far more memorable experience for the riders.

The cook had already arrived. His assistant, Vicki, had shown up a few days ago, the petite bright-eyed woman settling into her job with a happy haze hovering over her.

Cassidy had met the guides a few times—nice young couple with a good hand with horses. His job wasn't going to be too rough, not with how careful James and Dani were with their rides.

No, all the details for the job were exactly what Karen had promised when she'd hired him months ago. Just...

Cassidy stared down the long approach road, watching dust rise as the last of the arrivals got closer to making an appearance.

He had to assume it was some cosmic joke. Some rotten karma he was being paid back for, though he couldn't imagine how he could have been that shitty without knowing it.

In some ways he had Travis to thank for the job. Travis had introduced Karen Coleman to him over a year earlier, and with the Coleman family's reputation, he knew any job Karen offered was sure to be a solid one. A safe one, far away from Rocky Mountain House and all chances of running into a certain someone he was trying to avoid.

Travis.

Fucking hell, he was going to be in the same place as *Travis* for four months.

Did his friend know? They hadn't spoken since the previous

July. Cassidy had considered emailing, but in the end hadn't responded to the ones Travis had sent. It was easier to cut things off clean. It hurt too much to pretend everything was wonderful and awesome and...*damn it all.* Now he had to deal with Travis for the entire summer?

Made him a sick bastard that he was both dreading it and longing for it all at the same time.

Travis's familiar truck pulled into the yard, parking right next to Cassidy's. Cassidy frowned as he noted there was another vehicle still on the road, only a little ways back, but then distraction hit in the form of one long, lean cowboy dropping smoothly to the ground and stretching his back as he looked around.

At this distance Cassidy figured he was safe, so he indulged in checking Travis over hungrily. Nothing had changed. The dark-haired devil still drove him crazy. Travis reached into the back of the truck and pulled out a pack, slinging it easily over his shoulder.

Time to face the music. Cassidy stepped from the shadows and made his way toward the lot. Travis turned toward him, his welcoming smile fading rapidly to dismay.

"Cassidy? What—?"

He snapped his mouth shut and glanced away. Lips tight, obviously fighting a rush of anger.

Shit. "That answers my first question. I wondered if you knew I was working the camp for the summer."

Travis took a deep breath before stepping forward. "You bastard."

Cassidy laughed. "Nice to see you again too, T."

"Screw that noise." Travis abandoned his bag to the ground at their side and got right in Cassidy's face. "What the fuck?"

"I'm head wrangler. Your cousin hired me."

Travis shook his head. "I meant what the fuck were you

thinking? You were there and then you were gone. Not a trace, not a note. I had no idea what had happened. You could have been dead in some ditch for all I knew."

"I told you I was going."

Hands slammed onto his shoulders, fingers closing into fists as Travis grabbed his jean jacket. He leaned in, their faces only inches from each other. "You said I couldn't have what I wanted. You didn't tell me you were going to fucking pack up your life and never come back. Asshole."

Cassidy stiffened his spine and refused to give in to the urge to wrap his arms around his friend and hold on tight. Focused on the job—on what he'd have to do to make it through the summer in one piece without giving in to what Travis had demanded.

Focused on what he'd have to do to avoid falling for him hard.

There was one question to ask straight out. "You want me to quit working for Trailblazers?"

"Not my damn choice." Travis released his grasp so quickly Cassidy rocked on his feet.

He probably deserved a little of this bullshit. "I'm sorry I didn't give you a warning. I only got the news you were coming in Karen's place two days ago."

"It was a last-minute decision."

"I figured." Time to change tack. Maybe if they pretended they were meeting for the first time, they would survive at least a few days without blowing up. Cassidy pointed over his shoulder. "You've got a place of your own here to set up. I can show you around, introduce you to the crew tonight. Tomorrow we can ride to Second Camp."

Travis picked up his bag and settled it on his shoulder again. "Fine. Only let's wait until Ashley arrives. She was only a few minutes behind me."

Ashley?

"Oh, the photographer. Right—Karen sent word about her as

well." Good, Travis seemed to be game for changing the topic. "We won't have many guests for the first while, so I figured she could bunk in one of the guest tents."

Travis flashed his grin, all cocky and bright again. Warning signals instantly went off in Cassidy's brain.

"Oh, you don't need to find her another space. She'll be bunking with me."

A dart of jealousy slammed him in the gut. Cassidy beat the sensation down with a firm fist as quick as possible. He pasted on a smile. "Single cot in your cabin."

Travis raised a brow. "We'll figure something out."

Bastard.

Cassidy turned toward the parking lot, deliberately ignoring Travis's gloating expression. The sinking sensation in his stomach was stupid. This was great news. If Travis was fooling around with some woman, Cassidy had nothing to worry about. Simple.

So why do I feel as if I've been kicked?

He shoved his confusion aside and instead focused on the throwback-to-the-hippy-generation van rolling into the parking lot. The ancient vehicle with the artsy paint job was like something out of a sixties magazine. The blonde who stepped from the driver's door twirled, her bright gypsy skirt flaring around her as she raised her arms to the sky and squealed happily.

She was wearing beaded sandals, and Cassidy laughed. "Damn, Travis, did you use a time machine to pick her up?"

Cassidy's taunts fell away as she continued to pivot, the sunlight shining through her thin garments. Fabric pressed against her soft curves highlighting her feminine form with its high breasts and smooth upper arms. She faced them and another jolt hit hard. The woman wasn't the most beautiful he'd ever seen, but she wore a smile full of mischief, her lively gaze darting around the area to take in everything. Full, sensual lips combined with high cheekbones. He could imagine digging his fingers into the thick mass of her blonde hair and fisting it tight, tugging to expose her long neck for kisses all along the smooth column down to the soft skin bared by the V neckline of her top.

He was staring, he knew he was, but Cassidy was too caught up in admiration to care.

Until Travis cleared his throat.

Fuck it. Cassidy tore his gaze off the woman's curved waistline, off the hips he was already imagining catching hold of and—

"Ash, come meet the head wrangler." Travis's grin taunted Cassidy. "Cassidy, this is Ashley Sims."

The wild gypsy woman lifted her eyes, and Cassidy was tossed into a cloudless Alberta sky. In her gaze the full heat of a summer day blazed down on him as she checked him over far more blatantly than his examination a moment earlier.

She hummed happily and held out a hand. "Well, well. You feel the urge to round anything up, give me a shout. I'd love to see you in action with a rope."

Cassidy jerked to a stop, her fingers already in his, not quite sure how to respond to that comment as he accepted her firm handshake.

Travis rolled his eyes. "You want him to strip so you can look him over a little closer?"

Instead of blushing or getting embarrassed, Ashley's eyes lit brighter. "You're a genius, Travis."

She stepped forward and closed the space between them, and Cassidy found his chin captured by a set of strong feminine fingers as she examined him up close and personal. "You've got an amazing jawline," Ashley noted. "And the two-day stubble? *Rawr.* Totally perfect. I could easily snap a dozen shots of you."

Cassidy stood like a statue as she traced fingers over his face, her gaze tightening in focus as a tickle moved over his skin.

He wasn't sure what the protocol was for being checked out by an artist. "Umm, well, I don't have a problem with photos. Karen told me you were going to give Trailblazers help with next year's brochures."

Ashley touched the corner of his temple, brushing her fingers up and into his hair as she traced the scar she'd discovered. His hat fell to the ground behind him, but she had him trapped, unable to move away from her captivating touch. "I like that you're not perfect. You've got a few bumps and bruises to go with the pretty blond hair and those gorgeous green eyes." She peered in closer, tugging on his neck to get him to bend. "You're not wearing coloured contacts, are you?"

Cassidy felt a smile breaking out in spite of the crazy situation. "Nope, ma'am, just me."

Ashley patted his cheek then let him go. "You're nice. I like you."

"He's an ass," Travis cut in. "But you can still like him."

Ashley blew a raspberry at Travis. Before Cassidy could bend to recover his hat, she'd swooped in and knelt at his feet, reaching up to pass it back. "Sorry. I get a little enthusiastic at times."

Cassidy fought to stop from peering down the front of her blouse, the creamy scoop of her breasts right there and exposed. He cleared his throat and willed his body to stop reacting like some bloody teenage boy. "No problem. I like people who get into their work."

Ashley glanced between the two men as she regained her feet. "Hmm. Travis, come here."

She tugged him forward, and Cassidy found himself standing inches away from Travis as Ashley looked them over intently.

Travis sighed. "You want to get unpacked before you start making mischief, sweetheart?"

Ashley shook her head. "Mischief first, last and always. You know that."

Being this close to Travis made Cassidy nervous, and he shifted his feet to ease away slightly. "If you're ready, I can show you where you'll be staying."

She didn't seem to hear, she was too busy examining him and Travis. "I definitely need you two in shots together. God, you've got that angel/devil thing going on. Darkness and light, sinner and saint—"

"And we both know who the sinner is," Travis drawled.

Her smile bloomed again, gaze darting between their faces. "I don't know. Maybe Cassidy is one of the fallen-angel types. Looks like heaven and knows exactly how to get you to paradise."

Travis laughed, the sound breaking over them like a waterfall. Encompassing them, ready to sweep them away. He'd shifted position, and now stood close enough his body heat brushed Cassidy.

Between Ashley's provocative words and Travis being... Travis, Cassidy was walking a thin line of control. He took a couple of deliberate steps away and adjusted his hat. "I really need to get back to work."

Travis's cocky expression screamed an accusation. "We don't want to keep you from anything important."

Cassidy bit back the urge to call him an asshole.

A shadow crossed Ashley's face as she stepped closer to Travis's side, her intuitive gaze not missing anything. "Do you guys know each other?"

The urge to deny they had a past struck, but that would be not only insane, but hurt worse than the truth.

Travis waited for him to answer, one brow lifted as if in a dare.

Fuck him. "We've met." He ignored Travis completely and turned a smile on Ashley. "Anything else I can get for you?"

God, those expressive eyes of hers were going to kill him. Blue lasers that cut through him as if she could read into his soul.

The shrewd evaluation softened, though, as she nodded. "I'll need a place to plug in the camper, if that's okay. Karen thought you'd have the ability for me to set up. I have my, well, office as it were, all in there."

She pointed back at the hippy-mobile.

Cassidy leapt at the change of focus. "I'll find you an extension cord. You might want to tuck in behind the cookhouse." He eyed the camper. "There's a bright spot for your solar panels, and you won't be interrupted as often by the trail-ride guests."

She nodded. "Sounds great."

"I'll get right on it." He pointed up the hill, speaking to Travis but not looking him in the eye. "Your cabin is the second on the left. Feel free to raid the storage shed for whatever you need to make it work for two. I can help with carrying in about an hour. The others all went into town this morning to buy supplies, but I expect they'll be back in time for supper. I'll introduce you then."

"No problem." Travis managed to put his smirk into two words.

Stick to the basics. Cassidy ignored the desire to smack Travis a good one, instead smiling at Ashley who seemed to be excited about living in the bush for a while. "The ladies' shower house isn't working yet, but there's not a lot of people around. Until it's ready, we'll make up a warning sign to hang on the men's door when you or the other women need to clean up."

"Thanks." Ashley tucked a strand of hair behind one ear a moment before Travis captured her fingers and pulled her with him up the path. "I'll talk to you later about the pictures," she called over her shoulder.

"Deal."

Cassidy couldn't help it. He watched them. Ashley glanced

back once and gave him a smile that warmed him far more than he had a right, not when she was with another guy.

Not when she was with Travis.

The bastard never looked back. Cassidy felt like kicking his own ass for giving a damn.

6

———

Travis opened the door then followed her into the tiny cabin. His head full of memories, he was far more focused on the shock of discovering Cassidy than the actual living space.

Ashley dropped onto the teeny single-person bed, the springs squeaking ominously. "You sure you want me in here with you? I might have more room in my van."

Other than the bed, there was also a dresser and a small desk with a chair. A row of hooks along one wall, a towel rack under the window. "It won't be tough to keep the place clean."

He stared out the window, catching a glimpse of Cassidy heading in the opposite direction. What a mixed-up, fucked-up situation.

When he turned back, Ashley had ditched her sandals and wiggled onto the bed. She leaned on the wall and was observing him with an all-too-knowing look.

Fuck. "What?"

She raised a brow. "Snapping at me already. That's interesting."

"I didn't snap—" Her brow went even higher, and Travis gave up. "Don't pull that goddamn Vulcan face on me. Yes, I snapped. No, it's nothing bad. And you're sleeping in my bed, not your van, got it?"

A smile played about her lips as she wrapped her arms around her knees. "Cassidy's hot."

"For fuck's sake." She was merciless. Travis grabbed the chair from by the desk and hauled it around so he could collapse onto it. "Start the damn questions because I know you're about to burst over there."

She grinned. "All your secrets belong to *meeee*."

Almost true. "Cassidy and I met a couple years ago. He was working in the Rocky area, and we fell into doing stuff together. I thought he was about my best friend. Then last summer something happened and he took off, and I hadn't heard from him since."

"That was before we met then?"

Travis nodded.

Ashley frowned. "How come you didn't know he was working here? I thought Karen gave you all the employee information and that kind of stuff."

Travis could have kicked himself. "She did. Only the first page listed everyone by their initials, and I didn't bother to go through the rest of the pages before we got here. His last name is Jones—not like that would set off any warning bells."

"And it is a warning?" Ashley wiggled to the edge of the bed, her expression all earnest and concerned. "Before he took off, did you guys have a fight or something?"

The words *or something* stuck in his throat.

Sudden exhaustion hit like a two-by-four, carrying with it the recollection of pain. Travis stared into space and fought the rush of memories, and the confusion and the longings he had no right to have.

A soft stroke across his cheek made him glance into her dreamy eyes. "You're drifting, Travis Coleman. You gonna tell me what's got you all tangled into a knot? I won't tease if you don't want to share."

Travis laughed. "Don't take this the wrong way, but you let up on a secret? Bullshit. You're like a dog worrying at a bone."

"I can restrain myself if needed," she insisted. She tugged him onto the bed and crawled over him, cuddling in tight and draping her arms around his shoulders until she was a human blanket. "I'm a good listener if you need one."

Travis slid his hands onto her hips, stoking his thumbs over the soft stretch of bare skin at the waistline where her shirt had ridden up. He touched their lips together lightly, kissing her because he could. Ashley softened in his arms like always, leaning against him as if offering reassurance.

He pulled back far enough to watch her face as he spoke. He hated to confess, but maybe it was about time to give a little. There was no way he'd survive the summer without her support. "I hit on him."

Her eyes widened. Not shock—more like delight. Then amazingly, a flush stole across her cheeks.

Ashley blushing? Well, there was a miracle.

"You going to say anything?" he asked.

Ashley swallowed. "Well, first off, I'm trying not to be distracted by the mental images of my angel and devil getting naked together, because holy *shit*, would that be hot."

Travis's body tightened involuntarily.

Her smile twisted up into self-mockery. "I'm a little embarrassed I flirted with him when he's gay. No wonder he looked so uncomfortable."

"Sweetheart, he totally looked uncomfortable because he wanted in your pants," Travis reassured her. "Trust me, the guy likes women just fine."

Her clever fingers were tangled in the hair at the back of his neck. "But you hit on him, which tells me you've got some explaining to do."

"Fuck." Travis took a deep breath. "Fuck, fuck, fuck."

"You wish," Ashley teased.

"God, you have such a smart mouth." Travis accepted her caresses and the knowing expression in her eyes. Might as well leap all the way in. "I don't get turned on by a lot of guys, but he does it for me. And when you mix it up with fighting, I kind of lost my head."

She nodded slowly. "Fighting... So he knows?"

Travis gave in and gave up. "He knows I fight. He wasn't sure why."

"Do *you* know why?" The question whispered out. She was damn near holding her breath as if unwilling to interrupt him and break the spell.

He'd never come straight out and admitted it. Faced his needs, and the twist it gave him. But something called right now, and he had to admit that Ashley could probably understand part of his desire better than anyone.

He spoke softly, stroking her body as if drawing courage from the contact. "I like the pain. I crave it at times. It's not only a physical need, but mental. Somewhere in the mist that crawls over me when I'm getting beat on, peace comes. It's...more than pleasure, it's like the most focused mental clarity in the middle of what should be killing me."

"I knew about the pain part," she admitted, "but the rest is new. You like it when control is out of your hands?"

Travis shook his head. "That's the strange thing. I don't think so. It's not like how it turns you on when I order you around or tie you up. I still want to be in charge, which is why fighting works so well."

She kissed his cheek. His jaw. Nuzzled her face against his

and gave him comfort. "You are such a high-maintenance boyfriend," she teased. "Can't just get off on tying me up and fucking me blind. No, you need to be bossy and pick exactly how hard you get beat."

Her words made him smile. "Variety makes the world go round."

Ashley caught him in an enormous hug. "Damn right, and don't you forget it." She pulled back and stared at him intently. "You're one hot number, Travis Coleman. Don't you go thinking there's anything wrong with looking for what you need."

Confusion washed over him again as she threw him for a loop. "I thought you hated my fighting."

She rolled her eyes. "Don't be an idiot. I hated that you were getting into situations where you could get seriously hurt. If this is something you get off on, find a safe way to meet the need. Like with someone who will stop when you've had enough, especially if you aren't able to tell them when you've reached that point."

He'd done too much looking into it to have much hope. "If you're thinking about some fancy sex club you've read about, should I remind you I live in a small town in the backwoods of nowhere? Maybe down in California there's a place on every corner where they hand out every kink in the book, but I've got what I got—a fight club or a bar. There's no masters or slaves, or whatever the fuck they call themselves."

Ashley stepped off him, straightening her skirt and blouse as she slipped her sandals back on. "You're pretty tied up in labels for a redneck country boy, you know that? Use a little imagination. If you like pain I can use a crop on your ass, and I won't expect you to call me sir or anything."

He caught her hand and kissed her knuckles, fighting his laughter. "The idea of you whipping me doesn't do it for me. I could tie you up with one hand and stop you at any time."

"So it is about control?"

Travis paused to really consider the question.

Then the minx continued, her eyes bright with mischief again. "What about Cassidy whipping you? That idea sound any better?"

"*Fuck*." Instant hard-on.

Her grin mocked him. "Well then, there's part of your answer. And if you're wondering? There's another area I don't give a damn about labeling. If it's pleasure, I'm all for it. I have no issue watching you get it on with Cassidy, or helping you get it on with Cassidy. Or getting it on with you while Cassidy whips your ass. Or..."

He caught her against him and kissed her silent before he got overwhelmed with ideas triggered by her words.

She dug her fingers into his hair and gave back as good as she got. Only the fact they had to settle in stopped him from taking her right there on the skinny single mattress.

Sharing had been amazingly freeing even as he wondered where all this honesty was going to take them—and just how fucked he was that the idea of Cassidy standing over him with a crop made him shiver.

Cassidy pushed the final fifty-pound bag of oats onto the shelf and turned back to find the countertop was empty. "Is that it? We got it all put away already?"

The head cook nodded. "Never seen so much food vanish that quickly without me cooking it first."

Cassidy laughed. "Thanks, Ted. Let's see what the rest of them are up to."

Through the swinging doors in the common room of the cookhouse, they found the small gathering of men and women who would be setting up the Trailblazer camp over the coming weeks. "You all survived your trip to town for supplies, I see."

The youngest of the work crew, David, piped up. "It's a damn long trip. Glad we don't have to drive that too often." He held out a beer, and Cassidy accepted it gratefully.

"You're all good here for the next while. If you do have an emergency or things you need, make a list and someone will pick up what you need when we're grabbing fresh food once a week."

The door swung open, and Ashley stepped into view followed closely by Travis. Cassidy focused on keeping his expression neutral. "Come on in, I'll introduce you to everyone."

Travis pulled out a chair for Ashley before offering a hand to the oldest man at the table. "Travis Coleman. You must be Ted. Nice to meet you."

The cook grinned and nudged the worker at his side. "See? My reputation is epic."

Travis pointed at the dark-haired woman on the other side of the table. "Well, according to that one you're sort of a god of the cookhouse. Vicki's been sending message after message home to my baby brother for the past three days talking about how incredible you are. I heard about it every night—I think Joel was getting a little jealous."

Vicki came around the table to give Travis a huge hug. "You're a turkey."

Travis squeezed her tight before tweaking her nose. "You're lucky you're engaged, or you'd have all these wildcats after you, not just Ted."

Cassidy wasn't sure when he'd lost control of the meeting. Travis seemed to know everyone and was ready to sweet-talk them all.

He stepped in. "Vicki, this is Ashley. She's doing some photography work over the summer, and she's a friend of Travis's."

Vicki's cheeks bloomed crimson. "I know Ashley."

Oh God. Cassidy glanced up at Travis, not surprised to see amusement on the bastard's face. This was probably another tangled mess Cassidy didn't want to know about that somehow, undoubtedly, Travis was at the center of.

Cassidy rushed through the rest of the introductions then motioned for Travis to join him. "Some of the equipment Karen ordered arrived, but I'm not sure what came is right. Can you go over it with me so we can make exchanges if needed?"

Travis nodded, kissed Ashley on the cheek then headed outside with Cassidy to the storage shed.

It took over an hour to get to the bottom of the list, a half-dozen items set aside to be sent back on the next trip and replaced with new tack.

Working by Travis's side was awkward and yet so natural once he told himself to stop being an idiot.

The man had shown up with a woman who was obviously capable of keeping him happy in bed. All the sexual tension had to be on Cassidy's side, but no fucking way was he going there. Not even when they touched and bumped in the tight quarters of the storage shed.

Cassidy was ready to head out the door to escape to fresh air and a cold shower when Travis spoke about something other than nose ropes and stirrups.

"You know, when you took off I tried to find you."

This conversation had to happen sometime. Cassidy leaned on the wall, needing a solid base to hold him up. "I told you not to."

Travis shrugged. "You see me doing what I'm told very often?"

His deadpan dry tone only made it even more wrong, but Cassidy still laughed. "No."

Travis stepped closer, a lock of dark hair hanging over his

forehead, his dark grey eyes burning into Cassidy's. "I emailed you. I called. I texted."

"Stalking me."

His eyes blazed. "You'd been beat on, badly, because of me. I wasn't sure if you were dead or alive. Not sure what kind of asshole simply takes off and leaves his best friend in the first place, but I was worried about you for more than one reason."

Ouch, that one hurt. "I'm sorry. I know that part was wrong."

"It was all wrong," Travis snapped. "Even if I disgusted you, we're still adults. You should have told me to fuck off. I could have laughed it off, and we'd still be friends."

Cassidy's chest burned. "You didn't want to be simply friends, and like you said, how often do you do as you're told?"

"So you took off."

"Like a fucking shot." The longer Travis pushed, the higher Cassidy's temper rose. "I got out of there for your own damn good, and while I'm sorry about scaring you, I'm not sorry for stopping you from making the biggest damn mistake of your life."

"It wasn't your decision to make alone. We were best friends." Travis dragged a hand through his hair, his voice shaking as he fought his anger. "I went to your house, you know."

That was all it took for the bottom to fall out of his stomach. "You went where?"

"Your house—your folks' place in Drayton Valley. I figured maybe they would know where you were."

Blinding pain and white-hot anger rushed through Cassidy. "You had no right."

"I was worried, do you not get it?" Travis demanded. "But for the record? Your old man is an asshole."

Bitter laughter escaped. "Trust me, that's not really news."

Travis's face tightened. "You know, I've pissed off my daddy pretty bad a bunch of times—my brothers as well. Never had one of them take out a shotgun and point it in my direction."

Cassidy's legs threatened to give way. He held on to the shelf support like his life depended on it. "I'm so fucking sorry."

Then typical Travis—typical full-of-bullshit, spit-into-the-wind Travis had the gall to grin. "Yeah, well, he didn't shoot, so that was good."

They stared at each other. Cassidy's heart pounded so loud in the silence he wondered if Travis heard it as well. "So where do we go from here?" Cassidy asked. "You going to have trouble working with me all summer?"

Travis reached past him and adjusted a pile of horse blankets stacked on the shelf. "Already told you I didn't. The question we really need to ask is slightly different."

Cassidy refused to move, not even when Travis bumped into him putting the stack back in place. "What's that?"

A hand landed on Cassidy's shoulder, firm grip slipping down his arm until Travis's fingers were wrapped around his biceps. "Does your offer to help me still stand?"

Too much had happened over the past nine months. Too many times he'd played through what had happened that day, and he honestly wasn't sure what Travis was asking. "What kind of help?"

The tight grip on his arm lessened until it was a bare caress, Travis's confidence seeming to ebb away as his voice lowered. "I'm not sure what I need, Cassidy, other than a friend. A good friend like you. Ashley is amazing, but I missed you like crazy, and I need to know you've got my back. That you still care at least a little."

Caring only a little wasn't the issue. Cassidy patted Travis on the shoulder, gripping him firmly. "I'm still your friend."

The words came from his heart, even if being a friend meant that eventually he had to hurt Travis all over again.

7

Ashley stared at the chaos in the yard and, out of consideration for the others, tried not to squeal like a child. The rest of them were dirty and tired, and it was barely past noon, but she was having the time of her life.

Her projects were going to be so amazing.

One idea after another had struck. She'd be back at the Colemans' later in the summer with plenty of time to add shots of the rolling foothills, but being at the horse camp was like stepping back in time.

Some of the crew were building platforms that would become the base for the final canvas wall tents used for accommodation. Another couple was working the horses. Travis had stepped in and ignored the complaints that he was supposed to be the *boss man*, and was currently helping erect the tents.

Pictures in sepia, added water damage, scratches.

It wouldn't be the first time anyone had used a little poetic license in photoshopping, and the results could be gorgeous. At least, those were the shots she saw in her head. Now she raced from spot to spot to try to capture the images so she could make them come to life.

Searching for ideas was a fun part of the creative process, frustrating and rewarding in turn.

And right now, dangerously hot.

With the ease of men well used to working with their hands, Travis and Cassidy laboured side by side, the occasional low-toned comment all they needed as they raised the posts and secured them in place. It was the unspoken communication going on that made her blood heat and threatened to melt her camera lens.

They weren't even naked. Yet.

She didn't think they were aware of it. The cautious glances, a moment of physical contact held slightly too long. A lifetime of people watching made it obvious to her. The guys were definitely into each other in a more than "thanks for all your help, let me grab you a beer" kinda way.

Travis had taken off his jean jacket and tossed it to her over an hour ago, and she'd slipped it on, the fabric warm from his body. Cassidy's gaze drifted over Travis's back, lingering on his shoulders and firm biceps. He glanced away quick enough when Travis twisted to face him, only then the game began in earnest as Travis took his turn staring when he thought no one was looking.

It was a strange fact she'd discovered years ago. People seemed to forget that with a camera in front of her face, she could bloody well see *everything*.

See the response of their bodies to the labour, and to their mutual attraction. Muscles flexed, sweat formed on their skin. Travis brushed his hair out of his eyes then took a long drink from his water bottle, his throat moving in smooth, rhythmic waves. A pained expression crossed Cassidy's face, and he twisted away, casually adjusting himself.

Ashley made a point of being extra busy for a few minutes

changing her camera lens so neither of the guys would ask why she was grinning like a banshee.

Whatever had made Cassidy say no then disappear last summer, it wasn't because he didn't lust after Travis.

"Ashley, can you come help for a minute?" Travis called.

"Sure. One sec." She put her camera and gear bag up high where it couldn't be hurt, stripped off the bulky jacket and joined them. "You need me to do some heavy lifting for you, boys?"

"We need about a dozen more hands than we've got." Cassidy pulled the canvas tight, or tried to, but it was stuck on the far edge of the floor platform. "Can you loosen that side then watch so it doesn't snag again?"

"Got it," she said, dancing over to the far corner and tugging the stiff fabric free. "Go slowly, 'kay?"

Travis and Cassidy pulled steadily, lifting the sturdy green fabric up and over the rigid supports already in place while she guided from her side. The guys slowly disappeared from sight as she hurried back and forth, keeping the material movable.

"Okay, now come over here and thread this together. We can't let go," Travis shouted.

Ashley hurried around the corner, and a wild surge of sheer mischief struck as she spotted their precarious positioning. Travis had leaned around Cassidy to lock the loose edge in position. Their bodies were jammed together as they held the two massive pieces of canvas securely in place until she could finish her task.

Travis stood with legs wide apart, one leg between Cassidy's, their hips less than a foot from each other. She would have to crawl between them to get at the seam. "What do I use as thread?"

"The rope." Cassidy gestured with his foot in the general direction. "You'll have to guide us to line things up correctly."

"No problem." She coiled the cord in her hand and slipped

past Travis, brushing his torso and appreciating how everything about the man was so nice and hard.

Everything.

She leaned to the left as she squatted, this time knocking into Cassidy. "Oops. Sorry about that."

"It's fine." He tried to step out of her way.

Travis shot out a warning. "Stop, you're pulling me off balance. The whole thing will go to shit if you move."

Ashley had the thin rope worked through the bottommost eyelets on both sides and tied off in a tight knot. "I'm ready to lace. Anything fancy I need to remember?"

"Shove it in then pull it out," Cassidy ordered.

Dead silence for all of three seconds. That's how long it took before Travis burst out laughing. "What, no lube?"

Cassidy leaned his head against the support post. "God save me from your dirty mind."

"Just saying. I'd think you'd at least give it a kiss. Maybe rub it a little first or something. Get things warmed up."

Ashley snickered softly, down on her knees by their feet as she worked her way up the eyelets. She pulled hand over hand to drag the rope tight, her elbow sweeping Cassidy's thigh on every stroke.

When he shifted position this time, she took a deep breath to stop from humming happily.

Cassidy had a hard-on as well.

She threaded the rope through another set of eyelets, her body pinned between the two guys and the wall of canvas she was creating. Their limited banter fell to nothing, and only the sounds of the other crews carried on the air. Hammering drowned out the radio, but right next to her was where Ashley's attention was focused. On the warmth at her back, tight indrawn breaths escaping Cassidy's lips. The pressure as Travis leaned closer. It was like being in some glorious candy store where all her favourite treats were waiting for her to pick them and savour the sweetness.

Surrounded by two hot guys who were also hot for each other? Yes, please. Now if only she could have this positioning with their clothes off, and all parties on the go for some fun.

Slowly was the word of the moment, she supposed. They had all summer to get there.

The next holes were about chest level but she'd hit a snag. "Damn it, they're not lined up. Cassidy, can you pull your side down a bit?"

"I'll try." He adjusted position again.

"There. That's it. Now hold it." Ashley slipped under his arm and curled herself into place, feeding the loose end of the rope through as quickly as she could in the awkward position. He had lovely muscular arms—bulkier than Travis's. The need to keep her balance was a great excuse to grab hold of one, her fingers wrapped around the solid mass.

Cassidy coughed softly but didn't say anything, just waited for her to finish the next step.

By the time she'd done two more layers she was on her toes, reaching overhead. Her breasts made direct contact with Cassidy's forearm, her right hip rubbing Travis's groin.

There seemed to be less oxygen in the air than she'd remembered.

"You nearly done?" Travis drawled, his amusement clear.

"Nearly. I don't want to make a mistake and have to start all over." She twisted her head to the right and winked. "I'm sure you and Cassidy have much better things to do."

His gaze flicked to the side—to Cassidy—before coming back to hers. Travis's grin held a hint of something else. "Such a fucking tease."

"Oh, honey, a tease is the *last* thing I am. You know that." Words snuck out, lust-filled and low, though she wasn't trying to be obvious. There was no denying the facts. She'd give a hell of a lot to enjoy being sandwiched between them.

But then, she'd enjoy watching them crawl all over each other as well.

The final eyelets were too high for her to reach. "Someone's got to take over."

"Here." Cassidy put his hands over hers, slipping up to the rope end and grabbing hold. Ashley twisted, intending to get out of the way when, glory hallelujah, he leaned in to finish the task and every damn inch of him pinned her in place against the corner support post. His hard chest compressed her breasts, making her nipples tighten. His hips tight to hers, his rigid cock pushing into her softness. A rush of moisture hit between her legs. She'd been building to this moment all morning, but it was now confirmed—her panties were soaked.

The whimper of desire that escaped her could be misinterpreted as a gasp of surprise. Maybe.

Except she looked up to discover half-hooded eyes, fire in the depths as their gazes met. The green of his irises was nearly eaten up by the darkness of his pupils. Ashley wanted to wrap her arms around his neck and drag their mouths together. To strip them both and deal with the aching need.

What she got was ignored.

He couldn't back up and set her free, not without letting the rope loose, so she got to savour another moment of being trapped. Once he'd finished feeding the rope through the hole, though, he handed it to Travis.

"Grab hold and tie it off for me, T." Then as if he hadn't been rubbing her with a full-sized erection, he was off the platform altogether, gathering tools with his gaze deliberately focused elsewhere. "Well, that's done. Thanks for your help, Ashley."

She wasn't sure if she should laugh, or crowd in and start all over again. "You're welcome."

Travis stroked her arm softly before kissing her cheek. "You want to go get us a couple drinks?"

She dragged her focus off Cassidy to look up into dark grey eyes. "Sure. No problem."

"Oh, and Ash?" Travis helped her down off the edge of the platform. "Lots of ice."

Great idea. Maybe she'd pour some over her head until he was done for the day. "You are so getting jumped as soon as you're free," she whispered.

"Looking forward to it." Travis gave her a wink then turned to help Cassidy who was all business, attaching the bottom section of canvas to the underside of the platform. Studiously ignoring the both of them.

She took one final look before heading back to the pile where her gear waited.

Cold drinks would never take the place of hot fucking, and that was the truth.

"Sorry about that," Cassidy muttered.

Travis frowned as he grabbed a handful of screws and picked up his drill. "For what?"

"For getting too close to your girl. She surprised me there."

It was the last thing he'd expected to hear. "You're apologizing for...? Good grief. Okay, you're nuts. She's not my girl."

Cassidy paused, drill held in midair. "But you said..." Total confusion crowded his face as Cassidy tried to figure it out.

Travis leaned on the edge of the platform and waited.

"She's sleeping with you, asshole," Cassidy grumbled. "She spent the night in your cabin. What the hell?"

"Oh, that."

"Yes, *that*," Cassidy snapped.

Travis knelt and put in a screw. "Number one, Ashley is all woman, so forget that *girl* shit."

"Don't be more of a fuck than you have to be, Travis."

Cassidy was feeling snarly, was he? Travis had a good idea why. "Number two, I didn't see anything to apologize for, so this tells me you're the one with the filthy mind. What were you thinking of doing to her, you dog?"

"Shut up."

"She wouldn't mind getting dirty with you, you know," Travis confessed. "She as much as said it when we got here."

Cassidy choked, retreating from Travis, his expression gone skeptical.

Travis patted him on the shoulder. "It's okay, you can breathe. She's not cheating on me. She's rather...intense in how she lives life. Sex is something she grabs with both hands and has fun with."

"And you're good with that?"

"Why the hell would I want her to change? Not my business if she wants to look at your ugly mug while she's getting off."

For a moment he thought Cassidy was going to fall over. The evil glare his friend finally delivered was shaky at the edges. "You really are a bastard at times, aren't you?"

"Hell, you already knew that." Travis lowered his voice. "Think about it. You could come and give me a hand this afternoon. I was planning on tying her to the chair in my cabin and putting a scarf over her eyes. She loves it when she has no idea where I'm going to fuck her next."

Cassidy swallowed hard, his gaze drifting to where Ashley had entered the cookhouse, the door swinging shut and blocking her from view.

"She sucks cock like no one's business. Get her between us, and you can—"

"Enough." Cassidy pushed his drill into Travis's hands. "I'm not fucking around with Ashley. I'm glad you're so progressive and open, and you're not upset, because that's all I was apologizing for. We have to work together for the summer, and I didn't want there to be any misunderstandings, okay?"

"No problem."

Cassidy abandoned his tools and fled in the opposite direction from Ashley.

Travis flipped a mental coin. Heads, he slowed this down, tails, he kept the pressure up. Cassidy was damn hot under the collar, and if he wanted Ashley that badly and Ashley was game, what right did Travis have to stop them?

The teeny trickle of something in his belly nudged him toward slowing it down. He wasn't exactly jealous—Ashley was in charge of herself, and she'd made that clear many times in the past.

Only the idea of Ashley and Cassidy tangled together, all long legs and taut muscles and blond on blonde made his own limbs weak. If the two of them were going to be fucking around, he wanted to be in the middle, watching.

Plus, he really didn't know who he felt more possessive of.

Ashley.

Or Cassidy.

8

The crew spent a couple more days at Base Camp. They were nowhere near finished getting things ready, but a good start had been made before Cassidy announced it was time to head up the hill and add to the staging area.

Ashley had switched from clicking pictures to carrying around a pad and pencil. She'd discovered by climbing from the barn hayloft onto the small roof off the stoop she had a view of the entire site—and all the comings and goings.

It was a lovely place to witness the continuing dance between Cassidy and Travis. The coals of attraction were constantly being fanned, and she could hardly wait until they burst out and burned the place down.

In the meantime, Cassidy seemed determined to pretend he wasn't a walking hard-on. The bad part was Travis's frustration levels peaked after every encounter when Cassidy deliberately ignored all the subtle hints Travis tried dropping. The good part was he turned that frustration into the most inventive sex she'd had in years.

One more orgasm this morning and she wasn't going to be able to walk.

"At some point you should simply spit it out and tell him you're interested." She planted another kiss on Travis's chest, their breathing still shaky from him fucking her boneless. "It's not like you've ever been this subtle with me. Or I imagine any other woman you've been with."

"Yeah, well, kissing him out of the blue didn't work last time." Travis leaned up on an elbow, their naked legs still twisted together. He trickled his hand over her torso, fingertips lightly teasing her nipples before slipping to circle her belly button. "You're talking about Cassidy less than five minutes after I finish fucking you—I don't know if I should be happy about that or trying harder."

"Trying harder? Oh God, that might kill me. Trust me, I'm good for now." She captured his hand before he could reach her sex. "Stop, I have to ride a horse in a couple hours. I'll have trouble sitting as it is."

He leaned over and kissed her again, nibbling along her jaw to her ear. "I like that you don't give up, but give it time. We've got all summer, and while I'm interested in Cassidy, I'm crazy about you too. Don't go thinking I'm using you as some substitute while I lust after him."

"I know," she answered. "I know it's possible to care for more than one person at a time, as strange as that might seem to the world."

Travis rolled to his back and stared into space, a serious expression floating in as she crawled over him. She straddled his hips and waited.

He was quiet for a couple of minutes before he spoke. "You ever wish you could see into the future?"

The sudden change of topic not only surprised her, it cut into her soul like a knife slash. She wrapped up the pain that had burst forward, tying it tight to focus on Travis and the current situation, not the heartache of the recent past. "You feeling philosophical this morning, Travis?"

He smiled, hands resting easily on her naked hips. "Would make life a lot easier, wouldn't it? Knowing how people will react. What to avoid, when to move on. What will really make us happy in the end."

Ashley wished with all her might that she had a magic mirror to loan him. "Would make things predictable, though. You'd lose the thrill of discovering new things that make your heart race."

"Avoid the pain of getting your heart stomped on, or the frustration of hurting people you never intended to..."

Oh.

Ashley leaned over and kissed him. She put as much tenderness into her touch as possible while she played her fingers over his chest. "You got anyone in particular you're worried about hurting?"

He sighed. "You know it. My family. I've seen what it's been like lately with my younger brother Jesse. He's got the entire Six Pack clan on edge. He's not doing anything wrong, but he's obviously not happy with his life, and it seems as if he blames everyone else."

"Not your fault if he's being an ass," Ashley pointed out.

"Course not. But what he does affects the family. Years ago I never gave a damn about shit like that, but now it makes me wonder. Where's the line between doing what you need and what you should?"

She rested her chin in her hands and lay folded over him. "If you're really doing things that make you happy, and are good for you, it makes a difference. What you need and what you should do become the same thing."

He snorted. "That would be nice."

"It's true. You tell me—the shit Jesse's pulling right now. Is it moving him toward happy?"

Travis frowned. "I...I don't know."

"Bet it's not." Ashley tapped on the firm muscles under her fingers, loving that she could be buck-naked and having a deep heart-to-heart with the man. The level of trust that had grown between them made her smile. "I've seen your family, Travis. They want what's the best for you. For Jesse. If he was doing things that satisfied his needs, that's all they'd want."

Travis nodded, but he didn't seem to have completely bought in.

Ashley kissed his chest one last time before she crawled off him and got dressed.

It was going to be the summer of wait and see, was it? For more things than Travis and Cassidy coming to grips with whatever was going to truly make *them* happy.

She slipped through the rest of the morning in a kind of floaty mood. The ride up to Second Camp was long enough to give her a thorough appreciation for the old-time explorers who would have spent hours in the saddle, day after day.

The couple doing the actual guiding, James and Dani, continued on farther into the mountains to check the remaining backcountry campsites they'd use for the hardier clients who wanted a real trailblazer experience.

Cassidy and Travis got to work on the second paddock with the rest of the crew as Ashley wandered, camera in hand. She paused to arrange a picnic-type lunch that Vicki and Ted had sent on up. They'd stayed back at Base Camp to prepare supper for when the team was done for the day.

The afternoon heat rose and the men stripped off shirts, torsos gleaming with sweat as they laboured to get the vertical posts into position, digging the holes by hand.

"This is why setting up camp this far into the bush sucks. No electricity," one of the hands complained.

"We could haul in a generator," Dave suggested.

Cassidy shook his head. "There are only a couple tasks it would help with. All the work of hauling it in to dig a few holes? Man up and get that shit done."

The others laughed and picked up the pace, and the final uprights dropped into place before five p.m.

Cassidy wandered the perimeter with Travis, making notes of things for the next day, focusing on the job and not the man pacing at his side. For once Travis wasn't being a jerk and was keeping the sexual innuendo Cassidy had come to expect to a minimum. "What do you think? Time to call it for the day?"

"Is it going to stand overnight?" Travis joked. He grabbed hold of a post and hauled back, but nothing budged. "Real nice. You boys did well," he called to the crew.

"That mean we're done?" The youngest of the lot wiped his brow and pulled his shirt back on, drinking deeply from his water bottle as he waited for a verdict.

Travis checked his watch. "Cassidy? We'll make it back to Base Camp for a late supper if we go now."

Cassidy nodded. "Tomorrow we'll return and get the rails in place, while the others set up the tent platforms."

A shout rang out from up the hill. "Cass? The pump isn't working."

Shit. "I'll take a look at it."

"You want a hand?" Travis asked.

He hated to say yes, but... "I'm not very good with pumps."

Travis nodded, then motioned to Ashley. "You want to go back with the crew, or wait for me?"

She smiled. "I'll wait. Let me know if I can help with anything."

The crew cleaned up and mounted their horses, headed toward a hot supper and showers, and Cassidy was suddenly far too aware that there were only the three of them left.

It took ages to fix the damn pump, wrestling with connections, cleaning mud out of the line. Ashley stood to one side and watched them, her gaze heating him more than it should. It was hard enough to concentrate working side by side with Travis, damn near having to fold himself in two over the other man at times to reach the connections that insisted on jerking in the wrong direction if they weren't held solid.

Ashley leaned on the fence, a low musical hum escaping her. Cassidy flicked a glance her way only to see her eyes filled with amusement.

"Hmm. Always nice to see a couple of guys who know how to work with their hands."

Travis snorted and fastened the final coupling in place. "Don't push it, Ash."

She ignored him, speaking with a soft, teasing lilt. "You screwing that in nice and tight? See, that's all I'm talking about."

The laughter in her tone tickled Cassidy as if she'd dragged her fingernails up his spine. Goose bumps on his flesh along with an ache in his balls. Fucking great.

"Make yourself useful and take a bucket of water to the tent for us," Travis ordered. "I'll show you how good I am with my hands later."

"Promises, promises." She held the bucket between her legs. Travis directed the water into the pail.

It was the simplest of interactions, but Cassidy burned from watching.

Travis turned off the water before the bucket was too full, and she carried it toward the single canvas tent that had been set up days earlier when the crew had begun work on the area. "If you're about done, there are enough leftovers I can pull together something to eat before we ride back," she called over her shoulder.

Cassidy eyed the darkening sky. Nightfall had rolled in a hell of a lot faster than he'd remembered, and with the sun gone behind the hills, the canopy overhead darkened in a rush, stars already appearing on the horizon. "You know, since we have food, you don't have to ride all the way back tonight."

"We don't mind."

"Maybe not, but the trail is still rough and unfamiliar to your horses. I don't think you heading out now is in their best interest."

"You think we should stay for the horses' sake?" Travis grinned. "Well, head wrangler, I can't fight that attitude. Only you know there's a single wall tent set up so far."

"I'll put out a bedroll by the trees. It doesn't look like rain."

Travis spoke quietly. "Offer from earlier still stands, you know. The tent has more than enough room for three."

"Fuck off," Cassidy snapped, stomping down the trail toward the tent. Maybe *he* should ride home in the dark and leave the two of them to do whatever the hell they wanted, but his original complaint had been made for a reason. The trail wasn't safe yet, and if anything happened to the horses, he'd feel like shit for running scared. He paused and faced Travis. "You and Ashley make yourselves comfortable. I can handle sleeping outdoors," Cassidy insisted.

Travis shrugged. "Suit yourself."

That was two hours ago, and now, Cassidy regretted his cocky words with a passion. Regretted his own weakness and curiosity.

There was enough distance between him and the tent—that

should have been it for the night. He'd set his sleeping bag on one of the partially built platforms. The air was cool but not cold. Overhead the sky was completely clear. Stars danced against an inky wilderness backdrop, the small noises of nocturnal creatures whispering as they scurried through the bush.

Every time he closed his eyes, all he could see were Ashley and Travis tangled together.

His body hardened as he pictured it—images created from teasing words Travis had dropped over the past days. Ashley and Travis kissing, muscles flexing as they explored each other's bodies with firm hands. Ashley kneeling at Travis's feet, her blonde hair fisted in his hand while he fed her his cock.

Cassidy tossed off his sleeping bag and staggered to his feet, cursing inside as he crossed the dark campsite.

A long, low moan reached his ears, and he paused. Temptation struck briefly before he shoved it away. Curiosity roared up again, followed by disgust for what popped to mind.

You're welcome to join us.

Travis's words echoed and Cassidy gave in to the impulse, his feet following the musical Pied Piper gasps slipping from the tent.

It might be wrong, but it wasn't *creepy* wrong—Travis had invited him to do more than merely listen. Cassidy ignored the dry voice in his head pointing out his rationalization.

He was caught in a unique form of hell.

Another soft moan escaped Ashley's lips, and Cassidy's cock got that much harder.

"Hmm, sweetheart, that's it. Open yourself for me." Travis's whisper carried loud enough he could have been right beside Cassidy. They damn near were, only it was Cassidy's own fault for moving closer.

But whoever's fault it was, temptation twisted him from two feet away as he stood on the opposite side of the canvas wall. The thin fabric was all that separated him from where Travis and Ashley were fucking around.

Neither of them was quiet when getting off, either.

Cassidy didn't make it any easier on himself. In the moments when silence fell, he listened harder and tried to figure out exactly what was happening.

It wasn't really quiet because there were these soft lapping sounds—wet licks and what had to be finger thrusts as Travis went down on Ashley. Noises of pleasure escaped her. Every now and then Travis did something different, and she'd gasp, the sound dragging icicles up Cassidy's spine.

Cassidy opened his zipper, yanked down his boxers and fisted his cock, needing release more than he'd remembered in a long time.

"Hmm, Travis. Oh yes, right *there*."

"Take off your shirt," Travis ordered, the guttural command scraping in Cassidy's ears.

He fought the impulse for all of ten seconds. Then he gave in, shoving his shirt over his head to bare his chest as the debauchery on the other side of the tent continued.

With his eyes closed, it was easier to imagine what was happening as if the other couple were right beside him. As if he were the one under Travis's skilled touch. He trickled one hand down to cover his cock, stroking lightly. The other drifted up, fingertips flitting over his chest.

"Pinch your nipples." Travis again. Dark. Commanding. Cassidy circled one slowly, teasing himself, jerking as Travis snapped, "Harder."

He obeyed, slamming his lips together a half second too late to stop one small, explosive gasp of pleasure. Ashley's long groan of satisfaction was the only thing that saved him from being overheard. He listened to the noises Travis urged from her. Fist tighter on his cock, he played with the sensitive head. Wishing for more. Needing more.

Ashley came, her fluttering gasps echoing on the air, Travis's satisfied rumble layering over top.

A creak. Another.

"Open your mouth and suck me."

Cassidy pictured it. Her lush lips easing only slightly so that Travis had to push through them. Cassidy tightened his grip and moved in time with the creaks of the bed frame, his hand a sad substitute for the wet heat Travis would be feeling right now. Cassidy licked his palm and returned to stroking, spreading the precome down his shaft to ease his motions.

"Yeah, sweetheart. Oh, God, *yeah*. Use your tongue. That's it. All around the head."

Cassidy eased off the strokes and switched to teasing the sensitive underside of his cockhead, swiping his thumb back and forth as he set his teeth together to stop from groaning along with Travis.

A long sigh, tension shaking the edges, escaped Travis. "I swear you've got the sexiest mouth in all creation. Now, suck me. Hard."

The rhythmic creaking of the cot frame changed to a jagged rattle. Cassidy pumped faster, pressure building along his spine, tingling lines of anticipation at the base of his cock.

And when Travis swore, Cassidy came, semen jolting from him to land in hot, wet stripes on the grass at his feet. He stroked through the pleasure, wresting every last pulse from himself as stars floated in front of his eyes. His legs trembled as he fought to remain vertical.

He breathed as shallowly as possible as he fought to come back from his climax. Travis and Ashley were speaking softly, their bed slowly quieting as they settled down.

Cassidy pulled his clothes back together, making his way past the tent to the well to do a bit of cold water clean up. The wet cloth over his skin cleaned away the stickiness, but didn't do a thing to ease the fire still racing through his veins. He couldn't summon much guilt at being a kind of voyeur, though.

Odds were Travis knew what he'd started. Cassidy would bet anything on it.

Sure enough, when he turned to find his sleeping bag, Travis was approaching, his cocky grin all too clear.

Cassidy paused in the middle of the path. "You're an asshole," he muttered.

"You're not as quiet as you thought." Travis grinned wider. "I wondered... You get off thinking about her sucking you, or me doing it to you?"

The vision of Travis on his knees made Cassidy's head jerk back as he took a strangled breath through his nose.

"Yeah, either one would be good, right?" Travis stepped around Cassidy and headed to the pump. He twisted for a moment. "Heads up, I'm usually horny in the morning. I can't promise what we'll be doing, but if you want to watch, you have my permission."

Cassidy shot him the finger and escaped. He crawled into his sleeping bag, determined to wake at the ass crack of dawn and start the day's chores if that's what it took to avoid giving in again to temptation.

9

The most atrocious sound escaped her stomach, and Ashley glanced at the clock, surprised to discover it was already two p.m. She saved her computer work carefully before leaving the camper and heading to the cookhouse in the hopes of raiding the fridge.

Walking through the doors made her mouth water, the rich scent of tomatoes and onions floating on the air. The mess tent was empty though the long communal tables were already set for supper.

Ashley peeked through the double doors of the kitchen, smiling as she caught Vicki licking a spoon with something close to ecstasy on her face.

"You got some of whatever you're having for me?" Ashley asked.

Vicki whipped toward her, spoon held out defensively for a second before she lowered it and laughed. "Missed you at lunch. You know the rules—no dessert until you've had your vegetables."

"Screw the rules. Life's uncertain—eat dessert first." Ashley hopped up on the tall stool beside the workstation. "I was working on a project and forgot the time."

"You want something real to eat, then?"

"Don't want to make more work for you, but yeah. I'm starving."

Vicki opened the oversized fridge and grabbed a plastic container. "Not a problem, if you don't mind leftovers."

"Love them."

Vicki nodded and put a pan on the stove, working quickly while Ashley looked around the cookhouse. She should probably take a couple pictures for Karen's brochure. Plus a few artsy shots of the food.

Vicki had a plate in front of her in no time, savoury potatoes and slices of ham making Ashley's mouth water. "Oh, girl, thank you. I could kiss you."

A tiny snort escaped the other woman, and Ashley looked up in the middle of cutting into the meat. Vicki's face was far redder than it should have been from simply rewarming a few items on the stove.

Vicki cleared her throat. "You already did, or don't you remember?"

The outing Ashley and Travis had taken with his youngest brother, Joel, flashed to mind. Vicki had been along. One night under the stars—sipping moonshine and getting wild. They'd never talked about it afterward, and Ashley had wondered what had gone on in Vicki's mind. "I remember. I didn't know if you did. You were a little intoxicated—the liquor and all."

"We were both a touch tight." Vicki sat in a chair across the table. She forced herself to look Ashley in the eye, crimson with embarrassment. "I don't usually kiss girls."

"I do," Ashley admitted, trying not to laugh at the dismay spreading over Vicki's face. "Well, I kiss women not girls, because *ick*. And lately I've been kissing a lot more men since I'm seeing Travis."

"I don't understand."

Ashley silently ate her meal while Vicki worked it out. It was amusing to see the moment the light bulb went off in her brain. It was as if she literally lit up.

"Oh my God, you're gay."

Ashley licked the potatoes off her fork so she could wave it in the air without flinging food around. "You know, Travis has this same deep, dark desire to brand everything. Which, I don't know if you feel that makes it easier to put stuff into pockets or whatever. But if you're going to use labels, get them right. Gays are guys who like guys. Lesbians are women who are attracted to women. Bisexual like either, and just because you kissed me, it doesn't mean you have to hand in your heterosexual card. Well, not unless you want to."

Vicki grinned. "I'll stick with Joel, thanks, but I did wonder what the hell was going on. I mean...I know why I did it. Wasn't sure what you were up to."

Ashley shrugged. "Moonlit campfire on a cold night. You were dancing and looking hot. Travis got my motor going, and Joel was being a bit of a stick in the mud. I figured it wasn't going to hurt anyone."

"No. It certainly didn't." Vicki pushed a glass of juice her direction. "In fact, Joel turned the corner that night. So, thanks."

"But don't kiss you again?" Ashley teased.

Vicki wrinkled her nose. "Right. I'm sticking with my guy."

Ashley smiled. "No problem. I don't judge. I mean, I still think you're hot, but if you're happy, I have no intention of trying to convince you otherwise."

She took a long drink and waited for Vicki to spit out whatever else she was dying to ask. That she still had something on her mind was written all over her.

Sure enough. "You going out with Travis again?"

Ashley nodded. "He's sexy and fun, and most of the time he gets my kinks, so that's good."

"You got a lot of them? Kinks, I mean." Vicki wasn't shy anymore, leaning her elbows on the table. "You're not like anyone I know in Rocky."

"Is this a good thing or a bad thing?"

"Oh, trust me, it's good," Vicki assured her. "You don't seem to have a lot of the small-town biases I've seen my entire life. Where did you grow up?"

"If you think it was the big bad city, you'll be disappointed. I grew up in smaller towns than you. Well, usually outside small towns. We had a bit of a commune thing happening. Artists, growers. Back-to-the-earth folk. We traveled from one place to the next for most of my childhood."

"Really? That's kind of cool."

Ashley shrugged. "I learned a lot about accepting all kinds of people. And the fact my dad is good friends with my mom and her girlfriend kind of sums up most of the sexual norms I grew up around."

Vicki paused. "Your mom had a lover while your dad was around?"

"Actually, Mom and Tina have been together for years." Ashley cleaned the rest of her plate before finishing her answer. "Mom wanted a kid, and Dad didn't mind being a dad, and they all liked each other enough they figured they could deal with each other during the process. So—Dad stepped in and helped them out, and they had me. Over the years, all three of them chipped in to raise me best they could. It worked out okay."

The other woman was shaking her head. "You're right. Not at all like what I had growing up."

"It was normal to me. I like that I'm okay with being with whoever—sex is fun, and if it feels good, I don't see a reason to not. I mean," she reassured Vicki again, "I don't cross the lines in relationships, so don't worry about me trying to seduce you or something."

"Thanks for that." Vicki tossed her a grin. "Your family sounds like fun."

"Pretty much, except I wish they hadn't bounced around so often. We were as bad as those military families you hear about. No home base—always on the move."

"But Travis said you're hoping to settle in Rocky?"

"God, yes, I want that so bad. Somewhere to unpack my things and not have to pack them up ever again if I don't feel like it."

"I hear you. Joel and I are going to stick around—once I'm done this cooking job for the summer." Vicki gave a sheepish laugh. "It's weird to think I tried so hard to get away from Rocky, and now that I'm gone, all I do is wish I were back."

"It's because you've got Joel," Ashley pointed out. "He's the one who makes it home, right?"

Vicki nodded.

Ashley rose to her feet and gathered her dirty dishes. "Thanks for the late lunch. Can I help with anything?"

Vicki shook her head. "Got everything ready for dinner. What about you?"

"This afternoon I'm breaking out the paints and doing some actual art."

"Sounds exciting, if you know how to draw a straight line, which I don't." Vicki winked. "Have fun. If you get distracted again, I'll save you some supper."

"Thanks."

The younger woman paused in the middle of stirring something in the massive pot, offering a smile. "I hope you do find a place in Rocky. I'd like to get to know you better."

The rush of happiness that struck nearly made Ashley giddy.

"I'd like that as well."

Out of consideration, she gave Vicki a smile instead of a hug then slipped back outside. Her projects called, but there was a hint of something warm inside. A tiny feeling of putting down roots.

It felt pretty damn good.

Cassidy stepped into the shadows by the cookhouse as Ashley passed, her face shining with happiness. He didn't usually eavesdrop, even though he seemed to be doing a lot of it lately. But once the girls had begun talking he'd remained frozen in one spot, unable to walk away.

Their conversation explained a lot, from Vicki's earlier reaction to some of the questions Cassidy had about Ashley.

Explained more about Travis's torturous offers.

Since they'd gotten back from the embarrassing overnight at Second Camp, Cassidy had done everything he could to avoid the other man. He'd done all the paperwork possible, but mostly spent way more time caring for the horses than was needed.

The camp was slowly taking shape around them. Travis had turned out to be a good overseer. Cassidy had to admit Travis's work ethic was one of the best he'd seen. His push to get the job done motivated the younger hands, and yet the whole group seemed to be having fun.

The enjoyment of working in the beautiful mountain setting was made that much better by things going well, if not for the frustration that rode Cassidy.

The desire and the need he felt would kick him in the guts at the strangest moments. Coming across Travis pulling bales, biceps fully flexed as he manhandled the weight to the ground.

Rounding a corner and discovering Ashley with her face turned to the sunshine, body looking all soft and warm as she relaxed on a pile of building supplies.

And that was the hell of it. One side or the other, he was tempted. He was getting damn tired of jacking off in the shower.

But if that was what he had to do the entire goddamn summer, then he'd do it. Travis thought he was stubborn? Cassidy could be just as pig-headed.

He had reason to hold out.

After the crew knocked off for the day and headed to the cookhouse for dinner, Cassidy once again found his feet leading him to the shower house for a little relief.

He draped his towel on one of the wall hooks and cranked on a jet of water, stepping under the stream before it had a chance to warm. The rush of ice on his skin jolted his heart and picked up his breathing, but a cold shower wasn't going to be enough. Not today. Cassidy lathered his hands and stroked his torso as steam began to rise.

He'd barely wrapped a hand around his cock when the door opened, a creak of hinges warning he wasn't alone anymore. He muffled his curses and faced the wall, reluctant to stop even now.

A loud crash rang out followed by a not very quiet feminine voice. "Fucking hell. *Ouch.*"

Drat. "Ashley?"

"Oops, sorry. Didn't know you were in here."

Cassidy resisted banging his head on the wall in frustration. That was it—he was moving *finish the ladies' shower house* up the list to the next day's chores. "Maybe you can come back after dinner for your shower."

Another crash. "*Shit.* Damn toes. Well, Cassidy, I would, but that might be awkward. I won't be long, never mind me."

A bucket rolled past the open door of his shower enclosure

followed by more curses, and Cassidy couldn't stand it anymore. "Ashley, what are you doing?"

He stuck his head around the corner and froze.

Ashley was completely naked. She was also covered from head to toe with all the colours of the rainbow. A thin layer of paint turned her body into a canvas, every curve fully defined in living Technicolor. "Holy shit."

She glanced up as she toed off her sandals. "See, I can't wait."

Cassidy should have looked away, but he couldn't. Not only were the colours mesmerizing, her body had him trapped.

Full, high breasts, curving waist. Her hair poofed from the top of her head like some seventies disco diva, probably knotted up there in an attempt to keep the long blonde strands clean. She hadn't succeeded—the hanging tail ends of her ponytail were frosted blue and gold.

All of her made his mouth water, and the hard-on he'd been about to deal with simply got harder. "Jeez."

She glanced down at herself. "Fun, hey?"

He pretended they weren't holding this conversation while naked, him halfway hidden around the corner to keep his fully erect cock out of sight. "You look as if you were rolling in paint."

A full grin burst out. "I was. I dropped canvas in the backfield, then did a few rolls over the fabric. That's the first step for this project. I have to go back out once I'm clean to hang it to dry, then—"

"You need to wash that off," he interrupted, because standing and talking while she was naked— *God.*

"Right." She winked then vanished into the first open stall. Cassidy gasped in a couple breaths to stop the spinning in his brain.

He must have done something truly shitty to be tormented like this—he had no idea what, but he'd get down on his knees and say a thousand apologies to whatever gods necessary to make the punishment stop.

Another curse. "Fuck. Cassidy, can you come turn on the water for me? Stupid tap is too tight, and my fingers are slippery with paint."

The gods of karma tossed his apology back in his face.

What could he do? "Sure. Just...one minute."

He wrapped his towel around his waist and knotted it tight. For all the good it did as a barrier between them—didn't hide his dick or how turned on he was one bit.

She stepped aside as he leaned past her. The tap took a definite hard touch to get it started, and he was doused in cold water before he could step back. "There you go."

"Thanks." She ignored him and stepped under the spray. Eyes closed, she tilted her head and let the water pour down her torso.

He was a bastard, but he didn't leave. Not for a moment. He had to stay for long enough to watch her slide her hands over her curves, blues and reds mixing together and turning the swirling water at her feet purple.

She twisted, reaching around her torso and scrubbing her shoulder blades and back the best she could. Cassidy stared at the line of paint that remained between her shoulders, extending down her back where she couldn't reach.

Maybe the shower nozzle would scrub it from her skin. Maybe she'd use a towel.

Maybe he should put his feet to good use and run as fast as he could before he stepped back into her personal space and proceeded to clean every inch of her body with his hands and fingers then followed up all over again with his tongue.

Ashley ignored him as she twisted her long, sleek back and curvy ass toward him. He clutched the edge of the shower stall to keep vertical as she bent to scrub her calves and feet.

Dammit, he was going to hell for what he wanted to do. For watching the trickle of brilliant orange paint shimmer over her ass cheeks and between them.

He stumbled back to his shower, grabbed hold of the showerhead and flipped the temperature down as low as possible.

The fact he still had a towel around his waist only registered when the thing got soaked enough to fall to the ground. His cock sprang free, barely affected by the shockingly cold water pouring over him.

"Cassidy? Can I get your help again for a minute?"

He breathed out slowly and hoped his vocal cords would work. "What?"

"I should have thought about this sooner, but..."

She was outside his stall. His head snapped up, and he stared at the wall intently, as if keeping his backside toward her would hide anything.

"I can't reach my back. Can you wash it for me?"

He was a grown man. A naked woman wanted him to wash her back? Surely he had the balls to handle that without giving in to the urge to press her to the wall and drive his cock into her body.

She picked up the towel from the ground and thrust her hand past his waist. "Use this. I'll find you a dry one. Please?"

It was the only answer he could give her. "Sure."

He stepped aside and she paced forward, shrieking to a stop as the cold water hit her skin.

"You trying to save on the heating bill?" she asked, crossing her arms over her chest. Sure—cold, not modesty got her to cover herself. That's when he noticed her gaze had dropped. "How can you have a hard-on with the water like ice?" she asked.

He was going to die. "Turn around," he ordered gruffly.

He twisted the temperature gauge, grabbed the soap and put the towel to her skin. He could be done in under a minute.

She rocked on her feet. "You're going to push me over," she complained before grabbing the top of the stall, bracing her legs open. "There. Do your worst."

Naked.

Spread-eagle in his shower.

So close his hip grazed hers as he tried to soften his touch and still scrub the paint off.

While he worked, his brain went in dangerous directions. Went instead to wrapping one arm around her torso, fingers sliding up to clasp a breast in his hand. The other hand trailing between her ass cheeks and delving between her thighs to cup her pussy. He could drag a fingertip through her soft folds and make sure she was clean there as well.

Paint.

Scrub. Off. Paint.

Cassidy damn near held his breath until there were spots floating in front of his eyes, but he got her back clean without succumbing to temptation.

"Done." The word rasped over vocal cords gone tight.

She let go of the wall and twisted, naked breasts with taut nipples skimming the back of his knuckles where he clutched the towel in both hands. "Thanks, Cassidy."

She leaned in and kissed him—quick, like a rush of wind— then stepped away, ass cheeks swaying as he leaned out the stall door and watched her go.

A happy hum rose as she picked up her towel and rubbed herself dry, and he rocked back on his heels. His shoulders slammed into the shower stall as he reeled from the overdose of lust roaring through him.

When he'd spotted Travis's name in the email, he'd known he was in for a rough ride. No way had he imagined that he'd be just as tortured by an artsy blonde who didn't seem to have any sexual boundaries.

He wasn't sure he'd survive the summer.

10

For days Travis had ignored his building need, though the irritable sensation kept him on edge. Pretending it wasn't there seemed his only option until it morphed into a constant rub against his nerve endings.

"Get off the railing," he snapped at Ashley when she accidentally leaned on the post he was trying to attach more firmly. "Go take pictures somewhere else. You need to be underfoot the entire fucking time? I can't wipe my ass without you there."

She stood and adjusted her camera bag over her shoulder, chin rising. "That's it. That's the third time you've been a jerk in the last fifteen minutes, so fuck you. When Vicki gets back, I'll tell her to order you some prune juice to help get that stick out of your ass."

She gave him the finger, which made him laugh until he realized she had listened to his bitching and was walking away. The soft sound of her singing vanished as she disappeared behind the cookhouse, no doubt headed to her van to turn some of the photos she'd taken of him into twisted freak-show monsters.

He clutched his hammer harder and fought the urge to hurl it into the distance.

The past twenty-four hours had been a whirlwind as the first set of customers arrived for their May long-weekend excursion. Travis had worked with the crew to greet the party of ten. The hands stowed gear into saddlebags as each camper got paired with a horse before finally heading up the hill to get established at Second Camp. Ted and Vicki were already there preparing a "cowpoke lunch".

The season had officially begun.

Travis had elected to stay behind. There was enough work to do at Base Camp, and there was no reason to babysit James and Dani. Ashley said she needed electricity to work on some projects, so she wasn't interested in accompanying the first group.

And Cassidy...

Travis stared across the paddock at the man currying down the couple horses left behind. Like him, Cassidy had offered confidence in the guides' abilities and insisted he was needed at base.

Indecision rocked Travis. Did he ask? If he asked, what did he say?

For the two weeks since he and Ashley had arrived, there'd been nothing but tension between him and Cassidy—a lot of it caused by Travis's own stupidity. Even with all the teasing on his part, Cassidy had remained steadfastly silent.

Maybe Ashley saw something different, but as far as Travis was concerned, Cassidy thought he was trouble and nothing more.

Trouble or not, Travis needed help.

He laid the tools in the shed and calmed himself best he could. He'd ask it simple-like. Straight up. Find out what Cassidy thought would help. He'd avoid begging or pushing for anything but help with his one urgent, and getting more urgent, need.

It took a bit of time to gather his courage—and how fucked up was that considering he used to step into the boxing ring with little thought for anything but meeting the pain? Finally ready, he headed to the barn.

Cassidy walked out the door the moment Travis stepped in, and they collided, Cassidy clutching his shoulders to stay balanced.

A wave of something other than desire for pain broke in momentarily, and Travis fisted the front of Cassidy's shirt.

"Travis, what the—?"

Like a wild beast, Travis moved. He pressed Cassidy to the wall and took his lips. Aggressive and hot. Rough and dirty. Thrust his tongue into Cassidy's mouth as he pulsed his hips forward and ground their groins together.

For one second Cassidy had his hands on Travis's shoulders. For one second it felt as if Cassidy held him tight, groaning in pleasure through the wildness of the assault.

Then he smashed his hands against Travis's chest and shoved him away.

"Goddamn it, *no*." Cassidy shouted the words, his chest heaving as he gasped for air.

Travis reeled, dragging a hand through his hair. "Fuck, I didn't mean—I'm sorry. I wanted to ask you—"

"No." Another shout. Cassidy lifted his fists. "Keep. Away. From me. You got it? I don't want you, and I don't want this."

He stormed from the barn, slamming the door behind him.

Travis stood for a moment in shock. He'd damn near attacked Cassidy. Disgust filled him—he would never have treated a woman like that. That wasn't him, no matter what urges he had inside.

Loathing and nausea joined the frustration.

Then fury rose, and Travis lost it. He roared in anger and

rushed the stack of bales in the corner, crashing his body into them in the hopes of knocking some sense into himself.

All he got was a side full of itchy, sharp pokes and a sore shoulder.

He hunted frantically for something, *anything* that would help, searching his memory for what he'd tried in the past. Something that would allow him to let off a little steam.

A chain? Too dangerous with the mood he was in. A rope? Possibly. His irritation grew by the moment, and he slammed his fist into the wall. Pain blasted through him as he screamed curses into the air.

He felt ready to break, and there was no one to help hold him together.

The office door slammed against the wall. Cassidy was already on his feet as Ashley bolted through, her hair wild around her.

"You've got to come now. Before he seriously hurts himself."

All the frustration, all the anger he'd been nursing since tearing himself from Travis flipped to fear. "Where is he?"

"In the barn." She grabbed him by the arm and would have dragged him after her, but he hesitated.

Ashley exploded. The calm woman he'd seen floating around the camp vanished as she turned on him with eyes filled with fiery rage. She jerked him forward by the shirtfront. "I don't care what your issue is, or how you think you're saving him from some fate worse than death. There *is* nothing worse than death, so if I have to kick your ass all the way to the barn, you're going to help."

Cassidy caught her wrists and jerked himself free. "I care about him too. You're not the only one who—"

"Then stop wasting time and get your goddamn ass down there," Ashley shouted.

She wasn't listening to reason. He wasn't trying to get out of anything, not now, but he understood. She was as scared as he was. Just as powerless. More powerless in a way.

They sprinted all the way to the barn. Cassidy outpaced Ashley, bursting through the doors he'd run from less than thirty minutes ago.

Travis stood at the far end of the barn, pained grunts escaping him as he swung a rope, smacking the knotted end into his back again and again.

"Travis, stop," Cassidy ordered. "Stop, and I'll help you."

"Nobody can help," Travis snapped. "You don't understand."

Cassidy didn't understand, not completely, but this was his friend standing before him, tears of frustration marking his cheeks. Bloody knuckles. A torn shirt. A wildness in his eyes that needed taming. "I'm going to help, so shut up."

Travis laughed, a bitter, broken sound. "You'll help. Right, bullshit. You're part of the problem. If I could give it all up. Give it up—"

He grimaced and swung the rope.

Cassidy caught the cord in midair before it could land again. Instead, the knotted end walloped into his own forearm hard enough to bruise. "Fuck. I said *stop it*."

Travis swung his fist.

Cassidy ducked the blow and jabbed with his right. He made contact with Travis's diaphragm, catching him by surprise, and Travis folded in two as all his air rushed out.

Cassidy wrapped a hand around the rope and took advantage of the moment to jerk the other end free. He caught Travis by the shoulders and spun him, confining the other man's hands behind his back and pinning him against the wall. Travis struggled, but Cassidy had the size advantage to lock him in place.

He pressed his chest to Travis's back and put his head by his ear. "I promise I'll help you. Give me a chance."

Travis dragged in a ragged breath. Another. His upper body shook as he fought for control. But he stopped trying to escape, instead shivering in Cassidy's grip as if he'd been stripped bare.

Cassidy didn't move, only leaned in harder and hoped like hell his next brilliant idea would arrive soon.

Travis's voice trembled. "Give me your belt."

The words whispered out. Begging. Needy.

Oh fuck.

Bloody, aching pain wrapped around Cassidy's brain. With four words Travis all but destroyed him. Physical, mental and emotional agony.

As if he'd sensed Cassidy's alarm, Travis spoke again. "You promised," Travis insisted, his voice down to a whisper. "Please. I can't... I need it. And you promised."

"I promised," Cassidy echoed. How in the hell was he going to endure this? He'd expected to have to cause his friend pain—had worked that out long ago—that wasn't the issue.

But a belt?

He shoved away painful memories and took a deep breath. "Grab the wall."

A shudder escaped Travis, as if all the fight was going out of him. His hands shook as he obeyed, fingers spread wide on the rough boards.

A vision hit Cassidy—Ashley had stood like that in the shower. It was a strange echo, and yet encouraging. He'd made it through that impossible situation; he could make it through this as well. No matter that it felt as if Travis's request was rapidly dragging him to the edge of sanity.

He loosened his buckle as he stepped back far enough to kick Travis's feet. "Open your legs more."

Travis moaned as he obeyed.

Cassidy didn't want to be getting turned on, but fuck if he could stop it. The sound ripped through him straight to his balls, his cock hardening. And considering the alternative, maybe letting loose his desires would stop him from falling into the stinging pit of memories.

Neither of them was breathing very steadily. "You sure you know what you're doing, T?"

Travis nodded. "Please. God, *please.*"

If he was going to do this, Cassidy wanted to be in as much control as possible. That meant not simply beating on his friend without knowing what kind of damage he was inflicting. Cassidy lifted Travis's shirt, shocked to see red welts already marring the other man's skin. "Shit."

Travis took his hands off the wall for long enough to tear the fabric over his head. "If you stop now—"

He'd never done this before. "I don't want to hurt you."

The absurdity of the statement hit them at the same time, but there was no laughter. Tension hung in the air like a knife.

"I trust you." Travis spoke quietly. Low. "Just...don't stop, okay?"

Cassidy pulled his belt free from the loops, a soft slick accompanying the motion.

Travis sucked in air and braced himself. His shoulders bulged in the position he stood in, smooth bands of muscle wrapping around his torso and waist. Red marks dotted his skin here and there where the knotted end of the rope had landed.

Cassidy folded his belt in his hand. He held the buckle section firmly in his right hand and pulled the doubled section to the left, making sure there was nothing there but soft leather.

He held his left hand in the air. "I need to try this. I need to know I'm not going to—"

He couldn't breathe. Cassidy swung the belt and slapped his

own palm. Swung again. On the third attempt it landed with a solid *thwack*, stinging his flesh but not unbearable.

He could do this. For Travis. "You ready?"

Travis nodded, shifting on his feet. He rounded his back slightly and stared straight ahead.

The first blow hit too softly, wrapping partly around Travis's torso. Cassidy snapped back a curse and moved farther to one side. The second strike landed with a smooth slapping noise, and Travis's head fell back as a soft moan escaped him. "That's it. Again."

Surreal. Cassidy adjusted his stance and tried his best to aim, but the stripes of red showing up lay in clusters. He didn't change his force, didn't try to ease up but kept as close to that first strike point where he knew Travis felt it, but wasn't screaming in pain.

It seemed to go on for hours, one blow after another. The tongue of the belt rattled against the metal like an obscene church bell ringing over the prairies. A rhythm developed as Cassidy checked for signs that Travis had enough. Watched to see he wasn't permanently injuring his friend. If this was where they stopped, Cassidy might survive.

Of course Travis had to fuck that hope up with one bloody word.

"Harder," he ordered.

"Damn it, T—"

"Harder." Travis glanced over his shoulder, his dark eyes snapping bright. "I can breathe again. It's good. Only take me a little farther, Cass. You can do it."

"You're a fucked-up bastard," he said grimly, accepting they were going further.

Travis didn't give an inch. He stared Cassidy down, wetting his dry lips before landing his own blow. "You're my friend. I trust you."

The words had so much power in them, no matter how softly

they were spoken. No matter how much he'd rejected what was inside, Cassidy couldn't deny that belonging to someone, even as a friend, rocked him hard.

"Ten. I'll give you ten, if..." He swallowed hard and made a decision. "If you do *exactly* what I tell you."

Something flared in Travis's eyes, and Cassidy knew he'd guessed right. This wasn't only about pain.

It was about power.

"Face the wall," Cassidy snapped.

Travis turned in an instant. Set his shoulders and hunkered down as if he expected Cassidy to flail skin from bone.

His heart pounding, Cassidy moved forward and raised the belt. He snapped it, harder than before, but not much. The ringing sound of leather on flesh echoed in the silence of the barn, bouncing back from the rafters.

"Hear that?" Cassidy asked. "That's all I want to hear. You grunt or moan or make a single noise, I'll stop. If you keep quiet, I'll give you nine more. Understand?"

Travis nodded.

One last thing, but what Cassidy needed wasn't handy. He stepped in closer and reached around Travis's hips, undoing his belt and pulling it free. He tried to ignore the hard-on that was all too apparent.

"You going to beat my naked ass with your belt?" Travis asked.

Another shot jolted him along with the realization that was one situation Cassidy could never allow himself to get into. "No. Don't want you chomping off your tongue." He folded the belt in two and pressed it to Travis's lips. "Bite down."

He waited until Travis had a good grip before he stepped back and started again.

The leather cut through the air with a strangely hypnotic

noise. It landed on Travis's reddened back with a sharp *slap*. Travis jerked, muscles clutching.

But he didn't make a sound.

Three. Four. Five. Drops of sweat ran down Cassidy's forehead, and he paused to drag the back of his forearm over his face. He jerked off his shirt and tossed it aside, heat steaming from him as Travis waited motionless.

Silent.

The sixth stroke screamed through the air—but it was Cassidy who moaned, not Travis. Deep red welts stained white skin, but there was no blood except on Travis's cut and bruised knuckles.

Cassidy stared at the signs of Travis's earlier desperation, and steeled himself to finish.

Seven. Travis jerked hard enough his hands left the wall, arching violently, muscles tight. He set himself back into position immediately, not glancing at Cassidy.

His heart ached. His body—he swore he felt every blow as he struck it, but he had to finish this.

Eight...

Nine...

Ten.

The final stroke still ringing in their ears, Cassidy dropped the belt and rushed forward. He covered Travis with his body, bare chest to heated flesh. He pulled the leather from Travis's mouth and dropped it to the ground then simply stood guard over his friend. Offering his presence as a physical comfort while Travis came down from the whipping.

Travis's breathing was smoother than he'd expected. The tremors racing through his torso shook them both—intense, but passing quickly.

Cassidy didn't know which desire to give in to. To turn tail and run like every nerve warned him. Or to stay where he was. Stay and accept what he wanted.

Travis's head hung toward the floor, his fiery hot back like a condemning sentence against Cassidy.

Only, when Travis shifted his fingers on the wall slightly to cover Cassidy's hand, his breath caught in his throat.

Being with Travis was right. It was completely and totally wrong, but it was *right*.

"You okay?" Cassidy whispered.

Travis nodded.

He might have been motionless on the outside, but his mind was racing a million miles an hour. This wasn't the end. After what they'd experienced, Cassidy couldn't simply turn and walk away.

"Come to my cabin." He stroked his fingertips gently over the welts. "I'll put something on your back."

Travis didn't move for a moment, then shifted his head slightly to acknowledge agreement.

A barely there *snick* jerked Cassidy back as he recognized the sound of the barn door being gently closed.

Only to register a second later...

"*Ashley.*"

———

11

*A*shley ran. Inside she'd gone numb, and yet not nearly numb enough. Pain twisted in her gut and she took off, not quite sure where she was headed.

Her mistake had begun so casually. Snapping back at Travis without thinking. Stomping off like an offended child. Words couldn't hurt her—she knew better. She should have looked closer and seen the *why* of his behaviour. Maybe she could have guessed what he was reluctant to share.

Instead she'd pissed on him and left him. When she'd gone to scold him some more and discovered him in the barn beating himself up, everything had gone downhill from there.

Even knowing he craved pain, even having discussed the need with him, she hadn't *known*. Hadn't registered what seeking pain meant. She'd gone for Cassidy out of desperation but seeing them fight...

Seeing Travis stretched out and whipped—

A lifetime of chasing rainbows hadn't prepared her for the raw violence. Travis's yearnings weren't wrong in any way, but witnessing the beating administered had turned her upside down.

She ran, feet turning over again and again until she reached the trailhead leading into the wilderness. Heart pounding, eyes smarting with tears she paused, panting more from inner turmoil than from physical exertion.

Turn around. Don't go...

The words echoed in her head, and she wept. Stood in the middle of the path and let the tears flood down her cheeks. Everything was all mixed up. Memories of the horror she'd experienced in January. The shock of today.

Footfalls sounded behind her, rapidly approaching, but she couldn't move. Just stared off into the trees and wondered when life had gotten this confusing.

Life was *simple*. It was a game you played, and occasionally you discovered shiny moments or the next, sensual pleasures. Yet in the past hour she'd had another callous reminder that something had gone terribly wrong with her philosophy.

Warm hands slipped around her waist, tugging her tight against a solid torso. She wiped her eyes and tried to calm herself enough to face him.

"Ashley."

She tensed from the toes up. The wrong man was holding her.

"...Cassidy?" She twirled, staring into his face. "Oh, God, where's Travis?"

"I sent him to my cabin. Come with me. Come help me."

She wanted to shake her head, but she couldn't stay away. She would have dodged past him, but Cassidy blocked her path.

"You okay?" he asked.

Ashley laughed, the sound hurting her throat. "Is *he* okay? Go back—go be with him. He shouldn't be alone."

"He wants you. He was ready to go racing out the door to chase you down, but I promised I'd bring you."

Promise. Cassidy had promised to help Travis, and he had. She cupped his cheek and forced out the words. "Thank you for what you did. I know it was tough."

Cassidy nodded then tenderly linked his fingers with hers. "Come."

His strong hand held hers so carefully. The same hand that had held the belt that struck Travis, the sound still echoing in her ears. She shivered, and he tugged her closer, hesitant as he wrapped an arm around her shoulders.

"Travis is fine. I have some salve you can put on his back."

His fingers were so warm as he guided her down the path. Warm in contrast to her own that had gone icy cold.

After what she'd witnessed, she wasn't sure Travis wanted her around. "I think he'd like you to help him."

The grip on her fingers tightened briefly. "He asked for you. Don't turn him down."

Cassidy opened the door to his cabin. Travis rose from where he'd been seated on the edge of the bed. "Ash..."

The breath she took was ragged and uneven. "I'm sorry. I'm so sorry."

Travis wrapped his arms around her as she buried her face against his bare chest, the firm muscle hot against her cheek. "You've got nothing to be sorry for."

They stood silently for a couple minutes as her racing heart slowly settled. He really was okay—Cassidy had helped him, and Travis was going to be fine. Still, she couldn't stop from drifting her fingers over his skin, trying to reassure herself he was whole. "I shouldn't be here. I'm glad you're okay, but I'll let Cassidy take care of you."

Travis tightened his grip on her arms. "What?"

"I have to go. I have to—"

She tried twisting away, another involuntary shiver racking her body.

"What's wrong, baby?" Travis caught her by the chin. "Where's my singing gypsy who makes me smile?"

She shook her head.

Travis lifted her chin. His dark grey eyes examined her face carefully. "You're scared."

There was no way to deny the fear in her gut, so she nodded.

His smile grew. "Hon, remember, if I'd picked a fight with some big, bad guy in a bar, when we were done I'd have dragged myself to my truck and driven home. I feel like I'm being coddled right now. There's no beer soaking my clothes, no glass in my hair —hell, I might need to get Cassidy to step up his game next time."

A whimper escaped before she could stop it.

Travis's thumb skimmed her jaw as he made a soothing noise. "I'm sorry for scaring you. Really, I'm okay."

"I know." The words rattled past her teeth as she continued to shake. All the possible outcomes of the previous times he'd gone fighting mixed together with the memories she fought to keep away.

Too many hurts, too many sorrows.

"She's in shock," Cassidy said, curling the edges of a blanket around her shoulders.

Travis's gaze flashed up to meet Cassidy's. "But I'm fine."

"She's not," Cassidy insisted. A firm touch rotated her face toward him, those green eyes sparkling like hypnotic jewels. "Travis isn't bullshitting, you know. He's walked away from worse beatings before, including once carrying my sorry ass. But if it makes you feel better, you go ahead and baby him."

Something in the depths of his gaze made her wonder if Cassidy understood better than he was letting on how upset she was. If maybe he felt a little like she did.

Travis skimmed his fingers into her hair before leaning in to kiss her. "Distract me," he ordered.

And like that, the cutting edge of her panic eased. As if he'd taken away the choice of being fearful. Travis tilted her head to the side and angled his mouth over hers, and she kissed him back frantically. Hungry for proof that he was more than okay. That he wasn't holding anything against her.

Well, not anything but his hard, muscular body. Oh *God*.

Travis's lips never left hers as he caught her around the waist and used himself as a brace to hoist her into the air. He shuffled back until he could once again sit on the bed, arranging her in his lap as if he couldn't stand to be separated.

She folded herself against him, his warmth easing her pain. Forcing away the shadows that had threatened to knock her aside.

It might be wrong to ignore the truth, but she wasn't ready to deal with some things yet. Being with Travis, feeling his fire—that was what she needed right now.

She grabbed the opportunity with both hands.

Hard, muscular thighs pressed her legs as she straddled him. He explored her curves, hands tight on her hips to settle her into the position he liked before slipping upward. A soft caress of her waist followed. A slow, intimate cupping of her breasts. He pulled his lips from hers and stripped off her shirt, humming in approval.

The throaty sound he made wasn't the only noise in the room, and she stiffened lightly as she remembered where they were. Who had brought her there. Cassidy's gaze was fixed on her body as she twisted toward him, and the heat in the depths of his eyes washed her fear away.

With a nearly audible click, the final piece fell into place. She didn't check with Travis. Didn't stop to think beyond the here and now because this—*this*—was what she needed. What they all needed.

She held out her hand to Cassidy.

All the oxygen in the room vanished as his eyes darkened, gaze skimming up from her silently offered proposal. He was seeing it all—he had to. Her fear, her sadness, her desire.

Only he didn't stop with her, his examination continuing past where Travis was stroking her skin to Travis himself. Ashley knew what dark pleasure waited in his eyes—the boldness, the hunger.

She didn't dare look. Didn't dare *move* for fear she'd break the spell. One motion, one nudge in the wrong direction, and Cassidy would be gone.

He took her hand.

Heart pounding, she pulled him closer. As he dropped to his knees beside the bed, she wondered at the strange timing but wasn't about to complain. Not when Travis leaned back far enough to allow Cassidy to inch forward.

Her pulse flickered in her throat, and he kissed it. Lips soft against her skin. His voice a soothing layer of shimmering lust. "You're safe. Travis is fine. And I've been going crazy thinking about the two of you," he confessed.

"We'll make you forget being scared." The words drifted past her ear as Travis leaned in and kissed her cheek. "We'll make you feel so much pleasure you'll forget everything else."

Everything she wanted was right there for the taking. Cassidy's hand rested on her hip, Travis caressing his thumb in a relentless circle over her taut nipple.

Only...

"Your back," she protested.

Travis chuckled softly. He caught her free hand and tugged it downward until her palm covered the ridge bulging his jeans. "My back is fine, it's my cock that needs attention."

Cassidy's hand drifted up her naked back, making goose

bumps rise as his fingertips traced either side of her spine. "Come on, Ashley. Tell us. Is this what you want?"

She wanted more, but this was a start.

"Yes." Not a whisper, but firm and bold. "I want you. Both of you."

They surrounded her, and she gave in to the pleasure. Cassidy caught her by the back of the neck, gently turning her face toward him. The lighter flecks in his eyes flashed in the second before he covered her mouth with his. His kiss was somewhere between soft and hard, the fingers tangled in her hair trembling as if he was holding back.

She slicked their tongues together, teasing him. He tugged slightly, her back arching to keep them in close contact. Hot, wet heat wrapped around her nipple sending shards of pleasure to her core. Travis took advantage of her position to plump her breast and taste her again, rasping hard over the peaked surface.

Cassidy pulled his lips from hers and glanced down, hunger on his face as he observed for only a second. "Put her on the bed, T. I want to touch her too."

This time Travis didn't seem to mind being ordered around. She was twirled in midair then spread on the mattress like she was the dinner they were about to consume. Her breath hitched as Travis stroked her from shoulder to toes, stripping off the rest of her clothing in the process.

Cassidy grinned. "You're good at that."

"Practice. You too can learn from the master." The two of them exchanged glances. Travis's smile skidded slightly as Cassidy stepped away to join Ashley at the opposite side of the bed.

She'd seen it, though. Their attraction, and their hesitation.

Ashley rolled to a reclining position, breasts thrust forward, one leg pulled up. She licked her lips as she took in the tantalizing view before her. Two sets of firm stomach muscles, the dusting of dark hair on Travis's chest, the faint trail of hair leading down into Cassidy's jeans. "You need to be naked too, please?"

If she'd expected complaints or procrastination, she'd have lost. They both stripped far too quickly to be a tease, jeans and underwear discarded to the floor at the same time. Travis stood first, his familiar smile stroking her like a caress. Cassidy straightened slower, dragging a hand through his hair as he focused his attention tightly on her alone.

The two of them deliberately avoiding looking at each other.

So be it—at least for now. The sight of their cocks, both thick and fully engorged, overshadowed the rest of the arousing visuals. Tight butts and firm thighs were enjoyable, but their cocks...

She sighed happily, and Travis laughed. "What do you need, Ash? You want to tell us, or be told?"

This time the shiver that rolled her from top to bottom had nothing to do with fear. It felt so right to breathe out the words. "Take care of me."

Travis nodded, then placed a knee next to her on the bed. He leaned over, his weight pinning her in position. Clever lips and teeth were brought into play as he nibbled along her jaw and her neck, teasing her ear with his tongue until she quivered under him.

He spoke softly. "We'll give you what you need, but first— you want to fuck him? You want his cock in your pussy?"

Ashley glanced at Cassidy who'd sat on the mattress on her other side. "Your choice."

She wouldn't mind, but she wasn't going to push anything. And right now she didn't want to decide anything. She needed to feel alive, and if in the process she helped forge something between the two of them, all the better.

Travis kissed her neck, lifting himself enough to ease down the bed.

Ashley reached for Cassidy, pressing her palm against the sculpted curves of his chest muscles. She played her fingers over his skin as Travis worked his way to her breasts, his tongue painting a trail of moisture before finally reaching the aching tip.

Her hand shifted as Cassidy leaned over her to kiss her again, this time harder, exploring aggressively with his tongue. She joined in eagerly, not holding back. She didn't try to stop the noises Travis dragged from her as he scraped teeth over a nipple that had gone sensitive from his sucking.

It was satisfying to produce a gasp of her own as she found Cassidy's cock and captured it in her fist. Heavy and hot, she stroked the thick length lightly, and he groaned against her lips. "Shit, that feels good."

"You're telling me," she teased. Pleasure shot through her core. "Oh, *hell. Travis.*"

He'd tucked himself between her legs, opening her thighs to the sides and diving in as if he were starving. Tongue thrusting into her core, lips hard on her clit. Without any further orchestration Cassidy took over tormenting her breasts, and a haze of pleasure wrapped itself around her.

Two men fully intent on making her happy—it didn't get any better than this. Cassidy held her breasts, pressing them together as he alternated between one side and the other. Her nipples tightened. Tingled. Grew heavier, especially when he closed his lips around one and sucked, hard.

At the same time Travis sucked on her clit, and the combination threw her body into an arch, climax slamming her. Dizzy pleasure roared through and echoed in her ears.

Travis lifted his head and his eyes gleamed. "That's one."

She didn't need to count to know this was only the beginning. "Give me your cock," she begged.

"Not yet." He twisted her on the mattress, Cassidy's firm grip helping to slide her over the soft sheets. Only now Travis knelt on the floor by where her head rested near the edge of the bed, and it was Cassidy between her legs. Cassidy who planted his palms against her thighs and stroked slower toward her core.

"So soft," he muttered. "Like butter."

"Taste her," Travis encouraged. "Lick her right, and you'll make her scream."

"No screaming today." Cassidy pressed a kiss to the top of her mound, then paused as if reconsidering. "Well, maybe a little."

He caught her gaze and held it as he opened her with his fingers. Not looking away he stroked his tongue over her folds, each time dipping in deeper. Her breathing stuttered as he added his fingertips to the play. Circles and caresses on the edge of most sensitive skin.

"Hmm, she is sweet." Cassidy pressed a finger all the way in, palm toward the ceiling as he rubbed the front of her sheath. Ashley twitched as he stroked exactly right—and he smiled. The sorrow and shadow gone from his face as he pulled his hand back and did it again.

Travis leaned over and blocked her view. "Now you get to stop watching and start feeling."

Upside-down kisses followed, and Ashley laughed and moaned and then laughed again. Travis taunted her with his mouth and tongue while Cassidy applied full attention to what he was doing to her sex. Two fingers stretched her right when Travis stepped back far enough to grin down at her.

"You want me..." Talking while Cassidy worked her clit was nearly impossible. "...*God*, Cassidy. Right there, oh hell, oh, *yes*." She squeezed her eyes closed and fought off the orgasm she was hurtling toward.

Travis laughed. "If you're offering to suck my cock, no, not right now. I'm having fun watching you get ready to blow up."

He caught her hands and pressed them to his thighs, then he

stood over her, stroking his cock harder and faster than she'd have ever dared handle him.

She stared up the long, hard length of his entire body, the ridges of his abdomen that screamed for her to lick. The strong chest muscles that flexed in time with his biceps as he pumped. "Bet you'd like to put your cock in me right now," she proposed. "I'm going to come soon. You could be inside me when I do."

"Tease," Travis muttered.

Involuntarily her hips rose against Cassidy's mouth, her torso shaking as she rocked against him, begging with her body for the last push into another round of pleasure even as she mentally struggled to hold out.

She was so close to going over the edge, using all her strength to resist, Travis stepping away barely registered. When he picked her up, though, she noticed, as did Cassidy who complained bitterly.

"I wasn't done."

Travis rolled on a condom, tossing himself across the bed like he was going after runaway sheep. He put her in his lap again, only this time facing Cassidy. Her back pressed against Travis's chest, her ass hard against his covered erection.

"Put me inside you," Travis ordered.

She wiggled onto her knees and reached eagerly between her legs, tugging his cock forward far enough to slide the hard head through her folds and get him wet.

Cassidy had rolled back onto his heels, watching intently as she lowered her hips slightly, surrounding Travis's cock.

"So good," she sighed, dropping another inch, rising again as she worked him into her body. Travis lifted her hips, his strong hands gripping her tightly as he helped her find a rhythm.

In front of her, Cassidy moved in closer, picking up her feet and balancing them on the edge of the bed. "Travis, lean back."

Travis wrapped an arm around Ashley's waist and obeyed,

and Ashley moaned as she settled all the way into his lap, this time with his cock buried in her sex.

She rolled her hips, riding him smoothly, enjoying the feeling of being so full. She didn't expect Cassidy to touch her. To place his thumb directly over her clit and apply enough pressure she gasped.

"Holy shit, what did you do?" Travis asked. "She about burst into flames."

"Going to make her come like she asked, that's all," Cassidy said, but his gaze never left her sex. He teased her clit, catching it between his thumb and fingers, stroking and playing as Travis slid deep. Slowly at first, then faster, until Ashley couldn't think anymore. Couldn't do anything but feel their touch on her body. Travis's cock inside, Cassidy's unending caresses.

"That's it," Cassidy coaxed. "Oh, yeah, squeeze tight around him, baby."

A tremor started deep, rising like buried magma. At the same time he pressed on her clit, Cassidy traced his fingers along the seam where Travis thrust into her, and Travis jerked upward.

Ashley lost the battle. Her body rocked into Travis, arching hard. She might have sworn. Might have called out something, but she wasn't sure. It felt So. Damn. Good.

Cassidy rose and grabbed his cock, jacking his hand rapidly over the length while Travis pumped into her. Timing of their motions nearly synchronized. Ashley gazed through lidded eyes at the pleasure on Cassidy's face, at how his eyes tightened at the corners and his lips pressed together as he got closer to coming.

Under her Travis went off, slamming her down on his cock as far as possible, burying his face in her neck and groaning happily.

Cassidy arched as he came, semen flying from his cock to spray her belly and breasts, ribbons of seed that trickled in warm strands down her skin.

They were all panting as if they'd been sprinting. Ashley

reached for Cassidy and tugged him toward her, lifting her face for a kiss as he rolled onto the bed at her side. All tangled together, all naked.

There wasn't a whole lot of talking, not for the longest time. Travis at her back, and Cassidy tucked in front of her, both of the guys stroking and petting her as they came off their high. Travis dealt with the condom at some point. Cassidy grabbed a T-shirt, wiping her belly and breasts tenderly as she stared into his face and wondered what he was thinking.

She'd wanted them both—needed the blast of pleasure to set her feet back onto solid ground. But while it had been the right thing to do, it hadn't been enough.

Haunting memories lingered in spite of the physical satisfaction.

A careful roll brought her to her back between them, gazing into the rafters. The ceiling was built of rough timbers, the hand-hewn logs like the ramparts of a castle overhead, and the sight distracted her. "It's a rustic fantasyland."

Travis chuckled. "What?"

"It's like a ride at Disneyland, only for grownups. 'Enter the Log Cabin of Lust...'" she moaned, "'...*if you dare*.'"

"So we're on a ride at a theme park?" Travis asked.

"Or we *are* the ride at a theme park?" Cassidy had lain beside her, his head resting on his arm, eyes closed as his breathing slowed. He cupped her breast lightly as if he couldn't contain himself, continuing to caress his thumb slowly back and forth.

"That feels nice," she murmured in approval.

A faint smile tugged his lips.

"I don't know for sure," she responded to Travis. "But either way, that was awesome, and if this was a ride? I totally want to go back for a second round."

Travis leaned up on his elbow, dark gaze trickling over her naked body. He lingered when he reached the point where

Cassidy was still playing his fingers over her nipple. He didn't look upset, not really, more like he was considering hard.

Although, maybe it was her imagination because the next moment his grin was back. Lazy nonchalance in every inch of his body. "You got more itches to scratch, baby? Need us to give you more attention?"

"I have no trouble being with either of you," she admitted.

"Good." Travis tilted his head at Cassidy. "Maybe you'll stop being such a hard ass now that Ashley sweetened you up a little."

"Me?" Cassidy rumbled in surprise, pulled from his fixation on her breasts. "How did I end up the center of this conversation all of a sudden?"

Travis snorted.

There was one more matter that had to be dealt with. She hesitated. "You got more itches to scratch as well, Travis?"

His face tightened, and behind her Cassidy stilled as if waiting intently for the answer.

Travis's response was about what she'd expected. He shrugged, as if it were nothing. "For now, I'm good. And I don't want you to worry about me."

"You're my friend, I have to worry."

So much more to be said. There was so much more that needed to be figured out, but in the meantime she relaxed back and accepted their caring. Let them wash away her sorrows in a flood of pleasure and satisfaction.

It wasn't nearly enough, but it was a beginning.

12

———

Travis was a mass of conflicted hungers.

His balls throbbed harder than his back, the lingering whip marks cutting an uneasy blur of pleasure and pain into his every movement.

Sick bastard that he was, the constant reminder of having been under Cassidy's belt only made him feel more alive.

Spotting the terror in Ashley's eyes had shaken him to the core, though. She hadn't said anything more about what specifically had set her off, but he'd seen it. Known that there was more to her panic than simply being frightened for him.

He could only imagine what it would have done to one of his family to walk in on that kind of situation. There was no way that he was going to allow his family to suffer, but damn if he had any ideas other than keeping his secrets silent forever.

That, and the temporary solution of holding Ashley tenderly in the dark and soothing her when she called out restlessly in her sleep from the nightmares that had begun to haunt her.

He was an ass—tormenting the woman with his bullshit problems.

Work became a welcome distraction. Once the crew returned with the guests from the first of the trail rides, there was a ton to focus on. Dealing with the horses, and keeping up to date with Ted and the guides. Continuing to work on the physical camp setup took a lot of his day as well. He was surprised there were so few trips scheduled for the spring. While it didn't seem to make sense financially, Travis was glad of the extra work time because there was a lot more building to complete.

His weekly phone call with Karen put him back on track.

"No, you're right that we're only running at half capacity this year. We can't afford to run a full season and get things set up, but if we get the camp built, and run a solid ten rides this summer, it means that next year we can go in a month later and run a month longer and we'll break even." Karen paused, the connection buzzing slightly between them. "I thought you knew all this. Is something wrong?"

"No," Travis confessed. "My own damn fault for not going through all your notes more thoroughly. It's not like we can't get it done, but yeah—we're doing a lot more construction than I had at the last camp I worked."

Karen laughed. "You're just pissed it's not as soft a job as your dad joked about."

"Yeah. I'd like to see him doing the manual labour on this one." Travis stepped into the sunshine and stared at the cloudless blue sky. "Things are going well, and the weather's been great. That's helping. I figure we should have both camps pretty much complete by the June-first trip."

"That would be wonderful. We've got another small guest list set for that trip, but the following one over Father's Day is fully booked. Only Travis?" Karen paused. "Not that I think you need the warning, but it's a church group coming in that weekend. A father-son thing, so if you can warn the crew to watch their language? I'd appreciate it."

"Hey, they want to curse and end up with a good praying-over, who am I to stop them?"

"Bastard," Karen laughed. "Oh, and in case you haven't talked to your family, all the fields are ready and they'll be planting next week."

Travis was impressed. "Really? That's early. Maybe I should go away more often—they're working better without me."

"Drat. One sec," Karen mumbled, right before a bunch of strange noises carried on the line.

"Karen? You still there?"

"Yeah, I'm here. Had to...move to a better location."

Travis listened harder, slowly identifying the sounds in the background. "Karen, are you talking to me from inside a chicken coop?"

"Shut up," Karen snapped. "Yes, it's the only place I can go without being tracked down. Your family got the fields done fast because I sent the Marlette boys over to help to get them out of my hair."

Oh ho, Karen was having guy trouble. "Tell me they're all in their fifties with paunchy bellies, and I'll feel sorry for you."

"The oldest is thirty-four. I don't care how gorgeous he is, the man is the biggest pain in the ass you've ever met. Bigger than you," Karen grumbled. "His brothers aren't as bad, but—"

She went completely quiet, but for the creak of a door in the background. The chicken noises increased, and a deep male voice joined in, and Travis laughed.

Seems her hiding spot had been discovered. "I'll let you go, Karen. I'll call next week with an update. In the meantime, have fun with the chickens."

No answer.

He was still chuckling when he hung up.

Through all his work Cassidy and Ashley hovered in his mind.

He hauled another bale from the truck bed into the wagon, grateful for a reason to flex his muscles and forget about the rest. He took a side trip through the barn to grab a pitchfork and interrupted Cassidy loading grain into sacks.

"Why didn't you ask for help?" Travis hurried to give him a hand. "Far easier as a two-man task."

Cassidy's jean jacket lay draped over the railing, hat on the post beside it. His blond hair stuck up like a haystack. "Looked for you, but didn't find you."

"Bullshit right there." Travis grabbed the sack mouth and held it open. "I was in the office or just outside it all morning. Only way you couldn't find me is to not look."

Cassidy didn't answer him. Instead he scooped a shovelful and tipped the load into the sack. "How's Ashley?"

"You mean the woman who burst out singing this morning at breakfast and got half the crew clapping along?" She was impossibly gung-ho in the mornings. "I swear if she gets any more cheerful when she wakes up, I'm going to tie her to the bed and leave her there. It's bloody annoying at times."

"Good."

That was it. Good. Travis placed the sack with the rest Cassidy had started stacking along the wall. "Good. What's that mean?"

"Means I was worried she was still upset by what I did the other day. I know she's prancing around like a perky pony, but I wasn't sure if it was some kind of act."

"She's okay." Travis crossed his arms and stared at Cassidy, uneasy at the sensation in his gut. "But that's kind of you to ask. To be worried about her."

They worked in silence for another thirty minutes, moving from one task to the next. The entire time Cassidy looked as if he was about to start a new topic, then he'd close his mouth and point to the next chore.

Travis had a lot of experience with waiting people out. In a big family, you did a lot of waiting for your turn, or in his case, delaying until everyone else had gotten tired and had wandered off.

Privacy meant a lot to a boy who was keeping secrets. Maybe even more once he'd reached adulthood.

Travis was figuring the topic would take, oh, if he was lucky, a good month before Cassidy brought it up. So when he turned from the tack room to find a very stern-faced Cassidy blocking the door, he wasn't sure if he should shout *hell yeah* or cover his balls.

"What's up?" Travis leaned on the wall.

"We need to talk." Cassidy matched him in body language, going for nonchalant and nonthreatening. "About...a couple things."

"My issue?"

Cassidy nodded slowly. "T, I knew you liked it rough, but you gotta tell me more. Should I expect Ashley to be running in to grab me every week, or once a month, or what? Because it's not something I can handle happening out of the blue again."

"I'm sorry I freaked you out." Travis took a deep breath. "And I didn't really say thank you for what you did last time."

Cassidy wrinkled his face. "We got distracted taking care of Ashley."

Another of those zings to Travis's stomach hit at having frightened her. At not knowing how to make her shadows disappear. "I'm a fucking fool."

"You are, but you're also my friend, and..." Cassidy lifted green eyes to meet his, and Travis swallowed hard, terrified to hope, "...and I'm sorry I took off on you last summer. It wasn't right. It only left you hanging. I should have talked to you more, explained."

"Damn right." Travis shook his head. "In terms of me needing to get beat on, it's not like it's going to bust out and make me turn into some kind of madman in the middle of the mess tent. But if you were willing to help me, I can give you a heads-up and we can go somewhere private where none of the guests or crew can find us, and..."

Damn. He'd never had to figure this out before. And maybe that's what he needed to say.

"Cassidy, it's not easy to explain what I need. Pain feels good. It soothes something inside, but it's not like I want candle-wax dripped on me, or razor blades cutting my skin. Fighting has always worked."

Cassidy let out a sigh as he nodded. "Still...that can be dangerous."

"Fighting?" Travis thought it over. "Yeah. It could be, and Ashley was right when she told me I should quit. But the alternative is..." *Fuck.* "Why is saying this outright so damn hard?"

"Because it's fucking impossible to hear it as well. Tell me, dammit."

Travis's pulse picked up. "You know how hard it is to say to you that I want you to take your belt and whip me? Or maybe grab a crop and smack my legs and ass? Because while I want the pain, I want to be in control, and the few times I asked someone to help me—"

His hands were shaking, and he couldn't look Cassidy in the eye.

Boots moved closer, stopping inches away. Cassidy paused. "It turns you on, doesn't it?"

"*Fuck.*"

Cassidy caught him by the chin and lifted his head, dropping his hand away immediately, but there was no reason for him to hold anymore. Travis was trapped by those damn hypnotic eyes.

"While you crave the pain, you get off on it as well. Like sexually get off. Is that right?" Cassidy pushed again.

"Yes." The word snapped out.

Cassidy sucked in a deep breath. "That's the other thing I wanted to talk to you about."

God, they were both nervous as hell. Hope stirred, but not too hard.

"When you kissed me last summer I told you no. And I meant it. I didn't want to be anything but your friend."

Travis wanted to hold his breath, but he could hardly speak if he did that. "And now?"

Cassidy pressed a hand to Travis's shoulder. "If it's something that you need to deal with your pain issue, I can't... deny you help."

The statement was insane enough to drag a burst of laughter from him. "Oh, so this would be a sympathy fuck you're talking about?"

"*Jesus*, Travis." Cassidy jerked upright and stepped away.

Travis grabbed him by the shoulder and spun him before Cassidy could cover even two paces. "No...see, that's where this conversation went wrong before, and it's *not* going wrong this time. I told you I wanted you, and you know what? You never answered me. Let's start there and worry about the rest later. The bits about if you beat on me before we fool around, or if you beat on me while we fool around—none of that really matters until I hear you admit the truth."

He closed the distance between them.

Cassidy's eyes hardened. "You need me to say that I want you too?"

"*Yes*, damn it."

Cassidy didn't answer. He shoved Travis to the wall, easing their bodies together. Their groins made contact, and Travis's cock tightened. Cassidy planted his hands on either side of

Travis's head. They were both breathing hard, nearly panting, heat pressing between them.

When Cassidy finally spoke the words rumbled out like a curse. "I want you. More than I should. More than I *want* to want you, you bastard."

He brought their mouths in contact.

Travis was going to die right there and then. All the sexual aggression that usually burst free when he was turned on slid off explosive and down to a simmering high—manageable though ready to flare. He was turned on like crazy but at this moment totally focused on tasting Cassidy.

Tension tightened every one of Cassidy's muscles, yet his touch remained gentle as he fleetingly slid his tongue over Travis's lips.

Travis reached around Cassidy's back, pulling the other man closer as their breathing raced. He resisted yanking Cassidy's T-shirt off, choosing instead to wedge his fingers under Cassidy's belt and hold on for dear life.

Already this was enough to make his head spin. The pressure of a hard torso against his. An eager mouth working his. Cassidy's cock pressing into the rock that had sprung up in his own jeans. Travis rubbed their hips together, and Cassidy groaned into his mouth.

The sound pulled a trigger, and they both lost it. Not in terms of going wild, but things got way more intense damn fast. The pressure went up, and the heat went up further, and Travis found himself being kissed senseless. They ground together as if they were craving each other.

It wasn't going to take long, not with the tension building as fast as it was. The familiar ache at the base of his cock as his balls tightened made him clutch Cassidy that much harder. Crazy, wild sensations whirled through him, and when Cassidy jammed his hands into Travis's hair to jerk their mouths apart, the sharp stings sliced like a set of fingernails down his spine.

"Fuck..." He was a kid again about to lose control.

Cassidy kissed him, rocking his hips rapidly until there was no chance of stopping this runaway train. Travis blew his load, abdomen muscles clenching as the climax stripped away what little was left of his mind.

A couple thrusts later Cassidy hissed *yes*, his fingers digging into Travis's shoulders as he shook.

They rolled apart and semi-collapsed against the wall next to each other, shoulders still touching. Their uneven breaths rattled into the air as dust motes floated by peacefully in the stream of sunshine falling from the window to the dirt floor.

"God." Travis closed his eyes and sucked for air as hard as possible. Dry fucking Cassidy was one of the hottest things he'd ever experienced while still fully clothed.

The ringing in his ears hadn't completely faded when the sound of the barn door opening jerked his eyes open and his body to vertical.

Cassidy was fleeing through the doors.

Travis dragged a hand through his hair. As frustrating as seeing Cassidy run, *again*, this wasn't the end of it. It was only the beginning, and they had a long summer ahead of them. There were all sorts of ways this could go.

It wasn't going to end here.

Travis straightened the seed sacks still on the ground and made his way to his cabin to change.

And then...he had to find Ashley.

13

She'd seen guilt before, many times, but never on Travis. "You get caught in the kitchen stealing chicken carcasses for voodoo rituals or something?"

Travis glanced up from the stick he was supposedly whittling. "What's that?"

Ashley continued to play her guitar softly. Maybe if she wasn't looking straight at him he'd feel easier about telling her what the hell was going on. "You feeling the urge for...stress release?"

His laugh was tight—not the usual light and cocky response she should have gotten. "Stress release. I like that, but no, not really. Although I did talk to Cassidy earlier today."

They were seated in the clearing where eventually there would be a group fire pit with row benches around it for customers to use. Now there was only the fire ring, and Ashley had hauled in lawn chairs from her camper. They were in that between time of the day—after supper was done and before people were ready to officially give up for the night.

She figured there was about ten, maybe fifteen minutes

before the rest of the crew would start wandering in with drinks in hand. They'd sit and watch the fire and shoot the breeze a little before they hit the sack. Ashley had taken to bringing out her guitar, trying her best to keep them entertained, although their music requests ran the gauntlet from country to hard rock.

If she was going to get Travis to surrender any secrets, it had better be in a hell of a hurry.

"Talking to Cassidy is a good thing." She strummed lightly and glanced around to make sure they were still alone. "Is he going to help you over the summer?"

"Yeah." Travis leaned back in his chair. "You okay with it?"

What kind of question was that? "Of course. You said it wasn't something I could do, so why wouldn't I be okay with it?"

Travis fidgeted, and Ashley wondered harder.

"There something else on your mind?"

Something between a grin and a grimace twisted his face. "Well, you know that other thing you thought Cassidy might want to help me with?"

Oh. "Um, does this involve hot and sweaty male bodies grinding together in the dark? And can I watch?"

She thought he'd make a joke or try to brush it off, but something was definitely wrong. His continued uneasiness warned her to go slowly.

He shrugged. "Something happened, but Cassidy took off, and I'm not sure exactly where things are at."

Holy shit. Ashley did a mental readjustment. She'd wanted Travis happy, and if being with Cassidy could make him happy, so be it. But this wasn't making any sense. "So what happened? I mean, like where, and what?"

Travis rolled his eyes. "You want a play by play?"

"Yes, please." Ashley smiled hesitantly. "Well, I should have been paying better attention, I guess, but hey, good for you guys."

"You're not upset?"

Ashley waved a hand. "You can make it up to me some other time."

A couple of the crew called from by the cookhouse, already making their way toward the fire pit. Her and Travis's time alone was about to come to an end.

"This doesn't change anything with us. It doesn't mean we're not together." Travis leaned in closer and stroked the back of her neck. "You drive me crazy."

"I know, and you do a damn good job of making me blissful. But if you get a chance to have some fun with Cassidy, I'm not going to make a fuss."

He looked confused. "I feel as if I should be telling you not to worry more, but you really aren't upset, are you?"

"Nope." Ashley dug down deep, forcing herself to do the right thing. "I like you a lot, Travis. I came back to Rocky because I wanted to spend time with you as well as set down some roots, but most of all I want what's going to make you happy."

He nuzzled her neck, and goose bumps rose. "Hmm, maybe later I'll work on that *make you happy* business…"

"I'd like that."

The first of the crew arrived, chairs in hand, laughter ready to break free. Days of hard work led into this time of relaxing and settling in before nightfall, and as the stars slowly emerged in the darkening sky, Ashley played her guitar and sang.

And wondered if she should have been completely honest with Travis about what she thought about him and Cassidy. Because she wanted to watch, yes, but she also wanted to touch.

Be touched.

The next days as they worked dawn to dusk, more of the camp reached the final stages. Ashley caught herself watching the guys on the sly. Seeing if they were still sending out all those not-so-secret messages.

But what she registered more and more was her attraction to

Travis *and* Cassidy. Not watching them as a couple, but them as men individually.

It was midafternoon when she wandered out of her camper toward the residences and spotted Cassidy ducking into the old building they were turning into a sauna. She followed after him, curious.

He glanced up as she entered, a mouthful of nails poking from between his lips. He muttered around them. "Hi."

"Hi." Ashley picked up the boards stacked by the door. "You want some help?"

He nodded, pointing to where she could hold the end.

It took a couple minutes before his mouth was empty enough he could speak, a lazy smile escaping first. "Sorry about that, I didn't have enough hands."

"Glad I could help, then." She had to climb up on the wooden bench seat to reach the top of the next board he held. "I have to take regular breaks, or I'd get stuck behind the computer all day, and that would be a sin with how pretty this place is."

Cassidy hammered in nails as he spoke. "I thought you were working on your art projects. How can you have so much computer work?"

"Mixed media. I'm doing pencil drawings right now on a digital tablet then editing them on the computer."

He shook his head. "Pencil drawings used to mean a pencil and a pad of paper."

"I still do that. I have a sketchpad full I can show you." She wiggled to the side to let him reach the corner easier. "What else do you do, Cassidy? When you're not fixing things or building things or taking care of horses?"

"I fix things and build things and take care of horses." He dodged her fake punch. "I'm a ranch hand, Ashley. I do whatever needs to be done around the place to keep it going."

"Where were you working before you came here for the

summer?" She eyed him carefully. "Travis had to get someone to step in for him."

"Big spread down by Pincher Creek. They always have lots of spare help coming and going. When Karen offered me the job, it was a far better option for the summer. Pays more, and it's more interesting, even if it's a short season." He pounded in another nail then stared at the wall thoughtfully. "Kind of nice to be the one in charge for a change, instead of one of the hands."

"You like your independence. I hear you."

"I like playing cards and listening to music." He glanced her way. "You playing your guitar in the evenings—that's nice."

Cassidy made her smile. Not only was he delicious, there was a sense of something else—like an innocence, or an earnest need that made her want to pet him. And other more intimate touches.

She backed up to make room and stumbled.

"Watch out." Cassidy caught her, wrapping his hands around her upper arms and pressing her back against him.

Warmth rushed her as the sexual tension shot skyward. The full, firm length of him supported her, hard in all the right places, the scent of his soap filling her head. The contact between them was deliciously naughty, and she really hoped he'd make the next move. One little indication that he was interested...

"You're so soft." His hand slid down her arm slightly. A gentle caress. He might not have been aware he'd spoken, the words whispering into the stillness.

Ashley rotated in his arms and looked up into green eyes gone dark.

He brushed his knuckles over her cheek, his gaze darting over her face. Wordlessly he leaned in, and Ashley's heart fluttered as his lips moved toward hers.

Then everything changed. Cassidy snapped upright, his body tense as if a wall had dropped between them. A moment later he'd retreated to the farthest corner from her, hammer in hand as he examined the wall studiously. "Thanks for your help, but I've got it from here."

Whoa. Ashley hesitated. "Umm, okay."

She stepped back uneasily.

Loud hammering echoed in the small space, and Ashley escaped the noise, rushing from the sauna back into the sunlight.

That had been...weird.

She didn't know exactly what she'd done, but who knows. Maybe he'd remembered he had some deadline to meet, and getting distracted right then wasn't the best thing.

But it was still strange, and only got stranger over the next couple days until she felt like a yo-yo. She'd catch Cassidy staring at Travis, and then staring at her before jerking his gaze away, and it wasn't fun anymore. It was frustrating and confusing.

"You seen Cassidy much lately?" she asked Travis as they crawled into bed.

He shook his head briefly then frowned, a crease between his eyes as he pulled her toward him. "Well, yes, working around the place, but in private? No. He's always around the crew. Which reminds me—we're nearly done with the final setup. The entire camp will be ready by the weekend."

"Wow. Good for you. That's early, isn't it?" She snuggled into his arms and laid her head on his chest, needing some familiar warmth to smooth the uneasiness Cassidy had created with his confusing messages.

"Just in time, actually. We got a ton done this past week. But enough about work." Then he rolled her over and distracted her from her worries like he'd done so many times before.

The weekend campers arrived the next day, filing into the parking lot all morning. They were greeted by the guides and hands, and shuffled off to be geared up. The enthusiasm and excitement of the guests was entertaining, and Ashley watched with amusement from her perch on the stoop roof.

Lunch was served at Base Camp before the group headed up the hill, and Ashley found herself at a table while loud and happy voices rang through the mess hall.

A camper from a group of four guys nabbed the seat opposite her, eyeing her closely. "You a camper or a guide?"

"Neither." Ashley grinned. "Taking photos. You'll have to talk to one of the crew if you have any questions about the camp."

"No questions. I hoped you would be around for the weekend." The dark-haired fellow stared a little harder, his gaze lingering on her body. "Let me know if I can help you with your picture taking. I'm very photogenic."

Oh brother. Ashley got ready to cut him off at the knees—gently, since he was a paying guest—but found herself wrapped in a strong embrace as Cassidy took the seat next to her. He leaned in, turned her face toward him and damn if he didn't kiss her, right there and then. Hard lips to hers, brief but intense.

Hmm, nice. She was tingling in all sorts of lovely places after that.

Cassidy stared for a moment longer. "Thanks for your help this morning."

She wasn't sure what she'd done that morning, but she should really figure it out if it made him react like that. "You're welcome."

His hip touched hers, their legs pressing together he sat so close. Their shoulders rubbed as he turned toward the now polite-faced guest seated across from them. "You ready for your adventure?" Cassidy asked.

"Oh, umm, yeah. Looking forward to it." His buddies joined the table, and the conversation grew more general until their meals were done. The stranger escaped with the rest of his group after sending one final longing glance in Ashley's direction.

She held her amusement in until the man had turned his back. "Hysterical."

Cassidy slid away from her like she was contagious, creating a good foot clearance between them.

Okay, that was weird. She peeked at his face. "Something wrong?"

"No." He checked his watch. "I've got to run and make sure—"

"Cassidy." Ashley caught him by the wrist. "What is going on?"

He examined the room before carefully withdrawing his hand from her grasp. "Nothing. Just thought you could use some help warding off that guy."

"That's not the bit I mean. I could have dealt with him on my own, but your kiss did the trick, so, thanks. Only, do you think I have cooties? You jerked away from me as if my touch burns or something."

Cassidy shrugged. "You're a good-looking woman. I didn't want you to feel as if I was hitting on you."

She thought really hard, but no, that didn't make any sense either. "Umm, well, if you were hitting on me and I wasn't interested, I'd tell you no, same as any other guy. And if you want to touch me, I don't know why you don't just do it. I mean, I'm getting whiplash from wondering if you're trying to make a move or trying to run away."

He lurched from the seat. His gaze skipped away from hers as he mumbled, "You came here with Travis. Maybe you should remember that."

He took off, the doors of the mess hall swinging shut behind him.

Oh. Well, then.

In the background Ted and Vicki called to each other, packing the final rations as they prepared to head out. All nice, normal camp sounds that she could barely hear over the blood pounding past her ears.

It wasn't often that she got mad like this—the sensation was unfamiliar.

She didn't trust herself to be around any of the guests at that point. Hid in her camper and tried to work, but discovered that was an exercise in frustration. So she took her laundry and a sketchpad into the washhouse and did her chores, scrubbing her paint shirt by hand so hard the fabric should have screamed for mercy.

Stupid, idiotic man with his mixed-up, shitty, judgmental attitude. She spent the time waiting for the dryer to finish drawing pictures of Cassidy with a disproportionally humongous head. A green monster with purple spots on his muscular body.

Because she could.

She was still fuming when she made her way to the cabin she shared with Travis, laundry basket under her arm. She'd managed to avoid seeing the crew and the trail riders take off to Second Camp to get settled for their weekend. The entire Base Camp had gone quiet and empty again, and she was glad, because she didn't want to have to make nice with anyone right now.

Travis slapped her ass as she stepped past him into their cabin. "What's got that pretty face of yours twisted into a pout?"

"Cassidy gave me hell for being attractive. At least, that's what I think it came down to."

"What?" Travis laughed. "That makes no sense."

"Tell me about it. It's like he's pissed off that he's drawn to me, and so it's my fault. I'm supposed to *remember who I came out here with.*"

"He said that?"

Ashley nodded.

"Oh, Ash," Travis sighed. "He's trying to treat you with respect."

Ashley folded a shirt, working to keep bitterness from her

voice. "Well, I hope you're proud of that comment. Must be close to one hundred percent fine-grade bullshit in that one."

Travis paused. "What?"

Oh *jeez.* "You didn't hear yourself?"

"Yeah, I said Cassidy turned you down because he respects you."

Her fingers mangled the material of the shirt she'd been attempting to fold. "Respects me? Well, considering after that night we all spent together I said I had no issues being with either of you, it seems that who he's respecting is *you.* He doesn't want to touch me because of some macho ownership thing, and Travis? Just so you know for certain, I'll say it in small words." Her volume rose. "You. Don't. Own. Me."

"Never said I did," Travis protested. He eyed her cautiously. "You're awfully pissy today."

Ashley hit him with the dirtiest glare possible. "You make some smartass comment about *that time of the month,* or ask if I'm PMSing, I swear I will castrate you with my bare hands."

He took the shirt from her, tossing it on the bed and cupping her face. "Did I ever tell you it turns me on when you threaten me?"

"Fuck off, this isn't a joke." She shrugged out from under his touch, turning to glare up at his six-foot-whatever, darkly gorgeous and stupid-as-sin self. "Not only that, he's being a jerk to you as well. You should be as upset as I am."

Travis stiffened. "That's not the same thing."

"Bullshit, it's not. He's attracted to both of us, and while he thinks it's wrong for different reasons, he's still sitting in judgment on himself and then punishing *us* as the guilty parties. Well, fuck him."

He tried to back off. "You need some space for a while, Ash? I'm sorry you're upset, but I don't see what I can do to make it better. I can't make Cassidy fool around with us if it's not what he wants. He's got his own reasons and the right to them."

She knew that, but it didn't make the situation any easier to deal with.

Scream therapy right about now would feel pretty amazing. Ashley tossed back her head and let out a long, *loud* guttural shriek, up from the belly. When she stopped Travis was staring as if she was insane, which only made her that much more angry.

"You know what? Yeah, I need some room."

Tension rose between them.

"You going to head back to Rocky? Take off again?" Travis asked.

"Don't be a jerk. I'm upset, but I'm not running out on you." Her nerves snapped taut. "God, can't I be mad without you tossing that in my face? No, I don't want to go back to Rocky right now, but I don't like you or Cassidy or anyone else very much at this moment, so excuse me if I kick your ass out of here."

"It's my cabin," he drawled.

She jerked her hand toward the door, not daring to speak again or she'd say something she'd regret.

Travis grabbed his hat and jacket. He paused for a moment, but left without another word.

It might have been melodramatic, but throwing herself on the bed and settling in for a good, long cry seemed like the right thing to do.

14

Travis paced outside. He had to find a way to clear his brain. Too much inside threatened to burst out and break him, and the sound of Ashley crying?

He knew better than to go back and attempt to comfort her, but it didn't make his mood any better.

Cassidy stood at the edge of the paddock putting the final brushes on a horse's coat—it was natural to wander over and hang on the railings. Soothing to watch the other man move with an easy rhythm as he pulled the comb over the horse's shanks.

Travis sighed. What the hell should he do next?

"You two planning on killing each other anytime soon?" Cassidy asked.

"Shut up."

Cassidy shrugged. "You're living life damn loud. Good thing we've got the place to ourselves for a while—that's all."

Travis hadn't thought about the guests, he'd been too concerned about Ashley. "Didn't mean to disturb you."

Cassidy put the brush down. He patted the horse on the rump and sent her back into the main yard before cutting through the gate and back to Travis's side. "It's fine. I couldn't hear all the details, but you'll figure it out. A little shouting is simply another way of dealing with frustrations."

Travis growled. "This time was your damn fault."

"Mine?" Cassidy looked confused. "What did I do?"

Travis crossed his arms. It was on the edge of his tongue, what needed to be said, but hell if he knew how this was going to come out.

Still, he had to try. "Ashley insists there's no shame in taking hold of whatever it is that meets our needs. Like me wanting some hard, physical pain to scratch my itch. I mean, she wants me to be safe—that was always her biggest concern—but the actual need I have to get smacked around? She has no issue with. Insists that it's not dirty or perverse or wrong in some fucked-up way."

"She's right—to a point."

"To a point? You're going to make exceptions and say 'only if it's just you involved' or 'only if everyone is interested' or..."

Cassidy stared off into space as if watching ghosts flit about them. He turned back, his eyes guarded, all joking set aside. "It's not the itch-scratching that's wrong, T. It's the fallout I hate. The fucked-up attitudes and cruel situations *taking* can cause." He shook his head. "It's not worth it in the long run to enjoy a minute's pleasure and have to face a lifetime of hurt. That old phrase about picking your battles was right, only you've got to pick your pleasures as carefully."

Travis hadn't moved from his perch against the fence. The lost look in Ashley's eyes haunted him. It was the only reason he had the strength to carry on. "You're a damn hypocrite."

Cassidy jolted upright. "What?"

Things were mostly a muddy mess in his brain, but at moments they shone bright. Clear shots of understanding that made the world into something he could forge forward into. "Did you enjoy being with Ashley? When the three of us fooled around?"

"Hell, yeah. You know that."

Travis pushed. "Then why are you making her feel as if you're not interested in her? Coming on to her then shutting it off like she's dangerous, or worse, done something wrong?"

Cassidy paused. "You're shitting me. You want me to make a play for your girlfriend?"

"We already had this conversation. Does it matter that she was in the middle, or if she were alone with you? You'd still be touching her. Licking her until she writhed." Travis caught Cassidy by the arm. "And while we're talking about stuff that makes no sense, you fooled around with me as well. Does that make you my boyfriend? Because that would mean in whatever neat little boxes you're trying to tuck relationships, I'm cheating on you every time you're not there and I sink my cock into her sweet pussy."

Cassidy's nostrils flared, and Travis congratulated himself on a direct hit.

"We don't have a relationship," Cassidy bit out behind clenched teeth. "We're not together. We're friends, and what happened with us...it was a mistake."

"That's another load of bull," Travis noted. "Look, I get that none of this is straightforward. Being attracted to her and me and... God, I *get it*. The running-hot-and-cold shit though? It's making us all crazy. When you pretend you don't want Ashley unless I'm in the picture, you're hurting her. I can take you fucking around with my brain, but pushing her around is going too far."

Travis ran his hand up Cassidy's arm, the contrast between his strong, masculine build and Ashley's softer muscles and curves so clear in that moment. He glared at Cassidy, frustration and anger washing away lust. "Stop hurting her and give yourselves what you damn well want. I don't want to have to wipe away her tears when you dump all over her."

"I'm sorry."

"I'm not the one you need to say that to. And in terms of us and that *mistake*?" Travis slipped his hand to the back of Cassidy's neck, trapped him in place then kissed him. Harsh. Nearly brutal. Lips crushed together as they grappled and fought to get closer.

Fire turned on a moment from anger to lust...to disgust.

Travis tore them apart. "That conversation is not done either, but I can't stand the sight of you right now."

His lips burned, his blood rushed, but the damn near unquenchable ache wasn't there. Not this time. Like Ashley, all he wanted was some space.

He turned on his heel and stomped off.

"Where you going?" Cassidy demanded.

"Riding. I need time with a beast who's got a higher IQ than you."

He detoured into the cookhouse to grab some food and shoved a couple sandwiches into a bag. Grabbed some water. Packed it all into a pannier and saddled up a horse. The entire time he was getting the ride ready he felt Cassidy's gaze on him.

Well, fuck that. He'd had enough togetherness for a while. One night sleeping under the stars might put everything back to normal in his world.

He stepped into the stirrup and mounted, settling his hat more firmly in place.

Cassidy stood a few paces away, hand extended with a square black case in his grasp.

"What?" Travis demanded.

"Take it." Cassidy shook the box. "Sat phone and GPS. If you need anything, give a shout. Camp policy."

Travis accepted the load and shoved it into an empty flap by his right thigh. He stared at Cassidy for a long moment then turned and headed up the trail, into the solitude of the wilderness.

Eerie silence lay over the camp as the afternoon passed. Cassidy finished the chores, pausing every now and then to see if Ashley had moved from the roof of the cookhouse where she'd crawled to after finally leaving her cabin.

He was a shit. Travis was right, but Travis didn't know all of it, and Cassidy ached at holding back.

Would it be so wrong? To give in for the summer and let what he wanted be real?

He stopped in surprise when a loud clattering rang out, his gaze jerking toward the mess hall where Ashley stood, metal bar in hand as she struck the dinner bell vigorously.

Cassidy stopped in the wash hall and scrubbed the dirt from his torso, slipping on a clean shirt before heading into the cookhouse.

Maybe she was going to poison him or something. If so, he deserved it.

Overhead, storm clouds were rolling in rapidly, rain spurting down in occasional clumps. He hoped Travis would get back soon.

Pinned to the cookhouse door was a hand-drawn picture. Bright colours, like she'd used a crayon. It was clearly a picture of him, although in this portrait he had three heads and teeny tiny arms. He chuckled in spite of being the target.

He deserved that as well.

Through the door he discovered an empty mess hall, but a wonderful aroma hung in the air, and he followed it to the kitchen. There was another drawing pinned to the door at eye level. This one a pencil line drawing. A brief but beautifully rendered sketch that made him look as if he were in motion, stroking one of the horses.

Maybe he wouldn't get poisoned after all.

"Ashley?"

"Over here." She turned from the table the cooks used for food prep. She'd put out three bowls and some bread, a steaming pot between them. "I hope soup is okay."

"Soup is wonderful." He took off his hat and laid it aside, momentarily awkward with his hands.

She sat and grabbed the ladle, and he hurried to join her.

"I couldn't imagine sitting in that big hall with just the three of us. Too many chairs out there. I needed something smaller or I'd have felt like an ant."

Cassidy eyed the thick red soup she was spooning into his bowl, his mouth watering. "It's nice in here. And I didn't expect you to feed me, but thank you."

The wind rattled the windows, and they both glanced up. Outside the trees waved in the rising wind. "You think Travis heard the bell?"

"I don't know." The sat phone was burning a hole in his pocket, but giving Travis space still seemed the wisest thing. Only the misery on Ashley's face couldn't be ignored either. "Hey, he's fine."

She nodded slowly, dipping her bread into her bowl before staring at it unhappily. "Just worried."

"If he's not back after supper, we'll call him. Would that help?"

Her smile spread like the warmth of the sun. "It would. I know he can take care of himself, but..." Her gaze drifted to the windowpane where a spattering of raindrops scattered over the glass. "Yeah. I'd like to know he's okay."

Cassidy ate a couple spoons of the soup, his mouth smarting at the heat. "Wow—that's good."

"Spicy, right?" She shrugged. "I saw the clouds coming and thought if Travis was caught in the cold, he'd appreciate something to warm him up."

"It's spicy, but I like it. Definitely heats all the way through."

They fell silent for a bit, the food and the warmth of the kitchen in increasing contrast with the wind outside.

He had to say something. The setting couldn't be better to take this bad situation and turn it around, but their bowls were nearly empty before he found his courage.

"Travis isn't mad at you." Cassidy laid his spoon on the table. "He's pissed at me, and he's right. And I need to tell you something."

She stared at him, those sky-blue eyes tearing into his soul.

"I'm sorry."

A touch of mischief slipped across her face. "Go on."

He smiled. "You want me to muck this up and say I'm sorry you were upset by my actions? I know better than that. Travis told me about his sister-in-law Jaxi reading him the riot act once about non-apology, apologies. I'm sorry I acted like an ass and upset you. I've been trying—"

He took a deep breath. If this summer was going to change, if anything was going to move forward, she had to be fully onboard. Maybe it was old-fashioned, but he had to hear it from her. One more time.

"Travis and I had a couple conversations about this, but I should have been talking to you, not him. I'm uncomfortable. You're an attractive woman, and I want...things. I want things that if you and Travis were in a typical relationship I'd get my head knocked off for wanting. But Travis said you guys don't have a typical relationship."

She nodded, licking her spoon slowly. His body tightened, further proof he was going down dangerous paths.

"I like Travis a lot, Cassidy, but we're not exclusive."

Cassidy breathed out slowly. "Because you grew up in a lot more sexually accepting environment."

Her eyes widened. "Hell, no, it's not that."

Now he was confused all over. "But…"

She smiled sadly. "If I thought Travis would be happy with only me, I'd tie him down in a cold second. But I'm not enough."

Cassidy couldn't swallow around the lump in his throat. "You think he needs a different woman than you?"

All amusement vanished from her face. She didn't say anything, just stared and stared until the silence was far more condemning than if she'd smacked him across the ears. Smacked him for being a stupid shit, and a coward.

The worst thing was he couldn't look away.

Like a lash of condemnation from Mother Nature herself, the skies opened. Rain beat on the tin roof covering the kitchen area, loud enough to deafen them both. A flash of lightning filled the window accompanied by a rattle of thunder that shook the building.

"That was close." Ashley leapt up and pressed her hands against the glass to stare into the pouring rain.

He joined her at the window, watching water pool in the ridges left behind from their building efforts. "It's going to make a hell of a mess out there."

Another flash turned her face ghostly white for a second. This time he saw her cringe when the thunder rattled the roof.

"Travis…" She tugged on his arm. "Can you call him? Make sure he's okay?"

"Of course." He led her back to the table. "It'll take me a second, though. Finish your soup while it's hot."

She gave him a dirty look. "I'm not a child. I'm worried, but I don't need to be coddled."

"That's a reason to let your soup go cold?"

Ashley pulled a face. "Stop being logical and make the call."

He couldn't make it right there, not with the rain pounding so hard overhead that the nails in the roof must be shaking loose. Tin metal with a rain this fierce—they shouldn't have any leaks but the noise had grown loud enough to be deafening.

He caught Ashley by the hand and tugged her with him into the mess hall with its sturdier wooden roof.

Closing the doors behind them cut out some of the noise.

"The rain is crazy," Ashley said, moving once again to the window to watch it fall. She tipped her chin back to stare into the treetops where they were lashing the sky. "And the wind..." She turned toward Cassidy, and those eyes were haunted again. "You calling this century or the next?"

He got the phone fired up, hoping like hell Travis had his turned on. "If we can't get through, it's because he's shut it down, not that he's hurt, okay?"

She didn't answer, and he didn't look her way, because one more second of those enormous eyes staring through him and he was going to drop everything to make her feel better.

Static cut over the line. Another burst, almost as loud as a thunder blast. Cassidy held the receiver farther away and waited for the ringing in his ear to subside. "He's got it turned on, that's good."

Ashley stepped closer, and he kept the phone tilted so she could hear the response.

"Travis, you hear me?"

A deep voice was drowned out by the wind gusting rain against the side of the hall.

Shit. "Try that again, T. We're in the middle of the storm. You okay?"

Fainter this time, fading in and out as he spoke, but it was Travis, and he was okay. "Fine. I'm at Second Camp and tucking in for the night."

Ashley touched Cassidy's arm, her eyes bright with moisture.

"Good to know. Everyone else okay?"

"Campers think it's some special party thrown just for them, so yeah, okay so far. Horses are doing pretty well, none of them freaking out. There are enough hands here if we need to spend the night babysitting them. We'll be fine."

The fingers on his arm tightened. Cassidy touched Ashley's hand reassuringly as he spoke to Travis. "Be careful. Don't take any chances, you hear me?"

Impossibly, Travis laughed. "Yes, head wrangler. Now tell me how Ash is doing before I go."

Cassidy offered the phone to Ashley, but she shook her head.

He could understand it—probably too worked up to talk right now. Cassidy gave her a wink and answered Travis a lot more lighthearted than he felt. "She's with me, and she's not planning on cutting me anymore, so we're okay."

"That's what I like to hear. You take care of each other, right?" A sudden whistle cut over the line followed by a strange flapping sound. "Ah, shit, I've got to go. Lost part of the damn tent roof, so I may as well join the horses."

The line went dead, and they were back to nothing but the storm, him and Ashley, who still had a death grip on his arm.

He put the phone on the table and peeled her fingers free, stroking them softly. "Travis is fine, although it's also a mess at Second Camp. We'll have repair work to do in the morning once this thing blows over, but in the meantime, he'll spend the night there and take care of things. We have to mind the shop at this end."

Her expression was all the warning he needed to brace himself as Ashley threw herself into his arms and clung on tight.

15

———

Outside the storm raged on. The walls of the mess hall were solid log, and Ashley still wondered if the place was in danger of being blown over.

The sudden brutality of the weather contrasted with the apparent peace surrounding her. They had the noise to deal with, but they were warm and dry and sheltered. Knowing that Travis was safe with the rest of the crew also helped.

Now she had to decide what to do with the stubborn, foolish man she was squeezing.

It had taken until now to realize he was as afraid as she was. It wasn't some general anxiety holding him back from admitting his desire for Travis, but a deep, lingering fear.

Having grasped that truth made all the difference in the world.

She wasn't a frightened, weak creature, or she hadn't been before she'd been broken by the worst of situations four months ago. It was time she went back to making fearless decisions. Confronting the things that needed to be changed, seizing life with both hands.

Grabbing hold of the opportunities before her.

Cassidy held her like she was china, not pushing her away—he'd at least learned that lesson—but he was still acting more brotherly than loverly.

She slipped her hands across his torso, palms to his chest. "Thank you for calling Travis."

"I was worried as well. I'm glad he's safe." Cassidy stroked a strand of hair off her forehead, tucking it behind her ear. "Come on, let's get out of here."

"Give me a minute to clean up."

Walking back into the kitchen was like walking into a tin can. They both hurried to get the food put away, but abandoned the dirty dishes in the sink so they could escape back into the relative quiet of the hall.

"So much for our cozy atmosphere," Cassidy complained.

Ashley took the bull by the horns. "I don't know, I think we can manage something. You have a wood stove in your cabin, don't you?"

His smile bloomed slowly as she slipped her arm around his waist and walked him toward the doors. "I do."

She stepped in front of him and gave it her best shot. "Maybe it's crazy, but I'm learning as I go along that the right decisions are sometimes the craziest ones. I want you, Cassidy. I still want Travis, but I want you as well, and I can't pretend I don't."

"We've all got a touch of the crazies if we're being honest." Cassidy cupped her cheek, his fingers delicate on her skin.

"You ready to be honest?" she asked. "Really, truly, honest? Then how about adding in, I know you guys want each other."

He swallowed hard. "It's...not simple, Ashley."

She laughed. "And me wanting two guys is simple? Hello, this is all of us in the same boat, and it's time to decide if we're going to take the ride or bail."

A hesitant smile broke free. "Nice analogy in light of the fact we might need a damn ark to survive this storm." He slowed, turned more serious. "If I said let's take a ride, what are we going to do?"

An extra-loud rumble made them both jerk their heads toward the door. "You need to look in on the horses?" she asked.

"I should. Plus check the guests' cars in the parking lot, and the bunkhouse to make sure it's still in one piece."

"I have to check my van. Unplug everything and close it up tight. I can look around the parking lot and the bunkhouse, then join you in your cabin."

His smile faded. "I don't like the idea of you—"

"Stop right there." She pushed him back and grabbed her coat off the wall. "Don't like the idea of me getting poured on? Well, I don't like it either, but I'm a grownup, and I won't melt. So I'll let you do your job, you let me do mine, and then we'll see about getting your cabin warmed up so we can sit out the rest of the storm."

It was clear he wanted to argue. Instead he nodded then pulled her back into his arms before she could brace herself and step into the cold, wet night. "My cabin, as soon as you can."

This time when he leaned down he didn't stop. This time he kissed her thoroughly enough to make her toes curl and her body heat sufficiently to withstand any icy temperatures. He didn't simply put their lips together; he cradled them close, letting her feel every inch of his muscular body. Allowing her to feel his desire in the way his tongue played her. His teeth, his lips. So new and fresh and incredibly right.

The bright lights dancing before her eyes could have been from lightning flashes or his kiss.

Ashley hummed happily as he let her go. "Well, now that gives me an incentive to get my chores done in double-quick time."

Cassidy grinned. "I've got a bottle of Yukon Jack hidden away."

"Oh, I won't need any alcohol to warm me up. Not with what I have in mind."

There was no mistaking the anticipation in his eyes.

The dash from the backdoor of the kitchen to her van was only a dozen steps, and she was still soaked to the skin by the time she got inside. All the windows were sealed tight, the power disconnected from the cookhouse. She used the battery-operated lantern on the counter to gather some dry clothes and shove them into a daypack, wrapping everything in a plastic grocery bag first in the hopes of protecting them.

Protection.

She pulled out a strip of condoms and stared at them for all of two seconds before adding them to her load and zipping the bag shut.

She really was going to do this. They were going to do this.

The loop through the parking lot left her with mud caked to her boots. Water splashed up from the ground and soaked her jeans. It poured off the hood of her raincoat and dripped in sheets over her shoulders as she made her way to the bunkhouse.

The door snapped out of her fingers, torn from her grasp by the wind. She struggled to close it, surveying the interior with the small beam of light offered from her flashlight. So far everything was still in place, though the roof shook with every gust. She threw a tarp over the beds, using bungee cords to secure them in place. If the roof did go, at least the mattresses and personal items would be protected.

Her feet were icy cold by the time she was done padding barefoot back and forth over the rough timbers. She slipped her boots back on, cringing at the *squishing* noise and the accompanying soggy sensation between her toes. She double-checked the door was latched behind her then made the final dash to Cassidy's cabin.

~

Crazy weather. Cassidy was drenched by the time he reached the barn and slipped inside. The dozen horses left in the barn whinnied as he approached, saying hello. No panic in the lot of them, simply tails down as they stood in a group in the corner.

"Karen's trained the lot of you to be bulletproof, has she? Good job. Nice and easy."

He paused to turn up the music, letting the rhythm of the country station overcome the beat pounded out by the storm. He moved smoothly through the barn, taking each horse to their own stall, carrying hay for them to chew to keep their nerves settled if they wanted it.

At times like this he wished he were a chain smoker or a gum chewer or something to take off the edge off of *his* nervousness. It was true what Ashley had said. It was either time to move forward, accept what could be for the summer, or he had to bail and escape completely.

Having kissed her once, though, the decision was pretty much made. He steered his thoughts away from her in an attempt to keep his body under control, but it wasn't working.

Didn't matter the rain had soaked his T-shirt until it clung to his back, he was hot enough to hit his cabin and take that ride she'd mentioned.

Maybe a couple of times.

He turned off everything that didn't need to be plugged in. Pet the final noses that needed petting then locked the barn down for the night. Thank God for rock-solid construction. The building might be old, but it could take the weather.

All he had to worry about now was Ashley.

There was a pair of boots discarded on the stoop, the wind slowly dragging one toward the edge in spite of the mud weighing it down. He tucked them both under the bench, tossing his own alongside.

The light in the window showed Ashley as nothing more than a shadowy shape. He ducked inside and closed the door as fast as possible. The howling wind cut off, but a chill remained in the air.

She had the wood stove open and was carefully blowing on a pile of kindling to get it lit.

"You need a hand?" He stripped off his coat and hat, hanging them on wall hooks. There was already a puddle on the floor under the things she'd hung, and he turned to examine what she was wearing a little more thoroughly.

"Nope." She rubbed her hands together for a minute and smiled at him. "Don't worry, it's nearly there."

"Familiar with wood stoves?"

Ashley nodded. "Grew up with them. Had one in the teepee we lived in for a winter—that was an adventure."

"Me too. The woodstove, not the teepee." He was down to nothing but boxers, and the thin layer of fabric remained only because he didn't want to scare her with how quickly he'd gotten a hard-on.

The light from her lantern shone off smooth skin, reflected over curves that went on forever. She'd pulled on an oversized T-shirt, her wet hair in tangled strands around her shoulders.

She was gorgeous.

Cassidy stepped to her side and squatted to peer into the stove. She had things under control, so he sat on the edge of the bed and watched her as he dried his hair and cleaned up the mud.

She left the stove door open and stood. "Hopefully that helps warm the place up quicker."

He had a good idea what else would work to warm them up. "Crawl under the covers with me for a bit?"

That twinkle was back in her eyes as she accepted his hand. "I thought you'd never ask."

It was an older bed, with plain old cotton sheets and the hefty quilt he'd hauled with him as long as he could remember. Pillows he'd picked up somewhere in his travels. But the place was the nearest thing to heaven he'd ever experienced when she slipped in next to him and pulled the covers over their heads.

So many soft curves, some parts warm and some parts icy. Cassidy let his hands roam as their lips met. Their cold noses bumped awkwardly before warm lips connected. Ashley made a happy little moan deep in her throat, and his cock pressed the front of his boxers, threatening to burst free.

They'd fooled around once before, but this was different. This was him and her and no one else, and hell if he wanted to rush. Every moment needed to be savoured.

She slid a foot along his calf, and he let out an involuntary squawk, jerking his leg away only to find her chasing him.

"Your feet are like ice cubes," he complained with a soft laugh.

She pressed a hand to his shoulder and pushed him to his back, rolling on top as if that would pin him in place. "I know. You're gonna warm them up for me."

Well, if he had to. "I'll warm them up," he agreed.

He pulled her high enough he could reach her lips and started the kissing business all over again, this time spreading his hands on her lower back and slipping downward to catch hold of her ass.

Her naked ass. A shot of sheer lust rolled over him.

"God, woman, you're killing me. Where are your undies?"

"They were wet, and not in the good way, so I left them off." The imp snuck her feet under his thighs, but he didn't mind. The new position placed her sex directly over his groin, and that was one spot on both of them that was already more than hot.

He kept on kissing her, shifting her slowly over his cock. Rubbing back and forth until she was squirming.

"Now I'm getting you wet," she whispered.

"In a good way." He caught hold of the T-shirt and stripped it from her, cold air sneaking in briefly around the edges of the blanket.

There was barely light enough under the layers of fabric to see hints of shadows. Curves that made his mouth water and his body ache. He cupped her breasts, and she sighed happily, leaning into his hands as he squeezed thumb and forefingers around her nipples.

"Oh, yes, I like that."

He liked it as well. *Too* much. Trying to last longer than a randy teenager was going to sorely test him tonight.

She lifted her hips out of the way so she could surround his cock with her fist, and he sucked for air. "Ashley, don't."

Relentless, she stroked him firmly. "So many things I want to do to you. I want to lick you slowly, tasting and sucking your cock until you make those out-of-control noises. I want to touch every inch of you and learn what you like."

Cassidy squeezed his eyes shut, his thighs rock solid as he flexed his muscles and tried to hold on.

Then, hallelujah, she was rolling a condom down his shaft and angling him to tease the head between her folds. "But we'll have to do all that later because I can't wait."

They looked at each other, eyes locked together as she sank

onto him. Rocked her hips slowly to let him press in an inch at a time.

Wet heat enveloped him, and he had to fight to stop from thrusting into her softness. What she was doing was maddeningly good, but he wanted more.

Wanted...

Wanted to drive her as crazy as she was driving him. She liked dirty talk? He could do that.

"Next time we fool around I'm going to lick you first," he said. "I'll taste every inch of you until you've come a few times and then I'll sink into you and fuck you hard." She shivered, and he smiled. "I'll wrap your legs around my back and hold you under me. Give you my cock until you explode."

Ashley rolled her hips again. "Yes, please."

She planted her hands on his chest and leaned forward, her breasts swaying with the motion.

Cassidy threw back the covers, suddenly unbearably hot. He needed to breathe the fresh, cooling air so he didn't ignite like a volcano and blow the roof off the cabin.

One smooth undulation after another, Ashley rode him. Rocking her hips, bringing them together quicker and quicker. He cupped her breasts and curled upward to suck one tip into his mouth. Her head fell back, and she clung to his shoulders, increasing the pace and pressure on every move. Finding a rhythm like they were long-time lovers.

He captured her hips and helped her, thrusting up best he could, driving into her warmth and thrilling at the noises she made. The gasps and pleas and whimpers.

Then he reached between her legs and touched his fingertips to her clit, and her head snapped up, eyes focused on his. "Oh, yes..." she hissed.

He licked his fingers and reapplied them, slippery over her softness. Slicking over her clit as they pounded together.

Ashley dug her fingertips into his shoulders, and her body tightened around him. "Cassidy...oh. *Oh.*"

She shook, torso trembling as she came, staring into his eyes.

He let go of his control, thankful he'd survived long enough. Thankful to allow his release to tear free as spots danced in front of his eyes.

He clutched her tightly, their bodies more than warm. Sweaty in the growing heat of the room. He dropped kisses on her face, her temples, caressing her body again and again as aftershocks struck hard enough to make him gasp.

She caught him by both cheeks and examined his face as she took a deep, deep breath. Then she smiled, leaned in and kissed him tenderly, finishing by cuddling against his chest.

Cassidy stroked her for another couple minutes before placing her on the mattress and cleaning up, returning to her side and tucking her firmly against him.

She sighed, totally relaxed in his arms.

Outside the window the wind shrieked like an angry spirit, but inside the cabin for once the evil creatures that liked to torment him were silenced.

They were safe. They were together, and it was very clear that was a good thing.

"Travis will be back tomorrow," Ashley said.

She stroked her fingertips over the arm he'd wrapped around her. "I have an idea, if you're interested."

He went with honest. "Your ideas scare me a little."

Ashley wiggled in his grasp, pressing her naked chest against his, but more importantly looking him in the eyes. Her expression had grown serious. Intense. "One day, Cassidy. Take for one day —take everything you want and live life to the limit. Everything. I'm not asking for forever, or for you to pretend. I want to know if you think you can take one day."

The idea made him shiver briefly, but it was impossible to

feel the same terror that he'd experienced till now. He had to try. Had to make an attempt.

"One day." He couldn't promise more. *More* tempted, *more* stared him in the eye and enticed him, but the slope was still too dangerous to consider.

It wasn't his soul that would be destroyed when it all blew up.

"I knew you were a smart one." A soft kiss melted against his lips as she rewarded him for cooperating. Then her eyes lit up. "But before we talk about tomorrow, I'd like to try a few other things on that list we made earlier."

Cassidy paused. "List? Oh..."

Oh.

She pressed a kiss to his chest before working her way down his body, and suddenly the cabin was the hottest place on earth and getting hotter by the minute.

The storm could scream all it wanted. He was having the time of his life. One night.

Tomorrow? One day.

16

———

*H*is nearly completed to-do list doubled overnight after the storm, but Travis wasn't worried about getting things cleaned up. The hands had already proven they knew what they were doing, and the brilliant sunshine that greeted the day made the paying guests all the more eager to continue their adventure.

James and Dani had things under control at Second Camp, so Travis saddled up his horse and headed in the opposite direction. He paused along the way to clear aside trees that had fallen across the trail. Wondered if he was prolonging the ride because he wasn't sure what he would find at Base Camp, and this time he wasn't thinking about storm damage.

Cassidy and Ashley had made up, had they? The sensation in his belly was both unfamiliar and unwelcome.

He'd spent four months dating Ashley the previous fall and winter—and he'd thoroughly enjoyed it. Her full-fledged enthusiasm for, well, everything, had given him a kick. Their sexual escapades had been wild and varied, even wilder than he'd gotten up to in the past. They'd gotten along like nobody's business.

When she'd up and left him, he hadn't been that surprised. It had hurt, but he'd taken to holding everything he touched loosely. This ache inside warned him he might have been lying to himself, just a little.

He let out some of his frustrations by wrapping his arms around a thick trunk and dragging it to the side of the trail, muscles pushed to their limit with the heavy bulk.

He'd told Cassidy to stop turning Ashley down. *He'd* been the one to open the door to the two of them fooling around. So why did his stomach tighten as he pictured it? And how could he turn off the wild desire to get into the middle of it with them?

Maybe he was attracted to Cassidy, but he wanted Ashley as more than a casual fuck, and the realization hurt like slivers were being driven under his nails.

Such a stupid *shithead*. Couldn't figure out he was really attached to someone until he'd gone and blown his chances.

Back at Base Camp, conditions weren't as terrible as he'd expected. Water ran freely down the hill to pool on one side of the parking lot, but the horses were out in the paddock, tossing their heads and playing with each other. A couple rolled in the damp grass, bright sunshine turning the scene into some pastoral paradise. He sent his horse out to join them, smiling at Ashley who'd appeared on the path.

"Your boots kill me," he teased, determined to keep things light. "In case you never heard, rubber boots are supposed to be black."

She twisted a foot in the air and grinned. "I like my purple plaid, thank you. I'll buy you a pair."

"You wouldn't dare."

"In pink." Her grin widened as she stepped into his open arms. "I'm glad you're okay. I was worried about you last night."

Softness pressed tight, and when her eager lips rose to his, Travis ignored everything else to greet her properly. Damn if it didn't ease some of his fears, having her in his arms and holding her close.

When he finally let her go she was nearly purring. "Well, that was a lovely hello."

"Sorry I took off on you yesterday."

Ashley cupped his face tenderly. "Hey, I'm the one who told you to get lost. And I'm all better today. In fact, I have to run—got a bunch of things happening I need to keep an eye on. Cassidy is working on the roof of the ladies' shower house. Said something about it being the most important thing to fix." She backed away from him, sunshine and roses back in her smile, the happy-go-lucky woman he'd been so attracted to clearly showing as she bounced down the boardwalk, waving over her shoulder. "I'll see you at supper."

Well. She was cheery.

Travis braced himself for the second meet-and-greet, but Cassidy was also far easier to talk to than he'd expected. They got to work, and before he knew it, supper had rolled around. Travis watched Cassidy and Ashley while they ate, but other than no longer being on tenterhooks, things seemed normal.

Until after the meal was done. Ashley leaned back in her chair, mischief written all over her face. Travis poured himself another drink and waited. Something was on the horizon.

"Either of you guys want dessert?" she asked, leaping to her feet. "I spotted ice cream in the freezer, and don't bother to help —I'll get it this time."

"Three scoops for me," Cassidy instructed. "Travis only gets two since he didn't work nearly as hard as I did."

"Bullshit on that. Who was working hard? You sat on your ass on the roof while I dug a trench like a real man."

"Not my fault you're afraid of heights," Cassidy taunted.

Travis punched him in the shoulder, and they grinned at each other.

This was what he'd missed. Hanging out and relaxing with Cassidy. Shooting the breeze, and not really worrying about what the next day would bring.

Ashley placed two enormous bowls of ice cream in front of them before sitting down.

Travis glanced at the table. "You're not having any?"

"One scoop." She held up her hand to show him her cone.

Then she licked it. Her eyes closed, and she hummed as if she'd just experienced the best damn orgasm of her life.

Travis glanced at Cassidy. The other man stared slack-jawed as Ashley stuck out her tongue again and again, and worked that cone lewdly enough Travis was no longer so calm and relaxed as he'd been.

He slid his feet under the table and leaned back to ease the pressure off his cock as her lips closed over the top of the cone.

When she sucked, he forced down a growl of hunger.

"Hell," Cassidy breathed.

"You enjoying yourself?" Travis asked, amused at the direction this was going. Feisty minx had an agenda, did she? He could work with that.

Her tongue flashed pink for a second as she licked a dab of cream from the corner of her lips. She gazed at him from under hooded lids. "Tasty, but something hot would be better than this cold stuff. Still sticky, though. I like sticky."

"You're pushing it, sweetheart," Travis warned.

Ashley bared her teeth briefly before silently nibbling her way all around the cone.

Oh yeah. She was feeling troublesome tonight.

She popped the rest of the cone into her mouth and chewed, wiping her lips with her fingers before licking them clean.

Cassidy had his elbows resting on the table as he stared unabashedly.

Travis wasn't sure if he should be running for the hills again. Something had changed in a hell of a hurry.

Something big.

"I suggest a game." She abandoned her chair and crawled right up on the table, sitting cross-legged halfway between him and Cassidy. "While we're here and all alone. No holds, no limits. One night of fun between three friends, and nothing more."

"I wondered how long it would take for you to turn this into something dirty. Not that I'm complaining." Travis looked her over slowly as he spoke. "Strip poker?"

She waved a hand. "Takes too long, and I'm a card shark. You'd both be naked in no time..." Her eyes lit up. "Oh, well maybe we *should* play poker."

"High-low," Cassidy cut in. "Three cards dealt, whoever has the high card decides what the low card has to do for the next five minutes or thereabouts."

Travis didn't hesitate. "How far are we going with this? No limits leaves things pretty wide open, darling."

Only he looked at Cassidy as he asked the question.

The man's nostrils flared, and his eyes darkened. His hard-on was as obvious as Travis's. "As long as we're all enjoying ourselves, no limits." He paused. Glanced at Ashley then nodded. "I'm in."

Travis's vision blurred for a second as the rush hit. It was partly her, partly Cassidy, mostly the insanity of the situation. Whatever manipulations had led to this moment, he was no fool. Tonight wasn't going to be him and Cassidy only doing things with Ashley.

"I'll have to see—I'm not very good at following orders," Travis drawled.

Ashley slapped a deck of cards on the table. Folded her arms as if daring him.

He put his bowl and Cassidy's to the side, picked up the cards and shuffled them one-handed. "I'm in."

Her delight shone like a beam of light, and she reached for the cards. "Let me deal."

"Uh-uh. You admitted you're a shark." Travis offered the deck to Cassidy. "She deals off the bottom. You? I trust."

The layers of meaning in his message had Cassidy clutching the cards for an extra moment before nodding and pulling them closer. Ashley crawled off the table and into Travis's lap, tugging his cheek so she could kiss him.

"Thank you," she whispered.

He caught her fingers in his. "You wait and see what you're thanking me for. I've been saving up my wickedest fantasies since the last time we played this."

Three cards lay on the table in a straight line. Ashley leaned forward and flipped over the middle one.

Deuce.

Travis chuckled. "Looks as if we're starting the evening off right. Way to go."

She stuck out her tongue.

"That's right. My plans do involve your tongue, so get it all warmed up."

She jabbed him in the side. "Pick a card, and stop procrastinating."

Travis leaned over to the farthest one and turned up a jack. He grinned until Cassidy revealed the last card and beat him with a king.

"Well, damn. Okay, kids, what's the show going to be?" He pushed enthusiasm into his voice he didn't completely feel, but hey, it was part of the game, and the night was young.

Cassidy ignored Travis completely. Turned to Ashley and

offered her a hand as she found her feet. He kissed her knuckles then gently stroked her arm. There was a whole lot more warmth between them than the previous day, and Travis shoved down the urge to get possessive and call the game off.

Only the next thing Cassidy said was unexpected, and suddenly Travis wasn't sure what they were playing.

"Travis was right—you're all warmed up for what I have in mind as well." Cassidy turned her to face Travis and guided her to her knees, his hands tangled in her hair to tilt her head back. "Pull out Travis's cock and suck him."

There was no mistaking the shock on Travis's face as Ashley reached for his zipper.

Cassidy's heart pounded as his friend snapped himself back under control, a wide grin firmly in place as he slid his hips to the edge of his seat in anticipation.

Control—something Cassidy badly needed to find, and quick. *One day.*

One day of accepting what he wanted. Accepting what had been pushed so far down for so long that he wasn't sure he could set it free anymore.

But Ashley was right. This was the best time, best place, and if he was going to choose one chance to steal a moment—it was now.

Cassidy took a deep breath to steady himself, then turned to watch.

He'd fucked around with more than one set of partners in the room before. Had threesomes when the other guys on a ranch had brought women home and invited him to join in. Even the sex the other day with Ashley, though, he'd stuck to the unwritten rule. Don't gawk. Don't see anything but the woman being shared.

This time he let himself look at Travis. Really look. With his hands in Ashley's hair, Cassidy had a front-row seat, standing over her as she pulled Travis's cock free.

He was already fully erect, the head of his shaft rounded and smooth with precome glistening on the slit. Ashley held him at the base and twisted sideways to lick slowly from the bottom to top, her tongue leaving behind a streak of moisture on the thick vein marking the underside of Travis's length.

She got him good and wet, twirling her tongue around the head, going back and forth over the sides of his shaft until his dick glistened in the light. Then she wrapped her lips around him and took him in.

Cassidy's hands moved forward as Ashley dipped, and he widened his stance to let her move easier without letting her go. It brought his legs on either side of Travis's, Ashley kneeling between them. Cassidy's cock pressed the front of his jeans, raging hard and aching to have soft lips surround him as well.

Or maybe...not so soft.

Travis groaned in approval as Ashley worked him, sucking hard each time she drew back. Only Travis's eyes drifted up from her mouth, and as pleasure streaked his face, his gaze lingered on Cassidy. On the hard-on that was partly from thinking of Ashley and partly Travis's own fault.

One day—take the ride.

Ashley pulled off with a pop and smacked her lips in approval. "Better than any ice cream cone."

"You're stopping already?" Travis dropped his head back in exasperation. "Fuck, this game is gonna kill me."

"Pull the right cards, and you might get lucky again," Ashley teased. She kissed the tip of Travis's cock tenderly then let him go, resting the hard length back against his belly, the edges of his jeans still unzipped and open. "I don't think I can close your pants without hurting something."

Travis fisted himself. "Damn right."

She leaned on Cassidy's legs to make him ease back, then stood and kissed him. As her tongue slipped into his mouth, a shiver rolled up his spine.

That was Travis on her lips. *Travis* he could taste.

She pulled back and winked. She knew what had made him still. "Deal the next set of cards," she instructed.

They'd talked about this. Planned it even, but every step forward took courage to continue. Cassidy waited as the cards were laid out, and this time Ashley got control over Travis.

He leered. "If you're looking for a little licking, I'm game."

Ashley pretended to ponder for a moment before shaking her head. "Not yet. What we need is some visual entertainment. I'd like naked, please."

Travis rolled his eyes. "You're playing with fire, sweetheart, but I'll go along with it."

He rose to his feet, reaching for his T-shirt.

Ashley held out her hand. "Not your clothes. I want you to strip Cassidy."

All the regular sounds that usually faded into the background suddenly seemed extraordinarily loud. The fan in the kitchen, the hum of the refrigerator. The squeak of a tree limb against the hall roof.

Travis forced his cock back in his pants and did them up— putting on his armour? Cassidy waited to see if Travis would call the whole thing off right then and there.

He should have known better.

"Stand up," Travis ordered. He turned to Ashley and pointed at the table. "And you, sit there. You asked for it, so enjoy the show."

Travis stepped in close and caught Cassidy's gaze. For a good thirty seconds he stared, and then that wicked grin of his broke free.

"*Finally.*"

Cassidy wasn't sure how he'd keep his feet. Not when Travis slid a hand up his chest and fisted his shirt. "You rip my buttons off you're sewing them back on later," Cassidy warned.

A second hand in the fabric, this time on the left side. Travis leaned close enough his warm breath rushed past Cassidy's cheek. "You know what? Not a threat. Not a fucking threat at all."

He jerked his hands apart and buttons flew, landing on the floor with bouncing *pings*. Finding them all later would be an issue because Cassidy was caught staring into Travis's storm-grey eyes as the other man snapped his shirt back off his shoulders, pinning his arms behind him for a moment as the fabric slid downward.

Bastard tossed the first layer to Ashley like a token. "Here, hold them for us."

She wiggled on the tabletop. "You going to be all night about it, Travis?"

"I'll take as long as I damn well please." Travis snuck his fingers under Cassidy's T-shirt, separating the fabric from his jeans and slipping his palm against Cassidy's back. "Some things are meant to be savoured."

"Savour faster," she taunted.

Travis was right there, only inches away, the heat from his body increasing as he grabbed the bottom of Cassidy's shirt and peeled it upward. As their arms rose, their groins brushed, and Cassidy clenched his fists to stop from rocking harder into Travis. From grinding them together to get more pressure on his needy cock.

A flick of the wrist tossed the shirt to Ashley, then Travis dropped his hands over Cassidy's belt. Unbuckled it, pulling the leather apart. His knuckles were warm against Cassidy's stomach as he slipped his hand into the waistline to hold on as the top button snapped free.

Travis's fingertips grazed Cassidy's cock as it reached toward his belly button. Slow, cautious friction as if Travis knew exactly what to expect as the zipper descended. There was more room for Cassidy's cock now, but still not enough as Travis shoved his jeans over his hips and ground-ward.

"Whose bright idea was it to play games in the mess hall? He's still got his boots on," Travis complained.

Ashley rolled her eyes as she hopped off the table. "You're such a whiner at times, Travis Coleman."

She plopped onto the floor and caught the heel of Cassidy's boot. "Get behind him, Travis, and brace him while I pull."

Hard arms snuck around him as Travis tugged backward, and Cassidy ended up leaning on a solid mass of cowboy. Nothing but his boxers left as Ashley stripped off one boot and then the other, along with the jeans that had gotten stuck.

She vanished back onto her perch, and Cassidy was left in Travis's embrace. A long, hard ridge pressed into his ass cheek as firm hands began a slow, tortuous exploration.

Lips brushed his ear, right before Travis whispered, "You have any idea how long I've wanted this? Any idea what this is fucking doing to me right now?"

Cassidy stared straight ahead, his heart ready to pound free from his chest. "If it's anything like what's happening to me, yeah."

A small pause, barely there before Travis moved lower in his search. Tracing with palms and fingertips over muscles gone taut. Rubbing his thumbs briefly over Cassidy's nipples, over the ridges of his abdomen. Softly tracing the line of hair and, *holy fuck*, following it under Cassidy's boxers all the way to his cock.

When strong fingers closed around his shaft, Cassidy leaned

his head on Travis's shoulder and panted. "You so much as stroke me, and I'll lose it."

A second hand slipped over his other hip, also headed south. "Control issues," Travis goaded. "I haven't even got your boxers off."

"Which I'm not happy about." Ashley bounced to her feet and stood in front of them, her bright eyes shining and a sultry smile on her lips. "You distracted or something, Travis? You're supposed to be undressing him, not jacking him off."

"Just having fun. Feel free to help." Travis caught hold of Cassidy's balls, rolling them gently. "I'm busy."

It took every ounce of control Cassidy had to hang on as Ashley eased off his boxers. She paused as the head of his cock came free and kissed the tip, tongue darting out to tease the head as Travis took advantage of having more room to deliver a slow upward stroke.

"Jesus. Stop it, you two." Cassidy couldn't keep the pleading from his voice. He stood naked in the mess hall, begging for mercy from the man he desired and the woman who'd teased her way into his senses.

Both of them ignored his request.

"Ashley, strip," Travis demanded.

"You didn't deal any cards," she complained, but she already had her top off, wiggling her way out of the soft cotton pants she favoured over jeans. Nothing left but small triangles of fabric over her breasts and a scrap over her mound.

Not that Cassidy could see straight. "Fuck, Travis, I'm begging you. No more."

"Plenty more," Travis promised, but he stepped away and Cassidy snatched in air, bending slightly to get his balance.

Travis ran a hand over his ass, and more shivers arrived. It was insane and oh-so-good, and Cassidy was ready for anything, especially as a naked Ashley pressed herself up against him and raised her happy face for a quick kiss.

"What say we get Travis naked now?" she suggested.

"Hell of a good idea."

They turned as one in time to see Travis toeing off his boots and kicking them across the floor. "Do your worst, but once we're naked? I'm in charge."

"Bossy bastard." Laughter snuck out at the sheer pleasure rolling through Cassidy's veins. "Come on, Ashley, let's see if he can take it as well as he dishes it out."

17

The game tonight might be enough to put him into an early grave, but what a way to go. Travis stepped into the open and waited for the naked people in the room to come torment him.

Only they started right where they were. Cassidy cradled the back of Ashley's head and held her close for another moment as they kissed. Tantalizing flashes of tongue raised Travis's anticipation as Ashley rubbed against Cassidy, her eager hands skimming down his back before caressing the firm muscles of his ass.

Cassidy repaid the favour and cupped her breast, rotating them sideways to give Travis a clear view of everything he did. His thumb and forefingers closed over the tip, and he rolled them lightly. Ashley let out a gasp, arching hard.

Travis hated to interrupt, but fuck... "You want to undress me, or should I go ahead and start without you?"

Two heads twisted his way, sunshine in their hair and dark passion in their eyes. "Someone's feeling needy," Cassidy commented.

"You take the left, and I'll take the right."

Maybe he'd felt like an ass for complaining a moment before, but it was worth it to be surrounded on either side and have two sets of hands on him. All Travis wore up top was a T-shirt, and it was already coming off, Cassidy using his higher reach to pull the fabric free and toss it aside.

Hot air was the only warning a split second before two sets of lips pressed to his skin. Travis shuddered as Ashley used her tongue along his chest muscle, rising up to twirl around his nipple.

Cassidy seemed enthralled. He drifted his fingers over Travis's shoulder, pausing to kiss and bite lightly as he worked his way around to Travis's back.

"That's not getting my pants off," Travis pointed out.

Teeth grazed his shoulder as Cassidy took a nip. "As if you're pissed. Keep that bullshit up, and I'll give you an instant replay of what you pulled on me."

Oh, someone was feeling bossy? Maybe the response was irrational, but Travis whipped around and caught Cassidy, fingers tight in the hair at the back of his head.

Everything stilled.

Then Cassidy's nostrils flared, and he had Travis's pants unzipped in no time. "Said you were a bossy bastard. Looks like I was right."

"You ain't seen nothing yet," Travis promised. "Take off my fucking pants, now."

He might have made it an order, but they obeyed willingly enough, only he hadn't expected them to kneel in front of him. For a moment he thought he might pass out as all the blood rushed from his head and straight into his cock. "Jesus, you're killing me."

Ashley grinned upward momentarily before working with Cassidy to haul jeans and underwear down all at one go. Travis's cock snapped upright so quickly he looked like some kind of early warning system.

"Hey, Cassidy." Ashley leaned forward. "I've got an idea. Give me another kiss."

Travis held his breath as they leaned against him and made contact again, flashes of tongues more pronounced this time. Hard, hot chest pressed to one leg, soft curvy breast crushed to the other.

And in the middle? Ashley guided their mouths closer and closer to Travis's groin until those tongues were not just teasing each other but darting around his aching cock. Ashley licked with full-out enthusiasm. Cassidy more hesitantly at first, but with growing fervour.

If he closed his eyes and soaked in the sensations, Travis might last thirty seconds.

Watching?

Oh, God, if he kept watching he had ten seconds left, tops. But he couldn't pull his gaze away. Especially once they took turns covering him before pulling back, each time going a little farther, a little deeper as his shaft grew wet enough to slide smoothly between their eager lips. Soft and pouting, then harder and yet just as eager, Cassidy proving he could destroy Travis's mind as thoroughly as Ashley.

"That's it, Cassidy," Ashley encouraged him. "Suck harder as you pull back. Yeah, that looks awesome. Again. Use your hand, and go slower. Give him time to get really anxious."

While Cassidy continued to work Travis's cock, she caught his balls in her fingers—what was there as they'd pulled up so tight and hard, Travis was on the verge of exploding. She leaned in, sticking out her tongue to stroke the underside of his cock and over one ball.

Then damn it all if she didn't pause and turn her head

slightly toward him. "Oops, you said you wanted to be in charge, didn't you?"

Her big blue eyes stared up so innocently that if he hadn't been one second away from orgasm he would have laughed.

Instead all he could do was grind out a warning. "I'm coming."

"You ready to taste him, Cassidy?" she asked.

Cassidy nodded, which was good because the next moment with his lips squeezed tight, he'd sucked Travis's brains out the end of his dick. Semen exploded into Cassidy's hot mouth. Travis's body jerked as extreme pleasure tingled up his spine. Ashley teased the base of his cock with a smooth massage that seemed to double the sensation and his release rushed from him.

Cassidy pulled back and fisted Travis, licking his lips as he jerked the final spurts free, seed flying out to land on his chest.

Travis placed a hand on Cassidy's shoulder to stop from ending up in a puddle on the floor. "Holy *fuck*."

Ashley wrapped her arms around him while Cassidy rose to his feet and grinned.

"Give me a second, and I'm pretty sure I'll find my brains." Travis considered diving for the bench even if the wood would be cold on his bare ass. He was hot enough at the moment to put up with sitting in a snow bank. Only Cassidy stepped forward and leaned in, offering a supportive, if sticky, body to lean against.

They were all grinning like fools.

First, a moment of chastisement. Travis lifted Ashley's chin toward him. "That's not what I had in mind," he scolded.

She shrugged. "Seemed a good idea at the time."

He laughed and took her lips, kissing her and running his fingers over her back as he caught Cassidy and kept him tight to his side.

Hedonistic pleasure, maybe, but damn if it wasn't good. And damn if he didn't feel better in spite of the fact it was the three of them fooling around. Ashley's expression said all too clearly how much she cared about him. Cassidy's as well.

Later he'd take that information and revel in it. Right now, the two of them needed their worlds rocked as well.

He pulled back from his connection with Ashley and turned to Cassidy, catching him by surprise. With the other man's mouth already open, their breaths instantly mingled and tongues connected. Travis groaned in pleasure and planned his next move.

Doing a fist pump in the middle of the room seemed a touch too blatant, but inside Ashley was celebrating all the same. It was so deliciously decadent to see Travis and Cassidy opening up to each other. She had planned to do everything necessary to keep pushing them—well, they didn't seem to need any further encouragement. She drifted away to enjoy the sight of two strong, powerful men, naked and wrapped around each other. Cassidy's cock stood upright, Travis even after his orgasm had a semi—the man never seemed to lose it completely.

Ashley stepped back into her sandals, silently enjoying the show. Travis threaded his fingers into Cassidy's hair and tilted his head, examining his face intently.

"We're not done," he whispered, and that's all she heard before he lowered his voice further.

Cassidy's gaze flicked over Travis's shoulder and landed directly on her.

Uh-oh. This didn't bode well for her plan of hightailing it from the room to allow the guys some alone time. Not that she was opposed to having some fun herself, but this was supposed to be about them, not her.

Now both of them were staring intently. Cassidy dropped his gaze slowly over her naked body, and hummed happily. "We get to make her squirm? Because I could go for that."

"Squirm, and a bit more." Travis paused. "And then, your turn."

"Let's do it."

Oh shit. Ashley backed off a couple more feet, wondering if she had a chance of getting to the door, but it was too late.

Travis glanced up from examining her footwear, and his brow rose. "You going somewhere?"

She didn't answer, just took off like a shot for the door even though she figured it was useless. He caught her around the waist, and she was airborne, hot male flesh holding her firmly as he carried her. Travis plunked her on top of the table and leaned over her with both arms, his grin wide as he pressed their foreheads together. "I don't feel like streaking through the yard, thank you. You started the game here, we'll finish it here."

She pouted. "But this table is so hard."

Cassidy laughed and grabbed a cushion from the window seat. "Your throne, milady."

He laid the thick padding on the sturdy table, and she wiggled on top, pulling him over her and linking her hands behind his neck. "Kiss me."

"You are a bossy little thing tonight." Cassidy nuzzled her neck. "Between you and Travis, I'm feeling outnumbered."

His hips nestled between her legs, and for a moment she was tempted to wrap her legs around him and indulge in a good old-fashioned fucking.

Then that other bossy guy in the room interfered. "Shove over, Butch, I need access to some soft, womanly tits."

Cassidy rolled to the side, grimacing briefly. "I thought you'd forgotten that stupid nickname."

Butch? *Oh...* Ashley giggled. "Does that make Travis the Sundance Kid? Because, you know, that's just not right."

Travis settled at her side, leaning on an elbow as he slid his fingers over her breast. "You can be the kid. Now, shut up and take your punishment."

Two hands stroked her. Two lips caressed. Teased. Tasted.

This was the penance she had to pay? Willingly. She could handle it.

They were at her breasts, one on each side, warm tongues rasping in unsynchronized tugs and nips. She could handle the kisses they gave her in turn, tongues driving into her mouth and possessing her. Cassidy's smooth jaw, the rougher rasp of shadow on Travis's chin—both leaving behind sensitized skin that ached for more.

It was their touch that destroyed her. All the while their mouths took her to heaven, the gentlest of touches floated over her belly. Between her legs. Strong fingers stroked her sex before slipping into her pussy. Thrusting in deep, rubbing all the spots that made stars float in front of her eyes.

One finger, another. Pressure on her clit. Thick digits that pinned her in place then stretched her wide, and she gasped for control. Fought to hang on and not simply give in to the pleasure.

She had to see—had to know.

She struggled up on her elbows and stared down her body. Like feasting at some erotic food bar, their mouths returned to nip and nibble. Two hands rested between her legs, and both of them had a finger inside her at the same time.

Ashley moaned, her mouth captured by Cassidy's kiss as Travis eased back only far enough to make room for him.

Two men kissing her, kissing each other, tongues tangling then retreating. Combined with their fingers fucking her so forcibly she couldn't fight it anymore, Ashley closed her eyes and let her orgasm take her.

A minute later? Maybe two—she'd lost all track of time—Cassidy nuzzled her cheek softly, slowing his touch. "Fucking amazing."

Another kiss, this time Travis, his lips next to her ear. "You okay, baby?"

She made herself nod. "Uh-huh."

Even though she felt like a bowl of jelly, getting her jollies wasn't the end of the evening. She twisted toward Travis. "You're being an ass and leaving Cassidy hanging."

Travis laughed. "He hasn't been hanging since the minute you started working on that damn ice cream cone, woman."

"So?" she demanded. He wasn't stupid. He knew what she was asking.

"We're taking care of you first, that's all," Cassidy insisted.

"God, the two of you are impossible." She wiggled out from under them far enough to sit up, looking around to find the deck of cards. Seated naked, she ignored their grins as she shuffled a couple of times then slammed a card on the table in front of each of them. She flipped hers over to show an ace, then grinned at Travis. "Get Cassidy off. Now."

He exchanged an amused look with Cassidy. "I hope you're enjoying ordering me around, because it's not happening again for a long, *long* time."

"You playing?" Ashley taunted. She turned their cards to reveal a pair of jacks. "I'd have given you both jokers, but there were none in the deck."

Travis slipped off the tabletop, his cock back up to full again as he paced around the table to Cassidy's side. "Lesson to learn, Cassidy? Never bet with a woman who does card tricks."

Cassidy rotated to face him. "I don't know. So far everything's gone pretty damn well as far as I'm concerned."

"Going to get better," Travis promised. He planted a hand on either side of Cassidy's hips before twisting to speak to Ashley.

"And you. While you watch, I want those clever fingers of yours on your pussy. Once Cassidy loses control, I'm fucking you right here on the table while Cassidy plays with you."

A lovely shiver took her at his growly command. "Sounds wonderful."

Travis turned back, and Cassidy swallowed hard. Tension rose, a fine sheen of sweat on both their torsos glistening in the lights. Travis pressed his lips to Cassidy's chest. "Relax. You'll like it."

"That's not the trouble," Cassidy complained. "I'm worried I won't last more than three... Holy *fuck.*"

No holds barred. Travis simply fisted Cassidy's cock and surrounded him. Mouth sealed tight over the crown, Travis's cheeks hollowed, and Cassidy stiffened, hips rising off the table.

Even if Travis hadn't told her to, Ashley wouldn't have been able to stop from dipping her fingers between her legs. Rubbing her clit to ease the building pressure as Travis took Cassidy deep again and again. He sat on the bench, his own cock rising upward as he sucked Cassidy's hard length, leaving room to pump his fist up and down. Forceful, full, hard strokes until Cassidy gasped for air, his stomach muscles clenched to rocks.

Ashley couldn't stay away. She crawled in closer and brushed a hand over Cassidy's abdomen. Teased lightly to let him know she was there, then she pressed her palm to his chest and kissed him as she guided him to lie on the cushion.

"Ashley." He caught her around the neck as his eyes rolled back. She glanced down the table to see Travis had let go of Cassidy's cock. He'd pushed Cassidy's thigh out of the way and was playing with his ass. Still sucking his cock enthusiastically, noises of pleasure rising as Cassidy squirmed.

She stayed where she was, kissing Cassidy tenderly. "Feels good, baby? His mouth on your cock? His finger in your ass?"

Cassidy nodded, his lips tightly closed as if he were afraid to let go.

"Let it happen," she soothed. "Enjoy it all. His tongue. His touch. It's like getting fucked and fucking at the same time, right?"

She gasped as a strong hand pressed between her legs again, this time Cassidy dragging her hand over slick skin, their fingers linked as he rubbed her clit.

Travis worked Cassidy's dick like she'd worked the ice cream cone at the start of the night. His other hand was wrapped around his own cock and pumping hard.

Crazy, dirty sex. Perfect crazy, mixed-up sex.

Cassidy jerked without warning, curling upright slightly as he came. "Oh, *fuck*, yeah."

There was too much to see, to feel. Cassidy shouted again as Travis swallowed around his cock, the entire length buried deep. Travis's hand on his own cock faltered, picking up again to drag out another climax, shooting against his abdomen. Ashley's pussy squeezed around nothing, but that was fine—that was just *fine* as erotic tension pulsed in waves, and satisfaction rolled through her one more time.

"Oh. Fuck. *Yeah.*" Ashley repeated Cassidy's words enthusiastically. That had been about perfect.

Ashley moaned as she rolled to her back. Travis panted for air, and Cassidy...

Well, he had no choice other than to stay in one spot and allow the shudders racking his body to die away.

"That was awesome." Ashley smiled at the ceiling, looking a little like a cat that'd gotten into the cream.

He stroked her cheek, but all the while he was aware of

Travis. Of naked bodies and the scent of sex. Of the wetness around his cock, and his still-tingling balls.

"You two proud of yourselves?" Travis drawled.

"Ha!" Ashley waved a hand in the air. "Tell me you're pissed off. Just try to say it, so I can call bullshit."

Travis snuck his hand over her stomach, reaching until he made contact with Cassidy. Instant goose bumps rose as Travis stroked his fingertips over Cassidy's skin, caressing them both with one motion.

"Oh hell, I wouldn't dream of complaining, though I had talked about fucking you, little minx." She turned her smile on him, and Travis grinned in return, his cocky expression fading to far more serious. "And as much fun as your game was? It backfired. Now that I've had a taste, I don't want it to end."

Cassidy fought to keep from jerking off the table in shock. "What do you mean?"

Travis flattened his hand against Cassidy's chest and leaned farther to make direct eye contact. "We said this game was for tonight, but hell if that's enough. We've got nothing stopping us. No reason not to take for the entire damn summer. All three of us —that's what I want. I want you both in my bed, and as patient as I was tonight with Ashley ordering us around, I don't think I need to remind you that I'm stubborn enough to get my way."

"What if we don't want more than tonight?" Cassidy demanded, feeling his meager control of the situation slipping away. Even worse, he wasn't honestly disappointed by the fact.

A sharp snort of amusement escaped Travis. "Well, Cassidy, see that's why I'll get my way. If you really could say to me, 'T, I don't want to spend the next two and a half months fooling around with you and Ashley' then I'd listen, and that would be the end of it." He moved closer, his eyes mesmerizing. "But I know the truth. And the truth is you're longing for this as much as I am. So how about we cut the bullshit and make it official?"

Fear still hovered. "What if this—?"

"No," Travis snapped. Then softer, but just as earnest. "No what-ifs. It's not going to be perfect all the time—I know that. We'll deal with the stupid things we do as we do them, which probably means you guys calling me out for being an ass ninety percent of the time, but we're doing this. Are you in or not?"

Ashley curled her hands around Cassidy's biceps, blinking innocently. "We can handle it. Maybe between the two of us we can teach Travis some manners." She gave a little gasp as Travis's hand slapped her bare ass, but her smile stayed bright.

Cassidy would be a fool to turn them down. This was a once-in-a-lifetime opportunity. It wasn't forever, and it was everything he'd longed for. *Who* he'd longed for.

Travis's sharp eyes took in all of it. Cocky and bold and too damn addictive to ignore. It might be wrong, might be dangerous, but Cassidy couldn't resist.

He stroked Ashley's lips with his thumb, ignoring Travis for a moment. Focusing on her, because she was the reason this could happen—because she'd made the first moves, and she was strong enough to put up with him and Travis for the next while. "Not like I'd turn down the opportunity to spend the summer with a beautiful woman."

"Damn right, you won't," Travis muttered. "Shit for brains if you did."

"Asshole," Cassidy drawled back. "But I'm sleeping in my own bed, thank you. Bet you're a fucking bed hog."

Ashley's laughter rang over the room. "I love how you guys are so upfront and open about your emotions."

Travis nuzzled her neck. "Good. Because you got us into this, babe. And you have to deal with us for the rest of the summer."

From the look in her eyes, she wasn't one bit upset about that challenge at all.

18

"You want to go on a trail ride?"

Ashley glanced up from the teeny table in her camper van that she was using as a computer desk. The side door was propped open to let in the fresh air, and Cassidy filled the frame. His blond hair stood up in places, his hat held before him in his hands.

Hands. *Hmm.* The memory of his touch sent a shiver trickling over her. It had been a couple days since they'd had their little showdown in the mess hall. Since then she'd spent her nights in Travis's bed, without Cassidy joining them.

It wasn't as if the three of them had nothing else to do but fool around, but Cassidy seemed to be holding back. Travis had given the other man a few hard looks, but he hadn't pushed, so she'd followed his lead. Cassidy would come around, she was sure of it. They had lots of time, and there was something to be said for the thrill of the chase.

But having him come to her? Half the battle right there.

She patted the cushion beside her. "Nice to see you. What have you got planned?"

He stepped in and joined her, barely fitting his muscular body into the full-to-capacity van. "I was looking at the schedule, and if you want to go out riding for a day, this week works well."

More opportunities for picture taking. Ashley nodded. "Sounds like fun. Who all would go?"

"I'm giving the crew a couple of days off. James and Dani plan on staying here, so they can care for the horses. But Travis said he could wing a getaway."

Oh, better and better. This had potential to be more than simply a photo-gathering excursion. "The three of us, then? All alone in the middle of the wilderness?"

He grinned.

"Sign me up." Ashley paused, not sure if it was the right thing to do. Only she had to know. She laid a hand on his leg. "How are you, Cass? You've been awfully busy."

He cleared his throat. "You can say it. I've been hiding."

His instant honesty reassured her more than anything else he could have said. "Nothing wrong with taking your time, though I tend to rush in where angels fear to tread. Go as fast as you want, but I hope you know we want you." She squeezed his thigh. "And I mean more than simply sex-want. You're an awesome guy. I enjoy spending time with you."

"Thanks." His fingers pressed over hers. "Actually, I was thinking about that. Would you lend me your guitar?"

Well. "You play?"

He shrugged stiffly. "I did. Haven't for years, but I'd appreciate if you don't mind helping me brush up my skills. If you want."

She flipped her hand over so their fingers would mesh together. "I'd like that. Maybe in the evenings by the fire?"

Cassidy nodded. He leaned in slowly, and she tilted her head back to allow their mouths to connect. A soft kiss. Tender and brief, yet enough to make her toes curl.

He released her hand and crawled out of the van. There was a lovely warm spot inside her as she smiled after him. "The ride sounds super. Anytime you guys can make it. I can plan around your schedule."

He adjusted his hat before tipping his head in salute. "See you around?"

Her lips were tingling. "Oh yeah."

A little later Ashley found she was staring at the screen and not working more than working. Time for a break, or at least a change of scenery. With her portable easel and art supplies, she headed into the sunshine.

Travis found her in the field beyond the campsite. She didn't notice he was there at first, just leaned back one moment and discovered him sitting on the grass watching her.

She propped her paintbrush on the easel and wiped her hands clean. "Hey, you need something?"

He shook his head. "Taking a breather and wondered how you were doing."

Three steps took her to his side. She straddled his legs, sitting into his lap and draping her arms over his shoulders. "I'm doing lovely. The camp is gorgeous and inspiring, and thank you for letting me join you."

His hands landed on her hips, and he slipped his thumbs into her belt loops. "I'm glad it's working out. I like having you here," he admitted.

For the second time that day, she found herself being kissed tenderly. It was all too easy to give a response, to lean closer and kiss him back. This was the man who'd enticed her from the start. Take charge, lighthearted and cocky in public, and yet deep down, something more. Layers within layers—some of them only now starting to make sense as he opened up and accepted the things inside him.

Philosophical thoughts were pushed aside as Travis caressed

her. His mouth and tongue guiding her toward more intense pleasure, his hands drifting over her torso and up the sides of her breasts as if she were priceless and fragile.

"I love watching you work," Travis whispered. "You're so into what you're doing, it's as if you're pouring yourself out through your fingertips onto the canvas."

His fingertips were damn talented as well, brushing her nipples and prompting them to tighten to hard peaks. "I like watching you work, but that's because your flexing muscles turn me on."

He laughed. "Dirty girl."

"You know it. I can handle having those flexing muscles all over me anytime you like." She moaned as his touch grew rougher, arching her back to let him play with her breasts. "Sweet mercy, Travis, you starting something you plan to finish, or what?"

He lifted her hips and pulsed his lips around her nipple right though her shirt, nipping lightly before letting go with a sigh. "You're not wearing a bra, woman. You distracted me." He settled her again, pressing his knuckles under her chin and locking their eyes together. "You are a sexy thing, but you're more than that. You're pretty damn incredible. Sexy *and* smart."

Ashley preened under his attention. "Aren't you a lovely man?"

His laughter curled around them. "I'm an asshole and a bastard most of the time, but you bring out the best in me. Thank you."

The compliment was unexpected and so sincerely said that a shiver of delight rolled through her from head to toe. "That's about the sweetest thing anyone's ever said to me."

He tweaked her chin. "I mean it." Then his expression changed slightly, tightening. "Ash, I'm getting that urge. What did you call it? For some stress release."

She stroked his shoulders, trying to pass on reassurance. "You gonna ask Cassidy to help you?"

Travis nodded. "You want to be there or not?" His lips twisted. "I'm asking not because I expect you to, but things have changed. It's all mixed up, the urge I have for pain and the urge to fuck, and I don't want you to think I'm cheating on you if something happens other than me getting—stress relieved."

"You talking about if you and Cass fool around?"

He nodded.

Oh my, now she was torn. Pushing her selfish urges aside, she cupped his face and put as much sincerity into her words as possible. "The idea of watching you two fool around makes me hot, which might be all kinds of wrong, but I don't give a damn. I already told you that I didn't mind. You're not my possession, Travis. You don't have to ask my permission to enjoy being with Cassidy."

"I'm more than a casual friend, though, aren't I?" His eyes had grown darker as she spoke.

"Oh, definitely, you're more." She punctuated her answer with a kiss. "And, Travis, thank you for sharing with me. About you...having a *need*. I can't tell you how much it means to me."

He squirmed as if uncomfortable. "Yeah, well, you asked me to. And I didn't want you upset like last time."

Last time, when she'd wondered if she'd been the cause of another person—

A shudder racked her, and he offered a soothing caress, wrapping his arms around her. "It's okay, sweetheart. I'll be fine. Cassidy's not going to *hurt me* hurt me."

"I know." Damn the quiver in her voice. "It's not that. It's..." She stared into the sunshine and wondered how long the ice would stay in her soul. He'd trusted enough to come talk to her. She needed to take another step as well. "Someone close to me died over the holidays. I felt like it was my fault for not helping them."

His hug tightened. "Oh, baby."

"My cousin asked if he could talk to me, and I was all wrapped up in myself, and I walked out on him." Ashley wiped her eyes, unable to stop tears from rising. She blinked hard, fighting for control. "He committed suicide. I'm the one who found him the next morning."

"Ah, hell."

She buried her face against him, and Travis squeezed her close. Held her against him and gave her comfort.

When he spoke again, the words were low and tender. "Sweetheart, it's not your fault. You had no idea, and that's not the kind of thing you can anticipate."

She knew that. Had been told it, and told it to herself, but her selfishness still haunted her. Ashley pulled back and took a deep breath. "I know that in my head, but my heart is still broken. That's part of why I was so upset that first time you needed help. Because I wasn't listening to you. It's not the fact you needed pain that frightened me. It was me not taking the time to listen. I was wrong, and I'm so sorry."

"Shhh." He rocked her lightly, soothing hands on her back. "There's nothing to forgive. You've always done what you thought was best for me, even when it meant leaving."

"But that was wrong."

Travis shook his head. "No, baby, you walking away was exactly what I needed to get my head out of my ass."

He kissed her again, tenderness in his hands and lips as he wiped a tear from beside her eye. They sat together for a couple moments, and she finally found her breath.

It wasn't the end of her sadness, but it helped to know he didn't blame her.

She stood and held out her hand as he rose smoothly to his

feet. Travis hugged her tight for another moment, kissing the top of her head, and Ashley held in her sigh.

It felt so perfectly right to be in his arms, and yet she wasn't enough for him. Would never be enough.

The truth stung harder than any belt whip ever could.

Torn between nausea and anticipation, Cassidy pushed open his cabin door and paced in, Travis hard on his heels.

Since Travis had found him that afternoon and made his request, Cassidy had been uneasy. How sick was it that the idea of being the one to help his friend turned his legs to jelly and his cock rock solid?

All dinner he'd tried to come up with a solution before finally admitting he had no idea what was the best way to deal with this.

Maybe there was no *best*, there only was move forward and face both his hesitation to hurt Travis and his desire to be with him.

He stood by the foot of the bed and took a deep breath. "You got any idea how you want to do this?"

Travis shrugged. "You're the one who's got to deal out the pain. I figured you need to call the shots on that one."

A snort of disbelief escaped Cassidy. "Right, like you're not going to boss me around while I'm beating on you. Don't try to bullshit me about that."

His friend's stern expression slipped into a grin. "Yeah, well, what can I say? Someone's got to make the decisions, and usually that's me."

Cassidy hid his shaking hands by snapping a finger toward the bed. "Well, this time, I'm in charge. Strip and lay on your stomach."

Travis raised a brow, but he toed off his boots, kicking them toward the door. His shirt lifted upward without a word, sculpted muscles coming into view, and Cassidy schooled himself to stop from gasping for oxygen.

Travis's belt buckle loosened. He undid his jeans and pushed them from his hips along with his underwear, and that was it. Clothing abandoned to the chair by the door, nothing but primal male before Cassidy.

He'd seen the man buck naked more than once, but every time it was enough to blow his mind. Not only the muscles formed from labouring in the fields, but something else that made Cassidy's mouth water and his brain tangle so he couldn't think straight.

He eyed the sharp angles and muscles bulking his friend, starting at his calves and working his way up. Travis's legs were covered with a layer of wiry dark hair, and his cock rose from a thatch of solid black. A thin trail ran up his firm abdomen to his belly button, another dusting of black on his chest.

Cassidy was still staring when Travis adjusted his stance, pulling his gaze up to his friend's face in time to see his cocky grin. "You gonna look at me all night?" Travis asked.

Control—he had to take it, because Travis sure the hell wasn't giving it up. "Waiting for you to get on the bed like I told you to."

Travis sauntered forward, pausing inches away. Close enough that if he'd wanted to, Cassidy could have jerked their bodies together and gotten his fingers into Travis's naked ass cheeks.

Only Travis swung away and stepped to the bed. He paused again, glanced over his shoulder and then, fuck it all, if he didn't crawl onto the mattress with his ass presented toward Cassidy like some hard-core porn video.

Cassidy did the only thing he could in self-defense. He

turned his back and went for the things he'd gathered earlier. Took off his boots while he fought the urge to run.

Travis's soft chuckle said he knew exactly what was going on.

Enough. This wasn't getting them anywhere, and in the end, either he had the courage to give Travis what he needed or he didn't. As for the rest, it had been a hell of a long time coming.

Take. For one day, he was going to take.

Cassidy snapped out an order. "Spread your arms."

"My arms?" Travis sounded totally confused.

Cassidy slipped a rope around Travis's wrist and tied it off to the solid wood bedpost. He made his way around to the opposite side as Travis tested the hold.

"You want me to stop, you tell me," Cassidy said. "You protest or try to get free, I'm not going to listen, but you tell me no, and it's done. Got it?"

"Yeah, I got it. Just ain't ever been tied up before," Travis muttered.

Cassidy bet Travis had never relinquished control enough to let himself be tied up.

A final tug on the soft cord ensured it wasn't going to work loose, not without Cassidy releasing it. "Grab the ropes with your hands to protect your wrists."

Travis was still moving his arms into position when Cassidy caught his foot and looped it to a post. "Hey," Travis protested, "I don't know about that."

Cassidy ignored him.

He had to sit on Travis to stop him from thrashing, stringing him into position before the man finally stilled. "You'd think I was using boiling oil on you or something. Jeez."

Travis tested his bonds. "Feels...weird." The words came out deep and husky.

"Weird? Like, makes-you-want-to-freak-out weird or makes you horny?"

Travis laughed. "Everything makes me horny."

"Well, yeah." Cassidy ran his hand up the back of Travis's leg, spreading his fingers to caress as much skin as possible. "You're a guy. It comes with the territory."

Cassidy stroked all the way up to Travis's ass, cupping the flesh there and squeezing lightly. Travis sucked in a gasp then held his breath.

Not breathing seemed to be contagious. Cassidy let out the air suspended in his own lungs as he braced himself.

He lifted his hand from Travis's skin then brought it down sharply, the palm of his hand smacking soft skin with a ringing slap.

Travis jerked briefly before relaxing. "You gonna wear out your hand if you plan on doing that until I've had enough."

Cassidy smoothed his palm over skin gone faintly pink. "I looked up some stuff online," he confessed.

A sharp burst of laughter escaped Travis. "God, you didn't."

The ringing of the next slap mingled with Travis's amusement fading into a moan. "You're not the only person in the world that gets off on this. I didn't want to hurt you, and I'm not comfortable using a belt again. I found out there are ways to make it more...intense, quicker."

He stroked again, gripping firmer this time. Massaging and kneading Travis's ass and the seam where his legs and butt met. Travis fell silent for a few minutes, wiggling his torso when Cassidy reached for the bottle of oil on the side table.

Didn't complain, though. Not when Cassidy added a healthy shot to his palm and coated Travis from knees to mid-back, rubbing in the oil until his skin glistened.

"You're killing me," Travis muttered.

"Join the club." Cassidy's cock pressed like a rock against the front of his jeans, and the urge to strip was tough to resist. This was hotter than he'd remembered—although the last time was pretty much a blur in his memory.

"Cass..." Travis twisted his head to the side. "You're not going to like this, but my cock is going numb. Could you shove a pillow under my hips, or something?"

He should put in for sainthood. Cassidy snatched a pillow from the head of the bed and hoisted Travis's hips, pressing the material under him. A devil of mischief of his own moved his arm, and Cassidy slipped his hand lower and caught hold of Travis's cock.

"Fuck." The word whispered out as Travis thrust his hips forward.

Cassidy was basically at that moment sprawled over Travis, their thighs touching, bodies close, and his hand—

Adjusted Travis's cock before releasing the hard length to lie nestled in the soft pillow. Cassidy crawled off and picked up the new crop he'd pulled from the storage shed. A crop. Safe and familiar. No haunting memories.

"Tease."

"You still going numb?" Cassidy asked. "Because while I think you'd like me to get you off, it wouldn't solve your issue, so if you're comfortable, I'm going to finish what we started before moving to anything else."

Travis twisted his head and emotionlessly examined the crop in Cassidy's hands. "*Anything else* mean you plan on fucking me?"

Cassidy couldn't breathe again. *Stay in control.* "Right now, worry about the pain."

He brought the crop down rapidly, the soft leather flap on the end of the rigid handle snapping into bare flesh a hell of a lot harder than Cassidy's hand could.

Travis clutched the ropes, his knuckles going white, face turned into the mattress. Silence hung in the air between the cracks of leather meeting flesh. Cassidy worked a half-dozen smacks on each side of Travis's ass before pausing and once again using his palm to spread the oil. To give a contrast to the pain and sensitize the nerves faster.

Travis's skin was hot under his hand, hips fidgeting slightly, but he didn't say no. Didn't say anything but press closer to Cassidy's touch.

"Again?" Cassidy asked.

Travis nodded.

Time moved slower as Cassidy gave to his friend. Their breathing echoed in the room, the sharp nick of the crop an even metronome punctuated by the occasional grunt or low moan from Travis.

Cassidy's body heated as well as he stayed aware of Travis's every response. Watching for a sign it was too much. Too little.

A sense of power mixed with responsibility rolled over him. The pleasure was no longer only on one side.

Huh. That was...surprising.

Cassidy paused. Took a couple deep breaths—gave another soothing stroke.

Another set with the crop, this time slightly lower, on the upper part of Travis's thighs. Those blows brought a more intense response, making him cringe harder, and Cassidy slowed. Took more time between strikes, lingering as he stroked Travis's skin. Caressed and squeezed until Travis wasn't just rising up to greet his hand but groaning in pleasure every time the crop landed.

"Cass—" Travis turned his cheek up, sweat beading on his forehead. "God, Cass, I need..." He blew out a long, slow breath, tension pouring from him as he relaxed onto the mattress, all the fight gone.

Cassidy unhooked the ropes from Travis's wrists. His ankles. Oiled up his own hands again and started at Travis's feet. This time when he reached Travis's ass he stroked his thumbs over the red lines created by the crop, no longer hating that he'd caused them. Loving that Travis trusted him enough to ask him to.

He gave in to the pleasure that touching Travis's strong body gave him. He drizzled extra oil in the small of Travis's back and traced a finger through it and along the seam of his ass. It was all too simple to ease the slippery liquid farther in, separating Travis's cheeks slightly and teasing between them.

Travis reached back and caught his wrist. Strong fingers wrapped around him and held him in place. "Don't do this because you think you have to."

Cassidy leaned over until he could look Travis in the eye. This wasn't something he wanted to have any confusion over, and it was far past time for lying. "I want you. I've wanted you for fucking ever."

Somehow they ended up side by side, Cassidy clinging to Travis's neck as they kissed. Wilder and rougher than any prelude to a fuck that Cassidy had enjoyed before, but it was right. Violence and pain still hovered in the air. Cassidy found his jeans being torn from his hips, his shirt ripped over his head. It only seemed to take seconds before he was naked and a hot mouth was branding his skin.

He caught Travis to him and did his own exploring. Caressed the muscles flexing in Travis's back, reaching lower to clutch his ass again, this time knowing how hard and tight Travis wanted him to squeeze.

Then he couldn't wait. It had been far too long, and while hands wrapped around each other's cocks felt amazing, it wasn't enough. He caught Travis by the chin and held him captive. "Get back on your stomach."

Travis's pupils darkened further, a crease between his brows, and for a split second, Cassidy thought the word *no* was going to escape his friend's lips.

Then Travis turned, nestling against Cassidy's chest.

Rubbing them together so Cassidy's cock rested in the valley between his ass cheeks.

Cassidy eased him forward onto his hands and knees, holding firmly as he guided Travis into position. He caught up a condom and jerked it on, hands once again shaking. Then he moved in tight, covering Travis's body so he could press a kiss between his shoulder blades. "Tell me if you need a break."

"Just do it," Travis snapped. "God, you'd think you were…"

His words vanished as Cassidy pressed a finger into his ass. The oil from before and the lube Cassidy had coated his cock with made his finger slip in smoothly. He worked it a few times.

The tightness eased as Travis relaxed. Cassidy added another shot of lube to the valley between two fingers then spread Travis further.

"Oh, hell." Travis wiggled up on his knees, widening his stance.

"Okay?"

"God, yes."

The urge to hurry was there. Like a constant prod between his shoulders, but Cassidy took his time. Prepared Travis and teased him until neither of them could wait any longer.

He took a deep breath and put the head of his cock to Travis's ass, and pushed.

"Oh, sweet, *fuck*." Travis slammed back a hand and caught Cassidy's wrist again where he had gripped Travis's hip. "That feels so damn good."

Cassidy couldn't talk. Hell, he could barely breathe. Travis pushed his hips back as Cassidy rocked his pelvis forward, and suddenly his cock was buried to the root, all the way inside Travis.

Physical pleasure, yes, but the trust that had brought them to this point—that was what moved it from feeling good to something so incredible he couldn't describe. As he pulled his hips back, he smoothed his hand over the heated red lines still marring Travis's skin. He twisted his other hand, and their fingers ended up linked together. The touch made everything more intimate.

More intense.

He could have kept moving slowly, savouring every touch, but there was an ache in his cock and a warning bell going off in his balls, and he had to admit that he wanted more. He thrust forward, striking at an angle, and Travis cursed and arched. "Hell, *yes*."

Cassidy smiled. "You like that?"

He thrust again, and Travis's grip on his hand tightened to the point of pain. "Again," he demanded.

"Bossy bastard," Cassidy complained. "I've got my cock in your ass, and you're still trying to call the shots."

Travis laughed. "Did you expect anything else? Now, fuck me."

Cassidy held on tightly to both hips and drove his cock forward. Again. And again, the pleasure so intense he could have started a countdown and known exactly when he was going to blow. Ten more, nine, eight...

Only, not without Travis.

He reached around and gripped Travis's cock, jacking him hard in time with each thrust.

Travis twisted a death grip into the quilt cover. He alternately slammed himself back on Cassidy's cock and rocked his hips forward to thrust into Cassidy's fist.

"Damn." Cassidy saw white spots before his eyes and he was gone, semen spurting into the latex, his climax ripped loose as Travis's ass squeezed him tight.

Travis let out a guttural moan and gave in as well, strands of stickiness coating Cassidy's fingers, their bodies locked tight together.

Cassidy held on as long as he could before he had to collapse, which meant about five seconds. He rolled to the side, taking Travis with him. Cradling him against his chest and clinging to his hip so their bodies remained sealed together.

Their breathing rattled loudly in the quiet cabin air.

A strong hand slipped over his as once again Travis linked their fingers together. "You okay?"

Cassidy laughed. "I'm not the one who got his ass smacked with a crop."

"Not what I'm talking about, and you know it." Travis twisted until their eyes met. "All of it—the crop, the sex—you okay?"

It was a question that deserved a thoughtful answer. Cassidy paused and gave it a moment. It had been scary and horrifying before becoming invigorating and addictive, at least the last part.

He met Travis's frank gaze. "I'm not sure I like beating on you, but I like that I can care for you. Somewhere in the middle that makes it okay."

One edge of Travis's mouth snuck upward into that familiar grin. "I noticed you didn't say you hated tying me up, or the sex."

"I ain't stupid." Cassidy drew his hand over Travis's chest, trying to soak in that it was possible to be there. "You're fun to fuck."

Travis full-out laughed before wrapping an arm around Cassidy and pulling him close for an enormous hug.

All of it so wrong and yet perfectly right. Cassidy had no idea what else was going to happen for the rest of the summer. Travis and Ashley had more than turned his world upside down—they were rebuilding it.

19

———

hings didn't change overnight, but there was a smoother fit among all of them in the days that followed. Travis liked that he could look up and find Ashley smiling at him, her warm hugs and willing arms always there for him.

Cassidy was still more standoffish, but out of the public eye he was willing as well, and the three of them ended up in bed together in some form most nights, fooling around for a while before Cassidy would kiss them both and head back to his cabin to sleep.

It wasn't perfect, but seemed about as perfect as it was going to get. Travis was satisfied for the moment.

Two buses had pulled into the lot that morning, doors opening to release a flood of excited little boys and their slightly more groggy fathers. Travis leaned on the fence post to observe the bustle as the crew and guides got them all herded in the proper direction for their grand adventure.

One man guided his son along by a hand gripped in the back of his shirt, barely able to control the energetic bundle of boy.

Memories of doing things with his own father drifted in.

A soft hand snuck around his waist as Ashley cuddled in tight to his side. "You've got a twisted smile on your face. What deep thoughts are you playing with now?"

Travis pointed Ashley's attention down the hill. "Thinking about how my father survived raising us six boys. Couldn't have been very easy."

"What? You think you were difficult to deal with? Say it ain't so..." She laid a hand over her chest in an exaggerated tease.

"Probably the rottenest bugger of all of us." Travis made a face. "Forget *probably*. I was an ass a hell of a lot of the time."

"Oh, I doubt that, but if you were, you've changed a lot since then." She squeezed him tightly. "Your past made you into a better man today."

Travis stared silently for another moment. "You seen Cassidy this morning?"

She frowned. "Not since breakfast."

He dropped a slightly distracted kiss on her lips. "Bet he's hiding in the barn. Tonight—you want a campfire once the guests are gone?"

"You know it. Vicki got us the fixings for s'mores."

An exaggerated shudder shook him. "God, how can you eat that sweet crap?"

She laughed and headed the opposite direction.

Cassidy was working in the barn, the music turned down, most of the horses out in the paddock being prepped for the riders. Travis stood and watched as Cassidy raked, his hard muscles flexing with every motion. Ragged movements, though, as if he were on edge. Not the smooth and easy-like actions Travis expected, but strange jerks and sudden smacks tossed in at random.

"That pile of hay do something to piss you off?" Travis asked.

Cassidy jolted upright, his expression dark and clouded.

Ignoring the question, he turned back to his task, driving the rake into the pile and throwing the load into the wheelbarrow with far more force than needed.

Travis shifted around to get a better look at his friend. "Cass?"

Cassidy stabbed the rake so it stood upright then stepped back. "Got work to do."

He wheeled past Travis as if his task were the most important thing in the entire world.

What the heck?

Cassidy was back in a minute, rolling up his shirtsleeves and prepping to go again when Travis had enough. He stepped in and laid a hand on Cassidy's shoulder. "Hey, what's up?"

Cassidy shrugged him off. "Not in the mood."

Travis laughed. "With a yard full of guests you think I plan on seducing you right now? Get your brain in gear. I want to know what's wrong."

"Nothing."

The rake was up and killing the hay pile again, and Travis decided to ignore it for now. But not for long.

All day he let it go. Cassidy was interesting to observe, though. Like how at lunch, when the guests filed into the mess hall to grab their food, chatting excitedly, dads somehow controlling their rambunctious boys, Cassidy filled a plate and walked straight through the hall and out the door.

He ate his lunch on the stoop of his cabin, glowering at the campers as they finished their meal and got partnered up with their horses. The entire time the group was being prepped, Cassidy stayed far out of the way.

But he watched. And Travis watched him, and wondered.

"Is he okay?" Ashley whispered, tucking herself under Travis's arm and staring up the hill to where Cassidy still brooded.

He didn't know how to answer when he wasn't sure what was wrong. "He'll be fine." He smiled at her. "We'll get it out of him tonight."

"Resistance is futile." Her smile lit up the dark places inside.

That gentle smile was still in place hours later as she leaned back in her lawn chair and held her marshmallow-pronged roasting stick toward the flames. Overhead, stars were breaking through the night sky, tiny pinpoints of radiant light gleaming and winking.

"Pretty night," she declared. "But I'm not going to last long enough to enjoy it."

"You tired?"

She nodded, pulling off a marshmallow slowly and watching the insides stretch. "It's the satisfying-two-guys thing, I don't know how much more I can take."

He stared at her for a moment in concern, but she winked. "Teasing. I love being with you guys, that's not it at all. Getting that project done on time is making me nervous—I don't sleep as solid."

"You'll make it," Travis encouraged. "And if you need to hit the sack early, you go right ahead. I'm going to try and talk Cassidy out of his grump before I turn in."

They sat in comfortable silence while the fire crackled, until it seemed Cassidy wasn't going to make this easy. "He's not showing up tonight, is he?" Ashley asked, concern creasing her brow.

Travis stirred the coals then laid on another log. "I'll give him another half hour, then I track him down."

There was no hiding the enormous yawn that took her, and she stood reluctantly. "Let me know everything is okay as soon as you can. I can't keep my eyes open anymore, but I'm worried."

"He's on his way now." Travis pointed up the path at the shadowy figure slowly approaching. He caught her by the hand

and tugged her between his legs, bending her low enough he could press a good-night kiss on her soft lips. "Warm up the bed for me."

"Always."

She met Cassidy on the path, pausing to wrap her arms around him. Their outlines against the faint outdoor lights briefly slipping from two separate figures into one tightly meshed silhouette.

Travis considered how much things had changed. He tried to summon up jealousy at seeing them kiss. Ashley stroked Cassidy's face and whispered something too soft for Travis to hear.

It wasn't envy that tightened Travis's stomach, but need. Want.

Emotion rolled over him in a wave. He wanted to ease Ashley's fears so she could know what an incredible job she was doing on her projects. Every time she showed him her work, her talent floored him.

And Cassidy...

Travis admitted it. He had a deep desire to make whatever it was that was bothering Cassidy go away. He wanted to see his friend laugh wholeheartedly, wanted to alleviate his fears and be at his side all the time.

The man was hesitant, but so giving. Travis was reminded of his older brother Daniel in some ways, or maybe his cousin Gabe. Men who gave and gave without expecting much in return. When he'd been young he'd occasionally thought the two of them were idiots, but now their motivations seemed much clearer.

Strength, not weakness.

They cared more for others than for themselves, and that kind of unselfishness had never been a part of Travis's vocabulary. Cassidy and Ashley? They made him want to learn.

Cassidy put a beer down next to Travis's lawn chair before

settling opposite him, leaning back and stretching out his legs. "I'm getting to be a recluse. Too many people around, and I get the jitters."

It was nearly an acceptable excuse, only the explanation didn't sit right. Travis took a drink and pondered the best response. "Couple of the boys were so damn excited I thought we'd have to duct tape them to their saddles. First time on a horse."

"Good thing Karen's got the rides trained to deal with that kind of nonsense."

Nonsense? Even though he wasn't a kid person, there had been nothing but sheer enthusiasm in the lot of them. "You remember your first time on a horse?" Travis asked.

A silent shake of the head was all he got in response.

Seemed whatever was poking Cassidy was big enough to knock the chatter out of him, but Travis tried anyway. "I don't remember either. Seems like my daddy threw us up on them around the time we learned to walk. We've got a video of the twins sitting together on one of the oldest nags in the yard with my mom in the background wringing her hands, worried like they were being sent to their deaths."

Not even a smile. Not a crack.

Travis put down his beer. If this had been Ashley, he would have hauled her into his lap and held her until she gave up whatever she was holding inside. He didn't think Cassidy would go for being manhandled like that. But maybe...

He crossed the narrow distance between their chairs and knelt at Cassidy's side. That at least got his attention, Cassidy's blond head swung from where he'd been fixated on the fire. "What are you doing?"

Travis snuck a hand over the edge of the chair and caught Cassidy's fingers. He held on, smoothing his thumb back and forth to caress the strong hand that had cared for him and brought him pleasure over the past weeks. "Looking out for a friend. He seems to be having a shitty day. I'm wondering why."

Cassidy rolled his eyes and attempted to tug his hand free. "You been taking emo lessons from Ashley?"

"Maybe. Would that be a bad thing?" Travis asked. "Come on, spill. You've been pissed off and upset and worrying all day, and it's killing me."

"Fine, but haul your chair over here. I'm not talking to you when you're squatting next to me like you're—"

Travis flipped up a hand. "Enough. How about this instead?"

He hauled Cassidy to his feet and led him a couple of feet to the side where the hill rose gently. There was a log backrest, but the slope created a soft place to sit. Travis stretched out and waited.

Cassidy hesitated.

"Come on, you scared to lie beside me when we've got all our clothes on?" Travis patted the grass. "Humour me."

It took so long for the man to settle his ass to the ground, you'd have thought he'd been asked to strip and dance naked in the street. But he finally gave in, shoulders resting against the log, arms folded behind his head to give him something to relax against as he once again got lost in the flickering flames.

Travis rolled to his side, propping his head on his fist. One of his legs was right up touching Cassidy's, their bodies close enough that the warmth of the fire and the heat from each other made it perfect to lie still as the night cooled.

He examined Cassidy's face. "Well?"

"It's no big deal," Cassidy insisted. "You're making a fuss over nothing."

"Got your back up all day—that's not nothing."

Cassidy gave a weary sigh. "All those dads with their sons. Doing something fun together—hell, I didn't do shit-all with my dad other than chores. If he'd have taken me on a trail ride for an entire weekend, I would have thought I'd died and gone to heaven."

"Not every family is the same. I never actually went anywhere like Trailblazers with my dad either." Travis paused. This wasn't about the camping trip. He thought back to the stern-faced man who'd pulled out a shotgun and told him to get the hell off his property.

Yeah, this was about a lot more than just camping.

"You wish your family was different."

A brittle burst of laughter escaped Cassidy. "God. You have no idea how good you have it. Not only with your dad, but with all your brothers. I know you say they're a pain in the ass at times, but they're there for you. I'm so much older than my brother and sister I didn't do much with them. I barely knew them."

Travis laid his hand on Cassidy's chest. "I know how good I've got it, which makes life wonderful and shitty by turns. I love that they're there for me. I hate the thought of disappointing them."

Cassidy nodded firmly. "Damn right."

Such a small glimpse into something so important. "You never talked about your family before."

"Just...like you said. Not every family is the same. Not everyone has good memories to look back on." Brilliant green eyes turned his way, a sad sneer twisting Cassidy's face. "It hit hard today. Sorry I worried you."

"Nothing to apologize for. And I'm glad you said something." Travis thumped the side of his fist gently on Cassidy's chest. "Even if I had to drag it out of you."

Cassidy captured Travis's wrist and held him immobile. The memories that had rumbled inside all day weren't settling. It was good to admit a little of the pain, but the rest wasn't something he wanted to dump on his friend. Not now, maybe not ever.

But what he did want was to ease his mind. Loosen some of

the knots in his spine and make something other than bitterness spill through his body.

All it took was a gentle tug to roll Travis off his side and halfway over his own body. He slipped his hand behind Travis's neck and guided their mouths together. Sweet hops from the beer mixed with firm pressure from Travis's lips—intoxicating in a whole new way.

It wasn't about trying to get as riled up as possible. Pleasure, yes, but a softer, tender side that Cassidy needed right now more than he needed any kind of sex.

Travis lifted his leg, wrapping them closer. Getting his hands around Cassidy and caressing gently. A stroke over his shoulders. Another along the side of his neck until Travis cradled his face. All the while they kissed. Small nudges with chins and cheeks to move each other. Lips and mouths staying easy, tongues exploring.

The fire popped and crackled. Tendrils of heat and the occasional gust of smoke drifted over them. They rolled lower to move away from the log headrest, and Cassidy found his hand under Travis's shirt, hard hot skin under his palm.

He brushed his fingers back and forth lightly. Savouring the intimate contact as much as the kisses.

Travis groaned, but his touch remained controlled as he floated a fingertip down the side of Cassidy's throat.

Necking by the fire. Never in a million years would Cassidy have dreamed it possible, but everything about the situation was right. Achingly, beautifully right, and the only thing that would have made it better was if Ashley had been lying beside them. Her caring touch and giving heart as much a part of what he craved as Travis's.

Which proved he'd officially gone insane. Cassidy laughed, pulling back from Travis's kiss as he linked their fingers together and squeezed. "Thanks."

Travis grinned. "Hell, anytime. You ready to call it a night?"

He nodded. "I'll take a swing through the barn—"

"No." Knuckles stroked his cheek. "You already spent enough time in the barns today. I'll check the horses. How about you go crawl into my bed and cuddle up with Ashley. I know she was worried about you as well."

None of this was real—he had to remember that. It was a dream and a fantasy and only for the summer. But he was no fool. He wasn't going to turn down a second. "You joining us later?"

"Soon as I can." Travis grinned. "You should give up pretending you like sleeping on your own, and I'll build us a bed frame big enough for two mattresses."

"You'll still steal the covers," Cassidy taunted, pulling Travis to his feet.

"Sleep next to me, and you won't need covers. I'll keep you warm."

God.

Something inside not only cracked, it melted and threatened to pour out of him. Cassidy busied himself damping the fire so he didn't have to answer. Didn't have to look as Travis gave his shoulder a final squeeze before taking off toward the barns.

Only once it was safe did Cassidy pause so he could stare after Travis's retreating back. He had to wonder if the fantasy life overtaking his summer was going to end up leaving him a cold and empty husk when it came time to return to reality in the fall.

When he had to say goodbye, and leave Travis and Ashley forever.

20

———————

Spring merged into summer, arriving almost overnight as the camps switched from running over weekends to full-week excursions. Instead of hanging out Monday to Friday with the guys and the crew, and working on projects, Ashley adjusted to the busier summer schedule. The campers arrived on Sundays, and the place turned into a mass of noise and confusion for a solid day. She always stopped to observe the new people coming to camp, occasionally drawing sketches and chatting with them.

She might have been hanging around camp to spend time with Travis, and now Cassidy, but that didn't mean she couldn't lend a hand every now and then.

Some of the time helping out had led her into the kitchen, and she'd been slowly getting to know Vicki more, which was nice. She'd missed spending time with other women, and any lingering discomfort on Vicki's part seemed to have vanished as the weeks passed.

This week there was a group of girlfriends who had booked

time off together, arriving in two vans stuffed to the roof with multiple bags and suitcases.

Ashley eyed the sparkly fake gems on one woman's boots and carefully hid her grin.

"I saw that." Vicki climbed up the fence next to Ashley and rested her crossed arms on the top rail.

Oops. "Saw what?"

Vicki bumped her hip into Ashley's. "Even I noticed the clothing, and I'm not a real cowgirl. It'll be okay—the crew are all eager to help this batch do some proper packing." She pointed to the side where the two youngest staff were eagerly toting luggage into the hall for the women.

"Hey, you know me. I have no objections to people wearing what makes them happy. I hope she's not disappointed if they get some mud on them before the end of the trip, that's all." Ashley turned to smile at Vicki. "And what's this 'not a real cowgirl' BS? I've seen you out riding every day you've been around Base Camp, and I know you ride to Second Camp."

Vicki hung on the fence, arms fully extended as she stretched her legs. "Since I plan to be with Joel for the long-term, I figured I'd better keep working on it. We'll be living on the ranch, and I only got over being scared of horses this winter. I don't want to lose any ground."

"You're doing great. In fact, I took a few pictures last week. I wanted to know if I could pose you for some more. You interested?"

Her friend's face lit up. "You bet. Actually, could I get a copy maybe? Something to email to Joel?"

"I can go one step better. I'll take some pictures you can use for a special present for him—when you finish this summer, or maybe Christmas or something. Would you like that?"

Ashley found herself being impulsively hugged. "I would..." Vicki paused, setting Ashley free and stepping back slightly. "It makes me happy to think you're going to be around Rocky. I'm glad I came out to cook for the summer, but when I go back home I won't just have Joel, I'll have you. That's pretty huge for me."

Warmth she hadn't expected struck, and Ashley squeezed Vicki's hand. "Means a lot to me as well. And I'm not saying that because I love your baking."

Vicki's smile turned to instant dismay. "Oh, shit—*baking*. I've got cookies in the oven."

She whirled and sprinted back to the cookhouse. Ashley laughed as she pulled out her camera and headed around camp for another round of shots.

So far hanging out at the horse camp had worked well. The distraction of the guys had been lovely, but she was also getting tons accomplished. The first of her paid projects had been handed in the previous Friday. There were two more sets of digital work to finish over the next month, including promo brochures for Karen, and then she'd switch focus to more hands-on painting.

She figured once she went back to Rocky she'd toss herself full-time into producing everything she'd need for her show. Starting in August would be soon enough, giving her all of July to finish gathering material.

Including, if she had her way, not only shots of Vicki, but of Cassidy and Travis as well.

Inside the hall the ladies getting organized for this week's excursion had gathered around the wall map. Dani explained the layout of the camp and some of the trails they'd be taking over the week. Chatter was brisk, laughter bubbling up often in the group of friends.

Cassidy carried in a basket filled with extra gear, and the mood in the room subtly changed. Something rolled uncomfortably in Ashley's gut, and she sat back to figure it out.

Such small things, really. Normal reactions that never in a

million years would have bothered her before. A couple of the women smiled in Cassidy's direction, and he nodded back politely.

A lingering glance, a whispered conversation between two of the ladies as they eyed him...

For a second Ashley swore something foul had flown into her mouth. The realization she was experiencing jealousy didn't make it much better.

She didn't *want* other women admiring Cassidy. Or flirting with him, or—yet there was nothing specific she could complain about because none of their behaviour was wrong, rude or extreme.

In fact, with the sexual norms she'd grown up around, if Cassidy wanted to take the lot of them on, who was she to argue? A couple of months ago, Ashley might not have noticed.

But now? The idea of clawing the other women's eyes out was far too pleasurable.

She pushed herself off the wall without thinking and headed across the room.

"Will you be one of the guides for the ride?" one woman asked Cassidy.

"Afraid not. But you'll have the rest of the team to help you out." Cassidy pointed toward the hands.

The woman who'd spoken smiled sweeter. "We might need extra attention this time around. You should consider coming along."

He didn't get a chance to answer. Ashley slipped between them and casually wrapped herself around his hard torso. "Hey, babe, I'm having trouble with the power in our cabin again. When you're done with the campers, can you come help me?"

Surprise widened his eyes as his hands instinctively curled around her waist. "Ashley?"

She tilted her head back and went up on tiptoe to kiss him

full on the lips. Even if it was brief, it was intimate enough to stake her claim. When she pulled back and slipped out of his arms, she took in the watching campers as if noticing them for the first time. "Oh, I'm sorry. I shouldn't have interrupted. Have fun on your trip. The weather is supposed to be super nice while you're gone."

Moments later she'd escaped into the hallway where she slumped against the wall and kicked herself. Dumb. Stupid. Idiotic.

Not what she'd just done, hanging all over Cassidy in public, but getting possessive in the first place.

She'd never been the jealous type, but there was a very pronounced sensation inside—and she wasn't sure if it only was from wanting to stamp *property of* labels all over the man. Because she wanted to label Travis with the same tag, and how messed up was that when she really thought it through?

The door opened and a pair of concerned-filled green eyes trapped her. "Ashley? What's up?"

She wiggled uncomfortably. Shit. She wasn't going to get time to come up with a good excuse for her behaviour. "I'm sorry."

Cassidy was at her side in a couple of steps, lifting her chin and forcing her to look at him. "Now I know something is wrong. Are you hiding from me?"

"I'm pissed off at myself," she whispered, curling her fingers around his biceps. She stiffened her spine and admitted the truth, as embarrassing as it was. "And yet I'm not. Kissing you in public was my version of waving a big ol' warning flag."

Luckily he grinned, leaning over her with one hand on either side of her head. "I thought it was pretty hot, actually. You have nothing to worry about, woman. I'm not interested in kissing anyone other than you..."

He paused. Made a face.

Ashley laughed softly. "...and Travis. I know. It's a fucked-up situation, but damn if I can complain too hard. I like being with you guys."

"We like you too. *I* like you." Cassidy pressed her to the wall and kissed her. Far more commanding than her gentle peck moments earlier. This one demanded a response, and oh boy, she answered. Tongues tangling, her grip tightening on his arms as he slowly rocked against her.

Guilt at her earlier actions faded under the best kind of distraction possible.

The kitchen door to their right slammed shut, jerking Cassidy away from her lips. He sighed. "I suppose I'd better get back to work."

Ashley slid her hands up to his shoulders then down his back slowly, appreciating every second of touching him. "We can pick this up again tonight," she suggested.

"Once the campers are gone? Hmm, great idea." He brushed her hair off her forehead and tucked it behind one ear. "Now, stop distracting me. Between you and Travis, it's a miracle I get any work done at all."

Ashley waited until he'd paced out the main door, mostly so she could watch his ass while he strode away.

The scent of peanut butter cookies drew her toward the kitchen, and she slipped in to discover Vicki glaring at the cooling racks as if they were possessed.

"Did you burn the cookies? They smell good," Ashley reassured her.

The look of disdain previously aimed at the baked goods whipped upward. Vicki crossed her arms and managed to look far more intimidating than her five-foot-nothing height should. "You..."

She made a disgusted noise and stomped to the fridge.

Ashley paused. *Okay*—this was not the happy, friendly

woman she'd been talking with less than fifteen minutes earlier. "Me...*what?* What did I do?"

Vicki spun to face her. "I saw you in the hallway with your tongue down Cassidy's throat," she blurted out. She slapped her oven gloves against her leg. "God, if you've had enough of Travis, at least have the decency to call it off with him before you start fooling around with anyone else."

Shit. Ashley kicked herself for not dealing with this sooner. "It's not what you think."

"No? Because it's fine with Travis for you to be kissing Cassidy?" Vicki snapped.

"Actually—yeah."

Vicki's face was priceless. Her expression went from furious to confused to understanding then embarrassment in under fifteen seconds. "Oh, *jeez*, I should have known. Damn Coleman boys and their kinks." Vicki shook her head in disbelief. "They're both sleeping with you, aren't they?"

Plus a bit more, but the "bit more" wasn't Ashley's to share. "Yes, I'm with both of them, and they're okay with that." She snuck forward a little more hesitantly. She and Vicki had a budding friendship, and she really didn't want to ruin it. "Are you upset with me?"

Vicki shook her head. "I just..." Her cheeks had gone bright red. "I've got to be the most naïve person on the entire goddamn planet. Does everyone have threesomes or something?"

"I highly doubt it," Ashley reassured her. "And I didn't plan on this one, it kind of happened. I wouldn't do anything to hurt Travis."

Two cookies were held toward her. "Here, peace offering. Sorry for all the terrible names I was calling you in my head," Vicki said.

Ashley took the cookies, cradling the warmth in her hand.

"You might need to add a glass of milk to be truly forgiven," she suggested. "And some more chat time, if you're available."

A reluctant smile broke free as Vicki pulled out a chair. "Sit, and I'll make us chocolate milk. I've got enough time before lunch prep for a visit."

"We can have our cookies, then I can help you and Ted with lunch," Ashley offered.

Tentative friendships took nurturing. Both the sexual ones and the nonsexual. Ashley nibbled on the edge of a cookie and wondered when her life had gotten so full.

So complicated.

21

———

July rushed past in a blur of activity. Campers came through on a weekly rotation; supplies arrived and were transferred from one camp to the other. Travis soaked in the pleasure of working with a group of easygoing men and women as everyone fell into a routine.

What was more incredible was the time he got to spend with Ashley and Cassidy, which was neither routine nor relaxed. He never knew what to expect with Ashley—that hadn't changed, not even when it wasn't just the two of them fooling around, but them with Cassidy.

There were still times when he caught a shadow in her eyes, and he figured she was thinking back to her cousin. For the most part, though, she was the life and the joy in their days. He wasn't sure how he'd survived without having her around for so long.

Cassidy as well. Not for the *stress relief* the man offered, but for the conversations and sharing that had begun to stretch late into the evenings.

The stars were already high overhead when Travis stoked the fire then sat back to watch them closer. Cassidy strummed a simple chord pattern as Ashley accompanied him on the second guitar she'd had shipped in during a supply run. An old-fashioned folk melody wrapped around the campfire, enveloping them with its peaceful rhythm.

Cassidy still had to eye his fingers closely, but Ashley had no such limitations. A mischievous smile creased her lips as she played and watched Cassidy with approval. Travis thought both of them were incredible, firelight reflecting off their light colouring and making them shine as if under a spotlight.

Even as he admired them, Travis considered the new skills he'd learned over the past months. Maybe nothing so obvious as playing an instrument like Cassidy, but important nonetheless.

Lessons about how he could let others give to him without it meaning he was weak. He didn't have to always be right, or be in charge, and the lessons were slowly untangling fears built during years of holding back.

Ashley turned her gaze on him, and he fell into the endless blue depths of her eyes without worrying about hiding what was inside. If what he felt showed on his face, so much the better. Caring for her had always been easy.

Letting her see it? A hell of a lot harder, but he was trying.

Cassidy strummed on after Ashley's fingers fell silent, her stare fixed on Travis. "You got something on your mind, over there?" she teased softly.

"Thinking about you going back to Rocky. You sure you need to leave on Saturday?"

She nodded. "I know there are only a couple weeks of camp left, but I need to get going on my bigger projects. And I want to get settled into town—start making it home."

He liked that part of her plan even as he hated the idea of her being gone. "We'll miss you."

Cassidy's fingers stilled. He put the guitar away, and silence settled over them, brushing away the music. Travis understood. There wasn't much to say beyond they didn't want her to go.

Ashley slipped to Cassidy's side and crawled into his lap. She rested her head on his chest and stroked his jaw gently. The fire created the music now, blending with the fainter sounds of the horses settling in the barn.

Peaceful. Relaxing.

All of it shattered in an instant.

"When you're done here in mid-August, you coming straight to Rocky or do you have to go somewhere else first?" Ashley asked.

Cassidy didn't answer her immediately.

She frowned. "You are coming back to Rocky, aren't you?"

The thought that once again Cassidy had plans to disappear didn't sit too well with Travis. "Of course, he is."

"Didn't have it in mind. I was thinking about heading south. I can get back on with the ranch—"

"You can find work around Rocky." Travis couldn't believe this. "Why the hell would you want to go back to Pincher Creek?"

"Why not?"

"Because—" Travis snapped his mouth shut. The first response that leapt to mind was far too self-centered.

Ashley was no longer cuddled against Cassidy. She had pushed herself upright, back stiff, her expression filled with shock. "Because you need to come to Rocky, that's why."

"That's the last thing I need to do." Cassidy stroked her arm. "Damn it, Ashley, this shouldn't be a surprise. You knew all along the three of us being together was a short-term thing."

She jumped out of his arms and stomped a few steps before twirling and planting her hands on her hips. "I didn't know anything of the kind."

"One day." Cassidy barked the words far rougher than usual.

"That's what we started this with. The fact it's worked until now has made the summer special, but that's it. It's time to get that straight."

"Things changed," Ashley insisted. "*We've* changed. Short term isn't good enough anymore."

Cassidy raised a brow. "You think you can dictate where I live? What I do? You don't want to go there with me, Ashley."

Travis couldn't believe this. "The only reason you should be calling this off is if you've had enough, and I don't believe that for a minute."

His righteous indignation faded to misery as Cassidy glanced into the fire and refused to meet either of their eyes. "It's been good, but it's time it was over."

"Bullshit," Ashley retorted. "If it's been good, then we get ready for the next step, which is you coming back to Rocky and finding a job."

"Ashley, stop it," Cassidy begged. "I can't move to Rocky. I have no job, I have no place to stay—there's no reason to move there. "

"You've got Travis." Ashley pointed across the fire. "If you're saying walking out on him again is right, you're an ass."

"Plus you've got a place to stay," Travis cut in. He rose to his feet, confusion and anger swirling together. "But what are you talking about, Ash? He's got you as well, and it sucks that he thinks that's not important."

Cassidy dragged a hand through his hair. "Stop it, both of you. You're not making this any easier."

"If easy is you walking away, I don't want to make it easy." This was the last thing Travis had expected tonight—this kind of conversation. A turn in the path he hadn't seen coming that he definitely didn't want. "Look, Cassidy. Let's back up and start again. Maybe I've made some assumptions, but I thought things were going well. Was I wrong?"

Cassidy shook his head. "But this is here, it's not Rocky Mountain House. It's not the Six Pack ranch, and most importantly, your family isn't around."

"Wait. *What?*" Travis held up a hand. "You don't want to move because of my family?"

"You said we'd back up the conversation," Cassidy said. "Let's back it up a bit further, and how about you tell me why you've never let your family know you're interested in guys?"

The question jerked Travis to a standstill. He opened his mouth to answer, but got lost in the maelstrom swirling in his brain.

His friend nodded knowingly. "Because that's where this conversation has to begin. You've been in denial for years—and in a way, you still are. This summer has been a kind of fantasy world where it's been safe to be with me because Ashley's here. No one knows that you're with a guy, do they? No one knows that the tough redneck cowboy doesn't only love women, he gets off on men as well."

Oh, for fuck's sake. "Shut up," Travis ordered. "Goddamn bastard. Or are you having fun running off at the mouth? You don't get it."

"No, *you* don't. You haven't figured out yet that if I go to Rocky, everyone is going to know. This won't be some tidy little secret anymore, and I'm not willing to let your family hate you because of me."

Travis stomped over to Cassidy and hauled him from his lawn chair. He caught Cassidy by the collar and held him in place so there was nowhere to escape. "That's a pretty big burden you've laid on your shoulders. Ruining my life with my family. Trust me, if my family hates me, it will be for a whole different reason."

"You've been keeping secrets from them, admit it," Cassidy snarled.

"Hell, yes," Travis shouted. "But the secret was about me going off and damn near getting killed on a regular basis. That I crave something most people would consider sick. *That's* what I was hiding from them."

Cassidy stood as if frozen, his hands wrapped around Travis's wrists. "But I thought..."

Travis tugged Cassidy closer. "You thought wrong. Yes, I love my family, and the idea of disappointing them kills me. Maybe they will be surprised when I take you home to a family dinner. But..." It was his turn to hesitate. Confessions were good for the soul, right? "For as long as I can remember, I've been turned on by both girls and guys, it's true. But you're the first one that I not only want to fuck, but spend time with."

His friend turned his face away, a soft curse floating into the night air.

Travis slipped a hand farther around Cassidy's neck, easing off the pressure slightly, making it more about being together than pinning Cassidy in place. "That's what was freaking me out so hard last summer. I wanted you like I'd never wanted a guy before. It wasn't just about sex, it was more, and it threw me for a loop. This summer confirmed it. You're—special."

Cassidy snorted. "Yeah, right."

"And I wasn't keeping you some dirty secret," Travis continued. "We've been in a strange situation here at the camp, with the crew coming and going all the time. Yeah, maybe I didn't want any questions or to make them feel awkward, but not because it's *you*, it's you *and* Ashley."

"That does add a complication, doesn't it?" His friend nodded slowly, his gaze drifting to the side where Ashley had stood. "Shit, she's gone."

Crap. Another unwanted twist. "Come on, let's go find her."

Cassidy held him back for a moment, staring intently as if

trying to read his mind. "I'm sorry for assuming, and I'm still not comfortable, but I'm willing to talk about this more."

"We've got a ton to talk about, but we'd better find Ashley before she decides to hide all your clothes or something." Travis pulled his friend forward, his mind whirling with far too many surprises.

So much for a relaxing evening by the fire.

When the woman took off, she vanished well. Travis was the one who finally spotted her blonde hair, and Cassidy followed him toward the small stoop outside his cabin.

She was seated on the porch swing, staring into the darkness. The faint light from the barn shone past the fence posts and trees, casting vaguely human-shaped shadows. As if the settlers who'd abandoned the land so many years ago had returned, watching to see what would happen next.

"Ash?" Travis approached slowly. "You got company."

She wiggled all of an inch to one side. "There's room."

Travis sighed as he paced forward. "You couldn't make this simple, could you?"

Ashley sniffed. "Nothing is simple anymore."

"Not taking off in the first place would help, so stick around, you understand?" Travis sat on the swing, curling an arm around her shoulders.

Cassidy knelt in front of her. Her expression seemed far more heated than upset. "How much did you hear before you left?" he asked.

Ashley shrugged. "You don't want to move to Rocky because you don't want to be with us."

God, now he knew how raw hearing that comment really was

on the soul. "Okay, saying it like that hurts a hell of a lot. No, Ash, that's not it at all."

"Cassidy, I can only go on what I see you doing. What I hear you saying. So what is it? You joining us or leaving?" she asked.

Travis held his breath as well as they waited for him to answer.

"It's not that simple," he insisted. The "*ha!*" that burst from her forced him to smile. "Yeah, I know, but it's the truth. This isn't just me relocating. We can't leap forward and assume it's not going to cause a hell of a lot of trouble."

Fingers brushed his cheek as Ashley leaned forward and caressed him gently. "It's worth putting up with trouble for something valuable."

Cassidy caught hold of her hand and linked their fingers together. He needed the connection as they worked this through.

Ashley lifted her gaze to his. "So here's honesty on my part. For a long time I thought that once you two were together, I'd no longer be important. I was totally planning on leaving at that point."

"What the hell?" Travis growled. "Why would you do that?"

She pressed a hand onto his thigh and squeezed tight, clinging to them both. "Because there are things that Cassidy gives you that I can't. But you know what? The longer we've had out here, the more I've realized that we've all got something important to give. I'm good for you in ways that Cassidy isn't, and I like Cassidy for different reasons than I like you. It's a full circle, and hell if I want anything to stop us from being together."

"Even after the summer?" Travis asked.

She nodded. "I have to go back first, but once you're done here you guys come and..." Something between a sigh and groan of frustration escaped her. "That's what I was planning on suggesting tonight. I know my upbringing is far more twisted than most people, and I've seen some strange family combinations over the years, but I think we could make it work with the three of us living together. I want us to at least *try*."

Cassidy's heart ached. "At what cost? What if it meant that's all we'd have? The three of us?"

Her forehead creased, her blue eyes full of confusion. "Why would it be all we'd have?"

"You think Travis's family is going to accept that he's got both you and a male lover without a blink?" Travis opened his mouth to protest, but Cassidy cut him off. "No, let me finish. If you both want to know why I planned to leave, then let me have my say. Ashley, you're talking about setting up a permanent threesome, and while part of me is thrilled at the idea, I've also got a sick knot in my stomach. I don't think Travis realizes the big picture."

Travis slid off the swing and wrapped an arm around Cassidy, his strong hand resting on Cassidy's hip as if offering shelter. "I'm listening."

Cassidy took a deep breath. "It's not the typical homosexual hang-ups we'll face, it's the three of us. What kind of attitudes will we see from the community when we go to town? Or show up at the bar? What if we try to take in a movie? Hell, are they going to be shaking pitchforks or sending hate messages to us?"

"You have some faith in humanity, don't you?" Travis said. "Maybe they'll ignore us like they ignore most people, and all we'll have to worry about is your typical day-to-day shit that everyone deals with."

"When my own father beat the shit out of me for being a fag, you think other people are going to be more forgiving?" Cassidy snapped.

Dead silence.

He wondered if the shock of his words would be hard enough to knock some sense into them, even as he ached with the memories.

Ashley was off the porch swing and pulling him to his feet,

and five seconds later he was wrapped in two sets of arms as both she and Travis surrounded him.

She gazed up, grief in her eyes. "I'm so, so sorry. That's not just wrong, it's outrageous and cruel and unbelievably stupid."

Travis shook his head. "You said things weren't good between you, but you didn't mention how bad it was."

"When? 'Sure, I'll have another drink, and by the way, did you know I haven't seen my family since the night my father found out I was gay?' It's not the kind of thing you go around telling people."

"It's exactly what you share with close friends." Ashley pressed her hand against his chest and paused for a moment. "With people who care a hell of a lot about you."

His knees nearly gave out. "I couldn't."

Travis pulled him closer and supported him against his long, strong frame. "So you will now. All of it. I want to know, and then I want to talk this out until we come to a decision together."

He tilted his head toward the door, and Ashley rushed to open it. Cassidy had no choice but to follow her in.

There was a lump the size of an elephant in his throat, but a flickering flame of hope inside his heart. Maybe his fears were finally going to be washed away. Maybe there was something to look forward to other than sorrow and endless nights alone.

22

———

 shley sat on the mattress and waited. A flood of anger had quickly erased the disappointment that had struck as she'd listened to Cassidy's plans.

She was tired of accepting life as it came. It was time to grow up the rest of the way and take what was right. Take *and* give— and right now that meant giving to Cassidy.

Travis got the fire going. Cassidy perched on the edge of the mattress as if bracing himself for the rest of the evening. She slipped over and leaned against him, rubbing his shoulders to try to work out the rock-hard knots. Ashley kissed his cheek. "You know we only want the best for you."

He nodded then pulled her around to settle into his lap. "I'm sorry I chased you off earlier. I like it when you curl up against me. Feels as if you can't get enough of me, and you're soaking me in through your skin."

She smiled and snuggled in tighter. "Works for me."

They sat and watched Travis as the flames licked around the kindling and slowly took hold. He twisted to face them, pulling a chair over so he could be close. He nodded in approval at Ashley, then took both her and Cassidy's hands into his. "I don't care how long it takes," he said. "Tell us. We want to know."

Cassidy shivered, and she squeezed his hand encouragingly. "Whatever you want to tell us."

"It's pretty basic. He caught me looking at porn. Which usually would have been acceptable, since it was a manly thing to do, but this time the magazine was guys."

"Shit." Travis shook his head. "Yeah, that would be pretty cut and dried."

"You were curious?"

Cassidy nodded as he stroked her cheek. "I love women, with your soft curves and all, but guys were attractive too. I wasn't sure why and thought I'd look."

He met Travis's gaze. Travis frowned. "Wait. That's it? He caught you with a magazine, and for that he kicked you out?"

Sitting so close Ashley felt every change in Cassidy's body, and this time as he tensed, she slipped a hand around his back to embrace him tighter. To give him support as he stared at the roof and spilled the rest of it, words whispering out as if they were being pulled from deep inside. Painful to deliver.

Painful to hear.

"He ripped the magazine from my hands then proceeded to give me a thrashing, starting with his fists before moving on to his belt. He said he would 'beat that queer crap right out of me', and in a way, it worked. I didn't look at another guy for years. Every time I was tempted, I felt the pain from that night and I'd be sick."

The bitterness in Cassidy's voice closed Ashley's throat. There was a band of pain tightening around her heart, and hopelessness threatened.

"How old were you?" Travis asked, gentle as if to stop from spooking Cassidy.

"Sixteen." He shrugged. "I know what he did was wrong, but

to a kid who'd spent his entire life trying to gain his dad's approval, it cut hard."

"Did he ever apologize?" Ashley asked.

Cassidy grunted, more in pain than amusement. "Ashley, you don't get it. He *never* thought he did anything to apologize for. Not that night or before. I didn't have a father who gave two shits about me for anything other than getting the chores done—and I got beat at times for screwing up those. That night was the breaking point for us both. He didn't believe I could be interested in both girls and guys because that's how I was born—it had to be some sickness in my brain and something to be feared. He left me on the barn floor, and I figured things could only get worse. That night I snuck out of the house with a few things. Hitched a ride out of town, and never went back."

Ashley fought her anger. Swearing at a man who wasn't there had no logic, but it was what she wanted to do—Travis as well if his expression was an indication.

"No wonder he wasn't happy to see me on his porch last summer," Travis drawled. "If I'd have known, I would have had more on my agenda than a few questions."

"Giving him a beating ten years after the fact isn't a solution, T." Cassidy shook his head. "I'm glad I can tell you, but it doesn't change anything. Not really. I've got hang-ups because of what happened, but I've slowly been dealing with them. Thanks a lot to you two."

He dropped a kiss on her temple and squeezed Travis's hand.

"Oh, Cassidy, it changes things. Changes them a lot." So much more made sense now. Ashley leaned in close, staring into his green eyes in the hopes that he would understand. "You've been without a family for so long. No more. You've got me and my family—I tell you, my mom would be over the moon to welcome you in."

He pulled her in for a hug, and she tried to pass over what she felt in her touch. All of it seemed so inadequate, though. So limited, words and actions.

Ashley leaned away and cupped his face. "I told you before I was putting up an ownership flag on you. I meant it then, and I mean it more now. I want to be in your life, Cassidy Jones. Not only for this summer, but into the future. I'm looking to put down roots for the first time in my life. If you need a place to do the same, I want you with me."

Cassidy kissed her gently. "You've got a loving heart, woman. Thank you."

They turned without speaking to face Travis. Ashley had gotten it—Cassidy's fear that Travis would suffer the same fate. That he'd be ripped apart from his family over the issue and end up alone, maybe hating Cassidy and Ashley for what he'd lost. That possibility wasn't something Ashley could answer for Travis. She couldn't be the one to decide if he was willing to take the risk.

But she bet he was.

"First, I want to apologize for making you use a belt on me that first time." Travis shook his head. "You should have said something."

Cassidy snorted bitterly. "You weren't in a position to listen, and I dealt with it."

"You shouldn't have had to. There's a ton of shit you shouldn't have had to deal with." Travis's sorrow was clear in the tone of his voice, the position of his body. "I already told you it wasn't my attraction to guys I was keeping secret from my family, but here's me going out on a limb. If my dad ever heard what happened to you? He'd be the one headed up to Drayton Valley to beat some sense into your old man, even ten years after the fact."

"I like Mike," Cassidy confessed. "He's always seemed fair. I don't know what your brothers will think, though."

Travis paused, then shrugged. "I can make guesses, but bottom line is we won't know until we face them." He rose from the chair and leaned in, capturing Cassidy and Ashley in his strong arms. "If they turn out to be assholes, then they weren't my family in the first place. I'm with Ashley on this one, Cass. Let's build you a home. A real home, with people who care about you unconditionally."

"No matter that it could mean you lose yours?" Cassidy asked again.

Travis swore, pacing away and shoving a log into the stove as if looking for some time before having to answer. Ashley slipped out of Cassidy's lap and stood at his side, their fingers linked as they waited.

It was only a moment later when Travis faced them, the sharp line of his jaw set, the spark of amusement that always seemed to hover in his eyes completely gone. None of the anger of a few moments before, just sheer determination, and her anticipation rose.

This was the man she'd come back to Rocky for. *This* was the man she'd been slowly and steadily falling in love with.

She couldn't wait for Cassidy to realize exactly how much his world was about to change.

Looking across the room at Ashley and Cassidy only solidified Travis's resolve. The two of them were so different, and yet so much alike. Maybe in ways they didn't even know.

Cassidy stood nearly a foot taller than Ashley, his strong build contrasting with her softness. But his eyes were the ones filled with fear while she looked far more determined, chin lifted high as if daring Travis on.

Yet neither of them had experienced family and a solid home like Travis had. Time spent—well, some of it fighting, but most of it learning exactly what *real* family meant.

After all the years where he'd gone wrong, and all the times he'd disappointed them in the small things, never once had his family turned their back. There were issues and misunderstandings, and not everything was rosy and perfect, but it was real and full of heart. He saw that clearer now than ever before, and it made his time of holding back and hiding his needs seem childish. Foolish.

He'd grown up and found the truth, and it was time to make Cassidy understand.

"Family is about more than sharing a bloodline." Travis didn't speak loudly. Didn't have to with the quiet crackle of the fire the only sound in the room. Heck, Cassidy didn't seem to be breathing. "It's about choices and caring, and the two of you have made it clear you care about me a hell of a lot. I'd be a stupid-ass fool to not see it. I'd be even stupider to not want to give that caring back to you."

A slow smile bloomed over Ashley's face.

Cassidy—he was still a bundle of tension and fear, so Travis stepped forward and cupped his hand around the back of Cassidy's neck, leaning in until their foreheads connected and the entire length of their bodies pressed together. "My family will understand, but if it comes down to a decision—if they aren't the people I think they are—then I won't have lost a thing. I choose you."

His friend didn't answer, not in words, but the tension poured off him and his green eyes lit with hope.

Fingers snuck around his back as Ashley wormed her way under his arm, and Travis welcomed her into the embrace. "And you," he scolded. "I hope you got that sacrificial shit out of your system. I'm not letting either of you go, you got that?"

Ashley blinked hard, her eyes moist as she beamed at him. "Selfish bastard, ain't cha?"

"You know it. High maintenance, you called me that once."

This time Cassidy laughed before sagging. "God, that took a lot out of me."

Travis could think of ways to energize his friend. Only first... "You haven't said it straight out, so I want to hear it. We're all headed back to Rocky, and you two are moving in with me."

"Still think it's going to be a rough ride," Cassidy warned. "But yes, I'll move in with you. Find somewhere to work. Give it a try."

Travis wanted to make him change that final statement, but they'd already moved forward a long way. So he turned to the final part of the equation. "Ashley?"

"Gee, move in with two strapping men who worship the ground I walk on?" She poked Cassidy lightly in the side. "You do worship the ground I walk on, right? I already know I have Travis wrapped around my little finger, so... *Ohhh...*"

Cassidy had her in midair and tossed toward the bed before Travis could do it.

"Nicely done," Travis commented.

Cassidy grinned. "Thanks. You want to help me do some worshipping?"

Travis had ideas all of his own how tonight was going down, but allowing Cassidy to think he was in control wouldn't hurt anything. He stripped off his shirt and tossed it aside. "Of course."

Ashley wiggled back on the bed, her toes bare as she curled up and wrapped her arms around her knees. "You two first. I like seeing you get naked."

Before Travis could respond, Cassidy knelt on the bed and crowded toward her. "I thought Travis told you not to expect to call the shots for a long while. You get to be in charge, oh, I'd say sometime in December. Take off your clothes," he commanded.

She shivered, her expression bright with pleasure. Travis nodded in approval. Such a strong, powerful woman, and yet she had accepted that she got off sexually on being ordered around.

He'd learned a lot from her—more than he'd realized as he strode to the other side of the bed and watched her slip off her top. She skimmed her pants over her hips and took the elastic from her hair.

Long blonde strands fell over her shoulders, swinging loose over the pale pink fabric of her bra.

"What the hell is that made out of?" Travis dragged a finger along the elastic shoulder strap all the way to the swell of her breasts in the barely there material. "I can see your nipples right through the damn thing."

"Look," Cassidy said. "Here as well."

He'd stroked a hand up her thigh to trace the edge of her panties, the curls on her mound displayed against the front as he pressed his fingertips over them.

"Silk. Expensive silk, so don't get any ideas of ripping them off me," Ashley warned.

Travis hummed in approval. "They're very nice. Cassidy, take off your clothes while Ashley finishes what she started."

Cassidy jolted upright. "What—?"

"Strip." Travis folded his arms in front of him. "I can't fuck you with your clothes on."

A whimper of sheer pleasure escaped Ashley. "Can I help?" she whispered.

A response from Cassidy was slower in coming, as if he'd had to change mental gears. "You're going to fuck *me?*"

Travis didn't answer. Instead he moved to the side and grabbed a condom and lube. Removed the rest of his clothes. Taking that moment to separate the rising lust and the fiery anger still rocking his soul. The hurts of the past that had been shared were too raw and vivid, but he'd be damned if he let this evening finish with anything other than an attempt to wipe some of them clear. To erase part of the shadow from Cassidy's eyes.

He turned back to find Cassidy had stripped and settled next to Ashley, the two of them tangled together with arms and legs and mouths. Travis watched contentedly, wrapping his hand around his cock and pulling lazily as he admired the view. His body heated in response to Cassidy cupping Ashley's breasts, rolling the tightened tips between his fingers.

Ashley arched into his touch, dragging her fingers down his back, faint red trails remaining where her nails had dug into his flesh. She lifted a leg and rubbed her foot over Cassidy's calf. Cassidy slid down her body to suck a nipple into his mouth, and she squirmed happily.

Travis joined them, taking her lips for a moment as he ran a hand along Cassidy's naked back, ending with his fingers tangled in Cassidy's thick hair.

A slight tug on Cassidy, and he abandoned Ashley's breast reluctantly, his lips popping free as a throaty moan escaped her. Travis tilted Cassidy's head, and he took his lips, using his body to roll the other man to his back against the mattress.

Ashley joined in eagerly, her smaller hands slipping over their bodies, caressing everywhere she could reach. A soft drag over Travis's ass. A fingertip along Cassidy's neck and down to circle the flat disk of a nipple as Travis moved lower.

"So good," Cassidy moaned.

Ashley buried her hands in his hair and pressed their lips together again, covering anything else he might want to say.

But he didn't really need to speak. Travis could tell how much Cassidy was enjoying the attention. With two sets of hands on his body, he had nowhere to go. Legs trapped by Travis's body, arms pinned to the mattress. Travis kissed his way down Cassidy's chest, taking the time to lick his nipples, to caress his tongue along the edges of abdomen muscles gone taut.

Ashley whispered dirty words as Travis continued toward his goal. He settled between Cassidy's thighs, the thick erection rising before him distracting enough to force him to pause. He tormented Cassidy briefly with a firm grip, running a thumb back and forth over the flushed crown and smearing the precome that had beaded on the slit.

"So many things I want to do to you," Travis muttered. "Should I swallow your cock and drag you to the point you scream? Suck your balls while Ashley gives you a blowjob? Or maybe this—"

He grasped Cassidy's legs, bending them up and to the side, exposing his rigid cock, the tight sac below the straining cock. Cassidy's ass. Travis ran his tongue downward, starting at the tip of Cassidy's dick. Teasing his way along the hard length, stopping to suck his balls. Then he pushed Cassidy's legs apart and pressed in farther, wet tongue lapping lower and lower until he could circle the tight hole.

"Oh *fuck...*" Cassidy grabbed the back of his thighs and pulled, fingers gripping the muscle so tightly his knuckles went white. "You... That..."

He threw his head back and lifted his hips as if searching for more of Travis's touch, his words fading away into a long, low growl of pleasure.

Perfect. Travis teased again and again, stabbing his tongue against sensitive nerves, getting Cassidy wetter and wetter.

Ashley was between Cassidy's legs as well, her breasts swinging as she wrapped her lips around Cassidy's cock and sucked. She pulled back, and her cheeks hollowed. Travis pressed in farther and Cassidy shouted, the cry fading into gasps for air. "Travis, Ashley, *please...*"

It was time. "Use the lube, Ash. Help get him ready," Travis ordered, moving aside to cover himself.

Ashley smiled at Cassidy, pausing to press a kiss to his chest. "Oh, baby. You're going to like this."

She trickled a hand down his abdomen before dropping a nice size blob of lube on her fingers. She teased the slippery liquid over his hole. Cassidy's eyes widened as she stroked him gently, again and again. Each time advancing a little farther—a fingertip, to the knuckle, then buried deep.

Travis couldn't decide where to look. At her delicate fingers slipping into Cassidy's ass. At the expressions playing over Cassidy's face as she squeezed out more lube and added a finger. It was his eyes, though, that mesmerized Travis. He leaned over his friend, over his lovers, until Cassidy met his gaze.

"You're special. To me. To Ashley. This is what we want—to be with you. Any way, *all* the ways, and we're gonna do everything we can to rock your world."

Ashley rolled to the side and cuddled against Cassidy's side. "No running away, you got that?"

"I'm not going anywhere," Cassidy swore, his lips curling into a smile.

"Damn right, you aren't." Travis reached down to guide his cock, but Ashley was there already, her soft fingers around his length, aiming him forward.

An experience like he'd never had before—having her involved in this moment. His pulse was racing a million miles an hour as he stared into Cassidy's eyes. Heat met the tip of his cock, and he pressed forward at Ashley's urging, her hand slipping around his hip as if she were a part of them. As if while he pushed past the tight entrance and Cassidy gasped, Ashley was intimately involved.

Green eyes fixed on his as Travis pressed all the way forward until his balls were tight to Cassidy's cheeks. "Hell, that feels so fucking good."

Cassidy licked his lips before nodding. "Do it. Give me more."

More was Travis dragging his hips back then sliding in again, the pressure of Cassidy's ass threatening his control. Sensations roared up to the breaking point even faster as Ashley scratched his skin with her fingernails, the sharp bite of pain like an accelerator for the tingling pleasure gathering at the base of his spine.

He thrust quicker, lifting Cassidy's hips, adjusting the angle until his friend's eyes rolled back. Ashley had curled her fist around Cassidy's dick, jerking him off, and with both of them working him over it didn't take long. Cassidy came, stomach muscles contracting as he partially curled up, semen spraying over his belly.

Travis let himself go. Let pleasure roll over him and explode. It was more than physical satisfaction he felt as Ashley kissed Cassidy tenderly, slipping her hands over his chest and whispering in his ear. She turned her face upward and smiled at Travis.

Approval, and something else. Something tender and personal.

The climax left his arms shaking, his lungs desperate for air, but inside, there was that warmth and contentment he'd been missing for a hell of a long time. Contentment that drifted from the others as well as Travis ditched the condom then found a spot on the mattress next to Cassidy. Limbs entangled as they continued to stroke each other. Be with each other.

Cassidy let out a long sigh. "Ashley, I'm too well fucked right now to move, but I swear I won't leave you hanging for long."

She laughed, the sound breaking across the room carrying

brightness and light. "Don't waste energy on guilt. Watching you guys—jeez, so sexy."

Travis caught her fingers. "The night isn't over."

Ashley leaned up on an elbow. "Damn right, it's not. I'm so turned on right now, though. I might have to break out a few toys until you two are up to speed again. You don't mind, do you?"

Travis's cock leapt at the vision of Ashley fucking herself with a vibrator.

"Dammit, Ash," Cassidy complained. "I swear I'm getting a hard-on thinking about it."

"That's what I like. Men with good recovery time." She snuck a kiss onto his cheek then escaped Travis's hands to rise and stand over them, her beautiful eyes taking them in as if they were the feature item at a buffet. She dropped one hand over her chest, one between her legs, a mischievous smile escaping. "No rush. We're just starting, right?"

It wasn't only this night they had to look forward to, but a whole lot more. The truth of that rang in Travis's brain like caroling bells.

This was the beginning.

23

*A*shley accepted a spine-melting kiss from Travis, turned and got swept up by Cassidy's strong arms for a second breath-stealing, body-tingling farewell.

Both the guys wore wide grins as she crawled into her van and rolled down the window to say her final goodbyes.

"Did you charge your cell phone?" Travis asked.

"Done."

"I filled the van from the jerry can, but you'll need to stop and fill it up at least once," Cassidy reminded her.

Ashley fought back the laughter that wanted to come, pushing away her sadness at having to leave them for a couple weeks. "Yes, dear."

Cassidy made a face, and Travis leaned in the window for one more brush of his lips over hers. "Drive safe, and call when you get home."

"Go on. I'll be fine. You two take care of each other, and I'll see you in a couple of weeks."

They were visible in her rear-view mirror for the longest time, two tall, strong figures standing side by side.

She enjoyed the trip back to Rocky Mountain House, the long drive more than enough time to ponder ideas for her projects. She unlocked Travis's trailer and opened all the windows to let out the musty scent that had built up over their time away.

A quick call connected her with Travis, his deep voice sending a shiver over her. "You made good time."

Ashley laughed. "Hey, I told you I wasn't the one who made the trip so long the last time. You were the one constantly stopping for snacks."

"I'm a growing boy," Travis teased.

"Greedy thing. Hey, did you call your dad and get his okay for me to use some barn space for my projects?"

"Left a message. I bet he'll get back to me once he's out of the fields."

She eyed her van, itching to get it unpacked and start the next stage. "I'm going down to the wire here, Travis. You think it's okay to settle in?"

"Of course. Stop by the ranch house if you're worried, but it's fine. That old barn below my trailer hasn't been used for animals in nearly five years." He lowered his voice a notch, and the sexy turned up to high. "You should have stayed for the last couple weeks, woman. We're going to miss you."

"I'm not going to dignify that with a laugh. Yes, you will miss me, but since I'm the one who's sleeping alone tonight, don't try to make me feel guilty."

"Well, true, but we'll still miss you."

It was good to hear him joking. "I'm gonna get going, Travis. Give Cassidy a kiss from me, and we'll talk tomorrow."

The fridge was empty, the cupboards mostly empty as well. She'd have to stock up in the next few days, but for now the can of beans she found was enough to give her energy to slip out to the small barn by the river and get to work.

Hours later the echoing grumble from her stomach brought her back to reality. She'd moved everything barnlike aside, storing it in one of the stalls so it wouldn't be in her way. Then she'd arranged canvas and paint, setting up an entire studio. The spotlights she carried in her van weren't great for painting by, but perfect for organizing and rough work, and as tired as she was, it had been a successful afternoon. The entire place had been transformed.

She turned off the lights and headed into the trailer, ignoring her stomach temporarily and hitting the shower for a good long soak. The spider webs she'd knocked down made that an easy decision.

She was completely wrapped up in her mental to-do list and hot water when a strange thumping sounded.

A loud shout accompanying the banging pulled her from under the water, heart pounding against her ribs as she stepped out of the shower and twisted the door lock in a panic.

My God, there was someone in the trailer.

"Is anyone here? RCMP. I want to ask a couple questions." A female voice, loud and clear. "Hello?"

Ashley debated the wisdom of ignoring the summons, but her alternatives were limited. Pretending not to be there might end with the bathroom door broken down.

If it wasn't really the police, she was in more of a predicament, trapping herself in the bathroom. She turned off the water, hurriedly tugged her dirty clothes back on and shouted through the locked door. "I'll be out in a minute."

A pause. "I'll be outside."

Ashley waited until she heard the door close, then rushed from the bathroom to peer into the yard. The sight of a RCMP cruiser slowed her panic, but only slightly.

Great. There were *police* in the yard.

She took a moment to exchange her wet things for dry,

wrapping a towel around her head and approaching the front door with trepidation. "Hello?"

Two uniformed RCMP stepped from beside their car, the woman in the front seeming vaguely familiar. "I'm Officer Anna Coleman. I think I figured out the trouble—I tried calling the owner of the trailer, but couldn't get through. If you'd tell me your name..."

"Ashley Sims. Travis gave me a key, honest."

Anna waved off her partner. "It's okay, Nick. She's good."

He nodded and headed back to the cruiser.

"Can I ask what just happened?" Ashley fought down a shiver. "Although, first, I assume you're one of the unending Coleman relatives in the area."

The dark-haired woman nodded. "Yes, part of the Moonshine clan. It makes running speed traps on a weekend double the fun."

"I bet."

Anna looked her over carefully. "We got a call someone saw lights on here and in the barn. I knew Travis wasn't expected back for a while, and Mike Coleman didn't know anything. Wanted to make sure it wasn't vandals or some local youth looking for a place to fool around. Sorry if I scared you."

"That makes sense, no harm done." Ashley didn't get it, though. "Travis said he called his dad to let him know I would be here."

"Well, the message didn't get through. When I couldn't reach Travis, I tried Karen Coleman. She guessed it might be you."

"Hey, I'm glad you were looking out for Travis. Thank you." Ashley wiped at a line of water dripping down her neck. "The guys will be here in a couple weeks."

"We're already planning a gathering at Traders." Anna smiled and her face transformed, far less serious, more filled with traditional Coleman mischief. "If you don't mind partying with the local authorities."

"Not at all. Unless you cheat at cards."

Anna winked. "You'll have to wait to find out."

∼

Unbelievable. Travis got off the phone with Ashley and immediately called home.

His younger brother Jesse answered. "Joe's Pizza parlour."

"Give it a rest. It's Travis, is Dad there?"

"Aren't you a dick?" Jesse snapped back. "Whatever happened to talking to me? 'Hi, Jesse, haven't seen you in months. How are you doing?' That sort of thing."

Travis backed down because this time Jesse was right. "I'm sorry. How have things been?"

"Busy. Had the devil of a time getting things done around here all summer with you gone—hope you enjoyed your holiday."

"It was a good break, but I'm looking forward to being home in a couple weeks." It wasn't the time to point out that Travis had been working damn hard himself, and that there had been extra bodies around the ranch to help. "Hey, I don't mean to rush, but we'll catch up when I'm back. I wanted to know if Dad got my message. Ashley is back already, and she's in my trailer, so no one needs to worry about seeing smoke from the fireplace or lights or that kind of thing, okay?"

"Fuck." There were rattling noises in the background, and the sound of something falling to the floor. "You should call him."

"I left a message. I wanted to know if he got it."

"Leave him a message then."

Travis was tempted to shake the phone, if that would also shake his brother. "Jesse, are you feeling okay? That's what I just said!"

Jesse laughed, full-out explosive laughter. "You're not making any sense, bro. But we'll talk when you get home."

Then he hung up. Hung up the damn phone.

This time Travis did stare at the phone in his hand in shock. *What the hell?*

"You look like you're ready to kill someone." Cassidy stood in the doorway, slipping his hat farther back as he frowned. "Troubles?"

"Jesse is an ass." That was as succinct a comment as Travis could make it at the moment. "That boy gets more confusing to talk to all the time."

He debated not telling Cassidy what had happened with Ashley, only to save him the worry, but figured that was all kinds of wrong. They ended up calling her again so Cassidy could be reassured she was okay. Travis phoned Mike until he finally got through and got the all clear for Ashley.

The next two weeks were full. With final trail rides and getting the camp taken down, there wasn't much time to mope about missing the woman, though Travis wanted to head back to Rocky with something close to a physical ache.

Being around Cassidy made it better, though. Their friendship continued to grow, like stepping back a year in time but throwing in sex and the closeness that connection gave them. It wasn't only the attraction between them, but something more.

Something Travis had craved his entire life without knowing it.

Still, the days dragged. The crew members were given their final cheques, the horses were loaded up to be returned to Whiskey Creek ranch. By the time he and Cassidy closed the last building and locked the gate, Travis was damn near twitching. As uncertain as their next months would be, they wouldn't know if it would work until they tried.

And *tried* meant being back in Rocky.

Ashley came running up the hill as they pulled into the yard, one of his old shirts shaking in the wind as she flew into his arms. He swung her in a circle and savoured her kisses.

"Give her up, T. My turn," Cassidy demanded, and Travis passed her over with a laugh.

Ashley cupped Cassidy's cheeks as she beamed at him. "There's plenty of me to go around. You don't have to fight."

They pressed close and Travis wondered again at the lack of jealousy striking him. Never had been an issue seeing Ashley live life to the fullest, this time as she slow-kissed Cassidy, wrapped around tight and clinging like a burr.

Travis slipped into the trailer to discover she'd already laid out supper plates, something wonderful scenting the air.

"Hmm, is that stew?" Cassidy asked, stepping in the door with his arm draped over her shoulders.

"One of my few meals. I did warn you I'm not much of a cook, right?"

Cassidy waved a hand. "We'll take turns cooking. Crock-Pot and freezer meals."

She nodded. "Hey, T? I didn't know how you wanted to set us up in here. I don't have much stuff, so I picked up a dresser at the thrift store the other day. It's sitting in the living room."

Travis frowned, trying to figure out her reasoning. "Go on."

She shrugged. "You two don't share the covers very well."

Cassidy laughed. "I share very well, it's T with the issue."

"Yeah, well, I figured you two wouldn't want to share a room all the time, and then when Travis has early chores, he doesn't have to worry about waking anyone."

"You're sleeping in the living room?" Travis shook his head. "Bullshit on that."

"Hell, no. Just my clothes live there. You get your room, Cassidy gets the second bedroom, and I'll sleep with whoever is skipping the four a.m. alarm clock."

Cassidy pointed a finger at her as he winked at Travis. "That is one smart woman."

He had to agree.

All dinner they couldn't keep their hands off each other, though there was another itch scratching between his shoulders. Duller than usual, but still there. He got off the phone with his mother and joined Ashley on the couch, pondering if he should say anything yet or not.

Ashley climbed on him like she was claiming her own personal playground toy. "So, tell us..."

He shook his head to clear the cobwebs. "Family dinner Wednesday night. Coleman gathering at Traders pub on Friday, as usual, but there's going to be a big turnout."

"Shit." Cassidy leaned back in the easy chair across from them, his expression unoptimistic. "The countdown to D-Day begins."

Travis fought to keep the same sentiment from settling into his gut. "I'd like to take you over to Mom and Dad's a little early, if you don't mind. Give them a chance to say hello before the clan descends."

Ashley and Cassidy exchanged glances, then Ashley laughed. "Look at us. As if we're headed to the noose or something."

"Or something," Cassidy mock-moaned. He turned his frown into a smile instead. "I'm too happy to be here to worry much, so I'll stop being an ass and hope for the best. Tomorrow I go job hunting. There were a few leads in the paper, but it's better if I hit the pavement."

Travis held Ashley close and breathed in her scent, willing her warmth and softness to ease his frustrations, but it was no use. Casual-like, he announced, "I'm going to chop some firewood. Maybe you can come with me, Cass."

Cassidy's brows went up. He opened his mouth—probably to protest that the last thing he wanted after a seven-hour drive was to swing an axe. He snapped his lips shut again, pausing for far too long as he figured out what Travis *hadn't* said.

Then, damn if he didn't spill the beans. "Looking for stress relief?"

Travis glared at his friend. "Maybe."

A solid blow hit his shoulder. Ashley had risen to her knees and socked him.

"Ouch."

"Bullshit, *ouch*." She gave him another one. "Don't you try to hide that part of yourself from me ever again, Travis Coleman."

"I didn't want to upset you," he protested. "First thing you hear after moving in with me is I'm needy?"

"Get a clue, you're always needy, one way or another. I'm more upset when you're an idiot," she complained. "Besides, you should consider a few other things. I did some reading, and I now have all sorts of ideas to give you stress relief and kinky sex at the same time."

Travis released the fist he'd trapped to stop her from beating his shoulder. "Kinky?"

She waggled her brows. "You said you couldn't imagine me using a crop on you? Fine. Cassidy can do that, and I'll tease you other ways. Between the two of us, we'll keep you nice and stress free."

Good grief. "I've created a monster," he grumbled.

Cassidy dragged him to his feet. "It was mixing in the sex. She doesn't want to be left out."

"Damn right," Ashley muttered. "I'm no fool."

Travis didn't know what to expect with either of them anymore, but he knew this. He'd never felt so accepted and cared for in his life. He lifted Ashley's chin and nodded. "I won't keep it secret, but you try using feathers or some shit like that on me? I'll get you back, woman. You won't even know it's coming."

Ashley leaned up on her tiptoes and kissed him, her smile

dazzling as she eased back and gestured to Cassidy. "Come on, let's take care of our guy."

Take care of our guy.

Whatever else was handed their way over the coming weeks, hearing that phrase made all the uncertainty worthwhile.

24

Cassidy stood outside Thompson and Sons garage and eyed the *Help Wanted* sign. He'd spent the morning wandering through town to find out what was available for work, and this was the one place he figured he could use his skills and be happy.

It wasn't working the land, but the fall wasn't a great time to find long-term work, not with winter snows fast approaching. He could help with harvest, he hoped to give the Colemans a hand when he could, but he needed a full-time job to be able to stand on his own feet and contribute to Travis and Ashley.

Once again he was lost in a strange new world. No house of his own, no real job.

Only...

Last night he and Ashley had cared for Travis. The whole *dealing with stress relief* had moved past the uncomfortable point for him to a stage where having power over Travis was a head rush and physical turn-on. After the sparks and sex and showers were done, they'd all sat by the fire and watched the stars appear one by one. Ashley had played the guitar, but Cassidy had sat with Travis leaning against him, their fingers entwined, holding hands like romantic fools.

He'd slept with Ashley curled up in his arms, her soft body draped intimately close. Travis's early-morning farewell as he leaned over the bed and kissed both of them goodbye had been incredible. And hours later after they'd finished breakfast, Ashley had given him a slightly distracted kiss before she'd headed down to her workspace—

All those things were reasons to deal with the strangeness.

Behind the counter, an older man with his right arm in a sling across his chest struggled to his feet as Cassidy entered the door. "Morning. Can I help you?"

"Wondering about your help-wanted sign."

The man nodded, lifting his hand in the air slightly to show off his injury. "Damn car hood fell on me. Never knew cars could bite, did you?"

Cassidy joined the man in laughing. "Sorry about your arm, sir."

"My own damn fault, but we needed more help soon anyway. Here, I'll let you speak with my son." He slipped over to the entrance to the garage space and shouted through the door. "Clay, someone to talk to you."

Mr. Thompson waved absently then wandered off into the back as Cassidy waited.

One of the biggest men he'd ever seen walked in, wiping the oil from his hands on a rag. A rush of remembrance hit—while they hadn't spent tons of time together, Cassidy had met this man a couple times during the summer he'd spent in Rocky.

"How can I help you?" Clay paused, a crease folding between his brows. "Hang on, *Cassidy*, right?"

Cassidy nodded. "That's impressive. It's been about a year since I've been around."

Clay held out his hand and shook Cassidy's firmly.

"Welcome back, or are you passing through town and need repairs?"

"Back for a while," Cassidy admitted. "No repairs for you, though. Actually, I'm looking for work."

"Ahh." Clay looked him up and down. "You got experience?"

"Some. No formal training, but I can do all the grunt labour on an engine overhaul, and I know all the typical oil, air filter and sparkplug replacements."

Clay nodded. "Come in the back."

Cassidy followed him, for once feeling slightly on the small size. The Thompson boys were bigger than the Coleman family.

Clay rattled a wrench on the edge of the metal railing, a loud clanging echoing through the main garage. "Hey, guys, someone for you to meet. Anyone know Cassidy...?"

"Jones," Cassidy offered.

He found four additional sets of eyes turned on him as men rolled out from under cars and stepped back from leaning over hoods.

Make that five—adding in the dark-haired girl wearing a coverall who was unpacking items from boxes onto storage shelves.

She tossed him a shy smile. "I haven't met him before."

"Shut up, Katy," Clay growled. He turned to Cassidy. "My little sister."

The unspoken "hands off" registered loud and clear. Cassidy leaned forward and responded with a deliberate friendly but not too friendly smile. "Hi, Katy. No, we haven't met, but maybe you know my girlfriend, Ashley Sims?"

It was cheating of a sort, claiming Ashley and *only* Ashley like that, but worth it as the tension leeched out of Clay and the other guys damn fast. Cassidy stuffed down his amusement.

Katy shook her head. "Don't really remember that name."

Clay introduced his three brothers then pointed to the only

one in the room who didn't look like a Thompson. "That's my best friend, Gage Jenick—only the jerk is planning on taking off on me in a couple months to work the oil field."

"Progress, Clay. Can't hold back a good man."

"Yeah, you're an asshole looking for the big bucks up north."

Gage grinned.

Clay turned back. He named an hourly rate, plus a daily start and finish time. "You want the job?"

Whoa. Cassidy paused. Quickest job interview he'd ever had. "That's it?"

Clay shrugged. "You want me to make it up fancy, I'll get Katy to bake you a cake. She'll find the forms you need, and we'll do up the government shit, but if you're a hard worker, we can use you."

"I'm a hard worker," Cassidy promised. "And, thank you."

Another nod. Clay pointed to the sidewall. "There are spare coveralls over there, if you want to start on the clock right now. We're eight cars behind schedule. Every one and their dog decided this week was the time to do all the maintenance they should have done three months ago."

Cassidy couldn't wait to tell the others he had a job. "Right now is fine."

Clay shouted at his brothers. "What are you all looking at? Get back to work."

All of them flipped up middle fingers before quietly returning to their tasks.

Gage strode over to offer a handshake. "Good to meet you, Cassidy. Clay, can I steal him to help with the tires?"

Clay nodded. "Have at 'er. I'm fighting with the damn diagnostic machine again. If you can babysit Cassidy for the rest of the day, be my guest."

Gage winked at Cassidy. "We'll knock out half the work list without breaking a sweat."

"Ha. You do that, and I'll cover your tab on Friday," Clay offered.

"Deal." Gage tilted his head toward the back. "Come on, let's get you suited up, and we'll work on earning that reward."

It didn't take long for Cassidy to slip into the routine. While the setting was different, so many of the places he'd worked had the same kind of attitude. Everything in its place. One task at a time. The internal workings of a garage and a ranch weren't that different when it came down to it. Especially here in a small town where they had to deal with pretty much everything, from changing tires to engine rebuilds.

He pulled another tire off the rim setter and carried it to the stack growing along the east wall.

Gage wandered up, extra coffee in his hand that he offered Cassidy. "Four tires left? Damn, you are good."

Cassidy accepted the hot liquid, taking a grateful sip before answering. "Sometimes a mindless task is just what's needed."

Gage sat on the edge of a counter, nodding his agreement. "You living in town then?"

And so it began. Cassidy fought to keep from hesitating and simply answer the questions. If this was going to be their life, he had to prove there was nothing he was ashamed of or hiding. "No, Ashley and I have moved in with Travis Coleman."

The man frowned. "How do you know Travis?"

"Spent the summer out near Jasper working at Karen Coleman's trail-ride camp with him."

"Ah, right. Good people, the Colemans." The long pause wasn't on his side, but Gage's, as the man looked him over more thoroughly. He obviously had something on his mind, but he held his tongue and switched topics.

Cassidy appreciated Gage's restraint. It was a fine line right now for Cassidy, between wanting to get things out in the open and hoping in some ways that no one would ever find out.

One step at a time.

Like the *One Day* motto Ashley had gotten them started with during the summer, Cassidy grabbed on tight to his new mantra and repeated it throughout the day. He'd found a job, made a new friend. Had a place to head home to at the end of the day where two people would welcome him with open arms.

For right now, that was all he needed.

Travis thought long and hard about the best way to approach his family. He'd discussed it with Ashley and Cassidy, but in the end they'd agreed it was up to him to share the news.

He didn't want Wednesday night at the dinner table to be the first moment that he not only came out regarding living with two people but sleeping with them both. No matter how hopeful he was that his family would accept his decision eventually, he couldn't picture the initial moments going down without some trouble.

Fortunately he had plenty of chances throughout the workday to interact one-on-one with his brothers and dad, all of them except Daniel. And Daniel was the least of his concerns.

He caught up with Matt and Blake during a break, tractors paused in the field, the two of them sitting out in the fall sunshine drinking coffee and shooting the breeze. They both turned toward him, Blake frowning with concern as he rolled up on the ATV.

"Something wrong at home?" Blake asked, rising to his feet.

Travis shook his head. "Everyone is fine, only I needed to talk to you two."

Matt gestured to the thermos. "Grab a cup and a seat."

Travis rubbed his hands nervously. "I'm good. Just…"

He looked them over closer than he had in years. His two oldest brothers, both committed to working the ranch. Blake with his growing family was married to a woman who had known most of Travis's secrets since they were kids. Matt had married one of the most accepting and caring women Travis had ever met.

These were the guys who had kicked his ass when he needed it when he was young. Who had fought with him and fought for him, and...and why the hell was it so hard to simply come out and say what had to be said?

"Family dinner on Wednesday night. I'm bringing Ashley and Cassidy."

"Heard from Karen over the summer that you and Cassidy did a great job for her out at camp. She really appreciated it." Blake nodded his approval. "I'm glad that worked out for you, though we missed you around the place."

"Missed you tons. We had to do all the shit jobs we usually save for you," Matt teased. "Well, until Jesse started screwing up big time. Then we dumped them on him."

Travis didn't want to get sidetracked. "I'm glad I went, but it was time to be back." He lifted his gaze to meet theirs. "Feel like a fool right now, but I'll admit I missed you guys too. But I came out here to tell you something specific. Ashley has moved in with me. Cassidy as well."

Blake paused with the cup to his lips, lowering it slowly, his smile slowly fading to concern.

Matt cleared his throat. "You mean, like permanent?"

"I guess. We're seeing how it works, but we spent the summer together." Travis stilled his hands that were tapping uneasily on his thighs. "Call it dating or living together or...I don't the hell know. Only, it's the three of us."

"You mean you and Cassidy are both dating Ashley full-time?" Blake frowned. "I know the rest of you all had your share of threesomes, but how is that going to work, Travis?"

"There's more." Travis took a deep breath. "It's not just her with him and me, it's...me with him as well."

Matt slapped his hand on his knee and leaned back. "Well, hallelujah. It's about fucking time you admitted it."

The sense of panic in Travis's gut lessened at seeing Matt's grin. "You knew?"

Matt gave him a look. "You're not as subtle as you think, little bro. I mean, I never out-and-out saw you with a guy, but it was pretty clear you weren't just looking at pretty girls."

Blake, on the other hand was still frowning. "Wait. What...?"

"Dammit, Blake. Stop being an idiot. We've talked about this more than a dozen times." Matt shook his head. "Here, I'll use small words. Travis has a boyfriend."

Blake glared at Matt. "Yes, asshole, I got that part. But he's also got a girlfriend?"

The temptation to tease was too great. "There's too much of me for one person," Travis drawled.

"That's the smartass I expected." Blake shook his finger. "Still, you really thought this through? You think you can make a go of three people sharing a house and expenses and all the things that come along besides sex? Hell, I love Jaxi like crazy, and it's still tough dealing with life at times." Blake looked uncomfortable as he searched for words. "What about kids?"

Jeez. "Not thinking about kids for a long time, Blake. This is about us enjoying each other's company and caring for each other. We'll see where it takes us. Yes, we've thought it through, and no, it's not typical, but so far it's working. Only I don't want to have to avoid family events, or have them stay home when I come around the Colemans, so I need to know you'll treat them with respect."

Matt shoved him off balance. "Don't be a fucking fool."

"They're important to me," Travis insisted. "I won't allow them to be made to feel unwelcome."

"So bring them around family events. Works for me." Matt turned back to Blake. "You think we should leave that east field for a couple more days? It still seemed a little wet."

Blake made a face. "It's supposed to rain on Thursday."

"Cut it on Wednesday, then? Or wait until the weekend?"

Travis opened his mouth to bitch he wasn't finished talking when he realized what his brothers had done. They'd heard his announcement. They'd accepted it. Moved on. Without a word, which was more than he'd dreamed of.

He ended up phoning Daniel, who immediately tried to figure out what his kids should call Cassidy and Ashley.

"Good grief, have the boys use their fucking names," Travis snarked.

Daniel hummed. "Beth likes them to call adults Mr. or Mrs., or in the case of family, Aunt and Uncle. I don't know that she'll go for first names."

Travis couldn't believe it. "This is really your biggest concern, Daniel? I announce I'm bi, and you're worried if my boyfriend should be Uncle or Mr. Cassidy? Call him Mr. Jones, I don't give a shit."

Daniel snorted. "Sorry for not being more freaked out. You should have told me upfront you wanted gnashing and grinding of teeth, I would have practiced."

"Asshole."

"Shithead," Daniel responded without heat. "Hey, can you bring your friends for dinner here on Sunday? I need a hand moving some stuff, and now that you have a boyfriend, I can get double the labour out of having you over."

Travis couldn't stop a laugh from escaping. "I'll check with them, but that should be fine."

He headed home that afternoon with a strange sense of disbelief hovering over him. He hadn't had to confess a word about his cravings for the darker side of pain, and the other half of his secret had turned out to be not so secret after all.

Cassidy paced in after his successful day in obtaining work, hung up his jacket and headed straight for the shower. Travis worked to put supper on the table, phoning Ashley to remind her to stop painting and join them.

All of it far more domestic and homey than Travis figured he had any right to expect, but it was real.

Cassidy returned, fresh scrubbed from the shower, and joined him in the kitchen, pausing to rub a hand on Travis's back. "How did it go?"

Travis leaned on the counter. "Anticlimactic. Even my parents. Dad wanted to know what the two of you were doing for work, and my mom seemed worried about the trailer for some reason." He threw his hands in the air. "All that frustration and fear for nothing."

Cassidy shook his head. "Seriously? That's it?"

Travis stepped against his friend, holding him tight. Rubbing his fingers over the taut muscles in Cassidy's shoulders and the back of his neck. The tension in the words had said more than anything what pain was bouncing through Cassidy's brain.

Travis considered the entire day, the conversations with each of his family, and could only come to one conclusion. "It's probably not what they'd envisioned for me, but it's not their life. They're staying out of it."

Cassidy pulled away and went to lay plates on the table. "Still seems unreal."

"Agreed, but I'll take it." Travis laughed. "God, the last thing Mom said to me? She looked me straight in the eye, took a deep breath, then very seriously reminded me dinner starts at six, and we're not to be late."

It hadn't been perfect. Jesse had made a borderline rude remark before being shushed by Joel's fist meeting his arm. Then again, when didn't Jesse make stupid comments? Most of the family had expressed concern about the logistics of Travis being with two lovers. But not a single one of them had so much as blinked when it had been confirmed his sexual preferences ran to both men and women.

Ashley listened to the extended recap while they ate. When Travis was finished, she sat back with a contented smile. "See? I told you this would work."

"We're not in the clear yet," Cassidy warned. "That was Travis's immediate family, but yes. I'm very glad it turned out so well so far."

Ashley piled the plates on the tiny counter and pushed up her sleeves, wash water started. "You guys go relax, I'll clean up tonight."

Travis grabbed a dishtowel and stepped to her right. "We'll do it together."

"You want a chance to grope me, admit it," Ashley joked.

Cassidy hovered closer. "Is that one of the job perks for washing dishes? Because, if so, I'm on it."

Ashley laughed and tried to duck away, but there was no room in the small space for her to escape. Just the way Travis liked it.

25

———————

By seven p.m. Wednesday evening, Ashley's optimism had faded somewhat. It wasn't that there was anything wrong, per se, but awkward?

Gawd.

Of course, it wasn't necessarily anything more than meet-the-girlfriend nerves on all parts, compounded by adding in meet-the-boyfriend at the same time. Although neither of them was completely unknown to the family, the mixed-up relationship between Cassidy and her and Travis definitely added a new twist.

Thank God for Vicki. She'd swept in from the moment they'd arrived and taken control of Ashley. Beth had been pleasant enough from the first moment, and Jaxi as well, but there was something slightly off. Some lingering hesitation. Glances that lasted a little too long. Conversations that cut off a touch too quickly.

The old Ashley would have made some deliberately dirty comment to prove she didn't give a damn, only...

She did care. Far too much.

For the first time in her life, it wasn't about doing what she wanted. Taking what she pleased and damn the consequences. She'd gotten possessive over her guys in a way like she never had before. Maybe it was part of growing up, maybe it was about emotions.

Whatever reason, it was enough to make her bust her ass to try to smooth things over with the Colemans. She wanted to impress them.

Wanted to belong, for Travis's and Cassidy's sakes, if not her own.

Jaxi passed a bowl. "Cassidy got on at the garage. Are you looking for work in town, Ashley?"

She shook her head and explained about the art show.

"Plus she did the brochures for Karen," Mike Coleman reminded Jaxi. He turned to Ashley. "I saw a copy. Fine work on them."

"Thanks." She ducked her head to glance down the long body-filled table until she found her target. "I was looking at the website you have for your woodworking shop, Daniel. If you'd like me to make a new header, that's not a problem. Or a brochure, or whatever."

Damn, she sounded far too eager.

But Daniel smiled. "That could work. We'll talk more on Sunday."

Ashley turned to pass the bowl to Marion on her right and caught Travis's mom frowning, her gaze stuck off in the distance. Ashley lowered the bowl without saying anything, focusing back on the conversation between two of the boys in the opposite direction.

Uncomfortable, yes. But nothing that wasn't livable with. Under the table, she caught Cassidy's fingers and held on tight. She could accept *uncomfortable* for now, and give them all time to find their way.

By Friday she was more than ready to get the rest of it over, though. At least this time she could have a few drinks or drag one of her guys onto the dance floor when she needed a break from all the family togetherness.

She'd wanted roots, only she hadn't realized grafting into an established family meant so damn many branches were already in place. It was crowded at times for someone who'd had no one to consider but herself for years.

But tonight would be different. She attempted to distract herself by checking out everything passing them by. She leaned over Cassidy to peer out the window. "Oh, I like that truck. The red one, with the lift kit." She twisted back to grin at Travis. "Can we do that to yours?"

"Do it to your own vehicle," Travis said, turning into the parking lot at Traders and heading for an open space.

"Sure. My van would look so right with that. Not." She followed him out the driver's door, accepting his hand as Cassidy joined them. Butterflies danced in her belly. Stupid, really. These were people she'd met before. Some wouldn't care what they were up to, some wouldn't notice.

Vicki snagged her by the hand and dragged her away from Travis and Cassidy in the first ten seconds of their arrival. "I've been waiting for you. Come on."

Ashley glanced over her shoulder at the guys. "Have fun. I'll see you at closing."

Cassidy laughed. "Bullshit. Dance floor. One hour."

She winked and gave in to Vicki, following her to the area by the pool tables where the Coleman clan was already gathered. They'd pulled tables together and laughter rose from the group of women, loud and slightly dirty as they eyed the guys shooting pool.

Vicki banged on the table briefly. "Everyone, Ashley. Ashley —meet everyone. If you don't know their name, throw something at them to get their attention."

Hope patted the chair next to her. "But first, come sit by me. I want you to tell me about your art."

Ashley sat, but she looked around instead. "Let me count bodies, to see who I know."

Vicki held up a glass. "Beer? Pop?"

Oh hell, *yes*. "Alcohol of any form, please and thank you. If you've got pitchers going, I'm good."

Hope leaned in close. "You want to watch something entertaining, check out Karen Coleman. She's being stalked, and it's hilarious."

"What?" Ashley followed Hope's pointing finger to identify Karen, who she'd not yet met in person. "Who's stalking her?"

"Finn, one of the Marlette men who came out to help at the ranch over the summer." Hope chuckled, her laugh low and twisted. "It's funny when they're in denial."

Ashley watched over the edge of her glass as Karen leaned on a pillar nearby the table. She was chatting with Jaxi and the friendly, door-knocking cop, Anna. On the opposite side of the thick wooden post, a solidly built man had paused, his thick upper arms fighting with the sleeves of his T-shirt. He folded his arms and rested within easy listening range, but out of sight.

"I hope they're talking about him," Ashley said.

Hope sputtered into her drink. "God, you're eviler than me."

Vicki beamed. "Told you she'd fit in well."

"You did, now shut up and tell me about your classes." Hope rested her arm along the back of Ashley's chair, comfortably close and accepting. "Do you need a guinea pig for Baking 101 or bacon-wrapped anything days?"

Over the next hour, Ashley learned that Vicki was attending a few cooking classes and that Hope's quilt shop was doing well enough she'd hired a couple part-time staff to help her. Beth had left the local high school and was now teaching distance-learning math classes for homeschoolers using the computer.

Add in the cousins and the girlfriends and...Ashley's head was spinning. She loved people, but this? Was a little much.

Needing a break, Ashley slipped away from the table and headed toward where the guys were still playing. Travis was eyeing the arrangement and deciding his best shot. Cassidy stood behind him with his beer lifted to his lips. When Travis stepped forward and leaned over, reaching his pool cue forward, Cassidy's gaze instinctively dropped to Travis's ass.

Ashley grinned.

Grinned even harder when Cassidy realized where he was looking and snapped himself to vertical, turning away slightly.

She snuck to his side and tugged his mug from his fingers. "You have good taste in ass."

Cassidy's cheeks flushed. "Not so loud."

"Well, you do." She smirked before stealing a few sips of beer.

"Yeah, but I shouldn't broadcast it." Cassidy took back his mug before she could chug down the second half. "I know we said we wouldn't hide, but there's no need to shove it in everyone's face."

Oh, the images that leapt to mind at his comment. "You'd better finish playing pool soon so I can dirty dance with you. Give me a way to deal with all the naughty things drifting through my brain."

"Hey," Joel called. "You're up, Cassidy. Stop fooling around."

"He's not," Ashley said, swinging herself up on one of the tall stools beside their table. "He's practicing the fine art of public foreplay. All talk, no touch, but highly effective."

Matt laughed, wiping his mouth with the back of his hand before grinning. "Dirty talk does it for you?"

"Does for most women." She let the devil on her shoulder have free rein, leaning back to see the table where she'd left the ladies. "Hey, Hope?" she called loud enough to be heard over the music and voices.

Hope twisted toward her, most of the rest of the table following suit. "Yeah?"

"You get off on dirty talk? Matt wants to know."

A series of snorts and chuckles burst out around her, getting louder when Hope shifted upward in her chair and leaned in Matt's direction. Her long hair fell around her shoulders, and she lowered her chin to stare at him with half-lidded eyes. "Oh, he knows *exactly* what words get me hot, don't you, love?"

"Fucking right." Matt shook his finger at Ashley as the ladies rose from the table and headed toward their guys or the dance floor. "You busted up our game."

"Tell me you're pissed that you get to hang on to Hope and rub on her in public," Travis drawled as he stepped in behind Ashley. "Go on, try."

"Well, hell, no. Not a hardship at all."

"Lots of hard where I'm looking from," Hope muttered, slipping into Matt's arms and taking away his pool cue. "Dance floor, now, big guy."

Matt curled his arm around her and grinned at Cassidy and Travis. "Flip a coin, boys. We'll see you on the other side."

Travis brushed his cheek against Ashley's and breathed in deep. "You are trouble, ain't cha?"

She happily squirmed around to slip her arms around his neck. "Just like you. That's why we fit so well." She glanced at Cassidy. "Poor Cassidy is the sweet innocent one. We'll have to work harder on corrupting him."

Cassidy smiled, stepping to put away his cue on the rack. "I'm nicely corrupted already, thanks. So, we gonna dance?"

Travis helped Ashley off the stool and tilted his head toward the door between the bar side and the dance side of Traders. "After you."

"Hey, Cassidy, you want to do someone a favour?" Ashley asked.

The volume increased significantly as they passed the barrier and the live band grew louder. Cassidy moved in closer, right against her back as Travis pulled her through the crowd toward an opening on the floor. "Does it involve taking my clothes off?"

"Well, that too in about three hours, but right now? Find Karen Coleman and ask her to dance."

What the fuck? Cassidy stared after Ashley as Travis pulled her close and started swaying to the music. He draped her arms around his neck then smirked at Cassidy, basically gloating that he'd nabbed her first.

Bastard. Cassidy laughed, though. This was pretty much fine for now. Work people into the idea that this was about three of them slowly—he could handle that. Besides, he wasn't driving, and if things worked as planned, he'd have Ashley riding his cock before they were out of the parking lot.

He turned to figure out what mischief Ashley had triggered with her request.

The dance floor was full of faces that were slowly becoming more familiar. The Thompson boys from the garage, as well as all of Travis's relatives.

Katy Thompson was dancing with a man who glared daggers at Cassidy for glancing their way. Cassidy made a note of the face. The guy had balls if he was dating the lone female in the Thompson clan.

Karen stood in the corner with the tall dark-haired man who'd refused a game of pool to hang out with the ladies.

Which might have made Finn the smartest man in the building. Only now Karen was fidgeting as he leaned in close and spoke, the red flushing her cheeks visible even in the dim dance-floor lighting.

Cassidy gave a mental shrug. Wouldn't hurt anything—he supposed Ashley had her reasons. Not like Travis could dance with his cousin, and there was no reason he couldn't use this as an excuse to touch base.

He ducked his chin slightly to get her attention before speaking. "Hey, would you like to dance?"

Her eyes widened, and she shot from the corner as if jet propelled. "Yes, love to."

If looks could cut, the man left behind would have sliced a piece off him. Cassidy led her onto the floor as close to Ashley and Travis as he could. "You need some fresh air?" he asked.

Karen settled a nice un-intimate distance away—well, as far as she could get on the crowded floor. "Just needed some Finn-less time, that's all."

He nodded, glancing back at the man who had locked on them like he had radar. "Ashley told me to give you a breather. I wasn't sure if it was to make someone jealous or to save you. I thought Finn and his brothers came to help while you were laid up. Why are they still around?"

"Change of plans. I swear I'm being tormented for some evil in a past life." She grimaced then shrugged. "Anyway, good to hear you've decided to settle in Rocky. I take it the time at camp was more interesting than your end-of-summer report to me implied."

Cassidy wasn't sure how much she knew. "I had a good summer."

They both grinned but said no more.

"You need a ride home?" he asked her. "I mean, let me know if Finn is more than simply an annoyance."

She patted his shoulder. "Well, isn't that considerate? No...I can manage him. But thanks."

Ashley slipped between them, easing her arm around Karen as she settled tight against Cassidy's body. "Hi. Having a good evening?"

Karen laughed. "You sent Cassidy to rescue me. Thanks."

"I enjoy jerking people's chains. Finn looks like the type who's fun to tease."

"He's...different, that's for sure." Karen winked at Cassidy. "I'll let you two alone. Welcome to the clan."

Another heartfelt welcome. Cassidy settled Ashley tight against him and considered all the positive twists over the past days. He couldn't complain. Not so far.

Up on the stage, the band's lead guitarist had a familiar cast to his features, and Cassidy searched his memory for the name of Travis's cousin. Stan? Steve, that was it. "You know exactly how many Colemans are in the area?" Cassidy asked Ashley.

"A shit-ton." She smiled up at him. "But we only need the one."

He laughed and kept dancing. The floor was crowded, which made the rapid movement by a curvy blonde more outstanding as she forced her way to the front of the stage. Steve smiled down at her for all of three seconds before the woman lifted a full pitcher of beer and threw it in his face.

The music barely faltered as she whirled away. The guitar-playing Coleman, now dripping wet, abandoned his instrument and headed after her, a second band member stepping forward to the microphone to take up singing.

Cassidy and Ashley exchanged amused glances. "You have any idea what that was about?"

"He's a Coleman. Obviously did something to piss her off." Ashley curled up as intimately against him as she'd been a couple minutes ago with Travis.

As the momentary discussion regarding whatever had taken place with the band faded, there were more glances cast their way. One group of guys was doing a lot of talking and looking, obviously sharing a few opinions that might not be complimentary toward Ashley, or him and Ashley.

At that moment, Cassidy discovered his *give a fuck* was broken. "I wonder what they'd do if I went and grabbed Travis for the next song. Something slow and good to grind to."

Ashley lifted her head off his chest, and her eyes sparkled with mischief. "Oh man, I would give a ton to see that..."

"Probably blow a few blood vessels." Cassidy glanced to the side again. "Not worth it, but damn if I can't say I'm tempted."

"Yeah, I hear you." Ashley stroked her fingers over his ribs, easing around his back and all but riding his thigh as she positioned a leg on either side of his. "Tell you what, we'll do it when we get home. First song with clothes on pretending we're back here in public."

"The next with clothes off? Deal." Cassidy leaned down and kissed her, loving how eagerly she responded.

The rude looks and dirty comments were there, but as an undertone he could ignore. He turned off everything but staring into Ashley's tempting eyes, and relished holding her close as they swayed on the dance floor.

Ashley pushed the cart between the vegetables and fruits and considered how exactly she was going to convince her carnivores to join her in eating better.

Or at least add in a few things that were green and not deep-fried or slathered in calories. She picked up a head of purple cabbage and eyed it warily, wondering if the colour would disguise its true nature.

"If you want to sneak more vegetables in, I have some recipes for you."

She turned to discover Jaxi Coleman behind her, grocery cart filled with more children than food. "How did you know—?"

Jaxi laughed. "I recognized your expression. I've worn it myself many times. Blake usually eats anything that doesn't move, but when faced with a few too many 'rabbit meals', even he revolts. I can't imagine what having two of them to argue menu plans with would be like."

"It's more since we take turns cooking that I need some prepared food in the fridge in self-defense. Travis isn't *too* bad," Ashley conceded reluctantly.

"But Cassidy would pile three burger patties on a bun and call it a balanced meal? I hear you." Jaxi pulled a can from one of the twins' hands and put it back on the shelf, absently adjusting her cart to be farther from the shelves and out of reach of little fingers. "Rae, leave that alone. You get to pick out the juice, but for now, sit."

The little blonde sat, pigtails bouncing. Then two identical faces twisted to stare at Ashley. She smiled and felt warmth bounce back in the form of giggles and gap-toothed toddler grins.

"I'll email you the recipes. Spaghetti sauces with extra veggies, meatloaf with carrots grated in, stuff like that."

Ashley nodded. "I'd appreciate it."

Another shopper wandered past, eyeing Ashley for a moment before going wide-eyed and scurrying toward the next aisle. Ashley wasn't sure if she should laugh or sigh.

Word was getting around, that much was clear.

"Hey, ignore it."

Ashley glanced over at Jaxi.

The other woman shrugged. "Ignorant, stupid people are only satisfied when they're being ignorant and stupid. You make Travis happy, and that's what counts."

The truth in Jaxi's statement couldn't be denied, but it was the affirmation that warmed Ashley more than the children's acceptance. "Thanks, Jaxi. I can handle some dirty looks as long as the guys are content."

Jaxi adjusted the backpack she wore that held little girl number three. "I haven't seen Travis this relaxed in years. You and Cassidy are good for him, and anyone who thinks otherwise can take a hike."

Ashley motioned at Jaxi's more-than-full cartload of children. "You need a hand shopping? I don't mind helping," she offered.

Jaxi waved off her offer. "Thanks, but I'm used to this, plus Marion is somewhere in the store doing the bulk of the list." She rolled her cart forward and added a few items before offering an invitation. "We're making cabbage rolls later this week. If you'd like, we can buy extra ingredients and you can come over to help. You'll end up with a bunch for the freezer. If you have time—I know you've got a lot on your plate right now."

"If you don't mind teaching a beginner." Ashley paused. It wasn't her lack of domestic skills that might be a problem. "You want to check with Marion first?"

Jaxi tilted her head. "Why would I need to do that?"

Ashley shrugged. "I'm not sure Marion approves of me, that's all. Don't want to make things awkward coming around where I'm not wanted."

"*Pfft.*" Jaxi blew a raspberry. "Marion's okay with you. It's probably the same thing as I had to work through—I wanted to know you were going to do right by Travis. It was pretty obvious the other night at Traders that things are working out. Marion's got a mom-brain, and it's gonna take longer to convince her you and Cassidy are good enough for her little boy."

The idea of Travis as anyone's little boy made Ashley smile reluctantly. "I suppose."

"Trust me, I'm right." Jaxi grinned. "Ask Travis, I'm *always* right..."

Ashley's smile turned to laughter. "Fine. You're right, and I would love to make cabbage rolls. Call me, and let me know where and when."

She tweaked the twins' noses to their great delight then pushed on around the corner, hoping to finish the rest of the shopping in time to make some final adjustments to one of her projects before the guys were done for the day.

Normal, everyday activities. Working, shopping. Spending time together.

The forward motion helped soothe the moments of sadness that still struck when she remembered her cousin. Remembered a life that was cut short. Made her all the more determined to seize every good moment she could.

The next row Ashley turned down, she discovered where her earlier nosy shopper had gone. A gaggle of women were all bunched together, their carts blocking the path as they whispered furiously. One of them tapped the others to get their attention, and silence fell as embarrassed faces and a few frowns turned her way.

Bolstered by Jaxi's approval, Ashley didn't give a shit what other people wanted to waste their time yattering about. Only when she rolled forward and saw exactly where the ladies had picked to have their discussion, she couldn't resist.

"Excuse me, but I need to get at that shelf, please," she asked politely. All four heads rotated to the side, eyes widening and lips tightening as the women discovered they had blocked Ashley's path to the condoms.

One of the ladies proved she might not be a write-off as a hint of a smile appeared momentarily, the young woman separating herself from the others as she moved out of the way.

Ashley clicked her tongue disapprovingly as she reached for the shelf. "Really? A twenty-four pack is the largest box this store stocks? And none of them are ribbed. Damn." She tossed three packages and a couple of tubes of lube into her cart before smiling sweetly at the most indignant woman of the lot. "At least they carry large sizes."

She swore she heard sputtering behind her as she left.

~

Travis opened the main barn doors wide and waited for

Cassidy to enter in front of him. Up ahead, Ashley twisted her hands together as she bounced in place.

He and Cassidy had been back in Rocky since mid-August, and now, nearly a month later, Travis couldn't imagine being without the two of them. It was still two steps forward, one step back in some ways, but in terms of the things they were enjoying together?

He had no complaints.

"I thought artists kept their work secret until the grand reveal," Cassidy teased, pacing slowly into the high-roofed building.

"Well, I'm not your typical artist, and I'm not done everything, but I couldn't wait any longer." Ashley rushed forward and grabbed each of them by a hand, pulling them farther into the area she'd claimed as a workspace. "Come *on*, I've been dying to show you."

Travis exchanged smiles with Cassidy then followed willingly to where Ashley had put out a couple chairs. He sat, grinning harder as she fussed with the sheet-covered canvas. "I love it when you're like this. Giddy. Sheer energy."

Ashley twirled and beamed at him. "It's been incredible having this place to work. And I think I've done a good job. Fingers crossed the gallery agrees."

"You're not done, though, right?" Cassidy counted the canvases one by one. "Doesn't look like enough for a showing, excuse my ignorance."

"No, I'm not done, but it won't only be my work they're showing. There will be other artists as well. But I've gotten a super start, and I'm done the toughest of them. The rest of the month I'll work on watercolour and drawings— And I'm rambling. Shutting up." Ashley slipped to the right and grabbed hold of a sheet. "This is the first set. They'll be hung in a row, a little space between them."

Travis leaned forward as the sheet pulled back, and his jaw nearly hit the floor.

"Holy shit..." Cassidy breathed, rising to his feet.

It was as if she'd cut a section of land from the Six Pack ranch and magically projected it onto the canvas. From left to right the four pictures took in west to east on the land, the Rockies on the far edge fading into the foothills blending into the rolling grass of grazing land and the flatter cultivated grain fields.

Taken alone each picture was complete. A mountainous meadow, a ranch house with buildings, cattle and crops. Together, the effect was breathtaking.

"Ashley this is..." Travis abandoned his chair as well and moved forward to figure out exactly how she'd made the pictures come alive.

"You're not getting the full impact from this close," Ashley complained, but she was beaming. "You really like them, don't you?"

"Like? Love. God, woman, these are serious art." Cassidy slipped a hand around her waist and pulled her in close. He kissed her absentmindedly, gaze still fixed on the paintings. "I swear I can smell the country air."

"No cattleshit, though." Travis leaned in, hands held behind him so he wouldn't be tempted to touch. He wasn't much of an art critic, but he agreed with Cassidy. He turned and nodded. "You did damn good."

Ashley's grin stretched from ear to ear. "Ready for the second set?"

She made them sit again—something about getting the right perspective—before pulling off the drop cloth.

"Fuck." Cassidy dragged his hand through his hair.

Travis had been about to say the same thing. "Jeez. Ashley, you're going to get stolen away by New York City or Paris, or some other big fancy art place."

She'd done the same kind of three-dimensional voodoo on this set, only this time instead of landscapes the paintings showcased the people of the land. The faces weren't quite Cassidy or Travis or his father or Karen, but almost them. Working with the cattle, labouring in the barn. Karen stroking a horse's nose to settle him. Travis swore the beast had just finished tossing his head, his nostrils about to flare in the next second.

He faced Ashley. "I'm well and truly speechless."

"I did good, didn't I?" Ashley nodded. "I mean, they aren't your typical hang-on-the-wall paintings, not with all the crap I've added in layers, but my ideas worked."

"I can't believe you did all this in the past month and a bit." Cassidy caught her fingers in his and strolled closer to the pictures with her at his side. "I knew you were putting in long hours, but you've got some serious talent."

"I did a lot back at camp. All the preliminary sketches were done before I left, and I experimented back there as well. There are a couple of my disasters sitting in the burn pile behind the cookhouse—not everything I do works."

Travis stepped in front of her and cupped her face. "I'm so proud of you."

Her eyes sparkled as he leaned in and kissed her, the tender touch heating up as she snuck a hand around his torso and pulled them in tight.

Cassidy still had her other hand, and he laughed, laying an arm over Travis's shoulder. "There are more secrets to be revealed. If you two can come up for air for a while."

"Oh, yes." Ashley slipped away before Travis could pin her in place.

He glared at Cassidy. "Thanks for nothing."

Cassidy glanced at Ashley for a moment before sneaking Travis a kiss of his own to placate him.

Bold, demanding, the kiss was enough to set his blood

pounding harder. This was turning out to be a hell of an evening, and the night had only begun.

"Get your butts back in your chairs," Ashley ordered. "God, kissing all the time. You two are just...lechers."

Cassidy laughingly followed her directions.

Travis remained standing. "I'm going to be up in a second anyway. Show us the rest."

"Spoilsport." Cassidy tugged him into his lap, and this time it was Travis who laughed, escaping to return to his feet.

Ashley rolled her eyes then revealed the rest of her work. None of the rest were as striking as the original two sets, but all were impressive.

"Ashley, you're going to make a great showing at the gallery. I know it."

"Thanks, Travis. Bonus, I'm not as nervous anymore, now that I've got this much done. I can spend the final two weeks doing smaller projects." She paused by the final cover and took a deep breath. "One more to go, but this one? Is not for the show."

Cassidy frowned. "Why did you make it then?"

She rocked a little from side to side then looked him in the eye. "I had to make it. Call it inspiration or fate or whatever, it's the one idea that grabbed hold of me and wouldn't let me go. Close your eyes."

Travis smiled hard but obeyed.

Footsteps crossed toward them and her warm hand slid into his, linking their fingers. "Okay, you can look."

She'd made the painting she'd talked about that first day they'd run into Cassidy. Angels and demons—white canvas, black paint, shadows forming the picture.

Only it was him and Cassidy *and* Ashley, as if the viewer were standing slightly above them. Cassidy's head was thrown back in laughter or ecstasy. Travis's easy grin and relaxed slouch placed him at the center of the composition. Ashley stood with her bare feet firmly planted on the naked ground as the wind pulled her hair into a curve of energy.

None of them were touching, but their bodies echoed each other, as if the individual figures could be slid together and would click like a giant jigsaw puzzle. Independently strong, yet somehow more when they were together.

"It's for us. Well, for you guys."

"For us," Cassidy corrected. "Ashley, it's the best of them all."

"Told you I was inspired." She tugged their hands and turned them toward her, her face shining with her earnest enthusiasm. "I spent the time I was working on that thinking. Really thinking about how each of us is so different, and yet we work together so well."

Travis lifted her chin. "We do."

She stood between him and Cassidy, holding them both. She licked her lips, then blurted out, "I love you."

A shot like electricity went through him.

Ashley looked him in the eye, and then Cassidy. "I mean, screwed-up way to tell you or what, but I really do. I've fallen in love with you both, and that terrifies me and makes me happy at the same time. Even more foolishly, I'm enjoying feeling terrified and happy."

"Like you're on a high, and you're afraid you're about to come down?" Cassidy asked.

She nodded. "Except crashing would be almost as much fun as the floating part, as long as I get to crash into both of you."

Travis held her, the pleasure of her confession trickling down his spine. Cassidy's pleased glow was right there as well—the man clearly accepting what she so freely gave.

"I love you too, baby," Cassidy whispered. "Snuck up on me, but damn if you don't get under a man's skin." He cupped the back of her neck to pull her close for a tender kiss, more about being together than trying to consume her.

Travis stood beside them, the words on his tongue.

Hovering.

Waiting for him to say them, and yet...

He was spared his mental turmoil as Ashley broke free and grabbed his hands, tugging him with her. "Carry it inside for me? Can we hang it in the living room?"

"Hell, yeah." Something else to focus on, and he was saved for the moment.

Travis lifted the painting carefully, following Cassidy out of the barn as Ashley paused to cover her work.

"You're coming back inside, right?" Travis called to her.

"Be there in a minute."

Cassidy stayed pretty damn quiet as he opened the trailer door and helped rearrange things so Travis could put up the picture. Travis stared at the wall as a sense of great responsibility and incredible blessing rocked him.

Cassidy stepped behind him, tugging their bodies together as he rested his chin on Travis's shoulder. "You feel like you've been gutted and laid out in the sun, exposed?"

Apt words. "Pretty much."

There was a pause. "I don't expect you to tell her how you feel in front of me."

The laugh that escaped held a trembling edge. "I ain't good with those words, Cass. I can do my damnedest to show you and her how I feel, but spitting it out is like pulling tree stumps with my teeth."

Cassidy's cheek touched his. "You think we're too stupid to hear it if you don't say it out loud?"

God.

Travis rotated slowly, clinging to Cassidy, looking him in the eye and bracing himself. "You deserve to hear the words as well."

A mesmerizing green gaze caught him as Cassidy's grin widened. "They'll happen. When you're ready."

"*Ohhh*, are you two planning something?" Ashley asked from the doorway to the living room. "Because, game on."

Travis held Cassidy for another moment, not letting his friend, *his lover*, escape yet. "I've got lots of things planned, but the first involves two certain people, if they're willing."

Cassidy leaned in and kissed him. Open mouths, tongues slipping past each other. The scruff on his chin scratching Travis.

There were hands at his belt. Travis found his jeans stripped away as he willingly jerked his shirt over his head before doing the same for Cassidy. For Ashley. Clothes were tossed aside as the hunger between them increased.

Hands brushed everywhere for fleeting moments, caressing hips, slipping over the ridges of muscles, tugging one lover closer, switching to the other. They moved with an easy rhythm, all about giving, not taking. A kiss to one, then the other. Travis cupped Ashley's breasts and Cassidy accepted the offering, lapping at the tight peaks until she was writhing between them.

The long, heavy length of his cock rested between her ass cheeks, and Ashley rocked her hips, rubbing against him, egging him on. She ground over Cassidy's cock as well, her breathing picking up as they used their fingers to tease her.

"Looks like someone is in the middle today." Cassidy groaned as she stroked his cock. "You want to be in a sandwich between us, baby?"

She all but purred. "Hell, yes. *Ohhh...*"

Travis had moved in anticipation, grabbing the lube and slicking it between her ass cheeks. He played with the tight hole there as Cassidy's hands covered her sex. Travis stared over her shoulder to watch Cassidy slip his long fingers into her, thumb resting over her clit. Travis matched the motion, his finger easing lube into her tight passage.

Ashley dropped her head back on his shoulder. "I'm tingling all over."

Travis nuzzled her until she gave him her lips, Cassidy sneaking out to pull on a condom before taking over the kissing and letting Travis suit up as well.

Cassidy sat on the couch and patted his lap. "Come on, woman. Ride me."

No hesitation. Ashley crawled up and lowered herself over him, rocking slowly as she worked herself down on Cassidy's thick cock. They kissed again, then glanced over her shoulder in expectation.

Travis joined them, Cassidy's hands pulling Ashley's ass cheeks apart and giving him lots of room to place the head of his cock to her hole and press forward.

A long, low moan escaped her, and Travis damn near lost it. Watching his cock slip into her, feeling her heat surround him. And Cassidy—he slid his hands off Ashley's ass and stroked Travis best he could.

They were sandwiched together, perfect, so when Travis leaned forward he could kiss either of them. Hold on to them and look them in the eye and try to let it out how much they meant to him.

Cassidy thrust his hips up as they supported Ashley between them, two cocks fucking her. Cassidy's hard length was damn near rubbing his, separated only by the thin layer inside her body. Travis thrust in all the way and savoured the extra edge of pleasure he got from it being two of them giving to her.

The three of them, all tangled together as one.

"Oh, fuck. T. I'm going to come."

Travis slipped his hand between them, over Ashley's stomach to circle her clit, teasing the line between where Cassidy entered her body. "Hang on..."

"*Fuck.*"

Cassidy squeezed his eyes shut and Ashley laughed, using

her legs to unmercifully bounce herself harder on his cock. "Come on, Cass. You like it when I do this?"

Cassidy gasped, eyes popping open, mouth wide.

It only made Ashley laugh louder as she reached back to cradle Travis's neck and accept his mouth against hers.

A moment later she arched hard, a cry escaping her lips as she came, and that was it. Travis shuddered to a stop, buried deep, able to feel Cassidy lose it. Their cocks jerked inside her soft body, her torso melting on top of Cassidy as she went boneless but for the rocking aftershocks.

Travis panted, a slick of sweat over his body as he blanketed them, unable to stop touching. Caressing. A kiss between her shoulders. A nip to Cassidy's chin that made him smile as he relaxed into the couch cushions.

Travis hadn't said the words, it was true, but for now this was what he could give. His actions, not only during sex but the things he was doing to make them a home. To find a way that they could stay together heading into the future.

Once that was the only possible outcome, he figured the words would explode out.

Cassidy cupped his face, his green eyes boring into Travis as he nodded, then touched his lips to Ashley's temple, brushing her long hair out of the way.

Disheveled. Sweaty. Sex soaked.

"The picture looks good from this angle," Ashley whispered.

Travis twisted his head. Not toward the wall where her artwork hung, but to take in both Ashley and Cassidy as they sprawled under him. Her hair was tousled around her, Cassidy's fingers gently stroking through the strands. Travis clung to them both, his fingers linked with Cassidy's other hand where it rested on her thigh.

"The view is perfect from this angle as well."

27

___

The local fairgrounds were already showing signs of the full-out picnic activities planned for Saturday. Mother Nature had cooperated with a gorgeous fall day, the annual September event a familiar time to get involved in the community before the snow descended in late October.

Travis pulled into the gravel parking lot, waving at the fellow in the orange vest working the gate. The man smiled at Travis before glancing into the truck. His happy expression faded as he spotted both Ashley and Cassidy.

Ashley forced herself to look away, choosing instead to focus on the white-topped tents being raised on the grassy space, bright-coloured flags fluttering around the edges.

Not everyone would be happy to see her and the boys at the picnic, but not everyone would be jerks, either. What had Jaxi told her? Stupid people would act like stupid people—she had to ignore them.

Cassidy took her hand and helped her down from the high cab of Travis's truck, brushing a kiss against her temple on the sly before giving her more room.

"You headed anywhere in particular?" he asked as she reached back in and grabbed the package she'd brought as her contribution for a local fundraiser.

"Vicki said she and the girls were setting up coffee first thing. I'll meet them there, then we'll wander for a while."

Travis emerged from around the truck and slipped in front of her. "We're going to join in the baseball game later if you feel like cheering us on."

"You know it." She gave him a wink. "And barring that, I'll meet you at the pie tent, right?"

"She's got your number, T," Cassidy teased.

"Of course she does." Travis tugged her close and kissed her, giving her no opportunity to protest. She tried to wiggle free, but that only got her pinned tighter in place until she relaxed and accepted his caress, sighing happily when he finally let her go.

"I shouldn't have let you do that," she complained.

"You didn't let me do anything. I took what I wanted. Now get going, Cassidy and I have important things to do." He smacked her on the butt, directing her toward the food area.

"The colouring contest doesn't start for hours," Ashley taunted, skipping away as Cassidy offered to smack her ass as well.

"I'll get you for that later," Cassidy promised.

She took a few steps before pausing and glancing back at them. They were still watching her, standing side by side like light and dark bookends. Strong, solid—one with his gentle giving, the other intense in his passions.

The sight was becoming more and more familiar, her guys with their unique smiles and bright eyes. In contrast to the cocky lean to Travis's torso, Cassidy stood straighter, his shoulders pulled back and spine stiff as he rested about a foot apart from Travis. They weren't touching but they were together, connected in a way that was all too clear to her.

Yeah, life wasn't one hundred percent perfect, but the good bits were still making up for the rough moments.

She blew them a kiss then headed to find Vicki.

All the Coleman women were in one spot. Jaxi was hip deep coordinating the men carrying in chairs to place at the long dinner tables. Beth and Hope arranged tablecloths. Marion was measuring out coffee into two-foot-tall urns.

"Hi, all," Ashley called. "Put me to work."

Vicki pulled out another set of cups from a box and arranged them on the folding table they were gathered around. "Hey, you made it."

"Sorry I'm late. We would have been here earlier, but the guys took longer than expected to load up on firewood. Marion, Travis said you needed some at the house?"

Mrs. Coleman nodded. "Mike didn't get around to filling the wood shed this summer, but the boys didn't need to start on it this morning."

"The timing shouldn't have been a problem," Ashley insisted. "They were being lazy butts this morning and should have started sooner. They'll stop and drop off the load after the picnic, if that works for you."

"We appreciate it." Marion looked as if she were about to say something else then wrinkled her nose and went back to her task.

Ashley tried not to let it bother her, but this time it was pretty clear something was off. Beth and Hope exchanged glances before Hope left the cloth behind and stepped closer. "I have a job I've been waiting to do until you arrived. You brought something for the raffle table?"

Ashley held up her package.

"Oh, are you going over there right now?" Vicki wiped her hands and slid from behind the cups. "I have something to contribute, so I should come with you."

"What?" Beth laughed. "You're abandoning us?"

"You still have Jaxi," Hope pointed out. "She can get all this set up in about ten minutes flat if you don't get in her way."

"I heard that," Jaxi called. "You wait, Hope Coleman. I'll put you down to host Thanksgiving dinner this year."

Hope laughed, slipping her arm around Ashley and guiding her from under the tent area past Jaxi. "Not a threat, girl. I know damn well you want to host, so try again."

Jaxi winked, glancing back at Marion before lowering her voice. "Ashley, she's not mad at you. Really."

So Jaxi had said before, but Ashley was getting tired of the games.

Vicki popped up beside them, her feet turning over double time to keep up with Ashley's and Hope's longer strides. "So, after we drop these things at the raffle table, you want to find the guys?"

"I thought they were playing ball?" Ashley asked.

"Not until after lunch." Hope pointed the direction they needed to head. "They're supposed to watch the kids this morning, but knowing them? I bet Blake and Daniel are entertaining the lot while our guys have snuck off to the music stand or they're sweet-talking people into cooking them corndogs early."

Ashley wasn't sure she liked the sound of that. "I'm game for interrupting their sweet-talking..."

Vicki laughed. "Oh, girl. Don't be jealous."

"Exactly." Hope rolled her eyes. "I mean, tell the truth now, you really think Cassidy is going to look at someone else when he's got you?"

"Got you *and* Travis...?" Vicki snickered, then tugged Ashley to a stop. She glanced around to make sure they were alone. "Okay, true confessions. Back at camp, when I found out you were doing them both, I had this blazing hot streak of envy for all of three seconds."

Hope frowned. "It passed that fast?"

Vicki grinned. "Well, I remembered I was damn happy with Joel, but I also figured no way did I have the energy to keep up with two guys. You must be exhausted."

The teasing tone was real—Vicki truly had gotten over whatever concerns she had, and Ashley was glad. "Well, remember if I feel like telling them to go fly a kite, they cannot only deal with hard-ons themselves, but they have each other. And once they start fooling around, I tell you, my energy usually comes back damn quick."

"Is it just me, or is this an usually hot fall day?" Hope asked, fanning herself with her hand. She bumped Ashley. "Enough naughty tale-telling, let's get the goods dropped off so we can search out the sexy men in our lives."

Ashley carried a cheerful glow all the way up to the raffle table.

The stern-faced woman behind the counter knocked off a bit of her happy buzz. She glanced at both Ashley and Vicki then focused on Hope with only a slightly less disturbed expression.

"Hope. I wondered if you'd bring something for us."

"I had signed up, Mrs. Leigh." Hope placed a wrapped package on the tabletop. "Have you met the others yet? This is Vicki and Ashley. They both brought something to contribute to the raffle."

"Well, yes, I know Vicki." Mrs. Leigh didn't meet her eyes. "I suppose it would be all right."

Hope's gaze darkened, a spark of heat and anger in her eyes that reflected what was in Ashley's gut. "I don't know why it wouldn't be okay. This is a fund raiser for the pre-school and after-school care program, isn't it?"

"Well, yes, but the group is picky about who they take contributions from." Mrs. Leigh didn't even try to hide her sniff as she examined Ashley again.

Ashley's ears burned like fire. "So, only people with children, or only people who have lived in the community for years? I didn't see that on the request for donations that was posted in the grocery store."

"Hope, is there a problem?" A younger woman joined Mrs. Leigh who scurried off with a final look of disgust in Ashley's direction.

"Hi, Katy." Hope sighed. "Mrs. Leigh was giving us a sparkling demonstration of her bigotry. We're okay now, if you're interested in the items Vicki and Ashley brought to donate."

"Of course we are." Katy clicked her tongue after Mrs. Leigh's retreating back. "If she'd spend less time all *oh-my-goodnessing* at the nasty things in her brain, she might become a better person."

"It's okay. No harm done," Ashley offered. It wasn't as if being called dirty rubbage by someone whose opinion didn't matter should hurt.

Only...it did.

She focused on unwrapping her parcel. *Ohhhs* and *ahhhs* bounced back at her as Katy snatched up the drawing to examine it closer.

Bold lines leapt off the page. A pencil sketch of Travis on horseback, his hat pulled low but his eyes still visible as he grinned at her, the rolling land of the Six Pack ranch in the background.

"Wow, you did this?"

Ashley laughed at the awestruck tone in the young woman's voice. "With my own little hands. It's not much, but I'm in the middle of a deadline. That's one of my rough works for the larger paintings I'm preparing. Next year I'll know ahead of time, and I can arrange to do more."

Katy twisted the picture to face the three of them, shaking her head. "Now, don't you dare go cutting this down. It's incredible, and it's going to make a lot of money for the kids, so thank you."

"Gee, overachiever." Vicki hip-bumped her. "I only brought cookies."

Hope laughed. "You feed us, we'll keep you in quilts and paintings, right, Ashley?"

"Right." Like a yo-yo, her emotions were jerked up and down and up again. They passed over the charity items and paced slowly through the fairgrounds, the press of bodies increasing as the day grew later.

Ashley thoroughly enjoyed her time with the other women, laughing as Hope snarked out another sharp-witted comment. Vicki proved she had deadly accuracy on a few of the throwing games, the guys running them stepping back a little quicker after she'd knocked the piles of bottles over on the first throw a few times.

"Remind me not to make you angry when you're holding a ball." Ashley nibbled on the corndog she'd been handed by a girl who was maybe ten years old—nothing to worry about being sweet-talked there, she decided.

A group of teenage boys raced up, crowding around them. One whipped out a squirt bottle of mustard probably stolen from the picnic area and squeezed it hard, a stream of yellow stickiness spraying all over Ashley's face and chest.

He was gone before she or Vicki could get their hands on him.

"Darryl Hannes, I'm calling your parents. And Mark—and..." Hope shouted after the troublemakers even as Ashley caught Vicki by the arm before she could sprint after them.

"Don't bother," Ashley ordered. "I just want to get cleaned up."

"*Brats.*" Vicki glared after the boys then gestured to one side. "I'm so sorry. Come on, the washhouse is over here."

Ashley let herself be led away, the heads turning to rubberneck more annoying in a way than the childish assault. She waved off Vicki's help. "I'll be fine," she snapped.

Vicki jerked back.

Fuck. Ashley softened her tone and tried again. "Sorry, I'm a bit grumpy. Let me get washed up, and I'll meet you at the ball diamond."

"You sure?" Hope asked.

"Positive." A large blob of yellow slid down her chest and fell to the grass. "Gack, I hate mustard."

"We'll tell their parents. Beth will have all their numbers from the high school." Hope shook her head. "Little idiots."

Who were only following the cues of the big idiots around them. Ashley sighed. "Go. I'll be there in a bit."

Vicki refused to budge. "Deal with it. I'm staying. Hope can go rain down terror on the brats, I'm sticking with you."

There was a lump in Ashley's throat as Vicki tugged her into the washhouse, muttering under her breath. She soaked down a couple hand towels while Ashley did her best to remove the surface layers first.

Five minutes later Ashley was ready to burst out laughing. "I look like I bought a malfunctioning tanning lotion."

Vicki tossed the stained towels in the trash. "Gotta laugh or you'll cry, right?"

"Pretty much." Ashley leaned back on a stall door and gave Vicki a tired smile. "Thanks. For your help, and for understanding."

"I understand more than you know. People can be a pain in the butt, and I can handle it. It's when they hit me in the heart that I lose perspective." Vicki wrinkled her nose. "I'm still considered one of the town bad girls, you know. Hanging out with me isn't helping matters."

"Fuck that noise," Ashley snapped. "You're a saint compared

to the bullshit I see going on. And I'll own it—my life and choices aren't typical. But they are mine. If people don't like it, they should leave me the hell alone, not try to call down fire and brimstone."

She found herself caught in a tight embrace as Vicki latched on and squeezed. Nothing more, just a physical acceptance that closed Ashley's throat. She soaked in it for a minute.

"Again, thanks."

Vicki smiled, her eyes suspiciously moist. "Yeah, well, let's not tell Joel or your guys that we've been hugging, or they might get ideas about naked pillow fights. Us being the corruptors that we are."

Ashley choked out a laugh. She squeezed Vicki's fingers briefly then slipped into a toilet stall.

She was about to leave when she heard a mock whisper from a familiar voice. "It's disgusting, you know. No decent people would go out in public like that."

Mrs. Leigh. How lovely.

Ashley sat back down on the toilet seat and rested her head on the sidewall to wait out the catty conversation. She should march out and be done with it, but she couldn't take another round of evil eyes and outraged huffs. Besides, maybe it would be entertaining to discover what deviant behaviours the old gossip thought she and the boys were getting up to out in their evil house of sin.

Pretty much nothing interesting though. The woman needed a new vocabulary as she seemed stuck on *filthy, horrifying* and *morally disgusting.*

Only Ashley was disgusted and horrified herself when the conversation took a turn in direction.

"I'm not surprised, though," Mrs. Leigh continued. "That Marion Coleman has always considered herself above the rest of us. And see where it's gotten her? Sons who are attracted to the worst possible elements of society. One as good as a whore—breaks my heart to think of that sweet, young Joel tying himself to that Hansol creature. And Matt, well, sleeping with one sister before marrying the other?"

"Blake Coleman and Daniel have good strong marriages," another woman protested.

"Beth Coleman is a saint, and Daniel, but they got themselves off that cursed Six Pack land as soon as they could, you notice? And that Jaxi acts just as high and mighty as Marion, putting on airs and bossing around better women than her. I told Marion years ago she was setting up for a fall, and now she has. I called her last week and told her again. That lot will come to be nothing but trouble, and this new one is the worst to date. Sleeping with two men."

The whispers dropped to a scandalous hush. "I heard the two men are...*involved*...as well."

"Marion's not going to be welcome anywhere in town. Or Mike. There's talk—"

That was enough. Ashley slammed open the door and simply stood there in the doorframe, all her indignation hopefully clear and visible. "You know, shit-talk me all you want, but leave Mike and Marion Coleman out of it. They don't run their children's lives, and they're good people. Far better than those who thrive on nasty comments and dirty innuendo."

The women fled, dismay on a few faces, but mostly disgust—there was that word again. She figured if they had a scarlet letter with them they would have slapped it on her chest right there and then.

"And it's pretty incredible sleeping with two men at one time," she called after them, "but I won't bother to describe it because you'd probably just stroke off wishing you were me."

Soft arms slipped around her waist and hugged her tight

again, but this time Vicki's good intentions couldn't push aside the coldness inside.

Ashley twisted, staring into indignant brown eyes and a flushed freckled face. "You heard that crap?"

Vicki nodded. "The stinky attitudes are familiar, but you know what? They are getting better."

Ashley's face must have shown her shock because Vicki shrugged.

"Well, they are. It hurts and it's horrid, but...there were only a couple women talking dirt this time. For the most part they felt guilty when they realized you'd heard them. I bet they'll be thinking harder in the next while every time someone mentions you in a positive way. I mean, consider at the raffle booth. Katy Thompson loves you, and she's going to be singing your praises all day long. She's also got a ton of big brothers who she will have trained in no time to behave." Vicki held her close, lowering her voice. "I don't like it either when people are catty, but it cuts far less now that I have Joel who I know loves me, and the rest of the family."

"That's the part I don't know about," Ashley muttered. "Good *God*, no wonder Marion is giving me the cold shoulder. If she's being set on by bigots like Mrs. Leigh with rotten attitudes..." Ashley shook her head. "I never intended to upset the Colemans. None of us did—Travis and Cassidy and I just want to be together. We're not trying to tear the world apart."

"I know." Vicki gave her a final squeeze.

After considering all that she'd wanted to accomplish, this was the final straw. "I'm going home."

"But the guys are at the ball field. And..." Vicki sighed. Nodded. "...you want to go home. No problem. You need a ride?"

"Please?"

The fifteen-minute ride home was fairly quiet. Vicki stopped outside the trailer, engine still running. "You change your mind and want to come back you call me, okay?"

"I will, but I think I'll work on some of my pictures. Get my mind off the stupid people and back on the good ones."

"That's it." Vicki touched her hand. "*You're* one of the good ones. You really are, okay?"

Ashley laughed. "Thanks. You're a sweetheart, and if Joel hadn't already snapped you up, I'd fall in love with you myself."

"Stop flirting," Vicki scolded, shaking a finger at her. "I'm setting up a dinner with you guys and us this coming week, you got it?"

"Got it. And hey, I'm turning off my phone to work, so tell the guys I'm at home, will you?"

Ashley watched the truck disappear into the distance before heading into the barn. If her mind was going to be filled with anger and confusion, she might as well use the energy productively.

High one minute, low the next. It really wasn't right, in so many ways.

The love she felt for Travis and Cassidy hadn't changed, but moving back to Rocky had turned everything on its head. Maybe they had been in an idyllic setting before, cut off from the world. Had the isolation changed the truth? Blurred her vision and caused her to see things that didn't exist? Or was it *this* world that was wrong, cutting and cruel, where people were mistreated not for their actions but because of the judgmental opinions of others?

Marion Coleman might not have been on the top of Ashley's kissy-kissy list, but she was a good person. Travis had shared again and again how accepting and loving she'd been, and all the family clung to her as a solid pillar of support.

Hurting an innocent woman indirectly put a whole new twist

on the situation. Ashley could stick to her guns if it was just her being called names, but this...

She tossed paint at her canvases for a solid hour before climbing into the attic area and lying in the hammock Travis had hung for her in the eaves.

The gentle sway of the material cradling her helped her to slow down, her breathing settling even as her mind raced. Outside the window were green dusted fields, the meandering trail of Whiskey Creek visible by the line of trees following its banks.

Her eyes closed, and she saw Travis's bold grin, Cassidy's gentler beam. Felt their firm touches and caring actions. Like a beautiful scene painted in her mind, memories of time with them rose as sleep rolled in to silence the chaos. She swore she could smell the aroma of the campfires where they'd lingered each night, the hazy scent of wood smoke part and parcel of everything she'd experienced that summer.

Everything she cherished was a piece of a paradise, and the rest a touch of hell, and she wasn't sure how she was going to survive making a decision.

At what point did being in love mean she shouldn't stay?

28

It wasn't up front and obvious, whatever was itching Cassidy's nerves, but it was enough to make him wary. He sat in the lawn chair next to Travis while Blake Coleman and a slowly growing group gathered to talk about nothing.

The *looks* were there at times—not from Travis's family, but from the other guys. As if they were waiting for that moment when he or Travis would turn into something unnatural and come racing after them.

Or maybe he was being overdramatic and should get the hell over himself.

Blake shook his head. "I still say it's not likely we'd have a zombie apocalypse in our part of the country."

"What, the air is too clear or something?" Matt teased. "Hate to tell you this, but those stories are fantasy. They can happen anywhere the writers want to put them, and Rocky is as good as any other spot for the end of the world to descend into a pile of rotting limbs and flesh-eating crazies."

"But we'd deal with them far faster than the idiots on TV,"

one of the guys snapped. "I mean, seriously. *Shoot, shovel and shut up* works in more ways than one."

"You're such a class act, Mitch," Travis drawled. "You probably think you could simply outrun them."

Mitch shrugged. "Don't have to be the fastest runner, you know. Only have to outrun you."

"You can try. You. Can. Try."

Mitch shuffled to his feet and waved his beer bottle in the air. "I'll round up the rest of my team and we can hit the field."

"Deal." Travis frowned at Blake as Mitch disappeared. "Although how you plan on playing ball with three kids in tow is beyond me."

"Jaxi is coming to grab them. Trust me." Blake scooped up the smallest of the lot from the blanket he'd spread at his feet and wiggled her in front of him. "Although you, little princess, could be a fine distraction, couldn't you?"

He blew a raspberry on Lena's belly, which started all three girls shrieking as the twins crawled off their uncles and attempted to get to their dad in mock terror of being tickled.

A hand landed on Cassidy's forearm. "Welcome to kid central," Travis apologized.

"Hey, it's a part of spending time with your family. I don't mind much." He couldn't keep his eyes off the kids, in fact. Daniel's sons were older, but they too seemed content to hang around, the youngest taking total advantage of being small enough to have crawled into Daniel's lap. Robbie gloated as if he'd claimed prime real estate.

Family. Cassidy's soul soaked it up like a sponge.

Conversation wrapped around them. For the longest time Cassidy didn't realize that Travis was still holding him. It was so comfortable and easy. All Travis's brothers were there except for Jesse who had put in a brief appearance before vanishing.

Matt's gaze stalled for a moment where Travis had continued

to absently stroke his thumb back and forth on Cassidy's arm. Cassidy met Matt's eyes and waited on edge, ready to look away in self-defense if he saw any condemnation or disgust.

All that happened was Matt glanced at Travis, then back to Cassidy as one side of his lips twitched upward in a smile.

Every step forward brought Cassidy more hope.

Higher-pitched women's laughter drifted toward them, and Travis's fingers tightened briefly before slipping away, both of them twisting in their chairs, eager for a sight of Ashley.

She wasn't in the group of women blending in and grabbing on to their men.

Jaxi nabbed the baby from Blake. "You done riling up your women?"

Blake caught her close, and cradling Lena between them, he dipped her, kissing her soundly to the wild applause of the rest of the group.

When he finally stood them up, her cheeks were flushed. "You feel riled enough?" Blake asked.

Cassidy was out of his chair, looking around to see if Ashley was bringing up the rear. "Where's Ash?"

Vicki stepped forward, Joel at her side, his arm looped around her waist. "She decided to head home early. I dropped her off."

"She okay? Why didn't she tell us?" Travis pulled out his cell phone.

"She turned off her cell phone," Vicki warned. She wiggled on the spot before spilling the rest. "Ashley's okay. A little... pissed. Couple of women were talking out of line, and some kids pulled a prank on her. Nothing terrible, but she'd had enough."

Travis pulled out his keys. "I'm going to—"

"Travis." Blake shook his head. "Give her some space," he suggested.

"I think he's right," Vicki added. "She said she was going to get some work done."

"Play a game, then you guys can head home." Joel patted Travis on the shoulder. "Gives her time to cool off, and you'll still get out of clean-up here at the picnic. We'll do your share."

Travis glanced at Cassidy. "What do you think?"

He didn't like it, but it made sense. "If we leave right after the game."

Travis nodded, and the rest of the clan cheered.

The opposite team was assembling, and in spite of his concern over Ashley, Cassidy had to smile. "We're playing the Thompson boys?"

"And a few others. Gage Jenick, some of the volunteer firefighters."

The guys he'd been working with daily rambled in, and the dirt talk picked up.

Cassidy grinned at Clay. "Didn't know you guys played ball."

Clay shrugged. "We play anything to pass the time. Should have said you wanted on the winning team. We could have invited you to join our side."

"Ha." Daniel jabbed him in the chest, seeming unconcerned Clay towered over him by a good four inches. "We'll see who wins."

Matt and Clay eyed each other warily as they passed, and Cassidy was once again reminded these people had years of history together. It was going to take time to become a complete member of the community. Both he and Ashley had a long way to go, and the lack of instant acceptance wasn't really anything against them personally. At least, he could hope.

A couple of innings passed smoothly enough. The scowling man from Traders a few weeks earlier, the one dancing with Katy Thompson, had turned up on Clay's team. Simon hadn't gotten rid of that chip on his shoulder, either, although he seemed to turn on and off the shit talk like a tap when any of Katy's brothers were around. He saved his muttered insults for when Cassidy ran by first base, or when they passed on the field changing sides between innings.

Cassidy tapped Gage on the shoulder as they waited on second base for Gage's team to get another hit. "What's the story with him?" Cassidy asked, tilting his head toward Simon. "He's got that Jekyll-and-Hyde thing going on."

"Simon? He giving you grief?"

"Nothing I can't handle." Cassidy shrugged. "I didn't think he was Katy's type."

A low growl of frustration escaped Gage. "Don't want to talk about it."

Okay, that was telling. Cassidy kept a straight face. "No problem."

"Sorry, that girl gets on my last nerve." Gage glanced at Cassidy. "So. You're with both Ashley and Travis?"

Middle of the ball diamond. Awesome place for this discussion. "Yeah."

The batter missed his swing, and Matt got ready to throw again. Gage nodded slowly. "Cool."

Now Cassidy knew a little of the sense of unreality Travis had talked about while dealing with his brothers. That was it? Cool?

Cassidy would take it. "Thanks for not freaking out."

"Hey, I'd hit Ashley any day of the week, and while Travis isn't my type, he's a good guy. You're lucky to have them." Gage cleared his throat. "And you're not bad yourself. In a totally hetero-guy-making-a-comment way, if you hear me."

There was no way to hold back his laugh. "I hear you."

The ball flew into the sky, and Gage was off, racing toward third base as Cassidy sprinted backward to get a glove on the ball. He stumbled into Travis rushing in from the opposite side, and they crashed to the ground in a tangle.

Travis laughed as he scrambled to his knees and snatched up

the ball, whipping it toward home in a futile attempt to stop a run from scoring. "We have to stop meeting like this," he teased.

He helped Cassidy to his feet and brushed the dust from him, his grin widening as he smacked the dust from Cassidy's pants. But no matter how good it felt, this wasn't the place, and Travis should know better.

"Stop it," Cassidy warned as they pulled apart.

"Can't keep my hands off you," Travis admitted with a sheepish wink before returning to his place in the outfield.

Cassidy got the sentiment, but... "Play it cool, T."

Travis blew a raspberry over his shoulder.

The next inning Cassidy got a hit on his second swing, stopping with dread as he discovered Simon guarding first base.

Simon paced around Cassidy, glancing to see if anyone was nearby before settling in behind him and speaking softly. "Word is going around you like cock."

Cassidy ignored the rude comment, praying for a hit from his team so he could get the hell away before he was tempted to do something involving fists.

"I don't get it, though. It's not like you don't have a woman. I don't see why you'd feel the need to stick your dick in a guy as well."

"Drop it," Cassidy warned.

"I mean, fucking Ashley wouldn't be a hardship. I get that part of it." The guy didn't know when to quit. "But having to look at Travis—or maybe that's the secret. Turn him around and close your eyes, and you're just fucking any hole, right?"

Cassidy's hands were shaking, but he clung to his control. Planting a fist in the man's face wouldn't help make this a community picnic to remember in a good way.

Travis came up to bat, catcalls from the outfield resumed, and Cassidy inched his way to the side, ready to run.

The bastard on first didn't like to be ignored. He grabbed a hand of Cassidy's shirt, and as the ball sped toward Travis, Simon stuck his foot between Cassidy's legs and shoved, sending Cassidy sprawling.

Simon aimed a kick at Cassidy's legs to stop him from regaining his feet. "Or maybe that's the other part. Maybe you're the one on the bottom, the one being fucked, you freak—"

From the outfield a body slammed into Simon, tumbling him to the ground.

"Shut up, asshole." Gage Jenick had Simon pinned, taking a blow or two before nailing down Simon's flailing arms. He might have gotten in a swing at Simon's face in the process. "You want to be a jerk, do it on your own time and somewhere else."

"You like this faggot?" Simon sneered.

"None of my business what he's doing or who he's doing in bed, but yes, I like him. He's a hard worker and a decent guy, so shut your judgmental trap."

Simon struggled again, but Gage held him tight.

The rest of the game was on hold as Travis raced over and pulled Cassidy to vertical for the second time that day. "You okay?"

Cassidy nodded as he brushed the dirt off. "A slight misunderstanding."

"If you say so," Gage drawled. "Simon here was planning on going somewhere else, isn't that right?"

Travis glared at Simon who had staggered to his feet, wiping at the blood dripping from his nose. The man looked around, but finding no support, turned and fled the field.

It was uncomfortable and quiet for a moment before Clay shouted from the pitcher's mound. "You guys done dancing over there?"

Gage winked at Travis and Cassidy before turning to answer. "Hold on to your britches. I'm taking over first base—Simon remembered he's got an appointment."

Travis headed back to the batter's mound while Cassidy and Gage moved into position.

Cassidy offered a hand. "Appreciate what you did."

Gage shook it firmly. "Yeah, well, I've been wanting a reason to punch Simon for a long time, so thank you for the opportunity."

Cassidy laughed and stepped back into position. "You're okay."

"You're about to lose, but you're okay as well."

The crack of the ball flying into the air sent Cassidy racing for second base. Out in the distance, a cloud of smoke rose skyward, and Cassidy slowed to a walk. He was pretty sure he was looking north and if he was…that might be on Coleman land.

Right about then the fire alarm at the downtown station rang, and half the opposition abandoned their positions, racing toward the dugout, cell phones going off.

Cassidy jogged back to join Travis and the rest of the Coleman team. "That fire near your land?"

Travis nodded. "Come on, the game is over anyway. Let's check with Gage what he's heard."

They caught up with Gage near the parking lot. "What's the word?" Travis called.

Gage shouted over his shoulder. "Not good. Sounds like your place, Travis. Not the trailer, but down by the coulee. Some kids lighting grassfires that got out of control. One of them got scared and called it in. We're bringing the truck."

Cassidy's stomach fell. "The coulee? T, that's where the—"

"The barn. Ashley's studio. I know. Come on."

29

———

Travis shattered driving laws on the way home, spinning around corners as he took back-road shortcuts.

"She might be in the trailer." Cassidy clung to the dash as they bounced over washboard gravel.

"Try her cell," Travis ordered.

Only a moment later Cassidy shook his head. "Still offline."

"Call Joel. Tell him and Vicki to stop at the trailer and see if she's sleeping or something. He can let us know." He wasn't going to stop to find out. Her studio was the most dangerous place to be at the moment. "And have him warn everyone to leave the main road open for the fire truck."

Cassidy didn't answer, just followed directions then hung on tight, his other hand on Travis's shoulder, squeezing painfully hard. "She's got to be okay."

It wasn't a question, wasn't quite a comment, but either way Travis couldn't respond as his throat tightened.

Somewhere behind him there was a line of vehicles as the entire Coleman clan headed north. He had the truck in high gear, tires screaming as he took the back loop to the barn, skidding up to the building with growing horror in his heart.

The ancient structure wasn't going to last. The billows of grey smoke escaping from the open doors on the second-level hayloft warned there was a whole lot inside the building already on fire and smoldering.

Canvases were tossed haphazardly outside the large barn doors.

"She's here," Cassidy snapped, pointing at the pile. "God, she's trying to get her paintings out."

"The building could collapse, Cass." Travis was out of the truck and headed for the barn doors at a dead run. The entire time his mind pulsed with her name. With the urgency to swing her into his arms and keep her safe. Having Cassidy beside him only made it worse in a way. "Don't take chances," he ordered.

"Don't think of stopping me." Cassidy rushed through the open doors, Travis hard on his heels. "Ashley. Where are you?"

There was no answer to his shout, but plenty of noise. In the back corner of the barn, part of the second story gave way, an avalanche of bales cascading through the opening. They burst when they hit the ground, straw flying up, timbers crackling as flames hungrily licked their way across the tops of the wooden stalls.

Everywhere Travis looked, things were burning. The crates Ashley had stacked to use as storage for her paints glowed with flickers of pink and purple tossed in. Most of her remaining canvases were destroyed, the white sheets she'd used to protect them from the dust edged with black against a background of red.

"Ashley," Cassidy cried again. He twirled toward Travis, terror in his eyes. "In the loft?"

For a second Travis peered at the half-destroyed roof with sick fear shaking his limbs. Another section teetered on the edge of falling. "She couldn't be. There are paintings outside."

Which meant she had to be somewhere close. A waft of smoke blinded him, choking his breath. "Stay low," he warned Cassidy.

They fell to their knees. Travis snapped a finger to the left. "Check behind the paintings. See if she collapsed. I'll look in the storage area."

Cassidy nodded, his face tight with fear. "I love you, T."

He was gone before Travis could respond.

Travis moved forward, his limbs taking him toward the storage area even as his mind screamed a warning that was where the ATV was parked. An ATV full of fuel with extra jerry cans stacked along the wall.

His eyes watered as he peered back and forth in vain looking for some sign of—

A tangle of blonde hair, nearly hidden by a mass of straw. "Ashley."

Travis scrambled on all fours to her side, lifting off the heavy timber across her legs to reach her body. He eyed her for a moment, taking in the blood streaking her forehead. If this were a typical situation, he wouldn't have moved her, but the sounds of destruction around them continued to escalate.

He did the fastest visual check ever for broken limbs. "Ashley, baby. Open your eyes. We need to get out of here."

She moaned, lashes fluttering, gasping for air as she curled onto her side against him.

He lifted her, pressing her to his chest. "Sorry for hurting you, love."

Ashley curled her fingers around his neck, a sickening cough racking her. He cupped the back of her head and held her tight to his body then held his breath and raced for the main doors.

The sound of the first jerry can igniting echoed off the roof. It reminded him of the time he'd set off firecrackers in the barn. Loud, frightening, but mostly a warning of the more dangerous results that would follow, in that case when his dad got ahold of him to apply some well-deserved punishment.

There were more explosions to come, and the risks would only increase. He stumbled forward, waiting until he was back in the main area where there was a chance Cassidy would hear him. "I have her. Get out, get out now."

In the back, a second can caught fire, the sickening sound of all the available oxygen being consumed in a *whoosh* drowned out in the explosion that shot toward the ceiling. Another eardrum-shattering blast was followed by a horrifying creaking noise, and Travis risked a glance upward. Nothing but smoke, but that warning was impossible to ignore...

The ceiling was giving way.

A strong arm circled his shoulder as Cassidy joined them, directing their path through the near-whiteout conditions. The cry of a siren growing louder beckoned them forward. The increased visibility at the door gave Travis the strength to hang on, rushing out and away from the building with his precious burden, Cassidy half holding him up, half being supported.

Shouts rang from the right as the volunteer fire truck pulled in and men leapt out, hoses being pulled. Travis ignored them and kept moving, headed to the ambulance bringing up the rear.

"Come on, Ashley, open those pretty eyes of yours." Cassidy stroked her forehead, his voice tight from the smoke and fear. "You're safe, baby. We got you."

"My paintings." The words barely audible, wheezed out as she struggled to sit up.

God. Travis knew the damages were going to break her heart. "Lie still. You have to see the paramedics."

They were surrounded before she could protest. He and Cassidy had to step back. Had to open his arms and let the medical staff take her.

Something inside him broke.

Watching them pull a mask over her face, her eyes wide and frightened, twisted his guts to raw meat. Travis shoved himself forward to catch hold of her reaching fingers. He held on to his meager control with everything he had left.

Cassidy was there, his body close to Travis's, his fingers also wrapped around Ashley's. Grime and ashes were smeared on his face, his blond hair filthy with it. In the distance, water met flames and burst into red-hot steam, the sound rolling around them and echoing in Travis's ears.

"We need to look you over, Travis. Cassidy as well." What was probably a familiar face blurred before him. "You have to let her go. Just for a minute."

"I'm never letting her go," Travis whispered. He leaned in and pressed a kiss to her forehead. "Hang on, sweetheart. We'll be right beside you, okay? Me and Cassidy, we're going to be right beside you all the way."

She squeezed his fingers.

Travis let them place her on the gurney, watching closely as they started all kinds of medical procedures that rocked him even harder. Then the paramedics lifted her and she was gone into the back of the ambulance.

He twisted to find Cassidy staring, green eyes full of fear and sorrow. Travis stepped forward, ignoring the medical person at his side. He caught Cassidy around the neck and leaned their foreheads together until Cassidy was forced to look him in the eye. "Hey, listen to me. She's going to be okay. You got that?"

Cassidy blinked hard. "God, I was so scared."

"Me too," Travis confessed, the words sneaking past lips that felt like sandpaper. "But she's going to be okay, and we're going to make sure that nothing like this ever happens again."

Cassidy caught Travis's sleeves tightly with his big fists. "I love you, T. I love her. I can't lose either of you."

The pain that had hovered in his mind for years, the fear of not being accepted for who he was—all of his frustrations exploded like an echo from the fire. They rushed from him to be replaced by a burning need to give. He wanted to heal Cassidy's and Ashley's hurts and ease all their pains. There was nothing he wouldn't sacrifice for them. For the two people who had taken his world by storm and not only smacked him upside the head, but taught him that he could be himself and it was enough. That he could be himself and it would make him more than he'd been pretending to be while playing games.

Travis dragged Cassidy against him and hugged him fiercely before letting him go. "Come on, let the paramedic take a look at you."

He waited until Cassidy had given in before turning to find Ashley.

Nothing was ever going to be the same again.

Travis had finally given up and closed his eyes, leaning back in the chair beside Ashley's bed. The dark smudges under his eyes were nearly as deep as the ones under hers. The shower he'd stolen barely half an hour ago had washed away the grime, but couldn't erase the other results of the fire.

From his chair on the opposite side of the bed, Cassidy rubbed his thumb slowly over the back of her hand, staring at long lashes resting against pale cheeks. Oxygen tubes led to her nostrils. The thin sound of the machine dispersing its rhythmic dose created a consistent reverberation as if there were an additional person in the room. Eerie. Unnatural.

It had been hours since they'd made it to the hospital. He'd lost track of people in the frantic rush to get Ashley medical attention, but after they'd reached the hospital there had been plenty of family around.

Travis's family. His mom, most of his brothers. Their wives checking in to see if there was anything they could do. In the end they'd all gone home, reassured they would be updated if there was any change. Anything they could do.

The door opened quietly, and Cassidy glanced up to see Vicki and Joel had returned. He lifted a finger to his lips, and they nodded, slipping in without a sound.

Joel stared at his brother then let out a long sigh.

Vicki knelt by Cassidy's side and gave him a quick hug. "How are you doing?"

Cassidy checked, but even at the sound of her voice Travis didn't move. "We're okay. They're still monitoring Ashley. Some smoke inhalation, couple of bad bruises from where the beams collapsed on her."

He was repeating information they already knew, but he couldn't help himself. There was nothing else to say. This was the current reality, no matter how much it sucked.

Another hand pressed on his shoulder as Joel gave him a squeeze. "You want to hear the news now or wait until Travis is awake?"

"Travis is awake." Across the bed Travis lifted a hand in the air, his voice rough and low like he'd been chain smoking for years. His eyes focused quickly as he sat forward. "What's the word on the fire?"

"Vandalism that got out of control. A few of the high school kids thought it would be cool to do a circuit while so many people were at the picnic. Spray painted a few barns, tore up a few fields with their trucks." Joel grimaced. "By the time they hit your place they'd had a few drinks, and leaving rude messages on the backside of the barn wasn't enough."

"Rude messages?" Travis's question was clipped. Tight.

Joel's gaze dropped to Cassidy's for a minute, then back to his brother. "I'd rather not say."

"Don't try to spare my feelings," Cassidy said. "Homophobic slurs aren't going to kill..."

The actual *possibilities* implied in the unsaid part of his sentence crashed into him like an unexpected blow to the jaw. *God.* The band of fear across his chest tightened further, and he had to refrain from squeezing Ashley's hand too tightly.

Travis sat up straighter, his gaze on Ashley's pale face. "They lit the fires on purpose?"

"They said it was an accident. They decided it would be funny to burn a few boxes that were stored outside." Joel folded his arms. "Dad and Blake are looking into it. Deciding if there's enough to press charges. The only good part was one of the kids felt guilty and went back. Said he intended on making sure the fire was out, but it had gotten away, so he phoned it in. The kids certainly didn't know there was anyone around who could get hurt."

Vicki spoke softer as if to make doubly sure Ashley didn't hear. "We pulled aside the paintings that were outside, but they're pretty damaged. I don't know if Ashley can fix them or not."

Every part of the story made Cassidy ache harder. "First she has to get better."

"We won't stay." Joel paced over to his brother. "Just wanted to let you know."

"Thanks." Travis rose and accepted Joel's hug. "I'll call you later."

Vicki wormed into Cassidy's arms and gave him a fierce hug of her own. She pulled back, face tight. "Take care of them, right?"

"Always."

The room was back to silence but for the ventilator.

Silence, and guilt.

Cassidy forced his gaze off Ashley's shallow breathing to Travis. Waiting for a sign of condemnation. For anger.

What he saw was so much more.

"T?"

Travis rose and came around the bed toward him. He knelt and caught Cassidy's hand in his. "I'm sorry for everything that's gone wrong over the past weeks."

Cassidy paused. "There have been shitty moments, that's for damn sure. But I don't think you can take the blame for many of them."

Travis trapped him. Pulled him against his chest and took his lips. Kissed him as if he'd never get another opportunity. Hunger and fear—at that moment they tasted the same, and Cassidy had to shove aside the guilt that flared for feeling a rush of emotion when the woman he'd fallen in love with was still in danger.

But the *man* he loved was kissing him with a need and a hurt that had to be answered. Cassidy caught Travis by the back of the neck and soothed him. Accepted his frantic kisses but also slowed things down. Slipped his fingers over Travis's tight shoulders and pulled until there was enough room between them they could breathe.

Cassidy didn't stop rubbing until Travis stopped shaking.

Jaw firmly set, Travis caught Cassidy's hands. He lifted grey eyes framed by lashes darkened with moisture. "I love you."

The words were spoken loud enough there could be no doubt. Not a casual afterthought. A deliberate and forceful statement.

Cassidy met Travis's intense gaze. "I hear you. I've been hearing you say it for a long time, but it's nice to have the words and actions, T. Nice to have it both ways, because I love you too."

A deep breath shook Travis as tears welled up. "Bastard. Don't make this harder than it already is."

Cassidy couldn't help it. He caressed his thumb along Travis's jaw. "Is it my turn to be the twelve-year-old in this relationship and make a smartass comment about being hard?"

That brought a reluctant smile to Travis's lips. "Sure, we'll take turns. Like everything else."

"Can I have a turn too?" A soft, feminine voice, but raw and ragged.

They jerked apart, spinning toward the bed. Travis found his voice first. "Hey, baby."

Ashley reached up to explore the oxygen tubes looping across her face toward her nostrils. She wrinkled her nose at the IV in the back of her hand then shrugged, slipping her tongue over her lips.

"Let me help." Cassidy leaned over and kissed her gently before grabbing the small container of Vaseline the nurse had left on the side table.

Travis squeezed in, holding on to Cassidy as he reached for Ashley. "How you feeling?"

Ashley swallowed and grimaced. "Like a barn fell on me."

It was funny and yet horrifying. Cassidy caught her fingers and found himself holding Travis's hand at the same time.

"Anyone get hurt?" Ashley asked.

"Just you."

She nodded slowly. "I'll be okay. Once I give up my smoking habit."

Travis attempted a laugh, but the sound died away quickly. "The fire wasn't meant to deliberately hurt you, Ash. Some kids were being fools, and things got out of hand."

Her eyes widened. "Shit, really? I wasn't sure what happened. I was in the loft, thinking, and I must have fallen asleep. When I woke up, there was smoke everywhere."

"You got a lot of that smoke inside you. That's why you're on oxygen," Cassidy explained, stroking her hair back. Ignoring the tubes and brushing her cheek. Needing to touch her—to reassure himself.

"They warned me about that in the ambulance. I'm not freaked out or anything." Her expression tightened, the bright joy she usually exuded checked. "Did my paintings make it? I tried to take a few outside, and then a wall caved in and I got stuck. That part was scary..." Her voice faded away.

"Don't talk too much." Cassidy ignored her question. "Your throat must hurt like crazy."

"Cassidy," she warned. The fire was back in her eyes.

He shook his head. "The ones you took outside are smoke damaged and got bumped around. The rest are gone. I'm sorry."

She closed her eyes and lay back, a tear sneaking from the corner of her eye and breaking his heart. "That fucking sucks."

Travis wiped the moisture from her cheek tenderly. "Once you get out of here, we'll do everything we can to help you."

"Maybe I can get a postponement." Her face tightened in frustration and sorrow. "But...*shit*."

"Why'd you go home, Ash? Who upset you?" Travis asked.

The loss of her paintings had to cut hard, but Cassidy agreed —he wanted to know what had happened.

For a moment it looked as if she wasn't going to answer. Then she sighed and turned her blue eyes on them, sadness in their depths like her heart was breaking. "I know it's going to take time to settle in, and I'm not giving you two up, but you need to know I'm scared."

Travis's body tightened. "Scared of what? Of being hurt again? Because I swear that's never—"

"No," she laughed, the sound turning into a cough that took a few moments to calm. "God, no, not me. It's your mom I'm worried about. And your nephews, and heck, all the family."

Travis shook his head. "What are you talking about?"

"That's why your mom's been so quiet around me. Her

friends are turning on her because I'm here and ruining you. Me and Cassidy." She flicked her gaze to his. "See, you too can be a corruptive influence when you put your mind to it."

God. "Stop joking around, baby, or I'll paddle your fine butt, oxygen or no. Just *who* is turning on Marion?"

"People in town. I overheard it, me and Vicki." She caught Travis's hand. "I want you and Cassidy, but I can't stand to think of your mom getting handed crap because of me. Or little Robbie? Or what about those precious baby girls of Blake and Jaxi's? Down the road, are people going to attack them for being associated with us? People can be dicks to me, and I swear, I'll hand it right back and leave them fucking reeling, but that—?"

Her voice was down to almost nothing. Travis pressed his fingers over her lips to stop the tirade. "I understand. Now, stop talking."

She narrowed her eyes, but the next swallow she grimaced harder than usual. A reluctant nod followed.

"You trust me?" Travis asked, looking between the two of them.

Cassidy answered for them both. "Of course."

Travis cupped Ashley's face tenderly in his palm for a moment before kissing her. "Rest. I'll be back in a bit."

She nodded again, eyelids fluttering closed.

"She's going to be okay," Cassidy reassured him, partly for Travis's sake, partly for his own as they walked to the door.

"She will." Travis stared back at the bed with misery in his eyes. "Can you stay with her? There's something I need to do."

"Sure, but..." Cassidy paused. "Don't do anything drastic, T."

His friend shook himself alert. "Don't worry. I'll be a complete grownup. And for the first time in my life, I know exactly what that means."

He was out the door before Cassidy could stop him.

30

Travis dragged a hand through his hair, pacing back to the large front windows for the third time. The familiar setting of the home he'd grown up in was yet another reminder of what he was about to sacrifice.

Although *sacrifice* was the wrong word. The price was something he was more than willing to pay.

"Sit down," Mike Coleman ordered. "Blake will be here in a minute."

"I'm here." His oldest brother shouldered through the door, marching up to surround Travis in an enormous bear hug.

It helped, having that firm grasp, and it burned, because what he was about to say might hurt the family he cared deeply about. But if it protected the people he loved...

Travis smacked Blake on the back then retreated, facing them both and letting it out. "I can't let this go on. I can't let the people who mean everything to me be in danger like this."

"The vandalism?" Mike asked, pulling out a chair at the long family table and gesturing for them to join him. "RCMP are already looking closer into what happened."

"It's more than the vandalism." Travis shook his head, considering his words carefully. "Dad, I care about you and Mom. Care, hell—I *love* the entire family. More than I ever realized, and it's only hitting home now. You've always been there for me even when you've given me shit. I've learned from you that sometimes the right thing is the toughest thing, but you still do it."

His father nodded slowly. "What do you need to do?"

Travis took a deep breath. "I want to know what it would take to get a buyout on my share of the ranch." Blake's eyes widened. "Not all at once. The goal isn't to ruin the Six Pack holdings. And I'm not saying this is going to happen, because I haven't had time to talk to Cassidy and Ashley, but I didn't want to do that without talking to you first."

A long pause of near silence followed, the *click, click, click* of the pendulum in the cuckoo clock by the front door the only sound.

"I need to know there's another option. A way for me to take my family and set up somewhere they will be safe. Where we can live without worrying about getting hurt or hurting others."

Blake stared at his hands where he'd folded them on the table. "You think you're going to find a better place than right here?"

Familiar anger shot through Travis. "Ashley's in the goddamn hospital, Blake. Not only that, but she's worried sick that Mom is going to be ripped into next, or one of the girls, or the kids."

"What?" Mike demanded. "Why would she think that?"

"She heard the gossip from the horse's mouth. It's the reason she took off from the picnic to go stew on her own." Travis rose to his feet, pacing to steady himself. "Cassidy got roughed up by an asshole in the middle of what's supposed to be a friendly family event."

Memories of their conversation before they'd made the move to Rocky rushed him. Cassidy had warned things would be hard.

Ashley had said bad attitudes would be worth dealing with, but none of them had considered beyond themselves.

And none of them had considered being put in physical danger.

"It's bullshit to think we brought it on ourselves by being different, but in spite of that, we can deal with fucked-up attitudes. But none of us want to be the reason that Daniel's boys get picked on, or the Six Pack ranch gets vandalized more and more often. If we stick around, there are no guarantees that any of you are safe, and that's what none of us can stomach.

"But I can't give up on Ashley and Cassidy either." He lifted his gaze to his father's. "Maybe you won't understand this, but I love them. Both of them, and I know that might not seem right, but it's also the most right thing I've ever had happen. I'm not letting go. I'm holding on with both hands, and I'll do whatever it takes to keep them with me and keep them safe."

"You ready to fight all of society for this, son?" his father asked. "Because no matter where you go, there will be people who won't like what you've got. People who will tell you you're wrong, and that your choices are hurting others."

"What I do isn't hurting anyone else, and I've got enough love in me to share with more than one person," Travis snapped.

Mike grinned. "Damn right, you do."

He hadn't said much, but the squeeze of his father's hand that accompanied the words made his response as good as a shout.

Travis's throat tightened, and he had to take a moment to compose himself. *Goddamn.* He needed more practice with this emotional shit, because he was one step away from bawling like a bare-assed baby.

"Thank you."

Mike shook his head slightly. "You never do things the easy way, do you, son?"

Travis snorted. "I guess I don't."

Blake eased back into the conversation. "I'll put this out there. Every time my family grows, I learn about loving more than one person. I don't think you've picked an easy row to hoe, but you're also one of the most stubborn cusses around. I think you can do anything you put your mind to."

The words of praise from his big brother hit nearly as hard as those from Mike. Travis nodded, the tight sensation now wrapped around his chest.

"I want to suggest something, though." Blake glanced at their father. "Or at least start the conversation. I agree, it's bullshit for anyone to have to worry about vandals or the kids being set on."

The understanding was going to kill him. "So you'll help us find a new place to settle—"

"Like hell. I mean we'll find a way to make things work right here." Blake raised his brows. "Where else are there more people who've got your back?"

Mike nodded. "If you're going to buck tradition, why not do it with the weight of family behind you?"

Travis shook his head. "But what if—?"

He jerked himself to a stop.

Those were the same words he'd refused to allow Ashley and Cassidy to use when they started their summer together. He hadn't let them hide behind *what if*, and he couldn't allow himself now either.

*What if*s were to be dealt with. *What if*s only held you back if you let them become walls.

He nodded slowly. "I have to talk to the others, but if the family agrees this is a battle they're willing to take on, then I would love to stay. To make some changes in the community, and show people that families stick together, no matter what that family looks like."

Mike patted him on the shoulder. "That's my boy. Stubborn, especially when you're right."

"Finally," Blake teased. "Good to have you join the respectable side of the clan."

Respectable? Travis laughed. "I've got two lovers, and you're calling it respectable?"

"You are making it official, aren't you?" Blake paused. "Hmm, might have to be a family ceremony. I know you can marry Cassidy or Ashley, but I'm not sure about both of them at the same time."

Marriage? God, time to shut that one down fast. "Shit, Blake. Don't go ordering tuxes or anything. We'll be fine living together."

"Blake is right." Mike hit the side of his fist on the table. "Excellent idea. We could set it up during Thanksgiving, maybe." His father winked at him. "You know, before the kids start coming along."

Travis's skin crawled. "Stop, before I change my mind about wanting to stay close to you all. You're evil."

They both laughed, the layers of love wrapped up in the taunting.

He needed to get back to Ashley and Cassidy, though. To his *new* family. Tell them what their options were. See what they wanted to do and make a decision together.

Together. Travis liked the sound of that an awful lot.

Ashley's throat felt as if she'd swallowed a cat that'd then turned around and done its damnedest to escape.

There was an ache in her brain every time she thought about

the loss of her artwork, and yet part of her was already past the weeping.

Everything she'd prepared was gone. There was no way she could be ready in time for the show, and she was going to have to cancel or postpone her commitment. As much fun as continuing to gnash her teeth would be, it wouldn't bring back her work.

What was more, when she'd lain trapped in the barn, struggling to free herself, her main concern hadn't been about the paintings. It was the guys who she wanted to know were safe, and in the middle of the chaos and the fear, the realization of how much her world had changed hit hard.

The attitude that all relationships were casual was gone. That level of caring was now relegated to things that could be swapped or remade.

Her guys were irreplaceable and *hers*. No matter how stubborn and frustrating she found them.

Like now. She was hot and sticky from sleeping off and on since they'd popped her into the hospital bed, and no amount of sponge baths were going to rid her hair of the lingering smoke stench.

But no matter how hard she glared, Cassidy refused to let her sneak into the shower.

"Dammit, Cass—"

He shot up a hand as if he were blocking traffic. Grabbed the pad of paper from beside the bed and tossed it in her lap. "Save your breath and write what you're thinking."

Oh, she'd write it down, all right. In bold letters with a quick additional sketch of his face, horns sprouting from his temples. His eyes—bloodshot and glaring. She whipped the book around and held it toward him.

The jerk simply grinned. "Nice. It's missing my forked tail, but I like how both the a's in *jackass* are nice and round. Kind of makes me think of the tomatoes you want to throw at me."

"You two playing charades?"

They both turned to the door, eager for Travis's return. When Mike and Marion Coleman stepped through after him, Ashley pinned her smile in place though the edges might have gone a little ragged.

"Ashley seems to have forgotten she spent part of the day holding up a burning building. She wants to traipse around in the shower." Cassidy rose to his feet. "Mike. Marion."

"Sit down, son. We wanted to see Ashley again before they shut down visiting hours." Mike stopped beside the foot of the bed. "You look better, young lady."

"Thanks," she whispered.

Cassidy tapped the notepad and Ashley lost her cool. She flipped him the bird, arm thrust toward him before she remembered who else was in the room.

She twisted back to find Mike grinning and Marion examining her thoughtfully. Not the distracted *lost in space* expression the woman had been wearing recently, but more a considered one, as if she had a specific agenda.

Ashley debated closing her eyes and pretending to be really, really sleepy.

Her hopes were dashed when Marion twirled on the men. "You boys go stretch your legs. I want to talk to Ashley for a few minutes."

Cassidy moved reluctantly, looking to Ashley to see if this was what she wanted. Travis stood behind him, his chin dipping in encouragement. "Only don't you talk too much," he ordered. "Use the notepad."

Ashley rolled her eyes.

Marion sat in the chair Mike pulled to the side of the bed for her. He kissed her cheek then winked at Ashley. "Come on, boys. I need a coffee."

And...they were alone.

It should have been more awkward, but partly Ashley was too exhausted to be worrying about impressing anyone. Plus, now that she knew why Marion had been giving the cold shoulder, Ashley felt like shit.

She opened her mouth to apologize.

"I got something to say to you," Marion cut in before Ashley could speak. The matriarch of the Coleman clan leaned back in her chair and folded her hands carefully. "But first, I'm gonna ask this straight out. Travis told Mike what you overheard, and that you figured I've been distracted and maybe even upset by the gossip in town. Is that true?"

Ashley nodded.

Marion caught her hand, obvious sorrow on her face. "Oh, my girl. I'm *so* sorry. I had no idea that's what you thought, and I should have been paying better attention. Yes, I have something on my mind, but it's not worrying about what tongue-wagging gossips think about me and mine. I don't give two shakes about their opinions, and I never have. The only one I'm accountable to for my actions is God. The only people I aim to please are Mike and myself."

Ashley was now sitting poker straight as she attempted to soak this in. "You're not worried about me and Cassidy being with Travis?"

"Hush—don't you talk." Marion sighed. "Of course, I'm worried. I'm a mother, and I have to worry, but not about who in Rocky is looking and judging." She squeezed Ashley's fingers tight. "Honey, when you left suddenly last Christmas, Travis was pretty shaken. When I heard you were back I was worried he was going to be hurt again. You got my mama-bear instincts all riled up."

Ashley wasn't going to explain her reasons for leaving. "I didn't intend to hurt him."

Marion patted her soothingly. "I figured that out later, but the other part of the trouble was…well, I knew Travis leaned both ways, if you know what I mean."

There was no way not to smile at that phrasing.

"When you came back, I wasn't sure if Travis was still trying to hide liking boys by being a ladies' man. I didn't want him pretending anymore. Mercy, I've known he was gay since he was about eight years old."

So much for one of the things Travis thought was secret. Only Ashley had a point to make. "He's not pretending to like girls," she whispered.

"I know that now too. He seems partial to one in particular more than the rest," Marion teased. Then she straightened, and a fire came into her grey eyes that were so like Travis's. "And he also loves one man, and now that I see he's happy with you and Cassidy, I'm going to back off and let you be. If Travis has decided you two are who he loves, then no group of self-righteous, interfering tight-hearted women can possibly make me want anything but the best for my boy and the people he's chosen."

The self-professed mama-bear rose to her feet and opened her arms. Ashley leaned into them willingly and held on tight. It was good to have the support of this strong woman. Good to know that the bundle of energy and passion was on their side.

Marion sniffed. "Good grief, girl. Whatever did they do to your hair?"

Ashley coughed on the laugh that rose. "I stink, don't I?"

Marion pulled back and nodded. "Well, I suppose they had other things to worry about, but you hold on and let's see what we can do."

She had a cell phone out and a pair of reading glasses perched on her nose, and the next thing Ashley knew Marion was nodding happily.

"That's what I thought." She smiled at Ashley. "My niece

Tamara is finishing her shift, but she's going to come and give you a hand getting washed up."

"Thank you." For more than arranging for the shower, but Ashley wasn't sure how to add in her gratitude for sharing her concerns so honestly. For being accepting.

"Thank *you* for making my son happy." Marion paused, and a firm finger was pointed in her direction. "And if you ever assume that I'm upset with you again, I'll tan your britches. You'll *know* when I'm upset with you, young lady."

Ashley nodded, relaxing back on her pillow. She smelt like a bonfire and she'd lost months of hard work. Her head ached and her mouth tasted like old socks. But in spite of it all, at that moment?

She was happy.

31

____

$\mathcal{E}$ven though Travis knew his mom wanted alone time with Ashley, it was brutal to wait until she phoned to announce she was ready to leave.

Ashley was crawling back in bed when they returned to the room, her wet hair pulled back into a braid. His cousin Tamara adjusted the IV tube and the oxygen, helping settle her in. Ashley caught a glimpse of Cassidy and smirked.

"I got my shower." She stuck out her tongue.

Tamara laughed. "Give him hell, girl."

Marion picked up her purse and got ready to leave. "You rest, and we'll talk tomorrow."

The room turned into a whirl of farewell hugs, the door finally closing and leaving the three of them alone. Travis slipped to the bed, twisting until he could curl an arm around Ashley and cradle her carefully against his chest. "You get things straightened out with my mom?"

Ashley nodded. "We're cool."

"Mike told us about it," Cassidy shared, joining them on the opposite side and sitting as close as he could. He avoided the IV, but linked his fingers in hers.

"So it comes to this. We need to make a decision." Travis stroked her arm lightly. "And I'm not telling you to be quiet, but if you listen first, it'll save your voice."

He told them about their options. About leaving town, or settling in and fighting. About going somewhere else by themselves, or staying and having the backup of the Coleman clan.

The entire time he talked, Cassidy's expression grew more astonished until by the time Travis was done Cassidy was pretty much shaking his head.

"Your family just..."

Ashley squeezed his hand tighter. "That's the point, Cass. They're *family*. Real family."

Travis stayed quiet. He'd said his piece, and now was time for them to share. This wasn't his decision alone, and that made the idea of leaving his family tolerable, because he'd be with *family* no matter where he ended up.

Only both of them turned toward him. Two fair-headed angels with stars in their eyes as they smiled, lips curling farther as their grins grew wider.

"What?" he asked. "What are you two smirking at?"

Ashley stroked his cheek. "So serious."

Cassidy nodded. "You can't possibly think there's anything more to discuss about staying in Rocky?"

Travis waited, hoping, but not daring to say it until they did.

"Dammit, T. We're staying." Cassidy laid his hand on Travis's shoulder and held on tight. "No amount of gossip is going to scare us away, not if your family is behind us. That was my fear after the fire—that the vandalism was meant to hurt not only us, but your family. I couldn't bear for you to lose them."

"Marion? Is gonna kick some bitches' butts," Ashley murmured happily.

"You're really good with staying?" Travis asked.

Cassidy answered for them both. "We're in a better place than we were when we started a couple months ago, T. We've been making friends, been accepted by your folks. All of that is huge. We've got to give the community a chance, but in the meantime, we got each other."

"There's nothing more that I need." Ashley pressed tighter to him, and the knot in Travis's chest loosened slightly.

"Besides." Cassidy shrugged. "If some jerk on the ball field wants to get his ass beat, I'm good to give him what-for."

Ashley stiffened in Travis's arms. "What happened on the ball field?"

Shit. Travis bumped Cassidy in the shoulder. "Nice going."

Cassidy looked sheepish as he answered Ashley. "Nothing much. Nothing compared to what happened to you, but it doesn't matter now. Now? You go to sleep so you can get better, and we can take you home."

Home. Because wherever they ended up, if they were together, it would be home.

There was one more thing that had to be said. Travis slid himself up on the bed right next to Ashley and took a deep breath. "Ash?"

She hummed, her eyelids fluttering closed as she cocooned herself against him.

Travis glanced up to see Cassidy give him an encouraging nod. "Ash, I got something to tell you."

She cracked open one eye. "You really gonna say it now?"

He laughed. "Yeah, I am."

"Jeez. And me dopey on painkillers." Ashley snickered. "Fine. Go ahead."

Cassidy snorted.

Travis cupped her face and stared into her half-open eyes, the thin slivers of blue like the first glimpse of a morning sky. "I love you, sweetheart. I love your smiles and your energy and the way you never give up on me. The way the world lights up because you're around. I love everything about you with everything in me."

She took a deep breath and sighed happily. "That? Was lovely."

Her eyes closed again and her breathing settled.

Cassidy pulled the blanket over the two of them.

"Hey," Travis whispered. "I was going to let you hold her."

"You stay where you are. That bed won't hold three, but that's okay. I'll be right over here." Cassidy kissed Ashley, then Travis, laughing softly as he moved away. "Where's my poetry and mush?" he complained. "All I got was an *I love you.*"

Travis rolled his eyes. "We can wrestle and do the guy shit later."

"Deal." Cassidy settled into the chair beside the bed, stretching his legs out and staring up at the ceiling. "We're going to be okay, T. The three of us—we're going to be okay."

Travis drove them out of town, but he didn't turn on the side road that led to the trailer.

"Where are you going?" Cassidy asked. It had been a hard couple days waiting for Ashley to be released, but now that she was free to go, he wanted her home.

To be able to thoroughly reassure himself that she was okay.

"Side trip."

Cassidy didn't like that answer. "We should take Ashley straight home, T. She just got out of the hospital."

"Got a stop to make first."

Ashley laid a hand on Cassidy's thigh. "He's being a Sphinx again. It's really annoying. Like he's the one in charge or something."

"I've noticed he gets like that on occasion." Cassidy leaned forward to watch Travis's face. "Maybe we should lock him out of the bedroom for a couple days. Or tie him to a chair so he can't order us around, but has to watch."

Travis grinned. "You think being tied to a chair is gonna stop me from being in charge?"

Ashley wrinkled her nose. "He has a point."

Cassidy laughed. "He still missed the turn to the trailer."

Travis shook his head. "Never missed it, just got a place to stop first. Trust me, I know all things."

He turned them into the yard outside the second Coleman house, the one that Blake and Jaxi had lived in for the past three years. The rest of the clan were already there, trucks filling the parking space.

Ashley held Cassidy's hand as they followed Travis to the front door. "You know what the hell he's doing?" she asked.

"Not a clue." And this was one time he would have liked to be in on the surprise. He resigned himself to wait a little longer as they entered the living room to be met by most of the family. The only one missing again was Jesse.

Ashley got buried in hugs, and that made up for some of the wait.

They'd been accepted, they were being grafted into the family. Cassidy relaxed as that thought slipped deeper into his soul and healed a few more hurts.

Family was worth taking the time for.

"So." Marion pulled Ashley from Vicki, separating the

women who were chattering like magpies. "We have news for you, right, Ashley?"

Travis jolted upright.

Ashley smirked at him. "Who's the one who knows all things?"

Cassidy's laughter mixed with the others as Travis shrugged in resignation.

Travis's mom beamed. "The girls and I have been talking, and we've done a little rearranging. Well, started it at least. I'd been thinking for a while that big ranch house was too large for Mike and me. All that space to ramble about in—and I can't say that I love having six bedrooms and three bathrooms to clean. Since Blake and Jaxi seem to be doing their best to fill up bedrooms... What with a fourth baby on the way and all."

Heads jerked toward the couple as congratulations rang out.

Jaxi shook a finger at Marion. "That's the last time I tell you a secret."

"You didn't tell me, I guessed," Marion stated, but she was gloating.

Blake got smacked on the back. Jaxi rolled her eyes.

"When are you due?" Hope asked.

Jaxi wiggled her fingers. "January, thereabouts."

"So now is as good a time as any for us to swap houses." Marion nodded happily. "Blake and Jaxi will move into the main Coleman house and the babies will use up some of those empty bedrooms, while Mike and I take over the trailer across the road. Joel and Vicki will move into the trailer Travis has been using— it's a little more private and out of the way."

"Leaving the Peter's house, this one, for you three." Mike waved a hand toward the ceiling. "Mind you, it needs a little fixing. It's been lived in hard for a while, so I thought you could knock down a few walls, and replace some plumbing and...well..." He grinned. "Make it roomy enough for three adults."

It was more than he could have imagined. "No one has a problem playing musical houses like that?" Cassidy asked.

Joel stepped forward. "It's always been a part of how the family works. If it fits better for us to be out by the coulee, Vicki and me don't mind. And I finally got ahold of Jesse, and he said he's happy living with the Moonshine boys."

There was a slight pause at that. A sort of sad resignation on Joel's part, a hint of concern in Marion's expression. Cassidy realized since they'd returned to Rocky Jesse hadn't been around a lot, and it was clear his absence was being felt.

Mike broke the tension as he turned to Ashley. "I know you talked about the house swaps with Marion, but I have one more suggestion for you. We're all damn sorry your artwork got ruined. I'm glad you'll get another chance come January to have a show, and we're all going to be there. But in the meantime, if there's anything you need that we can help with while you start up again, you make sure you ask. Also, there's a building out back of here that will make you a good studio, if you can find a couple of strong guys to help you renovate."

Ashley grinned. "I think I know of a couple." She hugged Marion. "Thank you."

Marion sighed. "I'm still sorry I made you feel unhappy before. That wasn't right of me—my old brain was so focused on how we could fit everyone into new places I wasn't thinking straight."

"You made me happy now, so we're even. Forget it, please." Ashley closed her eyes as Marion squeezed her tight, and Cassidy warmed all the way down.

Ashley was getting to set roots like she wanted. He and Travis would do everything they could to make sure she stayed beaming like that, and he didn't much care which house they lived in if it made Ashley happy.

Mike paused then turned to Cassidy. "There's one more

thing. I know you've got the job down at the garage and all, but it seems kind of stupid to have a trained ranch hand working as a grease monkey and then hire some green kid on the side. What would you say to joining on the Six Pack punch-clock full-time?"

Cassidy's jaw fell slightly. He hadn't expected this twist to the day at all. "You'd hire me on full-time?"

Blake cleared his throat. "Actually, what Dad meant to say was we need another full-time worker, but we ain't going to pay you. At least not hourly. Hell, none of the others in the family get an hourly paycheque. You'd be full on the papers, same draw as us. Good year, you make a little more, bad years you get to go hungry like the rest of the family."

Unexpected, and the final straw. Cassidy felt tears rising, and damn if he could stop them.

He turned toward Ashley, but that didn't help, because she had ribbons of moisture running down her face. She'd understood exactly what that offer had meant.

It wasn't just a job offer; it was so very much more.

"You've got a family, Cassidy." She barely choked out the words before she threw herself at him. He caught her close and buried his face in her neck, thankful for the excuse to hide for a moment as he pulled himself together.

A strong arm enveloped his shoulders as Travis embraced both of them. "You're supposed to be happy, guys, not flooding the place."

"We're happy," Ashley insisted. She lifted her chin, and as flush-cheeked and teary-eyed as she was, Cassidy had never seen her looking more beautiful.

Travis held them close as he spoke to his family. "I have to answer for us all, seeing as you've pretty much knocked them off their feet. Thank you."

Cassidy pulled himself to vertical and dashed the moisture from his eyes. "Thank you from me as well." He took the time to meet each of the brothers' eyes, amazed at the acceptance he saw. "I'll make sure you never regret it."

Mike Coleman nodded. "You keep on doing your best like the rest of my boys, and you'll be fine."

He patted Cassidy on the shoulder, then Travis, then turned and shouted at Matt and Blake for something he'd spotted left undone the previous day. Joel stepped in to tease them for getting shit, and the rest of the family settled into groups to visit or get supper together.

Travis pulled Ashley and Cassidy aside. "I'm not sure what just happened. All I was told was to bring you two over for dinner."

Ashley had her arms around them both, her eyes shining. "I only knew about the house thing—you don't mind, do you?" she asked Travis.

"How could I mind? Anywhere you are is home." Travis kissed her, right there in the middle of the kitchen. A tongue-tangling, spine-melting affair that had her clutching him tight as he ignored that they were smack dab in front of his family.

They were both breathing damn hard when he let her go.

"Whoa," she said. "My head is spinning. Excuse me while I sit down for a minute."

Travis turned to Cassidy, and the fire and mischief and fuck-it-all passion that Cassidy remembered being so drawn to—all of that was back. This was the friend who'd become so much more. The friend who was his lover, and now his family—this was the man who stood before him.

Travis cracked off a grin and reached for him. "I'd warn everyone what I'm about to do, but I figure they pretty much already know."

Cassidy glanced over Travis's shoulder. Some of the family were watching, smiles in place. Some were busy at their tasks.

~

New York Times Bestselling Author Vivian Arend
invites you to meet the Colemans. These contemporary cowboys
ranch the foothills of the Alberta Rockies. Enjoy the ride as they
each find their happily-ever-afters.

~

Six Pack Ranch
Rocky Mountain Heat
Rocky Mountain Haven
Rocky Mountain Desire
Rocky Mountain Angel
Rocky Mountain Rebel
Rocky Mountain Freedom
Rocky Mountain Romance
Rocky Mountain Retreat
Rocky Mountain Shelter
Rocky Mountain Devil
Rocky Mountain Home

~

ABOUT THE AUTHOR

New York Times and *USA Today* bestselling author Vivian Arend loves to share the products of her over-active imagination with her readers. She writes contemporary, western, and light-hearted paranormal romances. The stories are humorous yet emotional, usually with a large cast of family or friends, and a guaranteed happily-ever-after.

Vivian lives in British Columbia, Canada, with her husband of many years—her inspiration for every hero and a willing companion for all sorts of adventures.

Find out more at www.vivianarend.com.